(1879–1958) was born Doro[...] Lawrence, Kansas, the daughter [...] professor, and Flavia Camp, an [...] spent a year in Paris with her [...] moved to Nebraska where she met Willa Cather who became her lifelong friend. After studying at Ohio State and Columbia Universities and at the Sorbonne, she was offered an assistant professorship at Western Reserve University in 1903. However, to avoid distressing her parents she took an administrative post at the nearer Horace Mann School and began writing short stories in her spare time. In 1905 she left to nurse her ailing mother.

Dorothy Canfield's first novel, *Gunhild*, was published in 1907 and in the same year she married James Redwood Fisher, with whom she had a son and daughter. They settled in Arlington, Vermont, the home of Dorothy Canfield's pioneering ancestors, but travelled widely. In 1911 she visited the innovative Italian school of Dr Maria Montessori, and on her return pioneered this educational method in America in: *A Montessori Mother* (1912), *A Montessori Manual* (1913), *Mothers and Children* (1914) and *Self-Reliance* (1916). Between 1916–19 she and her family moved to France to become part of the war effort. Dorothy Canfield founded a braille press and established a convalescent home for refugee French children, supporting these activities by writing, and her husband joined the ambulance service. She was later the first woman appointed to the Vermont Board of Education and was the first and only woman on the editorial board of the Book-of-the-Month Club for twenty-five years. During the Second World War Dorothy Canfield organised and led the Children's Crusade, encouraging American children to help young war victims. The death of her own son in combat in the Philippines in 1945 was devastating and she stopped writing fiction. She died of a stroke in Vermont in 1958.

A prolific and popular writer, Dorothy Canfield published poetry, translations, articles, patriotic reflections and children's books in addition to fiction and educational texts. Her other novels are: *The Squirrel Cage* (1912), *The Bent Twig* (1915), *The Brimming Cup* (1921), *Rough Hewn* (1922), *The Home-Maker* (1924), *Her Son's Wife* (1926), *The Deepening Stream* (1930), *Bonfire* (1933) and *Seasoned Timber* (1939).

VIRAGO
MODERN
CLASSIC
NUMBER
220

HER SON'S WIFE

DOROTHY CANFIELD

WITH AN INTRODUCTION BY
DOROTHY GOLDMAN

Published by VIRAGO PRESS Limited 1986
41 William IV Street, London WC2N 4DB

First published in America by Harcourt Brace Jovanovich Inc 1926
Virago edition offset from Jonathan Cape 1932 edition

Copyright © 1926 by Harcourt Brace Jovanovich, Inc.
Copyright renewed 1954 by Dorothy Canfield (Fisher)
Published by arrangement with Harcourt Brace Jovanovich, Inc.

Introduction Copyright © Dorothy Goldman 1986

British Cataloguing in Publication Data

Canfield, Dorothy
    Her son's wife.—(Virago modern classics)
    I. Title
    818'.52[F]   PS3505.A55/

    ISBN 0-86068-347-8

Printed in Great Britain by
Anchor Brendon Ltd., of Tiptree, Essex

Introduction

In some ways *Her Son's Wife* may appear to be nothing more than a conventional well-made novel, telling the life history of realistic characters in a simple chronological sequence; describing the years from 1908 when Ralph and Lottie Bascomb marry, until 1925 when their daughter Dids leaves home to go to college. But as the title subtly suggests, it is not the young married couple but Ralph's mother who is at the centre of the novel. Dorothy Canfield wrote to her agent that 'The story turns ... on the development and strengthening of a character, in this case after forty-five, the age when most people are set for life. A woman of forty-five meets calamity ... and struggles through great sorrow and misery, to an immensely deeper understanding and self-abnegation.'[1] The woman in question is Mrs Bascomb, widow, mother, mother-in-law, grandmother, teacher and diligent housewife, who attempts to come to terms with the weakness of her son Ralph and her selfish and worthless daughter-in-law Lottie, and tries to do the best she can for her beloved granddaughter Dids. As we might expect from a traditional novel it is the change which those experiences cause in Mrs Bascomb's character which demand our attention. By the end of the novel she has been transformed – by a series of gradual steps which the reader finds simultaneously astonishing and credible. The transformation permeates all aspects of her life: she learns how to laugh, her vocabulary becomes less prim, she even learns to accept 'the almost complete invisibility of the useful middle-aged woman'; but the most important change is in her feelings towards Lottie, which move from detestation, loathing and hatred, to pity and even love.

But *Her Son's Wife* was published in 1926 and despite the author's emphasis on character the novel is part of a more

1. Dorothy Canfield Fisher to Paul Reynolds, 3 Sept 1924. Paul R. Reynolds Papers, Rare Book and Manuscript Library, Columbia University.

complex and ambivalent literary mode than may at first appear. Set against the inner pyschological portrait of Mrs Bascomb, Dorothy Canfield draws a more impersonal picture of her characters in their social and familial roles. It may be significant that she rejected several titles which incorporated characters' names (e.g. *John Bascomb's Widow*) in favour of the final strangely impersonal title, which lays the emphasis on the relationships which her characters bear towards one another.

We are constantly reminded that while Lottie has her own personal history and character, she is also Ralph's wife, Mrs Bascomb's daughter-in-law and the mother of Dids, who we are similarly reminded is John Bascomb's granddaughter: 'long ago, Dids had figured out that there was more to relationships than she had thought, at first, and now knew quite accurately how the generations ... were tied together'. Mrs Bascomb herself exists not only in her own right but in at least three other roles. She is Ralph's mother (indeed she comes to realise that she is largely responsible for the weak, immature adult he has become), as well as being simply Grannie she tries to act as Dids' mother ('now she had the baby she had longed for all her life, John's child as Ralph had never been ... and now her own baby as much as if she had physically borne her within her own body') and by the book's conclusion she will have become Lottie's mother. What is more, Mrs Bascomb is quite aware of these different aspects of herself:

> Of late two of these women sometimes lived together in the same body, turning their eyes away from each other, as Grannie, holding the exuberant little body on her lap, tried to dress it for the daily outing; while Mrs Bascomb listened grimly to the crackling laughter and loud jocular voices from downstairs.

Indeed sometimes she can no longer remember who she is and what function she is fulfilling.

Significantly, as the book progresses, as Mrs Bascomb herself comes to put immediate human relationships and the development of human potential before outward persona, such descriptions grow less frequent. Lottie's stilted 'I do hope you're going to let me call you "Momma"' becomes the final anguished 'Oh, Momma! Oh, Momma!' Mrs Bascomb would have preferred the name Joanna for her granddaughter, a variant on her husband's name; Lottie chooses Gladys, from a movie heroine. When both are forgotten in preference to the child's self-given name, Dids, the book confirms the importance of human individuality and personal integrity over social roles and relations.

Dorothy Canfield suspected that her male audience would make little of any book which stressed human relationships in this way:

> I don't believe that it can interest any man. They have for too many generations had the possibility and the habit, of pulling on their hats and melting away out of the house, when family relations got too uncomfortably tense. I rather imagine that they will put on their hats and melt away from the book at about the third chapter. But I hope that women who have had, for generations, to stick it out with no escape, may have a certain horrified interest in the story.[2]

(The reader will remember how Ralph reaches 'unobtrusively for his hat and [slides] quietly out of the door' in Chapter 25.)

The book never falters from this belief that the family and human relationships are the most important things in life, and the author quite firmly rejects what she sees as the masculine response of evasion. For three years Mrs Bascomb abandons her family, telling herself, 'You have perfectly done your woman's task. Now live, as men live, for themselves and their work. Put those intimate personal relationships out of your head as men do.' She tries to make 'much of the idea of living like ... men of her age lived ... for themselves and for their work, with much external activity and no inner personal life'. But those three years are fruitless and barren and abandoned instantly when she discovers the depths her family has reached without her.

2. D. C. F. to Paul Reynolds, 28 March 1925. Paul R. Reynolds Papers, Rare Book and Manuscript Library, Columbia University.

Yet it would be a mistake to underestimate Dorothy Canfield and by a superficial reading of *Her Son's Wife* believe that it simply endorses the traditional female role. Though Mrs Bascomb is committed to family life, to the mother's task as educator and passer-on of the culture and to the housewife's position of holding the family together, she knows that none of this would be possible without her earnings as a teacher. More than that, her job gives her a professional identity which provides the strength enabling her to endure the demands of her personal life; the moment she entered school

she had left behind her Mary Bascomb, John Bascomb's widow, Ralph Bascomb's mother, for whom her own personal life was the universe ... she became 'Teacher' ... Her emotional life was forced into a saving momentary torpor by the mere passing over her head of hour after hour crammed with rigorously ordered occupation ... The austerity of this demand was an opiate for the pain of personal relations ... all of it, exerted on those teaching women a quieting, calming influence such as no home-keeping woman can ever know – left a prey as she is to the reflections from the convex mirrors of home-objects which can show to her nothing but ever-magnified images of herself.

Such sentiments are not uncommon in Dorothy Canfield's work; as early as her second novel, *The Squirrel-Cage* (1912), she attacked the social regime which condemned women to aimless and frustrating lives.

Dorothy Canfield recognised the importance of work in her own life. Born in 1879 she grew up in mid-Western American university towns where her father was a professor of economics and later a university president. With such a background it is not surprising that after deafness thwarted her hopes of a musical career she looked set to become an academic herself, gaining a bachelor's degree in French from Ohio State University and then a doctorate from Columbia University on the English translations of Corneille and Racine and their presentation on the English stage – incidentally she also spoke Italian, Spanish, German and Norwegian. In 1903 she was offered the position of assistant professor in French and German at Western Reserve University in Cleveland, Ohio, but she suppressed her ambition when she saw her parents' distress at the thought of her leaving them. She turned down the post and accepted the less demanding one of local school secretary. Even that did not last long; in 1905 her mother became ill and Dorothy, the dutiful daughter, gave up her job and stayed at home to take care of her. But after her marriage in 1907 she never stopped working. She wrote ten novels of which nine were best-sellers, eleven volumes of short stories, several books for children, a dozen or so works of non-fiction on mainly educational and historical subjects, some poetry, a play and hundreds of articles. During the First World War her husband went to France as an ambulance driver, where she soon joined him with their son of seven and their daughter of three. There she was actively engaged in war work – especially taking as her task the support of those blinded by the war. She served as a member of the selection committee of the Book-of-the-Month Club from its inception in 1926 until 1951, reading on average fifteen novels a month and influencing the taste of the American reading public for a quarter of a century. As a worker for Black rights, she was especially proud of their decision to recommend *Native Son* by Richard Wright, a savagely frank novel portraying the depravity and despair to which social injustice condemned American Blacks: indeed she wrote an introduction to it. It seems a fitting comment on her unremitting labour that when in 1931 she took on the additional task of translator, it was of Adriano Tilgher's *Work: What it has meant to men through the ages*.

Dorothy and John Fisher had an unconventional marriage in that she was the breadwinner: her husband was active in local politics and acted as her literary editor and advisor but the financial security for their rural life in Vermont was earned by her pen. She tackled the subject of role-reversal directly in her sixth novel, *The Home-Maker*, which immediately preceded *Her*

Son's Wife. In this book Evangeline Knapp, compulsive home-cleaner and demanding mother, finds liberation when her husband Lester is paralysed in an accident and confined to a wheelchair. They exchange jobs and both are more successful and much happier in their new roles: he becomes an imaginative and caring parent and home-maker who rescues their children from the frustration which their mother's regime had imposed on them and she becomes a successful and fulfilled career woman, earning more than Lester ever did. The second crisis of the novel occurs when one after another they realise that Lester may well recover and that they could not withstand the social disapproval which would inevitably follow if they then retained their preferred way of life. A conspiracy of lies between husband, wife and doctor preserves the happiness of the family, but at the cost of self-respect and personal integrity.

It seems clear that two years after the publication of *The Home-Maker*, Dorothy Canfield was still considering some of these same issues in *Her Son's Wife*. Here too the financial security for the family comes from a woman; here too personal moral sacrifices are made for the greater good of the family; here too children's needs are foremost. Dorothy Canfield wrote of *The Home-Maker* that 'it should be taken, as a whoop not for "women's rights" but for "children's rights"'[3] and the same comment could be applied to *Her Son's Wife*. From the opening chapter which unsympathetically reveals the unreconstructed Mrs Bascomb's attitude to her young charges and their parents, to the ending when Dids departs for college, we are never allowed to forget the importance of the rising generation. But again we must beware of the temptation to underestimate *Her Son's Wife*. It is more than a simple chronological account of Dids' education and growth to maturity. To understand her development we must understand Mrs Bascomb and Lottie too. We watch them perform an elegant and persuasive dance in which they change not only places and roles, but even generations. Mrs Bascomb effectively achieves her desire to

3. D. C. F. to Alfred Harcourt, 4 October 1924. Papers held in the Dorothy Canfield Fisher Collection at the University of Vermont Library.

become Dids' mother ('*Her* baby now') and supervise her growing up. All the formative influences on Dids are for good – but we slowly learn not to blame Lottie for her inability to provide them. It is telling that on those few occasions before the end of the book when we pity Lottie she is presented to us as though she were the child; she is 'just a kid': 'Mrs Bascomb caught a glimpse of... a pretty, childish, foolish face, brimming with pleasure, the face of a school-child on the playground at recess time, filled with the delight of the precious ten minutes' reprieve from lessons ... Why, it was Lottie!' Dids might easily have become like her mother as the three parallel scenes at the soda-fountain in Chapters 10, 21 and 34 make clear. In fact on those occasions they almost seem the same person and through Dids we get a picture of Lottie's earlier years. Mrs Bascomb discovers the tragedy of wasting human life that Lottie represents as she realises that without her intervention Dids will be brought up to be another Lottie. At one point she despairs of rescuing her: 'the best thing she could do for little Dids was to clasp her close and leap with her into the river'; she comes to recognise that Lottie too was 'a helpless, desolate child who ought never to have been born'. When Lottie's father reappears towards the end of the novel we are ready to understand that Lottie 'never had no chance ... If she'd a-ben looked out for, the way you've looked out for Dids ... Nobody ever learned us any better'.

As Dids grows into maturity, Lottie declines into dependence: originally she is a threat to Mrs Bascomb, 'a looming black figure' then a 'cheap, ignorant, vulgar ... phantom'; but by the conclusion of the novel she is 'a forlorn little phantom ... ignorant, unprotected, warped, stunted ... standing there all these years waiting for a mother'. By the time Dids has become an independent adult, her grandmother and surrogate mother has another child to care for, Lottie, who is finally recapturing the childhood she never had.

With Dids' independence Mrs Bascomb has achieved her goal; the painful necessity of letting go has been achieved. She recognises that Dids 'had forgotten that her grandmother existed. That was right. That was as it should be.' This attitude reflects another of the author's strongly held beliefs which arose from experiences in her personal life. In 1911 she visited Dr Maria Montessori's school in Rome, and returned to America enthusiastic about a method of education which taught children to become independent and to grow to maturity by gradually assuming responsibility for their behaviour. Characteristically she wrote four books on the subject, *A Montessori Mother* (1912), *A Montessori Manual* (1913), *Mothers and Children* (1914) and *Self-Reliance* (1916). Although John Bascomb's dictum that 'Character is destiny'–reverberates throughout *Her Son's Wife*, it does not make it a darkly deterministic novel, for character can be formed, as Dids' was and Lottie's was not. Dorothy Canfield found this belief heartening. She felt that the success of the Montessori method of education gave some proof of the inherent goodness of man; that the worst sin is the wasting of human potential; that parents and educators have the whole future of democracy in their hands. Ralph Bascomb's attitude to his daughter's upbringing – 'It's good enough, good's the average' – will not do. Only the best is good enough for each individual.

Earlier than her Montessori experiences we can find another clue to the social mission which Dorothy Canfield felt was part of the function of her fiction. In 1899 when she was twenty, she and her mother went to Madrid and visited the Prado, where she became fascinated by one of Velasquez' court dwarfs. She wrote, many years later:

Above his dwarfed body, there looked out a full-grown man's face, terrible in its quiet sadness. I could not pass along that wall without stopping to meet his darkly shadowed eyes. It was as if he had a wordless message for me, a compelling one. In the end even the hard, adolescent crust over my shallow undeveloped young heart was pierced with an involuntary, persistent compassion for human ills ... The sad-faced dwarf, bearing with patience the ignominy of his misshapen body, was a victim of man's inability in the seventeenth century to cure glandular lacks which now our modern medical skill easily sets straight. The tragedy of the dwarf man, the dignity of that helplessly suffering face … opened my heart to share the sorrow of the victims of modern man's ignorant inability to mend flaws in the social structure and standards, which cause just as much misery as glandular lacks ever did centuries ago.[4]

There is little doubt, I think, that in her novels and short stories as much as in her non-fiction and the numerous liberal causes which she espoused, Dorothy Canfield was attempting to right social wrongs. She brought to the task an optimism which we may feel to be more nineteenth than twentieth century, an optimism which made her much admired by Humanist critics.

To this nineteenth-century optimistic belief in progress she added a fair amount of turn-of-the-century regionalism: that literary movement, largely carried on by women writers, which explained, defended and justified a particular regional culture in portraits of small towns and villages, their rural inhabitants, their antecedents and small domestic routines. Indeed, her first published work was a fantastic ghost story about football which she wrote as a schoolgirl during the winter of 1893 in collaboration with Willa Cather, who was then a college student. Called 'The Fear that Walks by Noonday', the story won a prize and was published in the 1894 University of Nebraska Year Book, *The Sombrero*. In itself it was not important, but her friendship with Willa Cather was. The influence of this great novelist, one of America's leading regionalist writers, is evident in much of Dorothy Canfield's work. Again, her personal life bore out her fictional beliefs. When she and John Fisher married, to the amazement of their friends they turned their backs on city life and went to live outside Arlington, Vermont, on land which had belonged to the Canfield family since 1764, and it was this area she wrote about so often, from the early *Hillsboro' People* (1915), right up to

4. D. C. F., *A Harvest of Stories* (Harcourt, Brace and Co., New York, 1956), p. xx.

Vermont Tradition: the biography of an outlook on life (1953).

While *Her Son's Wife* may not immediately announce itself to be part of the regionalist tradition, we should recognise that this is the source of its domestic detail – 'the little surface things of life' – remembering the descriptions of Mrs Bascomb cooking and Lottie's haphazard washing-up, the jumble of cutlery in its drawer, the marks on the dining-table; remembering how much of Mrs Bascomb's emotions is described in terms of her house and furniture – 'The familiar furniture glared at her menacingly, like crouching demons, swollen with anger'; how the spiritual degradation into which Lottie is dragging Ralph and Dids is symbolised by the squalor in which they live. Mrs Bascomb's 'spotless kitchen [was] invaded by a savagery of slovenly ways and slovenly speech'.

In a review of her friend's work Dorothy Canfield wrote: 'I offer you a hypothesis about Willa Cather's work: that the one real subject of all her books is the effect of a new country – our new country – has on people transplanted to it from the old traditions of a stable, complex civilization.'[5] It is perhaps true to say that she herself was developing that same subject, looking at how the new society was developing its own traditions, stability and complexity. When she said that 'I can write nothing at all about places, people, or phases of life which I do not intimately know, down to the last detail'[6] and that 'Everything I write, or about everything, is written not in English but in *American* and that is true not only from the standpoint of language but the underlying state of mind as well',[7] we should accept it and recognise how *Her Son's Wife* is structured around the traditional time scale of an American small town: school terms, local sporting fixtures, the Winter Carnival, Lincoln's Birthday, the Community Club lectures and Dids becoming president of the Senior class in High School.

5. New York *Herald Tribune*, 28 May 1933.
6. Quoted in Bradford Smith, 'Dorothy Canfield Fisher', *Atlantic Monthly*, vol. 204, 1959, p. 76. © The Atlantic Monthly Company, 1959. Reprinted with permission.
7. Quoted in Louis McCallister, *Dorothy Canfield Fisher, a critical study*, unpub. doctoral dissertation, Case Western Reserve University, 1969.

But in Dorothy Canfield's writing there is another aspect of American literary history that we must not forget. As early as 1933, an article on her writing by Edward Post was entitled 'The Neo-Puritanism of Dorothy Canfield', and along with nineteenth-century optimism, early twentieth-century regionalism and the functionalism of the 1920s there exists an older, darker New England Puritanism; her characters may be able to take charge of their own lives, but they will have to pay the price. In its simplest form it appears in the inner dialogue of her characters: at night Mrs Bascomb wrestles with her conscience. It would not be fair to reveal to the reader the steps which Mrs Bascomb takes to rescue Dids, but because of them we are forced to face up to the fact that Mrs Bascomb – the woman who matures spiritually, who comes to understand the importance of personal relationships and becomes skilled in nurturing them, who rescues her granddaughter and rears her into a fine young woman, who eventually learns to love and be loved by her daughter-in-law, who saves her son from despair – may also be a monster. Why does Ralph think that his mother 'looks as though she had killed Lottie'? Why does she begin to wash her hands in such a neurotic manner? Why does she stop wearing the locket with her husband's portrait in it?

In her last novel *Seasoned Timber* (1939) Dorothy Canfield wrote, 'Responsibility for others [is] not a burden but an enlargement of personal life.'[8] Yes, indeed, but in *Her Son's Wife* she also considers the possibility that sin, evil and guilt can be concomitant experiences, integral to human development, central to personal life. Is it possible that we must completely reassess Mrs Bascomb? Is the final almost Jamesian irony of the novel a gauge both of Mrs Bascomb's ultimate moral triumph and ultimate spiritual degradation? Is it possible that when Dids leaves home she leaves behind a grandmother who like Frankenstein has at last created what she has always wanted, the baby that can never be taken from her, will never leave her,

8. D. C. F., *Seasoned Timber* (Harcourt, Brace and Co., New York, 1939), p. 105.

will never grow up? Although she may believe that she has learnt that 'a mother is not a person to lean upon, but a person to make leaning unnecessary', the final image of the book is of her willingly, even joyfully, accepting a burden of her own making.

Dorothy Goldman, Canterbury, 1985

PART ONE

Chapter 1

To the downcast little girl murmuring earnestly, 'But, Teacher, I never meant to –' Mrs. Bascomb said, with upraised forefinger: 'Sh! Didn't I hear somebody knocking?'

The group of plainly dressed women and children standing in the aisle to wait their turn, stirred, and one of the women said eagerly, propitiatingly, 'Yes, Mis' Bascomb. Yes, ma'am. I been hearing somebody knock, quite a while back.'

Mrs. Bascomb rewarded her with a faint smile, and towards the door said musically, on two notes, '*Come . . . in.*'

A slight change in the expression of the waiting women showed that they recognized the teacher's accent as different from the one they would have used. An even slighter shade of satisfaction in Mrs. Bascomb's face showed that she knew they had so recognized it. The door opened. A tall, fair-haired, mild-eyed girl looked in.

'Oh, come right in, Margaret,' said Mrs. Bascomb; 'I won't be long.'

The women in the aisle looked at each other, understanding that the last phrase was intended for them.

The girl glanced at them. 'I'd better go back to my own room,' she said.

'No, no,' said Mrs. Bascomb easily, again on two notes, 'No need for that. Just sit down and wait. If you can crowd yourself into a fifth-grade seat?'

With a docile smile the newcomer sat down, her slim, long body drolly twisted between a low seat and desk. She put her chin on her hands and settled herself to observe a cross section of the older woman's life. A faint consciousness of this coloured the wistfulness in Mrs. Bascomb's face.

From the back of the room, the girl could hear but one side of the dialogues which followed, and see only Mrs. Bascomb's expression. The others presented their backs to her,

5

and their voices came to her only as a badly articulated mumble, against which Mrs. Bascomb's refined speech chimed out crisply. It was like hearing a telephone conversation.

'But Annie dear, if you hadn't intended to, you wouldn't have struck Isabelle. It can't be true when you say you didn't mean to. We only do what we mean to. Somewhere in your heart there must have been anger with Isabelle. And anger is a poison. You must put it right out of your life or it will make you do worse things than hitting a little schoolmate. Isn't that so, Mrs. Dempsey?'

A pause for Mrs. Dempsey's murmured answer.

Then the sweet, rather melancholy voice again, 'Yes, of course it is hard. Anything worth doing is hard. But it is perfectly possible. I always say to young people that if they will fill their lives with beautiful thoughts, the evil ones will have no chance. Now, I'm not going to punish Annie. I don't believe in punishments. I just want her to think over what I have said, and to write out twenty times and bring to school to-morrow, this sentence, "I love Isabelle and will make her my friend." '

A murmur from Mrs. Dempsey, not quite so inaudible, of which the words 'that darned mean kid' were distinguishable. She was interrupted by Mrs. Bascomb's voice saying gently, 'Oh, yes, she can if she tries. I always say there is *something* to love in every one. And if we look for it, we can bring it out. That's a lesson Annie must learn and it's every bit as important as the multiplication table.'

As the unpunished Annie and her mother moved forward, Mrs. Bascomb's eyes for an instant sought those of the girl at the back of the room. Pleasant messages of admiration and acknowledgment were exchanged while the next group came forward to the teacher's table. It was with a complete change of expression that Mrs. Bascomb transferred her attention to the shabby little boy and the small, bent old woman.

A mumble of two voices together, broken by Mrs. Bascomb's voice, reasonable, quietly ironical, 'I believe I could understand you better if you took turns in saying what it is you want me to hear.'

An ungraceful silence, each waiting for the other.

6

The clear voice again, with a little impatience, 'Well, Michael –'

The little boy's voice, apologetic, ashamed. Then the old woman, leaning forward, talking in a still lower tone, trying to convey something without saying it. An embarrassed shuffling of the little boy's feet.

Mrs. Bascomb's voice, round and full with reproach, 'But where is Michael's mother?'

The old woman leaning still farther forward over the table, laying a shaking, withered hand on the row of books standing at the edge. The little boy hanging his head very low. From the two silent women, left standing in the aisle, an emanation of comprehension. They looked down at the floor and away, as if to show they were not listening.

Mrs. Bascomb's voice, grave and rich, 'But Mrs. Malone, a wife's place is with her husband, always. Marriage is a sacred thing. You can't solve problems by running away from them. When people marry, they take on certain responsibilities, and just because things turn out to be harder than they thought, they have no right to. . . .'

The old woman's voice, very low, in a brief statement.

Mrs. Bascomb's again, shocked, 'Oh, that was much too young to marry! What makes parents allow such marriages. But even so, there is always some way of arranging things, if the people concerned really *try*.'

At this the old woman's back became agitated, less placating, and although very much bent, no longer so respectful. It shook with the energy of what she now began to say. Her voice carried even to the back of the room in disjointed phrases, snatches of description. . . . 'Grabbed up a poker and went for her. . . . Put her out of the house at one o'clock in the morning and snow on the. . . . The neighbours had to come in and. . . . Less than three weeks after Michael was born, didn't he. . . .'

Her voice was shrill, her accent vulgar – the accent of one used to coarse words. She struck the tops of the standing books with her knotty old hands.

The little boy's hanging fingers twitched nervously, his loosened shoulders and knees made him look lower and smaller than ever. The women in the aisle were listening now, greedily, humanly.

7

Mrs. Bascomb drew herself back. An expression of energy came into her face which for the moment did not look in the least wistful, but masterful. She tapped commandingly on her desk. 'There is nothing to be gained by going into unpleasant details in public, Mrs. Malone. None of this concerns me. I simply wished to tell you that Michael must have some quiet place in which to do his home-work, because if he does not do neater work than of late I shall be obliged to have him put back a grade.' She paused to let this threat sink in, and went on with finality, 'I merely thought it would be kinder to warn you beforehand, and give you a chance to make good.'

By the turn of her phrase, by gathering together some loose papers on her desk, by shifting in her chair and looking past the excited old woman to the next one in line, by a certain expression of her mouth and chin, she conveyed as though by a push on Mrs. Malone's back the fact that her interview was at an end.

The old woman stopped short, her lips still moving. She caught her breath, fumbled an instant with the fastenings of her cloak, looked around her vaguely, looked once more at her grandson's teacher, and taking his hand made her way to the door, dragging her feet. As they passed outside in the hall, a faint sound of repressed weeping from the little boy could be heard.

Mrs. Bascomb glanced at the young girl, and shook her head with a resigned gesture.

The next woman in line, a thick-waisted blonde with a flaxen-haired little girl beside her, stepped forward, but as she opened her mouth to speak, the door was pushed ajar and a pretty woman in a handsome velvet cloak made a rustling entrance. 'Oh, I'm *so* glad to find you still here, Mrs. Bascomb,' she said exuberantly, 'I was so afraid I'd be too late. How do you do? I haven't laid eyes on you since the last meeting of the Bridge Club. How splendidly you're looking. But you always do. My husband often says to me that it doesn't seem possible that both he and I went to school to you, and you looking just the same now as you did then. I declare I've got more wrinkles this minute than you have. But I'm worried into wrinkles. About our Freddie. That's what I

8

wanted to see you about to-day. Freddie's arithmetic.
If we . . .'

As she talked, her eyes had roved impartially and un-
seeingly over the desks and chairs and walls and waiting
women. But she now caught sight of the girl at the back
of the room, and recognized that there was another person
in sight. 'Oh, hallo there, Margaret Hill. What's a first-
grade teacher doing up on this floor?' she cried gaily.

Even as she spoke, her face and voice were coloured by
a recollection of the probable reason for the girl's presence.
It made her look good-naturedly mischievous; and it made
the girl blush, not displeased.

She answered with composure, but with some self-
consciousness, 'How do you do, Mrs. Marvin?'

Mrs. Bascomb smiled faintly, not annoyed by the un-
spoken implication which had passed between the two
women. 'I'm alone for a few days, you know. Ralph has
gone over to Harristown to see about some work for his
summer vacation. And I asked Margaret to have supper
with me.'

'Oh, yes, I *see!*' said Mrs. Marvin with an arch glance
at Margaret. 'Your Ralph graduates from the University
this coming June, doesn't he? Mercy! How time flies.
It doesn't seem possible he's old enough to graduate. But
of course, when you come to count up – I was in the
Eighth Grade, I remember, when he was a cunning little
tyke in the First.'

'Ralph was born in '87,' said his mother. 'He was only
three years old then. He was too young to come to school
at all. But of course I had nobody at home to leave him
with.'

The phrase was spoken with a drooping cadence, to
which Mrs. Marvin answered sympathetically, 'Yes, now
that I have children of my own, I often wonder how you
ever managed, left all alone when Ralph was little.
Goodness me! It's all I can do to keep track of mine, and
me with nothing else to do, and a husband to back me up.
How you ever took care of Ralph and earned the living
too! But of course Ralph was always such a sweet little
fellow. He never made you any trouble, I don't suppose.
Still I guess that was because you know how to manage

9

him so he wouldn't. I'm not so smart, I must say. I never can get Freddie to mind me, the way Ralph always minded you . . . all you ever had to do was to look real hard at him. Gracious! I tell Freddie's papa, often, I could look my head off at Freddie and he'd never even know it. Ralph always used to have his eyes on your face, waiting to see what you wanted him to do. What a lovely head of curls he used to have, too. I wish our Freddie's was like that. His is just as straight! And stringy, too. No matter what I put on it.'

It had cost Mrs. Bascomb no effort whatever to listen to all this, and now, very favourably disposed towards Freddie and his arithmetic, she said invitingly, 'Was there something I could do for you?'

At this, the stoutish woman with the little girl, who had been submissively waiting, stepped back and disappeared from sight, until the matter of Freddie's arithmetic had been discussed in detail and settled and until Mrs. Marvin had made all her last, cheery, chatty farewells.

When the door finally closed on her, the waiting woman once more became visible and once more took her place before the teacher's desk. Over her head Mrs. Bascomb glanced at the clock, but her tone was carefully patient as she asked, 'What was it, Mrs. Langwetter?'

Mrs. Langwetter hastily laid a murmured petition before the woman at the desk, who considered it, looking down at her white hands. Then, indulgently, 'Why, yes, Mrs. Langwetter, I think I could allow that if Greta would be sure to bring in all her written work.'

Mrs. Langwetter confounded herself in thanks and moved on.

Mrs. Bascomb turned her eyes on the last woman, who had been waiting from the first. 'Mrs. Armstrong, could you come another day, just as well?' she asked persuasively. 'I have a great deal I want to talk to you about. Jamie's writing needs attention, and his reading. I want him to do some oral reading at home in the evenings. It's rather long to explain, and I have been so much delayed this afternoon. I feel very tired. I'm not very strong, you know.' She added with the air of leaving it entirely for the other to decide, 'Of course, if it is just as convenient for *you*.'

Mrs. Armstrong hastened to say that she could *just* as well come another day; that it was *no* trouble at all; that she was so anxious for Jamie to get on well at school, and his papa was, too; and they were so grateful to Mrs. Bascomb for the interest she took in him; and of course if there was *anything* they could do at home to . . .

Over her head Mrs. Bascomb glanced fleetingly at the clock. Mrs. Armstrong lost the thread of what she was saying, not very well in hand at best, glanced hastily around her as if looking for something, seemed to remember that there was nothing she need look for, seized Jamie by the hand, and nodding and smiling anxiously, got herself out of the room, murmuring incoherencies about being *so* much obliged to Mrs. Bascomb for taking an ·interest in Jamie.

As the door closed, Mrs. Bascomb drew a long breath and relaxed in her chair, looking expectantly at the waiting girl.

Margaret wriggled herself out of her cramped seat and came at once to the desk. 'Oh, Mrs. Bascomb, how tired you must be!' she said intensely. 'All this after your day of teaching! How do you stand it, frail as you are. But how perfectly wonderful you are with them. It's an object lesson to see you. But I could teach for years and never learn how to take each one in just the right way, as you do. It was wonderful!'

'You dear girl,' murmured Mrs. Bascomb. She put her left hand to her forehead as though her head ached, but she looked up into the girl's face with a brave smile which spoke of weariness conquered.

Chapter 2

HALF-WAY down the hall Mrs. Bascomb stopped, 'Oh, I mustn't forget to call up Hammond and Babcock. They are going to send a man to see to the plumbing in my bathroom this afternoon. I was to telephone as I started home so that they'd know I'd be there to let him in.'

She disappeared into the booth in the office, leaving

Margaret to stand at the window, staring down at the black-beetle tops of the automobiles parked up and down Main Street, two stories below her. In spite of the muffling of the booth's double-door, the sound of indignant expostulation soon made itself heard, so that the girl had her sympathy ready when the door was flung open and Mrs. Bascomb, ruffled and resentful, stepped out.

'They say "they *haven't* any man to send this afternoon"!' she announced, giving an angry caricature of the presumably nonchalant accent at the other end of the line. 'Just like that! No excuses! No apologies! When they've promised and *promised* to send somebody!'

Margaret drooped under the sternness of Mrs. Bascomb's look on her. She had, of course, no connection with the missing plumber, but her certainty of this was not enough to protect her from that responsibility for the world in general and its mismanagement of which Mrs. Bascomb's eyes accused her.

'It's simply dreadful!' she hastily proffered the most emphatic superlative she could think of. 'It's simply *dreadful* how they break their promises.'

But she had not been superlative enough. 'Dreadful's no word for it!' said Mrs. Bascomb severely, rebuking her for lukewarmness. 'People nowadays have no conscience. They'll say *any*thing!'

'Is it something very serious the matter with your plumbing?' asked Margaret, casting about for the right thing to say. She was instantly aware that she had said the wrong one. Mrs. Bascomb turned away without answering, as if the question were too trivial to consider.

Margaret followed her out meekly, and walked down the hall after her, trying to guess from the look of her back whether her indignation had cooled down enough for a new topic to be safe. Their footsteps echoed hollowly in the after-school emptiness of the halls. At the head of the stairs, Margaret lengthened her step and overtook her companion, casting a cautious, practised look of inquiry into her face. She saw nothing in it now but the usual fatigued resignation, and ventured to bring out shyly, 'Have you any news from Ralph? I haven't heard from him, myself . . . not even the comic post-card he threatened

12

to send to me here at the school, to shock Miss Latham.'

The moment she mentioned the comic post-card she was sorry. Mrs. Bascomb had no taste for jokes and her patient manner of listening to pleasantries took away all their savour. Margaret hoped she would not ask 'which comic card?'

She did not. She also agreed tacitly to let the subject be changed, and to permit the recreant plumber to drop out of sight.

'No, I haven't heard from Ralph, either,' she said, snapping the wrist of one glove shut and beginning to put on the other. 'He'll be back so soon he probably didn't think it worth while to write. He had decided, you know, that if he didn't secure the promise of a position with the Telephone Company for this summer, he wasn't going to stay in Harristown to try for another. His University classes begin again on Monday, you know.'

'Oh, I didn't really *expect* him to write,' said Margaret disclaimingly. A door, in the basement two stories below them, opened with a crash, and confused voices burst up towards them, mingled with the sound of loud, unrestrained weeping.

'Oh, *dear!*' said Mrs. Bascomb, stopping short and looking alarmed, 'What do you suppose is the matter now? I can't stand anything *else*.'

Someone came bounding up the basement stairs, three steps at a time. A tall, raw-boned, wild-eyed boy it was, who, hearing them above him, stopped, leaned out over the railing and glared up at them to see who they were.

When he recognized Mrs. Bascomb, he cried loudly in a shaking voice, 'Say, are there any teachers left in the building? Miss Plummer? Mrs. Jeffries? May Monaghan has just heard her mother had to be taken to the hospital this afternoon, and she's carrying on dreadfully. We don't know what to do with her.'

Mrs. Bascomb looked relieved. 'Yes, yes, I'm sure that Miss Plummer is still in her room,' she said hastily, beginning to move on down the stairs. 'I saw her there with a lot of children as we passed just now.'

The boy leaped up past them, his face white, his eyes

outrunning his feet. From the depths, the hysteric cries rose up louder and louder.

The two women hurried down the stairs and out into the street, shutting the door of the building behind them with relief.

'I suppose I ought to have gone to try to quiet her myself,' said Mrs. Bascomb, looking disturbed, 'and if there hadn't been someone else in the building, of course I would. But it seems as though I'd had my share this afternoon, with that dreadful old Mrs. Malone shouting and making such a scene. And Miss Plummer is so good with that sort of person. She doesn't seem to feel things as I do. It sets me all trembling to be with people who have lost their self-control, as those big Irish girls do, when they scream and take on. And there's nothing anybody can do for her, after all. Miss Plummer will . . .'

The girl broke in, leaning towards her fondly, 'You ought to be protected against that sort of thing, always,' she said. 'People not so sensitive as you, are the ones who should . . .'

'I know it's a weakness of character,' said Mrs. Bascomb with a sigh, 'but it's the way I'm made. I just can't help it.' She caught sight of her reflection in a window as they passed, and pushed her hat slightly more forward.

The girl asked with eager sympathy, 'How do you do anyway, these days, Mrs. Bascomb? I've been worrying about those sleepless nights.'

'I'm not troubled so *much* with sleeplessness now,' Mrs. Bascomb measured her words with the care of a scientist conveying exact information about important natural phenomena, 'although I never have a *really* good night. But lately I've had another trouble. It starts with a heavy feeling, *here*.' She laid her gloved hand on her right side, 'and after that come shooting pains that run clear up to my shoulder. Sometimes when I wake in the morning, I have scarcely strength enough to crawl out of bed. But of course . . .'

They were turning away from Main Street when she began this report. They were many blocks farther along, very near to her own street, when she finished it, saying

14

bravely, 'But I don't suppose it's very serious. Just something else for me to live through.'

'I should certainly see a doctor,' said Margaret.

'Oh, Dr. Dewey never does anything for you unless you have a broken leg.'

'Why, don't you try this new Westopractor?'

'I haven't heard anything about him. Who is he?'

'A youngish man. Dr. Pell. Just moved into the Cheney Block. They say he's wonderful. The new modern treatments, you know. Only better. Partly bones and partly complexes.'

'Pell?' asked Mrs. Bascomb. 'Did you say Pell? What are his initials?'

'I don't remember. Oh, yes, Dr. M. Buckingham Pell.'

'Why, for mercy's sakes, that must be that little guttersnipe of a Maurice Pell who gave me so much trouble, when I had the fourth grade, years ago.'

The girl instantly threw over Dr. Pell. 'Aren't you wonderful!' she cried. 'Everybody always says there's no fooling you about anybody in town. You've had them all in your room in school. And with your memory . . .'

'I'd not be likely to forget that worthless little liar! I never saw such an unreliable child. The word of truth wasn't in him.'

The girl had not the slightest interest in Dr. Pell, a fact which now made itself impalpably felt in spite of her effort to continue her conscientious interest in anything Ralph's mother might say.

'I certainly hope you find *some* doctor who can help you,' she murmured.

'Oh, I'll get along,' said Mrs. Bascomb, evidently thinking of something else.

There was a long silence, through which the girl felt her companion finding her way through associations of ideas which Margaret could not follow, to quite another plane from the one on which they had been talking. She felt the silence filled by something grave and deep – and remote from her. Glancing timidly sideways, she knew that Mrs. Bascomb was thinking of her husband. Margaret had seen before that brooding stillness in the older woman's face, and knew that nothing brought it there save a thought of

15

the man dead for so long, but not forgotten, who had been Ralph's father.

The girl shivered responsively. She wished she dared ask Mrs. Bascomb about her husband, get her to talk freely of her short happiness, and her long sorrow. She felt that such talk would be a draught for the thirst of her own heart. The little surface things of life seemed so dry and trivial to her now, her heart filled as it was with hope and doubt.

She felt an inner trembling, and presently she knew that, through her silence, something of her emotion was being communicated to the other woman. As they turned into the pretty, well-kept yard, in front of the white, green-shuttered cottage, Mrs. Bascomb took the girl's hand in hers for an instant.

But, as they took off their hats and set about getting supper, they talked only about the little surface things of life. From the blue-and-white dining-room, where Margaret was setting the table for two, to white enamelled kitchen where Mrs. Bascomb in a fresh cretonne apron was managing oil stove and fireless cooker, there was an interchange of sober, house-wifey talk.

'You'll find the forks in the upper left-hand drawer, Margaret.'

'Oh, Mrs. Bascomb, how perfectly sweet the drawer looks! It's a picture! The forks all laid together and the spoons cheek to cheek.'

'Yes, I always think that the moment's extra time taken for *real* order is well-spent. Do you like your potatoes mashed or fried?'

'Oh, *mashed!*'

'I'm glad to hear you say so. We Americans eat too much fried food, I always say.'

'Where shall I find the salt-cellars, Mrs. Bascomb? Oh, yes, I see them, the little old darlings. However do you dare use such valuable antiques?'

'That's the advantage, I always say, of doing your own work. You *do* dare use your nice things. Those salt-cellars were part of my grandmother's wedding outfit. She was a Massachusetts Peabody. The buffet is one of the things that came down to me from her family. Have you about finished, Margaret? For you'd have time to run up to the bathroom and wash your hands before I start to serve. Open the two little white doors on the west wall, and you'll find the clean towels. I hope you won't mind that my toilet soap is all scentless.'

'Oh, Mrs. Bascomb, I *loathe* perfumed soap.'

And yet, as they settled their lady-like persons at opposite ends of the daintily set table, they smiled intimately across it at each other as though they had been exchanging confidences.

They went on chatting in the vein which talk always took with Mrs. Bascomb: – of the way the janitor at school oiled the floors, of Margaret's novice work down in the first-grade room, of queer old Miss Plummer and her awful hats ('though she is very good-hearted, we must always remember that, I tell people'); of how hard Margaret found it to 'handle parents' ('My dear girl, just remember that all parents are afraid the teacher will be hard on their particular child. You've only to make them feel that, once or twice, and you have no further trouble with *parents!*'); of a new method of teaching fractions which was being tried out in Newark, New Jersey; of the engagement of a schoolmate of Margaret's and the linen she was beginning to collect; of a spring lecture course which the Community Club was arranging because the winter lectures had been such a success. Mrs. Bascomb asked if Margaret had heard whether this new series was to be on household decoration, or the Commission form of municipal government. She had heard that both subjects were under consideration. They were sure to be splendid, in any case, because the Community Club got such fine speakers. 'I never miss one,' said Mrs. Bascomb.

They even talked about the movies, and Mrs. Bascomb confessed to a weakness for them. 'But then, I think it is good for a teacher to get out a good deal in the evening,' she said. 'There's so much in life that's sad, one needs to forget it all, sometimes. And life often looks very empty when you're past forty. I always try to get out three evenings every week, as a matter of principle, even when I'm very tired. It keeps you up with the times.'

17

Margaret spoke of music, of a series of concerts to be given, and Mrs. Bascomb acquiesced, 'Oh, yes, of course I like music, too. Very much. It's so pleasant of an evening, especially when made by your friends at home. I often say I like it better than cards. Though I must say I do like a good game of bridge.'

But Margaret felt that they were using this chat as a boy whirls his sling around and around his head – the better to loose his stone. After the meal was finished, the dishes dispatched, and the fern-dish set back on the polished old mahogany of the dining-room table, she knew that the real moment had come at last.

Although it was still early in April, it was warm enough to sit out for a time on the porch, where Mrs. Bascomb sank down in a wicker arm-chair, and Margaret coiled herself on a cushion, her arm over the other woman's knees.

'How just *right* this porch and its furnishings are!' she said. 'It looks so like *you*. All the house does.'

'Yes, it's been a dear little house for Ralph and me, a real expression of our personality. That is what a home should be. Every littlest thing in a house is so precious when it is part of your past.'

'Yes, yes,' murmured the girl in perfect although somewhat preoccupied accord with anything Mrs. Bascomb could say. She was not thinking of the house at all.

But Mrs. Bascomb was. She went on, 'And when you've struggled for it . . . ! We had it only partly paid for when I was left alone. Everybody thought I was foolish to try to keep it, with a mortgage. And Ralph to bring up. But I couldn't have given it up. Ralph's father had selected it. I came here as a bride. Ralph was born here. It was sacred to me. Ralph was ten years old before I had paid off the mortgage. But he has always had a home.'

Margaret lifted her eyes. 'He's always loved it, I know.'

'Yes, Ralph has always been a good son,' said Mrs. Bascomb, answering what she had thought the girl would be sure to say, 'a real comfort. He has never given his mother one minute's anxiety, I'll say that for him. And what more can you say for a young man? I've always managed him through his affection. One sad or grieved look from me was enough.'

'Everybody always speaks about how perfect your relationship to Ralph has always been,' murmured the girl.

'It's a great responsibility to bring up a boy. I've always thought the best way was to keep his confidence. He has always told me everything.'

There was a silence. Both women looked off into the darkness, their faces untroubled and dreamy. Then Mrs. Bascomb remarked, 'It doesn't seem possible that my little son is a man now. Think of his having passed his twenty-first birthday.' She drew a long breath and said with the accent that suited the words, 'But he'll always be just a dear little boy to his old mother.'

The girl reached up, took her hand and gave it a sympathetic pressure. Then with a long breath, she laid her head down on the other woman's lap. The action was a shy avowal. Mrs. Bascomb bent over the smooth, well-brushed fair hair and stroked it gently.

She went on now, as to someone with the right to know, 'It's been hard to help Ralph to choose his life-work. Of course I wanted to leave him *perfectly* free to follow his own inclination. But I'm very well satisfied with his choice of the law. My father and grandfather were lawyers. It seems very suitable for my son to enter the same profession.'

Margaret said, 'He worries, I am sure, about being an expense to you so long, while he's in law school. But he plans to work ever so hard during the vacations, and earn as much of his expenses as he can.'

'Oh, that's of no consequence,' said his mother handsomely. 'I've given my life to Ralph gladly, and I will always be thankful to do anything for him. Any mother would feel so.'

She went on, 'You feel that it is *worth* making sacrifices for a son who is a credit to you. And Ralph has always been that. I've always been proud to show Ralph to my friends.' After a moment she continued, 'Of course a long preparation for a profession sometimes means a rather late marriage. And I don't approve of late marriages. I'm

19

not one of the grasping mothers who want to keep their children for themselves. Though, of course, it'll be a terrible wrench to give Ralph up. He's always been so *mine.*'

'But Mrs. Bascomb, any girl worthy of Ralph wouldn't *want* you to give him up. The idea! Of course, he'll always be *yours!*'

Mrs. Bascomb pressed her hand and said, 'That's very sweet of you to say, dear.' (But her tone took it as a matter of course, as the least that Margaret could profess). 'And as to the money difficulties of marrying young, if Ralph married a girl with a profession of her own, she could help out during the first few years.'

'Yes, of course, of course,' agreed Margaret, self-consciously.

'A little hardship at the beginning of married life doesn't hurt young people, I always say. When Ralph's father and I were married, we were really poor. The house wasn't at all as it is now. Just a bare little shell, built to sell, as Ralph's father used to say. I have only carried out what we had talked of together.'

Margaret looked up, hesitated, and finally ventured, timidly, 'Is . . . is Ralph very much like his father?'

'Not at all, not in the *least!*' said Mrs. Bascomb, the answer bursting out with the effect of something spoken before she had had time to think. She felt the girl's surprise and added, her voice shaking, 'Of course nobody in the world could seem to me like my husband.'

Margaret had never heard her use any phrase other than 'Ralph's father.' 'He must have been wonderful,' she said in a low, abashed voice.

Mrs. Bascomb was silent. Then, as if coming to a decision, 'Did I ever show you his picture?' she asked.

'Oh, no,' breathed the girl, much moved.

Mrs. Bascomb pulled a thin gold chain about her neck and detached from it a little oval locket. 'Take it into the house where there's a light,' she said. 'I'll sit here.'

But before the girl could reach the electric light on the table inside, the woman was beside her and had the locket again in her hand. 'I'll open it for you,' she said.

The two gazed in silence at the face that looked at them from the gold oval. 'I see what you mean,' said Margaret, 'he doesn't look a bit like Ralph. The eyes . . .'

'He had the finest eyes in the world,' said his widow sharply, as if the girl had criticized them. 'When he looked at you, you wanted . . . you . . .' Her voice died away as though she had forgotten that the girl was there. She held the locket in her hollowed hand, looking down at it steadily. Margaret looked with her and saw that under the glass of the other half of the locket was a piece of paper with some words in handwriting. Mrs. Bascomb turned her hand so that they were legible.

'Read it aloud,' she said.

Margaret read, 'Character is destiny.'

'After his death I copied that from the little note-book he always carried. He lived that sort of life. I never was his equal. I couldn't follow him.'

Margaret, too, had not followed him. She did not make much out of the words she had read aloud, except that they sounded solemn and like something heard in church. She felt embarrassed and did not know what to say next, for fear of making the wrong comment.

She glanced from those disconcertingly deep steady eyes and ironic mouth, to the large framed photograph on the piano from which Ralph's bright gay face laughed out at her, and thought to herself that Ralph was forty times hand-somer than his father had been, and looked a great deal easier to live with. She did not like the face in the locket at all. She murmured, 'Yes, he looks wonderful! But I think I would have been a little afraid of him.'

'I was very much afraid of him. I still am,' said his widow, 'the way you are of your conscience. If he had lived . . .'

She shut the locket, put it back on the chain and dropped it into her bosom again. She looked sternly at the girl as though she were blaming her for that long-ago death. They were far from the bland composure of their earlier talk. Margaret had said she would have been afraid of Mr. Bascomb. She looked now as though she were rather afraid of his widow, as though she did not recognize in her the woman of whose approval she had been so happily sure, an hour ago, on the subject of scentless soap and mashed potatoes.

'I believe I'd better be going,' she said, although she noticed that the clock showed only half-past eight.

'Oh, it's early yet,' said her hostess, in the tone which does not detain the guest.

Margaret went hastily back into the hall to look for wraps. But when she returned to the living-room, her pretty, pale-blue cape on her shoulders, she found the Mrs. Bascomb she had always known, her patient face framed in waving, grey-brown hair, her head tipped a little to one side, her habitual faint mixed smile on her lips.

'What message shall I give Ralph for you, if I write?' she asked.

'Oh, just my best regards,' answered the girl correctly.

'I'll tell him you are looking sweeter than ever, that's what I'll tell him,' said his mother.

Margaret made a little rush, threw her arms around the other's neck and kissed her with ardour.

Mrs. Bascomb patted her gently on the back. 'You dear girl,' she murmured.

Chapter 3

AFTER Margaret had gone away, Mrs. Bascomb stood for some moments, her eyes fixed and absent. She was regretting that she had spoken to the girl about her husband. The thought of John pierced too deep. Strange that after all these years, she still felt the pang . . . half of fear as she had said . . . as if there were disappointment in that well-remembered deep gaze of his. She put up her hands to protect herself against that look now, gathering together hastily a defence against that inexplicable reproach. What was that disappointment? What more could she have done? Had she not always done what was right as far as she could? And by 'right' she did not mean only reading her Bible every night and going to church . . . no, she had worn herself out in the service of other people; she never did what she wanted to do; she had made her life one long self-abnegation . . . why was it then that when a sudden deep thought of John thrust itself into her life, she always began thus tremulously to defend herself against his eyes?

With a rush, up from the depths, there came a cry of pure sorrow, 'If John were only here, he would tell me! If John were only with me!'

The tears rose brimming to her eyes. But she did not allow them to fall. She always put away hastily that upward surge of grief. She told herself that it was weak to give way to it, that it was morbid. In reality, she was terrified by it as a timid swimmer is panic-struck to feel deep water under him. To what, away from her traditional moorings, would it sweep her, if she let it have its way with her?

By long practice she had learnt how to escape from it, filling her mind and hands with little material processes. Now, in a moment she had once more pushed it all down below the surface. She was thinking quite collectedly of her housekeeping – her handbag lying on the sideboard, a magazine out of place on the living-room table, a picture a little awry on the wall, her waterproof cloak still hanging on the hat-rack in the hall. She stepped about the business of restoring to the house its usual meticulous neatness, and felt the normal tick-tick-tick of her usual thoughts within her head.

With them came her usual depression, settling down like fine dust, powdering with grey her every thought, tingeing with weariness even her approval of what seemed more and more certain – Ralph's choice of Margaret Hill. Everything made her weary, nowadays, it seemed, even spending an hour or two with a gentle, biddable girl like Margaret. It was the perspective of living with Margaret . . . of going on living anyhow . . . that wearied her. Nothing was ever quite right. Margaret had certainly been too open in showing that she was ready for Ralph to reach out his hand and pluck her. But girls hadn't got the reserve they used to have. However, it would do no harm to have Ralph's wife a little crazy about him. And the money Margaret would inherit would do no harm either. Though of course she would not wish Ralph to consider that. And she knew he would not. Whatever else you might say of Ralph, nobody could accuse him of being mercenary or calculating . . . the beautiful, game-loving big boy!

She half suspected him now of staying on in Harristown to see the opening of the baseball series there. He was always running over to Harristown to see basket-ball or baseball. What a strange passion men and boys had for games! Sometimes it seemed to Mrs. Bascomb that they really cared about nothing but competitive sport . . . *really* cared, with heat and passion. She certainly never saw anybody anywhere get so excited about anything as she had often seen men over a football game. She thought it very childish, although familiar, her father and her brother having shared in this weakness. Ralph was like her side of the family, anyhow. Just like his Uncle George. Yes, George had been just such a handsome, taking boy, although he had grown bald and stout so soon it was hard to remember that at Ralph's age he had had something of Ralph's dashing good looks, and bright gay ways. She ought to have told Margaret Hill nothing more than that Ralph was like the Evarts and not like the Bascombs. She wished again she had not been led into talking with the girl about John. A weak, clinging vine like that had no idea what love could be. . . . And she never would have! Ralph would never . . .

She stopped short in the midst of this thought, gathering her forces together to repel a familiar enemy, the sort of thought she did not approve of, the thought that Ralph would have been more to her if he had been like his father. She told herself that it was not 'loyal to Ralph' to allow herself to feel this. In reality she was afraid of the hurt it gave her.

She put it away with a resentful push and, once more on the plane where she willed to live, she continued her progress towards the kitchen sink where she was carrying the dining-room fern. She was proud of the invariably flourishing condition of her house plants both here and in her room at school. She had a good deal of contempt for women who did not succeed with them, and enjoyed seeing those in other classrooms wither and droop, while hers were always crisply green. It was the one thing she did not

24

approve of in Margaret Hill, that she had no hand for plants. She felt it as not a good sign.

But, she thought, sighing, nothing is ever just right. If there was one hard lesson which life had taught her more than another, it was that. She was getting worn out with it all. She had had so much more than her fair share of hard things. Her work all these years had told on her. Everybody said she was overworked, teaching school and housekeeping too. And at school it wasn't just the teaching. The interviews with parents for instance, absurd as parents were. And that lying firm of plumbers! Yes, she was worn to the bone with it all. As Margaret said, she felt things too intensely. In the first moment of indignation over some outrageous incident like that, she simply *boiled!* This afternoon the heat of her resentment had seemed beating back on her in hot waves from the walls of the telephone booth; the round nickel mouth of the receiver had taken on an angry look as though it reflected her indignation. Nobody could feel things so intensely, and not be worn out afterwards.

And she was the one who always had to see to everything. Ralph was so careless and heedless. He was a good boy, Ralph was, but not quick to see changes in his mother's mood, absorbed in his own trivial interests. She often had to exaggerate her expression before he took note of it. Although it was true that when he had been selfish and careless and had hurt her, he was uneasy till she allowed herself to smile and forgive him and be cheerful again. Yes, Ralph was much easier to manage than many boys would have been.

As she often did when she was alone, she now drew a long sighing breath, and, leaving the watered fern to drain, she turned out the light. The sudden darkness seemed to come from within as well as from without. She told herself that it was the shadow cast by approaching old age. She felt old . . . old and used up. Her wish to live had dwindled till now when she woke in the morning, she could not think of any real reason for getting up and grinding through another day. There would be nothing in it for *her*, any more than in any of the other empty days.

These were thoughts which she made no effort to put

25

away. They came faster and faster, zestfully flapping their black wings. Yes, she had worn herself out in the service of others, without ever getting anything for herself. To be worn out at forty-three! But she had always worked so hard, twice what other women did.

She must begin to think of herself now. She ought to spend what was left of her energy in safeguarding her peace and security. It was time. And soon she would be able to. As time goes, Ralph would soon be independent. She saw him as he would be, a successful lawyer, respected, feared, prosperous, and deeply aware of what he owed his mother. Of course Ralph would always provide the necessities of life for her. But she wanted something of her very own beside that, for the little comforts of life, so that she could have things . . . at last . . . as *she* wanted them. It was due her, after her life of self-sacrifice. She had so little money in the savings bank, barely a thousand dollars. But she could soon begin to save more, to lay by something for herself.

She began a mental calculation of how much she could save in a year, after Ralph was earning his own living, and how much income that would mean. Annuities always brought in more than anything else. Something in this train of thought brought up the picture of the financial page of a newspaper, and that made her remember that she had forgotten to look in the mail-box for her evening paper when she had turned into the walk with Margaret. By this time she had turned off all the electric lights in the house, but had not yet locked the front door. She opened it, went out of the house and down the path towards the mail-box.

She stepped from the box-like walls of her house into infinity. Over her head the sky rose, boundless and black. From the far end of the street, where it ran off into the country, came the shrill quaver of frog song, rhythmic like an inner pulse. The moist air, charged with the pungent odour of life renewed, rose and fell in sighing breaths. Immensity brooded over the earth.

Mrs. Bascomb put her hand into the mail-box, thinking fixedly, 'It's only right for me to begin to think about

myself a little. To have things more as *I* want them. It's
high time I did. After all these years!'

A letter came with the newspaper. Probably a bill. She
walked back up the path. Before the fixity of her thought,
infinity shrank to nothing – to being a dark night in
April.

She remembered that she had not yet put out the milk-
bottle.

Stepping into the passage, she walked securely in the
dark, knowing every board in the floor, over to the button
which controlled the electric light, and pressed it. Oh, she
saw from the handwriting that the letter was from Ralph.
It was a pity she hadn't thought to look in the mail-box
before Margaret left. They could have shared the news
together. She liked to read out Ralph's letters to Margaret,
omitting certain parts which she read silently to herself,
while Margaret waited.

Still standing by the electric button, she opened the
letter. She read it at a glance.

DEAR MOTHER:

I am writing to tell you something that will surprise
you, I know. Mother, I was married this afternoon. It
was rather sudden, of course, but it seemed best. Charlotte
Hicks is the name of your new daughter, and I hope you
will like having a daughter. You know you have always
told me you believe in early marriages. Of course, I know
I am very young, but I am of age, and I'm ready to work
hard to support my wife. I'll have to give up the idea of
being a lawyer, and hustle right out to get a job, as soon
as I graduate. But I think I will like that just as well, if
not better, than going on studying so many more years.
Lottie is not used to luxury. She is very anxious to meet
you. Her own mother died when she was a little girl and
she is looking forward to having a mother again. I hope
you won't mind too much our not letting you know. We
didn't have any wedding to invite anybody to. Just went
before a justice of the peace, with no fuss about it at all.

We both send love,

Your affectionate son,
RALPH.

In a hurriedly scrawled postscript, 'Mother, Lottie's not your kind, but she's all right. Ralph.'

The first movement made by the woman who read this letter was a wild look around her, as if to make sure that no one could see her, that no one had seen the news in the letter.

No one was there. But everything she saw looked at her hatefully, malignantly. In the interval between the moment when she had dropped her eyes to the letter, and the moment when she had raised them to look again at the world, everything had changed. The familiar furniture glared at her menacingly, like crouching demons, swollen with anger. She gave a cry of terror at the sight, and with a startled reflex gesture turned off the light.

The darkness came like oxygen to a man suffocating. It seemed to save her life, her physical life.

But for an instant she was quite out of her mind, there in the darkness. She was wondering passionately who she was, what woman it could be standing in this hate-filled, strange house. She must get away, out of some appalling danger which threatened her. The paper rustled in her hand with an ominous sound, and more terrified than ever, she pressed the button frantically to have the light once more.

The vision which had come with her momentary madness had gone. There was nothing there but her own house, her own furniture, her own property, docile, passive, dear to her.

She sank into a chair feeling sick. What was the matter with her? She had had the preposterous idea that Ralph had written to say that he . . .

Her eyes fell on the piece of paper clutched in her hand and as she stiffened, her eyes followed the words. She was aware once of thinking, 'The postscript is not like the rest. She probably stood over him as he wrote, and all he could really say, himself, was what he scrawled at the end when she was not looking.'

Every time the word 'she' came into her mind, she felt a looming black figure behind her, filling the room with peril. But she could not turn her head.

28

Other than this thought about the postscript, nothing came into her head, although she continued automatically to read and re-read the letter, innumerable times, thousands of times it seemed to her, coming to the end and starting again at the beginning, unable to stop herself.

DEAR MOTHER:

I am writing to tell you something that will surprise you, I know. Mother, I was married this afternoon. It was rather sudden of course, but it seemed best. Charlotte Hicks is the name of your new daughter, and I hope you will like having a daughter. You know you have always told me you approved of early marriages. Of course, I know I am very young, but I am of age and I am ready to work hard to support my wife. I'll have to give up the idea of being a lawyer, and hustle right out to get a job. But I think I will like that just as well, if not better, than going on studying so many years. Lottie is not used to luxury. She is very anxious to meet you. Her own mother died when she was a little girl and she is looking forward to having a mother again. I hope you won't mind too much our not letting you know. We didn't have any wedding to invite anybody to. Just went before a justice of the peace, with no fuss about it at all.

We both send love,

Your affectionate son,
RALPH.

And in the hurried scrawl which seemed like Ralph's very voice, 'Mother, Lottie's not your kind, but she's all right. Ralph.'

After a time, Mrs. Bascomb became aware that she was in great pain, and she connected this feeling in some way with her prolonged sitting in that chair. She felt that if she could move she would be relieved. But she could not move.

And yet, when she heard a sudden knocking, she sprang to her feet and rushing to the door, fell upon it locking and double-locking it noisily.

'Don't be startled, Mrs. Bascomb,' said Margaret Hill's

voice from the outside, 'it's only me. I forgot my handbag. And it was so early I thought it would be all right to come back and get it to-night.'

'Oh,' said Mrs. Bascomb. She did not recognize her own voice. It seemed years since she had heard the sound of it.

A clock behind her struck nine. When the last stroke stopped vibrating she heard the ticking of the clock again. Of course she must open the door. At once. If she did not, Margaret would suspect that something had happened.

She had never conceived of any strain like the effort with which she now fought her way up through circle after circle of her inner chaos till she felt herself able to turn the key in the lock.

Margaret Hill had not noticed that there had been a pause longer than the one natural to a timid feminine woman, like Mrs. Bascomb. When the door opened and she stepped in, she saw Mrs. Bascomb's back, walking away into the kitchen.

'Where do you think you left it?' asked Mrs. Bascomb's voice over her shoulder, as she disappeared into the kitchen.

'Oh, I remember exactly where. In the bathroom. I took it up there because my powder puff was in it.'

She ran quickly upstairs. When she came down, Mrs. Bascomb was just coming out of the kitchen, the fern dish in her hand, the green of the leaves freshly varnished with water. Margaret saw that she had interrupted Mrs. Bascomb in the nightly ceremony of watering her fern. How fussy she was about her house plants. It was a subject on which Margaret allowed herself to feel some irritation with Ralph's mother.

'How beautiful your fern looks!' she said enthusiastically.

'I always think the maidenhair a little more refined looking than the common Boston fern,' said Mrs. Bascomb, setting it down on the table.

'Well, good-night again,' said Margaret. 'Sorry to have bothered you.'

'Good night,' said Mrs. Bascomb, walking towards a window and raising her arm to draw the blind.

Margaret thought she walked a little stiffly. After all,
Mrs. Bascomb was really not young any more, thought the
twenty-year-old girl. As she ran down the porch steps,
she heard again the sound of the key turning in the front
door.

Chapter 4

MRS. BASCOMB was sitting stiffly in a dining-room chair,
her knees under the dining-room table as though she were
expecting a meal to be served. She did not know that she
was there, rather than anywhere else, all her capacity to
know anything being concentrated on knowing that Ralph
was married, had married without letting her know, had
been carrying on a surreptitious love-affair without
breathing a word to her, had been lying to her, perhaps
for months. . . . Ralph for whom she had done everything a
mother can do for a child.

Margaret's entrance had shocked her back to full consciousness. All her intelligence was aroused . . . gone now
the insane vision of everything glaring upon her with hate,
gone the paralysed inability to rise from her chair. Now
she felt a frightful limitless energy, felt that she could
have risen from her chair, and walked forty times around
the world, if that would unmarry Ralph and give him
back to her as she had had him . . . as she had thought she
had him.

But nothing could now give her back Ralph. The
deadly certainty of this was what was being served to her,
as she sat there straight in her straight chair, her arms
laid on her well-polished dining-room table.

She felt the deadly poison of this certainty filling her
body. But she did not die. There she sat, Mary Bascomb,
who must go on living. By nine o'clock the next morning
she must have found some way of going on living.

She had not told Margaret Hill. No, as instinctively
as she would have stepped back from the edge of a precipice
she had recoiled from letting Margaret know. But to-
morrow morning at the opening hour of school she must
walk off the precipice, her eyes wide open. For it would

be of no use to try to hide it. It would be in the newspapers. Everybody would know that Mrs. Bascomb who always boasted so about having her son's entire confidence. . . .

She started back from this thought and fell ragingly to scorn of Margaret Hill. What a weak, cold fish that girl was, she thought, with all the opportunity that had been given her, not to be able to hold Ralph. Girls, nowadays, had no blood in their veins! She had always thought Margaret a poor stick, and now she knew it. And yet the girl would make a scene when she heard the news, would weep and feel aggrieved, and perhaps expect Ralph's mother to sympathize with her. Mrs. Bascomb's indignation boiled at the idea of thus being called upon to pretend that another could be considered as suffering even a part of what she felt. She detested in advance the pathetic look which she knew Margaret would put on. It was rather late in the day for her to look pathetic!

Abruptly she stopped thinking of Margaret. She had other things to think of. What was she herself to do? What in the world did Ralph expect her to do? Without a penny in his pocket except what was left of his week's allowance from his mother. With two months' class-work between him and his diploma. It was crazy. There was nothing that could be done.

But something had to be done. And before nine o'clock to-morrow morning, when she must face her world and have some attitude to take. She tried to visualize it, her appearance in the assembly hall for morning exercises, and afterwards in the halls, and in the lunch-room at noon. She could not imagine herself there, bare to all those prying eyes full of what they would call pity but which would be satisfaction that after all Mrs. Bascomb's wonderful Ralph . . .

She sat there stiffly, hour after hour, consuming the gall and poison which were being served to her.

At intervals she roused herself and tried to consider practical ways and means. Come, come . . . what could she do? Something must be done at once. If Ralph and this . . . if both of them could only disappear at once . . . go to California, to Canada . . . But how could they live? Ralph had no money, no profession, was only a boy.

If only she had money. She could mortgage the house . . . sell it.

After such frantic flights as these, she came back to quieter thoughts relieved by her own intemperateness. After all, it might be all right. In spite of the postscript which showed Ralph was ashamed of her, the girl might be creditable, or might be made to appear so; whereas to have Ralph disappear would make everyone think there was something disgraceful about his marriage. Yes, that had been a crazy plan. She put it away and tried to think of another. After all, Ralph had said the girl was 'all right.'

The clock ticked with sombre insistence, and at intervals struck another hour.

At half-past five she rose, trembling with weakness, made herself a cup of strong black coffee, drank it hot and walked down through the April concert of the shouting birds to the telegraph office in the railway station.

The young night-operator was still behind the counter, pale and puffy-eyed with sleeplessness. Mrs. Bascomb recognized him as a boy about Ralph's age, who had been in her class in school and in Ralph's class in High School. 'How do you do, Jimmy?' she said. 'I didn't know you worked here.'

'Good morning, Mrs. Bascomb,' he said, surprised to see her out at that hour.

'May I have a blank, please?' asked Mrs. Bascomb, getting her fountain pen from her handbag.

She wrote: 'Your letter received. Mother's home always yours. Bring Charlotte home and we will talk things over and make plans for the future. If arrive afternoon train, key in usual place. Go in and make yourselves at home. Love, Mother.'

As he read this, the operator could not hide his astonishment. Mrs. Bascomb had braced herself for it; she answered gently, 'Yes, my bad boy has gone and married. Rather sooner than I thought. But I have always believed in early marriages.' (She thought it likely that the young man had already heard her express this opinion).

After his monotonous, empty night, the telegraph operator welcomed news. 'Funny thing,' he thought, 'I had a notion that Ralph Bascomb had been running

33

around with that Hill girl a whole lot. But his real girl must have been in Harristown. So that's what he's been up to, beating it off over there all the time to basket-ball games.'

He read the telegram again, pencil in hand, counting the words. He was thinking, 'Just like Ralph to go and do it on the sly. Those pretty, smooth-spoken boys that the old ladies fall for . . . they'll bear watching. I'll bet Ralph's mother would be surprised at the clip he's been hitting up since he got away from her at the University.'

To Mrs. Bascomb he said, 'Well, at that, it's an awful nice message to send after a runaway match. It's not everybody who'd be so good-natured about it, I'll say. Seventy-six cents, please.'

She smiled faintly and laid down a dollar bill.

As he looked in the change drawer, the operator was thinking tolerantly, 'Oh, well, shucks! can you blame him, at that? A fellow's got to have some fun in life, more'n Mrs. Bascomb's sewing society crowd'll give you. Ralph's just a kid. And a kind of triflin' kid, too. No real harm in him.'

Aloud, as he counted out the change, he remarked, 'Charlotte. I always liked that name, sort of.'

'Yes,' said Mrs. Bascomb, picking up the silver pieces. 'It is rather a pretty name.'

She went back to her house, took in the waiting milk-bottle, and sitting straight at her dining-room table, ate a dish of oatmeal and cream. When she finished, she still sat on, before the empty dish, in the silent room, whose silence seemed waiting for some sound.

Presently, the clock behind her began to strike seven, and as if this were the sound she had been awaiting, she bowed herself forward as though someone had dealt her a brutal blow on the chest, and began to weep loudly.

Chapter 5

JIMMY WALTON, the night operator, boarded in the same house with Miss Saunders, the second-grade teacher, and Miss Preston, secretary to the Principal. Hearing the others at the breakfast table comment on the surprising item of news in the morning paper, he spoke of having seen Mrs. Bascomb. Of course he did not tell them what she had telegraphed, because that would have been against professional etiquette. But as the two young teachers remarked, walking to the tram together, 'You could see well enough what Mrs. Bascomb has done. Just forgiven the young lovers and taken them right to her heart.'

'She *would*, you know,' said Miss Preston, who was a great novel-reader. 'She's a wonderful mother. Just given up her life to that boy.'

'I wonder who the girl is?' asked Miss Saunders. 'Did you ever hear of any of your Harristown cousins speak of the Hicks family?'

'There are some *Dicks*, who own the big furniture factory in East Harristown,' said Miss Preston, finishing the sentence in a hurry, because they saw the tram approaching from a distance and seized on the pretext to stretch their nimble young legs in a gallop. It was such glorious spring weather! The air made you want to shout, and turn somersaults . . . or run away and get married.

'My! What a grand day!' said one to the other, as they settled themselves in their seats, the fine texture of their young cheeks delicately pink like flower petals. 'I bet you the hepaticas are out. Let's go and look for them in Pearson's woods this afternoon, shall we?'

They had both forgotten all about Mrs. Bascomb and her new daughter-in-law. After all, Mrs. Bascomb was by no means the centre of their universe.

But after they reached the school building, and separated to go to their different floors, they found everybody talking about the announcement in the 'birth, death, and marriage' column of the paper. Having one more item of news than anybody else, they talked too, by which it happened that at noon everybody in the Main Street School knew that Ralph Bascomb had run away with the only daughter of a well-to-do manufacturer (he was such a pretty boy, he always had some girl crazy about him) and that Mrs. Bascomb had apparently known about it beforehand, because she had gone right down to the station to telegraph them her congratulations and to tell them to come straight home to her. There was some criticism of Mrs. Bascomb for having let Margaret Hill delude herself with false hopes, but the general opinion was that Margaret had been much too open in the way she had run after Ralph and fastened herself upon Mrs. Bascomb. Margaret did not appear at school that day, nor indeed for all the rest of the week, sending word she had a touch of influenza and could not leave her bedroom. Some of the younger teachers felt sorry for Margaret, sorry and a little scornful.

So when Mrs. Bascomb went into the lunch-room at noon, the pedestal was standing ready. She had but to step upon it . . . to step, in fact, from one to another.

By that time her own inner pendulum, having reached its extreme swing in one direction, had started back. She had intensely dreaded to go back into the school-world, but it had had its usual quieting effect upon her. The instant she entered the building, there had fallen upon her a thousand steadying professional associations of ideas. The centre of gravity of her personality had shifted, as it had all the other thousands of mornings when, at the threshold of her classroom, she had left behind her Mary Bascomb, John Bascomb's widow, Ralph Bascomb's mother, for whom her own personal life was the universe, and who was, in the nature of things, the fore-ordained centre of that universe. As she hung up her wraps in the cloak-room, instead of this woman for whom everything which touched herself personally was of poignant importance, she became 'Teacher,' one of many exactly like her. And 'Teacher' was valued solely for her ability to transfer into forty little brains, many impersonal items of information; such as how to divide fractions, and why seaport cities have an advantage over inland towns. Her emotional life was forced into a saving momentary torpor by the mere

36

passing over her head of hour after hour crammed with rigorously ordered occupation.

Again and again she had experienced it, often unwillingly, always helplessly, this thrusting aside of her own affairs by the school routine . . . arithmetic from 9.15 to 9.45; reading, 9.45 to 10.15 . . . and all the rest of it. In that world her happiness or misery mattered not at all. What mattered was that by June, all those varying atoms of grey-matter in the forty little skulls before her, must have absorbed what was laid down for them in the State Course of Study. The austerity of this demand was an opiate for the pain of personal relations. For the time being, clamour though they might, they were pushed from the centre of the stage.

It was not only one classroom which thus temporarily freed one woman from the age-old, traditional, aching conviction of the frightful importance of her own affairs, but every room all over the building. The relentless roughness of the process was made more tolerable by the certainty, always reassuring to the gregarious human mind, that it was shared by many others. The very look of the building from afar; the odour of the school-air, chalk dust, floor-oil, hot steampipes, window-plants; its audible note, silence shot through with young voices murmuring from behind closed doors; all of it, exerted on those teaching women a quieting, calming influence such as no home-keeping woman can ever know – left a prey as she is to the reflections from the convex mirrors of home-objects which can show to her nothing but ever-magnified images of herself.

Mary Bascomb, raw and quivering with anger and resentment and fear, walked into her classroom and felt her personality relegated to the background by the frozen indifference of the world, visibly going on its own way with its own affairs as usual. It gave her a breathing spell till noon.

And at noon she heard what everybody else had heard, that Ralph Bascomb had run away with the only daughter of a well-to-do manufacturer, and that Mrs. Bascomb, wonderfully sacrificing herself to him as always, had taken the young people right home without a word of recrimination.

37

As she took the bowl of tomato-bisque soup in the lunch-room, she was wondering with intensity, behind her down-dropped, quiet eyelids, why under the sun she had not thought of that possibility before, why she had gone off at 'half-cock' over Ralph's phrase, 'not your kind,' why it had not occurred to her that he might have meant frivolously and fashionably brought up. Her spirits reacted with a bound. After her long waking nightmare, this new possibility seemed more than endurable.

At half-past four when she turned into her own front path again, she felt infinitely more like herself than at dawn she would have thought possible. She was very tired, as was natural after her long vigil, but she was not feverish, or numb, or nauseated, as she had been, at intervals, all the night long. She was again Mary Bascomb, ready as she always was to do her duty.

This might not, after all, turn out to be so difficult. A not unpleasing picture of the situation took shape before her inner eye: – there was the new person in her world; Charlotte, very young perhaps, a gay little boarding-school thing, but still in the formative period, shy, timid, terribly anxious about what Ralph's wonderful mother would think of her (Ralph would of course have talked a great deal about his mother); there was Ralph, moved, grateful for his mother's magnanimous attitude, immensely relieved that she was not going to make any fuss about it (she knew Ralph!); and there was herself, generously ignoring the slight they had put on her, helpful, admired by Charlotte's family as such well-to-do families always did admire her. Family counsels . . . she saw them . . . 'these heedless children! But still we must do our best by them . . . youth will be youth!'

She remembered with distaste her frantic emotion of the night before. To lose her self-control was very disagreeable to her, she thought again as she had thought so many times in her life. She did not believe in it. People shouldn't.

But her knees shook under her with an excusable physical weakness as she walked up the steps of her house and fitted the key into the lock. Before she turned it, she drew a long breath and took one resolution that come what might, she would never quarrel with Ralph's wife. She despised women who couldn't get on with their daughters-in-law. One of the many axioms which she had always repeated with entire conviction was that it 'takes two to make a quarrel.' As she opened the door to her house, she was setting it down as a foregone conclusion that she would never, never be one of those two. With her first contact with this strange girl, she would set the note she meant to keep: kind, motherly firmness.

She stepped into her hall and saw hanging on her hat-rack a bright green hat, of an eccentric shape, made of very shiny, varnished, coarsely-braided straw, which she recognized as one of the cheap models of that season. Below it, leaning against the wall, stood a bright green cotton parasol, with a thick, bright green tassel hanging from the handle. Mrs. Bascomb, gazing at it fixedly, saw that the fibres of the artificial silk had worn off in places and showed the rough jute thread of which it was made. The air was heavy with perfume . . . the sort of perfume that would go with that hat.

Automatically, implacably, Mrs. Bascomb's opinion of her son's wife was settled.

All that foolish talk at school about her being the daughter of a well-to-do manufacturer! . . .

She felt sick with the reaction from what such talk had led her to expect. She stepped into her kitchen and saw her enamel-topped table littered with dirty dishes and bits of food . . . as she had never seen it in her life. A frying-pan, yellow with dried leavings of scrambled eggs stood on the oil-stove.

Not a sound in the house. They weren't there. They had not even had the common decency to be there, waiting for her return. They had come in, taken possession of things, and then gone away to amuse themselves, leaving her to be greeted by their dirty dishes.

She stood there, in the disordered kitchen, staring at the smeary and littered table, till the enormity of it filled the universe.

She went upstairs to her own room, as to a refuge, and found it redolent of that awful perfume. Her dressing-table showed white patches of scattered face powder. *She*

39

had been in here, too, then. The house was stifling with her!

Mrs. Bascomb had started towards a window for fresh air, when she heard a door on the floor below her open and slam shut. There were hurried, racing steps on the stairs. Young voices. Laughter.

She became rigid where she stood, could not have turned her head.

The door burst open and Ralph's voice filled the room, gay, high-pitched, 'She's beat us *to* it! My watch *was* slow!'

His arms were around her from behind, her face pulled sideways so that he could give her a great rumbling kiss. Her hat was half pushed off by his boyish roughness – she must be looking ridiculous with it over one ear . . .

'Here we are, Mother! And you'd better believe I gave humble and hearty thanks for your telegram. We surely were up in the air till it came. But I knew you'd come across like a good old sport. I told Lottie you would.'

He talked, Mrs. Bascomb thought in the instant she looked into his excited face, close to hers, as though he were drunk. But his eyes had never been brighter, his young colour fresher. His breath on her cheek now was as sweet as that of a kitten's. She remembered . . . no, he did not look as though he were drunk, but as he did when he came in hoarse with yelling for a home-team, frantic with excitement over a close game.

He turned now, keeping one arm around her waist, and pulled up to him on the other side.

So this was Lottie.

Mrs. Bascomb, trying with one hand to retrieve her hat, bending her tall frame to kiss the powdered face tipped up to hers, was aware that Lottie was very small, very pretty, and smelled abominably of that perfume. Of something else, too. Mrs. Bascomb's sensitive nose caught an acrid whiff which told her that Lottie's abundant much-curled black hair needed washing.

She was appalled by the unexpectedness of everything, by the contrast between the well-ordered scene for which she had prepared, and this one! The bitter inward rush of her new impressions met the rushing outward ebb of her

40

hopes. The two dashed themselves together in her heart and boiled up in bewildered excitement. For an instant she was deafened by their tumult.

The only moving force in her was what was left of the momentum from her former mood. She said mechanically, just what she had decided to say, 'I'm glad to welcome my son's wife to his home.'

To which Lottie, kissing her on the mouth very energetically with moist, soft lips, answered in a phrase as evidently prepared beforehand, 'I do hope you're going to let me call you "Momma." '

Chapter 6

SHE had said in her telegram that they would 'talk things over and make plans for the future.'

Well, they did, that evening, Ralph and his bride, sitting close together on the sofa, their arms around each other, Ralph's mother opposite them.

Her lips were dry. From time to time a nervous tremor ran over her from head to foot. She could not have told which hours behind her had contained the greatest shocks . . . the preparations for supper, with her spotless kitchen invaded by a savagery of slovenly ways and slovenly speech, the supper-table with its revelation of personality as shown in table manners, or the cleaning up afterwards – Lottie's plump, short-fingered hands with their glassy, sharp pointed finger-nails piling all the dishes together into a dish-pan of lukewarm greasy water, Ralph to the tune of noisy jocularities wiping them without rinsing, and both of them, save when she spoke to them, as unaware of her presence as of the stove. Not a word, not an accent from them to show that they understood what she had done for them, the sacrifice she had made.

She had gone from one burst of resentful wrath to another, each embittered by the very evident fact that what she felt was nothing to Ralph and Lottie.

As, finally, she sat opposite them in the living-room, she was wondering how they could help crying out in terror over the ashy greyness of her haggard face. She caught sight of herself in the mirror and was frightened by her own aspect, pinched and drawn, her eyes sunk in her head, ten years older than she had looked the day before. She turned this ravaged mask reproachfully upon the two who were the cause of it and saw that Lottie's rounded arm was around Ralph's neck and that Ralph's lips were once more upon that full, slack mouth, the moist softness of which still clung to her own, despite all her attempts to wipe it off. They were not alarmed at her frightful, stricken expression because they did not see it.

The well-worn channels of communication between herself and her son did finally carry to him some message from his mother. He looked at her uneasily with his habitual dislike of her disapproval, and said, pushing Lottie away playfully, 'Here, Lottie old boy, we've got to talk business. Got to sit up and be practical.'

Lottie straightened herself, folded her plump hands, drew down her pretty face, rolled her liquid dark eyes towards the ceiling, and began to twiddle her thumbs rapidly. Ralph fell on her with a yell of amusement, kissing her so violently that she fell against the arm of the sofa, laughing and trying to push him off. With every one of their turbulent gestures, a fresh wave of that perfume was wafted to Mrs. Bascomb.

She was cold with disgust. And she looked it. But there was no one to see.

'Now, Ralph, you be good !' said Lottie, pushing him to the end of the sofa.

Ralph turned towards his mother again, saw with annoyance that her expression was cold and severe, and looked at her with the resentment a rollicking child feels for a tiresome drill-master.

The three pairs of eyes met expectantly. Mrs. Bascomb resolved fiercely that *she* would not be the one who brought up the question of what Ralph was to do. She would wait. She would just wait and see what Ralph had to say for himself.

Apparently, he felt no need to say anything for himself beyond an impatient, rebellious 'Well, Mother . . .'

'Well, Ralph . . .' she answered, with an intense dryness.

They looked at each other with hostile eyes.

'I thought we were going to talk things over!' said Lottie, pouting pettishly.

Ralph glanced at her, forgot about his mother, leaned swiftly towards her and dropped a kiss behind her ear.

She remained provocatively motionless, her chin dropped, looking at him sideways from under her lowered eyelashes, smiling slyly. They had both again forgotten that Mrs. Bascomb was there. From them there came now more than the odour of cheap perfume . . . hot gusts of passion.

Mrs. Bascomb caught her breath. She would not stay there to be insulted in her own house. They had no sense of decency. She stood up rigidly.

At once the young people before her became only a boy and girl, self-conscious and resentful at being made to feel abashed.

'Oh, Gosh, Mother,' said Ralph, 'yes, we'll sober down. But when you were only married yesterday . . . have a heart.'

She sat down and tried to fold her quivering hands to stillness.

In this manner they 'talked things over' till nine o'clock, by which time it had been decided (if you could call anything 'decided' on which such casual odds and ends of attention had been bestowed) that Lottie would stay there, with Ralph coming and going from the University till June, when presumably Ralph would have his diploma and be ready to earn his living and Lottie's. In the meantime they were all to be on the look-out for some suitable occupation in which Ralph could engage at once after graduation, starting at the bottom and working his way up . . . 'though not too darn near the bottom, either,' Ralph said, only half joking. 'A married man can't take any office boy's job. He's got responsibilities on his shoulders.'

At this, he and Lottie exchanged a glance on which later events supplied a commentary.

Ralph had put aside with emphasis any discussion of the plan of his becoming a lawyer. 'Nix on that. I always hated that idea. And I'm tickled to death that I've got a good reason for getting out of it.'

43

'But Ralph! You always . . .' began his mother.

'No, I didn't,' he caught her up breezily. 'No, I never. You just had me talked into a corner, that's all.'

His whole manner was changed, already, Mrs. Bascomb thought, loosened, coarsened, roughened, indifferent to all that she had tried to teach him. It did not seem possible to her that this was her boy, her obedient little son who had always been such a comfort. The tears came to her eyes at the thought. Nobody noticed them but herself. She wiped them away visibly, and knew that the gesture had gone unheeded.

'Well now, that's all settled,' said Ralph briskly, looking at the clock. 'Bedtime now. Bedtime for little Willie who's got to take a train back to History A to-morrow morning.'

Lottie began to complain that they were to have no honeymoon at all, as everybody else did . . . that he was going to go away and leave his little girlie for days and days as though he didn't . . .

Mrs. Bascomb shut her ears to this, rose without being noticed and went out into the hall. The moment had come to decide about the rooms for the night. She must face it. The bed in Ralph's room was no wider than a soldier's cot, was in fact his childhood bed left on in his young man's room. The only double bed in the house was the one in her room, the bed which she and Ralph's father had bought; the bed on which Ralph had been born; where his father had died, in the room which had been hers and hers alone for twenty-two years.

She stood at the foot of the stairs for a long time before she had the physical strength to say, 'You'd better take my room, Ralph. It's the only one that's big enough for two people.'

'All right,' said Ralph, 'anything *you* say.' He went on, 'Lottie, want a bite to eat before bed?'

'I could take a glass of beer and a cheese sandwich if somebody should tie my hands and put it in my mouth,' said Lottie good-naturedly.

'By George, that *would* taste good,' said Ralph. 'But we never have anything like that in the house. We'll have a case sent up from Kahn's to-morrow. But come on, let's see what there is.'

44

Literally petrified by this dialogue ('*we* will have a case sent!') Mrs. Bascomb stood at the foot of the stairs listening to their gay raid on her ice-box. If she could have opened her mouth, she would have shrieked at them, 'What are you doing? How *dare* you?' This was too much! There were limits to . . .

But her lips were too dry to speak. And in an instant she knew that if she could, she would not. Ralph and Lottie were inconceivable leagues away from her . . . it would seem only petty domestic tyranny . . . she could hear Ralph's voice as he would say, 'Great Scott, Mother, can't we get a little snack before we go to bed?'

She shuddered at his forgetfulness of her, of any decent feeling, and finding it hard to put one foot before the other, climbed slowly up the stairs.

She took sheets and pillow-cases from her immaculate linen shelves, and opened the door to her room. For an instant, before her in the dusk, stood a figure which every time she looked in through that door was thereafter to confront her in that room. The spot where she had first seen Lottie could never be like any other spot in the world to her. On it, that first night, as through the years to come, stood Lottie . . . cheap, ignorant, vulgar . . . everything which Mrs. Bascomb detested . . . there she stood and triumphed coarsely over the mother of the boy she had fooled and caught.

Mrs. Bascomb pushed a button and the glare of the electric-bulb emptied the room of the phantom. She made up the bed with her usual firm neatness, looking about her strangely as she did it. Then, going to the closet she swept her clothes by armfuls from the hooks and carrying them to Ralph's room, flung them down in heaps on the floor, as never before in her life had she handled any possession of hers. She took up by its four corners the embroidered cover of her dressing-table and carried it away, all her dainty breakable toilet articles tinkling together with a delicate crash of splintering glass and clinking silver. She lifted her eyes to the walls and snatched down a reproduction of the Sistine Madonna which she had had from her girlhood, and flung into the waste-basket the calendar of optimistic day-to-day mottoes which

45

always hung near her table. The room, stripped in a twinkling of its personality, looked now like a bedroom in a boarding-house. It was with a cold fury that she realized that neither Ralph nor Lottie would notice or care how it looked.

On her way to Ralph's room she stood for a moment in the upper hall, listening to the sounds from below; – laughter, little shrieks and squeals, broken bits of dialogue:

'You needn't try to . . .'

'Yes, I will too, if I . . .'

'All right, Miss Madam, look out for yourself then!'

'Ralph, let go of me or I'll . . .'

Mrs. Bascomb felt a curious sensation in her mouth and was aware that she was audibly grinding her teeth together. This gave her a fright, 'Oh, I shall never live through it. I shall never live till June, till they go away.'

She called down the stairs in a hard, strong voice, 'I'm going to bed now. Good night.'

There was a pause in the chattering talk, an instant's silence. She recognized it already. Whenever her presence was forced on their attention, it always took them an instant to remember that she existed.

A chair grated. 'Hold on a minute, Moth,' called Ralph unexpectedly. She heard him come out into the lower hall, and standing at the head of the stairs, she saw him turn and leap up towards her. The hall light was full on his face, his flushed, sensually excited face, which did not look to her in the least like the face of Mary Bascomb's son, but like that of a common man in the grasp of a common woman. What was he coming up there to do, she wondered.

What he did was to put his arms around her neck and lay his head for an instant on her bosom, saying, 'Say, Mother, you mustn't think . . . you needn't think that I don't . . . Mother, you're a mighty good old sport.'

He lifted his head and for an instant his eyes looked deeply into hers. From the shock given her, she realized that it was the first time their eyes had really met since his return. For longer than that. When *was* the last time that Ralph had really let his eyes meet hers? Years ago.

What did she see in his eyes now? From behind the flushed sensual mask of the excited young man's face, did

46

his little-boy eyes look out at her for an instant with a little boy's frightened, helpless . . .

'Oh, Ralph! Ralph!' she cried, straining him into her arms wildly.

Whatever it had been, it was all over. 'Yes, Lottie!' he cried, 'coming.'

He kissed his mother's cheek, just his usual matter-of-fact boy's kiss, and plunged back down the stairs.

'Good night, Momma,' called Lottie's voice gaily.

Mrs. Bascomb went into her son's room and sat down on the edge of the bed, her feet in a clutter of her own clothes. She did not pick them up. With trembling fingers she undid the fastenings of her garments, slipped on her night-gown and crept into the little bed.

Presently Lottie and Ralph came upstairs and went into her room. Through the thin walls she could hear them moving around, just as she had heard Ralph, all the years of his growing up. But now there were voices for her to hear. Not loud as they had been downstairs. A low, intense murmur, which only occasionally broke the long, thick silences.

Ralph's mother lay in Ralph's bed, her body drawn into a knot, all her being taut with hatred. After her wholly sleepless night, her bodily exhaustion was so great that although she could not sleep, she could not wholly wake. Her thoughts moved crazily from one broken image to another . . . her dishes, her grandmother's delicate old china in grey water with a rim of grease . . . a hand with shiny, sharp-pointed nails holding a fork as if it were a dagger . . . the murmur in the next room . . . the hat-rack with the cheap bright-green hat and the cotton umbrella below . . . she would never live through it, never! What had she ever done to deserve such misery . . . a thick tassel made of jute, covered by fibres of artificial silk . . . frogs shrilling, where had she heard that? The sound brought back to her sickeningly the sensation of the letter in her hand as she withdrew it from the mail-box . . . she could never live till June . . . she would go insane . . . the silence in the next room.

Presently she fell asleep as though she had taken a **drug,**

47

and dreamed of the look in Ralph's eyes which had so horribly moved her, dreamed that he had opened a door there in her own house, a door she had never seen before, but now she knew it had always been there . . . had opened it and disclosed a vast, dark, empty room . . . empty. And yet now she knew it had always been there . . . empty.

She woke with a start, the clock downstairs striking eight. She had not slept so late on a school-day for years. The dream dropped into oblivion.

An hour of desperate haste in the untidy house, silent except for her hurried, furtive movements as she dressed and prepared her breakfast. And then, as on a thousand other mornings before, as on thousands of mornings to come, she found herself once more stepping into the school building and leaving her personality, her wrecked and battered personality, behind her as she entered the formal, impersonal usefulness of 'Teacher.'

Chapter 7

SHE had concentrated all her strength on living through till June, till Ralph's graduation, and she soon saw that it would take all her strength and more, to endure what was laid on her at school and at home.

At school she saw, day by day, in the eyes of her colleagues, the advance of their enlightenment about Lottie. Mrs. Jeffries remarked in an effusive tone, 'Oh, I saw your new daughter-in-law down at the drug store to-day. Such a *pretty* girl!' Mrs. Bascomb knew by the intonation of the phrase that everybody was seeing what had so shrieked itself out in the hall of her house, as she stood looking at the cheap, shiny hat and the artificial silk over the jute tassel.

When she found Miss Saunders leaning over Miss Preston's desk, with the unmistakable aspect of satisfaction which accompanies the hearing of gossip, and when both girls started apart on seeing her enter, Mrs. Bascomb knew that Miss Preston's Harristown cousins had found out, what she herself had long since heard, that Lottie's father was nightwatchman in the shoe factory there, and that Lottie had been saleswoman in a cheap, men's-clothing store on South Street. She imagined that they were adding what she had guessed, that Lottie had been more or less 'talked about.'

The other women in the school looked at her with sympathy, it was true, but with a sympathy coloured with pity, and pity was intolerably offensive to her. It was her experience that you only pitied people on whom you could look down. It was, in fact, looking down on somebody to pity him. She knew, having pitied people herself.

How *could Ralph* have made such a return to her for all she had done for him! A thousand times she asked herself this unanswerable question.

Margaret Hill showed neither sympathy nor pity for anyone but herself, and yet did not escape Mrs. Bascomb's resentment. The girl's first reaction had been a broken-lily grief which exasperated Ralph's mother by its absence of the slightest self-respecting concealment. How could anybody parade her feelings around in public so, she thought irritably, observing Margaret's pale face and drooping, fair head.

Someone else observed them with more sympathy than Mrs. Bascomb. Ralph had not been married a month before Mrs. Bascomb saw Margaret out in the shining new Buick belonging to Mr. Lathrop, cashier of the principal bank in town; and Mr. Lathrop beside her, bending on her a foolish look of middle-aged sentimentality; Mr. Lathrop whose middle-aged wife had not been dead a year, whose grown-up children were college-mates of Ralph's at the University. The sight filled Mrs. Bascomb with the corrosive irritation which almost everything in those days caused in her. 'Sickening fools, both of them!' she thought.

It was from a distance that she saw the rapid progress of the Hill-Lathrop affair, for not only had Margaret never made the emotional scene with her which she had dreaded, but as a matter of fact the girl had never gone near her at all. Few people did in this period of her life. Or not more than once. She was as far as possible from parading her feelings around in public; always kept her voice well-modulated, her face quiet, her eyes under control. But people transacted hastily what business they had with her, and left her speedily.

'I feel as though she'd be hot to the touch,' said impressionable Miss Preston, after having gone to Mrs. Bascomb's classroom on an errand.

'Well, I wouldn't risk touching her to find out,' said Miss Saunders.

All this at school. At the house which had been her home . . . there are no words in which to speak of the life in the house which had been her home. All her energies there were fixed on sternly ignoring that which she could not but see, on refusing to be aware of what she knew was common knowledge to every woman in their street. Fiercely, unwaveringly, she marched forward to the impassable stone barrier before her, as if the road lay open.

A week or so before Commencement Day, the Commencement Day which was to have marked her deliverance, on returning from school, she found Dr. Dewey at the house. As she came in, Lottie went hurriedly upstairs, and it was Dr. Dewey who told her in his brutal medical jargon, mincing no words, dotting all the i's. Lottie was pregnant and would probably be confined early in September.

They went forward then into a phase which made the last months at school seem easy and relaxed. There was nothing to do but to keep Lottie till her baby came. Even after Ralph had found work, his beginner's tiny earnings could not furnish living conditions possible for a woman within three months of her first confinement, especially any woman who took it as hard as Lottie did. She suffered so much from nausea that she was obliged to have her breakfast in bed, and to lie there till after ten every morning. And when she had dragged on her clothing, she was fit for nothing but to drop down on the couch in the living-room or the hammock on the porch and lament her lot.

For she detested the 'whole business' as she called it,

50

and when she was feeling particularly low-spirited, she cried out on herself as a fool for going through with it. She fully expected to die when the baby was born, and if not, she knew that never again would she regain her health and good looks. She was outspoken in her blame of Ralph and of herself too, for 'not having known better.' She and her silent mother-in-law were in accord upon one thing at least, and that was in a complete absence of any welcoming affection for the child-to-be.

'Lottie's baby!' thought Mrs. Bascomb contemptuously, as she sewed with a venomous rapidity upon the little garments. Lottie's sole contribution to the layette had been her insistence that everything should be lace-trimmed. Until Mrs. Bascomb's return to the house at the close of the school-year, nothing had been done in the way of sewing, beyond the creation of a little more disorder in the heap of white materials which Mrs. Bascomb had bought.

'I'll pay you back later, Mother,' Ralph had said uneasily, happening to be in the house when the big bundle of dry-goods was delivered, and having thus forced upon his attention the fact of his mother's continued expenditures for him.

His mother felt a mixture of disdain and pity for him as he said it. Ralph had troubles enough of his own, without trying to pay his own expenses, she thought ironically. For, as far as she was able, Lottie made him share her own hysterical discomfort. She insisted that he 'cheer her up' and yet if he ventured to enter the house looking moderately calm, she cried out at him for caring nothing about her misery. But she seldom had this reason for upbraiding him. Ralph's returns to the house were far from gay. He had found a job in the office of a printing establishment and was staggering under the shock of his first contact with the business world. Nobody in the office knew that the new boy had an ailing wife and a grimly silent mother at home, or would have cared if they had known. No allowances were made for his fatigue after nights when Lottie could not sleep and would not allow him to. He must learn the new business not in the way he had till now learned everything, as a good-natured concession to people paid to teach him, but in the face of people's brutal absorption in their own affairs. It was nothing to them whether he learned it or not. If he did not, there were plenty more where he came from. In the three months' time between his scraping through his University examinations and the birth of his child, Ralph's face and bearing altered more than during the ten years before. His mother, on the rack herself, could not but pity him, bitterly as she blamed him.

She shut herself up in a self-contained fury of silent martyrdom and hard work. At first she had tried to live till June. Now it was until after Lottie's confinement. Once the baby was born, and Ralph had his first rise in salary, certainly they could go their way, leaving her to what shreds of peace life might still hold for her.

In the meantime she would see that she had nothing to reproach herself with. She uttered never a word of reproach, and indeed few words of any kind, to the frightened, unreasonable girl; she accepted in a rock-like silence Lottie's enormities as a house companion. Ten times a day she set her teeth and 'cleaned up' after Lottie as the girl took her listless untidy way from bedroom to bathroom, and from bathroom to hammock. With the exception of Mrs. Bascomb's necessary trips for marketing, neither of them went out at all. These trips she made early in the morning before other people were abroad. She had no wish to meet her decent associates till Lottie and Ralph were out of the house. The young couple might not seem to be aware that their baby was to be born only five months after their hasty marriage, but it was a fact of which Ralph's mother was fully conscious.

The incredible way in which they disregarded this crying fact seemed to Mrs. Bascomb to sum up the incredibility of the whole situation. They had from the first showed no sign, not one, of appreciating all that she was doing for them; and they now made no pretence of appreciating the disgrace they were bringing upon her. Mrs. Bascomb was hourly shocked by their callousness to her suffering, by their selfish absorption in their own passing sensations, Ralph in his detested job, Lottie in her discomfort.

Their three acrimonious grievances against life filled the little house to the brim during the hot, dragging days. There was no room left for any concern with the new human being who was slowly coming into being. Lottie's grievance was, however, the only one that was articulate. By the time Ralph had struggled his way through his day's work, he was too beaten down by fatigue to have the energy to resent the situation at home even if he had dared, in the face of Lottie's claim on him, to have any claim of his own. He bowed his head before it dumbly, as a shelterless man turns his back to the rain, hunching his shoulders and stoically taking it because he can do nothing else. His mother said as little about her feelings as he. She took an immense pleasure in repressing her righteous indignation . . . how extravagantly righteous! . . . under a hermetically sealed contemptuous dignity. To listen in a fierce silence to Lottie's complaints gave her a wry perverted satisfaction. It filled to overflowing her conviction of having all the right on her side. From the contents of that cup, familiar to her all her life, she now drank deeper and heavier draughts than she had ever dreamed possible. How *could* Ralph and Lottie continue to pile up all the wrong on their side!

Mrs. Bascomb's sense of decent family feeling kept her from mentioning the state of affairs to any outsider (indeed she was from this time on cut off from her old friends because of this necessary silence). But it gratified her beyond measure to be so sure of sympathy for herself if anyone ever should know. The approval, the indignant approval of such an imaginary spectator of her actions was one of the intoxicating elements of the orgy of her rightness. It kept her strung all through the summer to a supernormal state of endurance. Never had she worked as she did during those vacation days, which before this had always been dedicated to a justifiably self-indulgent recovery from the fatigue of the school-year. All the things which Lottie should have done and which she outrageously did not do, Mrs. Bascomb herself did, in an ecstasy of self-approval.

During this period she saw practically no one whom she knew; partly because she avoided them, partly because all the activities of school and church and club were suspended during the heat of summer and most of her school associates were away on summer vacations. She was

53

profoundly thankful for the temporary absence of the people of her world. The baby would be born, Lottie well again, and all three out of her house, she hoped, before the return to town of her friends. Lottie was not more concentrated than she, upon the day of liberation in September.

That day passed as such days usually do, excitedly, hurriedly, not at all as it had been planned, with certain things left undone in spite of the preparations, the doctor coming and going, an expensive nurse in a white uniform ordering Mrs. Bascomb about. Ralph did not go to business. He paced palely up and down the house, or sat on Lottie's bed, holding her hand, horrified to faintness by her cries of suffering.

These had rather a different effect upon the nurse. As she and Mrs. Bascomb stood together an instant in the hall outside, she said with some impatience, 'My! Don't she make a fuss! She's getting along all right. What'd she expect?'

Mrs. Bascomb made no answer. It would have been beneath her dignity to comment on Ralph's wife to a stranger. Besides, what could she say? She had no words to express what she felt, even to herself. Ever since her first glimpse of Lottie she had been shut up in the unreal dumbness of a nightmare. As she rose up and lay down, she often felt that she was in a long nightmare, rather than living in her own house. She had not been able to wake herself up out of it since Lottie's kiss.

That day was the culmination of a nightmare. Her house, her cherished spotless house, in hideous disorder, stained, soiled, smelling of antiseptics; herself, her sensitive, impressionable person seized upon and forced to labour like a charwoman in a hospital! And all as a matter of course. This last was the dreamlike element of incredibility. No admiration, no surprise, no gratitude from anyone; not even any sign of comprehension of how she was being treated. Nobody indeed noticed her at all, save as hands and feet to order about. As she ran up and down stairs on the nurse's endless errands, her amazed resentment was mingled with cold disgust 'at the whole business' which she had all along shared with Lottie. 'All this because a boy could not control himself. This is the way the world is peopled with Lotties.'

And yet there were moments of ecstasy when she thought, 'This is the end! I shall have done my duty to the last. If I can live through this, the nightmare will be over.'

At ten that evening, the nurse telephoned the doctor to come; at midnight as Mrs. Bascomb stood at the door of the sick-room, the doctor handed her a blanket-wrapped roll, saying carelessly, 'Nice little girl. Listen to her coo. You take care of her for a minute or two, will you, while nurse and I fix up the mother?' He added, although Mrs. Bascomb had made no inquiry about Lottie, 'Perfectly normal delivery. She isn't hurt a bit.'

Inside the room, in a thin shaking voice of horror, Lottie was saying, 'Never any more, Ralph. *Never any more.*'

And Ralph, the sweat running down his white cheeks, answered sobbingly, 'Oh, no, Lottie! Never again!'

The doctor and nurse looked at each other with a cynical smile.

The grandmother turned away carrying the new inhabitant of the world at whom its parents had not so much as glanced.

She went into the bathroom and sat down on the chair before the little bath-tub on its folding stand. She was at the lowest ebb of revulsion from life. Lottie had not been the only woman to be horrified by the gruesome details of a confinement. That she, of all people, had been forced to undergo this frightful experience; she, unable to endure the sight of blood, or to hear people scream. It was hideous.

The blanket-wrapped roll on her knees stirred and murmured. She turned back a fold of the blanket and looked down unlovingly on the new strange person in her house.

The baby girl was lying on her back, her face as calm as that of a Buddha, her eyes wide open, gazing up fixedly. As their gaze met, John Bascomb's widow woke from her long nightmare.

The eyes were the eyes of John Bascomb, set under John Bascomb's brow.

Chapter 8

FOR the period of Lottie's illness, Ralph had been banished to a corner of the attic which for this occasion had been roughly furnished as a bedroom. A cot bed had been set up in Lottie's room for the nurse, but for the first few days she did not wish to have the baby there. So the little crib had been put beside the grandmother's bed, and she had been asked to take care of the baby during what was left of the night.

By two o'clock Lottie was comfortably asleep, Ralph had staggered off to bed, and the baby was being washed by the nurse. The rough, elderly doctor looked in on this process before he left the house. 'Usual number of fingers and toes?' he asked. 'She looked all right to a hasty glance.'

'She's a beautiful, beautiful girl,' crooned the nurse with professional enthusiasm. She turned the sprawling atom over on her immaculate lap, 'Just look at the back on her! She's going to be an athlete.'

The doctor grunted, 'All new babies look just alike.'

'No, they don't either,' said the nurse, bringing up seriously a bit of the lore of her trade. 'No, doctor, you're all off there. When they're brand-new in the first hour or so, they often look more like themselves, like what they're going to be, than later on, when they've settled down to just being a baby.'

'Well, I don't know but they do,' the doctor conceded, with the faintest possible interest in the matter. 'Now that you mention it, seems as though I had noticed family resemblances in very new babies, more than later on. How about it, Mrs. Bascomb?' he said, turning to the grandmother, dim in a shadowy corner of the bathroom, 'Have you noticed anybody that your new granddaughter looks like?'

After a pause, the shadow stirred and murmured, 'I haven't had time yet really to look at her.'

'You'll probably have plenty of time for that in the next ten days,' surmised the doctor. 'Nurse is going to have her hands full with the mother. Don't you let her put it over on you too much, nurse. She's in splendid shape. Sound as a nut. She could get up and do a washing to-morrow, if she had to.'

He added, 'I don't believe I'll come back again at all, unless you send for me. I'm getting old and crotchety and losing my patience. I'd fling out and say something I'd be sorry for.'

'Oh, I can manage all right,' said the nurse, with a nurse's enthusiasm at seeing the last of the doctor. 'We'll be asleep in half an hour, all of us.'

Mrs. Bascomb slipped from her shadowy corner and followed the doctor down to let him out of the house. He shook hands with her formally. 'My congratulations on your new dignity,' he said. He could think of nothing else he could say to express his sympathy for her. She had never been any favourite of his, either as a woman or as a patient, but you had to hand it to her, he thought; she had acted very well in this exasperating business of her son's fool marriage.

Gosh! What a girl Ralph had picked out! He'd never had any use for Ralph, you could tell from the way the old women thought so much of him for always minding his Momma that he was either a poor rag or as sly as a cat. But, by George, he was almost sorry for the poor kid now. What hash the Momma's darlings did make of getting married, anyhow. This must have been a frightful blow to his mother. She was gamer than he had thought her. Must be pretty good stuff in her, after all, in spite of her being so far from hating herself.

'You've been a great help to us to-day,' he said impressively, trying to make his tone express more than his words. He had always noticed that Mrs. Bascomb's appetite for appreciation of her efforts was a vigorous one, and this time, he didn't grudge it to her.

But Mrs. Bascomb made no answer, scarcely seemed to hear what he said, and as she stood there, her hand on the knob of the door, something about the expression of her face struck the doctor's professional eye. With his hand half-way to his head, in the act of putting on his hat, with a foot advanced to step out of the open door, he halted and turned to look at her sharply, his medical instinct aroused. In his long experience with an unchanging clientèle, he had often seen in the face of a patient with whose aspect he was very familiar, some impending change in health announced by an indefinable change of expression. But, look sharply as he might at Mrs. Bascomb, he could not recognize or label the change in her face. Perhaps it had been his fancy. He was dog-tired and nervous. These confinement cases with struggling, shrieking women took it out of a doctor. He ought to leave them to the younger men. Perhaps Mrs. Bascomb was getting old. Yes, that was it he decided, and completed the various gestures he had begun, put his hat on his head and finished striding out of the open door. Yes, she had just passed the boundary line, and for the first time had begun to 'show her age.'

'Good night,' he called over his shoulder, walking with his long, loose steps down the front path into the blackness.

'Good night,' said Mrs. Bascomb, standing in the open door and looking after him.

When his echoing footsteps had quite died away in the silent street, she moved and went forward out of the house, down from the porch, out under the sky.

She stepped forward into infinity, and she felt its mightiness brooding about her. But it did not dwarf her. It magnified her. She shared it. She lifted her face to the stars. She found that, alone there in the darkness, she had stretched up her arms to them.

John had come back to her. Out of living eyes he had looked at her. He had not dropped into nothingness. He had been there all the time, waiting . . . somewhere . . . somewhere in all this starry greatness.

She saw again the solemn gaze of the new-born child fixed on her, and began to tremble and weep.

'Mrs. Bascomb,' called the nurse in a low tone from the head of the stairs.

She ran into the house, locking the door behind her, saying breathlessly, 'Yes?'

'If you're ready to take the baby now? . . .' the tired nurse put it discreetly, like a suggestion.

'Yes, oh, yes!' cried Mrs. Bascomb softly, running up the stairs and holding out her arms. 'Yes, I'm ready to take the baby.'

Chapter 9

MRS. BASCOMB turned in at her own path hurriedly. It was half-past four. She had been detained at school. Lottie always wanted to go down town at least once every day and always expected her to return from school by twenty minutes past four. She opened the front door. The baby was crying. Was she sick? Hadn't she looked a little pale this morning? She took the stairs in one rush and ran into her own room. The baby's voice came from there. The child was in her crib, screaming her heart out. Where was Lottie? Had she simply decided not to wait? Had she gone away leaving the baby alone?

The bathroom door opened and Lottie's voice came out together with a whiff of scorching hair. Lottie was curling her hair. Oh, she was not dressed yet. She was probably late herself. Lottie's voice said defensively, defiantly, 'She's just got her rag out, that's all. That book you made me read *said* you should not take them up just because they cried.'

The grandmother checked her dash towards the crib till she had time to pull off her heavy coat and to tear the gloves from her hands, cold with the chill of the October day. She rubbed her fingers together hard to warm them. She was quivering to the baby's shrieks as though they were issuing from her own throat.

Now she was warm enough to touch the crib. She bent over it and snatched aside the blankets, twisted about the little body by the child's lusty kicks and struggles. The baby was chilled, was wet, was tangled into an absurd and uncomfortable position by the disordered blankets. Her little legs and feet were like cold marble. She was furious, too, her face screwed into a thousand wrinkles, her toothless mouth stretched wide, the screams coming from it almost like something visible.

The grandmother, with an indignant exclamation, took her up and sat down before the radiator, snatching off the cold wet cloth which had slipped down about the little legs. She laid a dry cloth to warm on the radiator and drew her chair closer to the steam-pipes, so that the baby would feel the warmth on her bare feet and legs. She rubbed them gently with her hands, stooped low over the little body, murmuring inarticulately, 'darling . . . darling . . . poor baby darling . . .' She felt the cold and wet and anger of the child in her own heart, in her own body.

She felt too, as sensibly felt as if against her own bare flesh, the soothing warmth which in a moment made the baby stop crying, and lie stretching out her feet, wriggling her toes gently, and gazing with a wide satisfaction at the ceiling. The two brooded together, in rapt, shared, physical comfort. Mrs. Bascomb's active mind was as vacant of thought as the baby's face. Her darling was warm, was pacified; she herself was filled with peace, with warmth, she who had been so filled with coldness and wrath a moment ago.

Presently she roused herself, reached for the warm diaper and put it on, pinning it firmly about the little body so that it would not slip down. Her fingers touched the baby's satiny skin, as she swooped to kiss the little feet, fiercely.

As she smoothed the long dress into place, she saw that it was rumpled and dirty, the front breadth stiff with ill-smelling yellow spots of soured milk. With one gesture, she pulled the garment off and, carrying the child up over her shoulder, stepped out into the hall to the white-enamelled chest of drawers she had bought the week after the baby's birth. She opened the top drawer and looked into a swirling confusion of crumpled clothes, a dirty pink sock on top of the heap. She shut that drawer energetically and opened the next one. It was quite empty save for a vile-smelling, small knit blanket. She opened and shut all the others swiftly. The bottom one was jammed full of soiled clothes. There *were* no clean dresses for the baby. There never were. And she had dozens of everything. Mrs. Bascomb set her jaw.

The bathroom door opened. Mrs. Bascomb's face dropped its belligerent expression. To the splendidly curled Lottie who stood there, one white, round shoulder emerging from her clutched-together wrapper, Lottie's mother-in-law said in a guarded voice, 'The baby's dress is not very fresh. I thought I'd put on a clean one.'

She had not made it guarded enough. Or else the quick, angry slamming of one drawer after another had been audible in the bathroom. 'There aren't any clean ones,' said Lottie, putting her chin out. 'Nobody on earth could keep clean clothes on any kid that throws up her dinner all the time the way she does. What's the use of changing her clothes all the time? She just gets them dirty again in a minute.' She looked at the baby, nestling in her grandmother's arms, and then up at the older woman's face. Her own face darkened. She stretched out her arm and took the baby roughly, 'Here, give her to me. I bet she's hungry.'

'Is it time to nurse her?' asked Mrs. Bascomb neutrally.

'I haven't looked at any clock,' said Lottie with emphasis, carrying off the baby to the front room.

Mrs. Bascomb went back into her own room and shut the door. Her fingers were trembling as they often did with the effort she put upon herself to be silent. She hung up her cloak in her cupboard, took off her hat and put it away with her gloves. It took the strictest system to achieve any order in that small room which must contain all her things and many of the baby's. She forced herself to look about and see what other small task she might undertake to keep herself from thinking. The baby's disordered crib. She took out the twisted blankets, shook them straight, and leaning from her window hung them to air on a line she had arranged with a pulley from her window to a near-by tree. *Now* what could she do? She could try to devise some way of getting a clean garment to put on the baby, who was at present in her little flannel petticoat. 'Flannel is so hard to get clean once it is spotted with milk,' Mrs. Bascomb said to herself. But she was not thinking of that. She could think of nothing but the baby in the next room, hanging on the beautiful, white-skinned, blue-veined breast. Her own breast ached with longing.

She said resolutely to herself, 'There is the little blue flannel wrapper. Perhaps that's clean.' She was thinking, 'Will she never give the baby back to me?'

Lottie's voice outside the door, 'Do you want the baby? She won't nurse any more.'

Mrs. Bascomb could not restrain her feet from a hurrying rush, her hands from shaking as she opened the door.

Lottie looked good-natured. One of her inexplicable changes of mood. Perhaps she had been relieved by the child's nursing. 'You can keep her if you want to,' she said, with the indulgent accent of one granting a favour. 'I've got to finish dressing.' She went back into her room and shut the door.

Mrs. Bascomb took the tiny, healthy, well-fed animal into her arms with a long breath. She sat down in a rocking-chair and began to sway to and fro, the baby held up against her shoulder. The little creature nestled, fumbled with tiny hands for a comfortable position, dropped its forehead into the hollow of its grandmother's neck and with a sigh abandoned itself to a trance of well-being. The grandmother crooned softly to herself under her breath, something that had no air, no words, that came as unconsciously from her heart as the tears which stood in her eyes. She was aware neither of the song nor of the tears, of nothing but the need to cherish and protect this warm germ of life, so small, so living, so great. She had forgotten that she herself existed; all her capacity for living poured into the morsel of flesh in her arms.

Presently, coming a little back to herself, she laid the baby on her lap and looked at her. The round face did not often look like anything but what it was, a pink empty baby countenance, featureless human dough, vague, impersonal . . . a beginning of things. But once in awhile (three or four times so far in the two months of her life) as she wriggled from one position to another, as the light fell this way or that across her brow, the grandmother had suppressed a cry to see again that likeness which had made her seem like a reincarnation.

She did not see it that day. The baby lay, a cocoon of animal satisfaction, kicking her legs against the dragging folds of her long flannel skirts, grunting gently from time to time, the only expression on her face being the reflection of various, vague, not disagreeable sensations in her tiny body. Mrs. Bascomb's face bending over her, took on a look very new for it, a look of whimsical amusement. 'You little pig!' she said adoringly. 'You little piggy-wiggy!' As if in answer, the baby grunted once more and her grandmother laughed aloud.

The sound startled her. She did not often laugh. And the clock downstairs chose that moment to strike five. It was time to stop this absurd communion with the baby and go downstairs to start supper. She dressed the baby in the little blue wool wrapper as she had planned, and carried her down into the kitchen.

The dirty dishes from Lottie's lunch were piled up in the sink. Lottie always said it wasn't really worth while to wash up such a little mess of things, and it was better to leave them till they could all be done together. You didn't notice them, along with the others, she said. Mrs. Bascomb looked at them ragingly, and forgot the baby. She told herself that she simply would not wash them another time. It was nothing but cowardly weakness, the way she and Ralph gave in to Lottie. She would assert herself like a human being, remind Lottie that this was *her* house, and they living in it on sufferance, largely at her expense! She would bring the girl to her senses with a round turn. Before she would wash those dishes again, she said inwardly, she would let them lie there till they stunk. She rejoiced in the strong vulgar word. She rejoiced in her resolution and in her hardened heart.

Moving around the kitchen, using one arm awkwardly, holding the baby on the other arm, she began preparations for supper. She was indignant that Lottie did not come down to help her, and infinitely relieved not to have her in the kitchen, bungling, dropping breakable things, leaving the gas turned on full head under an empty kettle, scattering flour on the floor, wiping out a greasy frying-pan with a fine linen towel, burning a hole in her apron by using it for a holder (a hole which would never be mended till Mrs. Bascomb set her own needle in it), doing everything wrong, and bristling from head to foot with defiance of any criticism or suggestion however carefully phrased.

63

Those dreadful scenes upon which Ralph had so many times opened the door, his wife half crying, half furious, flushed to the roots of her hair, his mother cold and white-lipped, trembling with silent anger!

'Well, goshamighty! what's the matter *now?*' was his usual comment, in the traditional tone of the weary man coming back to unreasonable, quarrelsome women.

Lottie was always in the right, and his mother always in the wrong. Of course Lottie was always right, she who flung her warm young body palpitating against Ralph's, who put her white arms around his neck, who pressed on his young mouth the moist, melting softness of her lips.

'I used one of the holy silver forks to stir the potatoes!' she would cry out, and over her head Ralph would look at his mother in reproachful astonishment at her pettiness.

'Say, Mother, can't you take your housekeeping a little easier?'

Mrs. Bascomb was perpetually amazed that anyone always right as she was, could be made so often to appear in the wrong.

Yes, though it left her all the work to do, it was far better to have Lottie stay upstairs, powdering and putting perfume on her ear-lobes and eyebrows, and re-arranging her hair a thousand times, and changing her transparent silk stockings from one foot to the other so that the hole in the heel would show a little less. Lottie's mother-in-law arranged a nest of pillows for the baby on the couch in the living-room, and hurrying now with all her might, darted back and forth between the dining-room and the kitchen. That evening marked the beginning of the Community Club course of lectures, and she did not wish to be late. She had attended them regularly for more than ten years now.

At half-past five Ralph came in, opening the door cautiously, and asking at once, 'Where's Lottie?'

His mother, her accent strictly neutral, gave him the information that 'she hasn't come downstairs yet. She's still dressing.' For her the essence of that statement was that Lottie had left her to prepare the supper unaided. She supposed that Ralph would see that too. But it seemed to have another meaning for him. His thin shoulders

drooped with fatigue as he stood facing her for an instant.
His face and hands were grimy with street and office dirt.
'Did she say anything about wanting to go to the movies?'
he asked.

His mother started. She had spoken several times to
Ralph and Lottie about that Community Club lecture,
and had let them know how much she was looking forward to it. 'No, she didn't say anything about it,' she
answered.

Was it *possible*, she thought, that they were simply
going to ignore the lecture, and cut her off from the only
pleasure she had left?

Ralph hung up his hat in silence. Conversation between
him and his mother now consisted in calling out to each
other over the high wall of things they did not say, bits
of information about facts of daily life.

'I guess I'll go and wash,' said Ralph. Lottie was
always talking about the elegantly manicured hands of the
'men-friends' she used to have in Harristown.

'I'll be ready to serve in a few minutes,' said his mother.
'You might tell Lottie.' She added, though Ralph had
not asked, 'I've got the baby down here, asleep, on the
couch in the living-room.'

Ralph went upstairs with a dragging step.

Mrs. Bascomb took the potatoes out of the oven, dished
up the peas, and poured her beaten eggs into the omelette
pan. She was trying to shut her ears to the murmur of
voices upstairs which had begun when Ralph opened the
door to the bedroom, that low murmur, half sentimental,
half sensual, which she heard every night from her bedroom. She set her jaw hard, and turned the omelette
deftly upon the heated platter.

'Supper's ready,' she called up the stairs, the hardness
of her accent cutting short the murmur.

Ralph and Lottie came down. Ralph's freshly washed,
delicately featured face, pale without its grime, the circles
under his eyes dark in spite of soap and water. Lottie was
abloom with youth and cosmetics. Her brown eyes were
as bright and liquid as a squirrel's. Her round arms were
white as milk. The skin on her neck was like the finest
white velvet.

65

As Mrs. Bascomb carried in the potatoes, she caught sight of her own face in a mirror, grim, middle-aged, with withered, yellowing skin. She was the only person who looked at it.

Lottie saw the pile of pillows on the couch and made a rush for it.

'Look out! I think baby's asleep,' cautioned Mrs. Bascomb sharply.

Lottie picked up the little blue-flannelled form, holding it high above her head. 'Muzzer's darlin' sing!' she said. 'I des bet bad favver hasn't looked at his baby dirl. Come here, bad favver!'

The baby, wakened as she was from sound sleep, drew down her little face drolly, stretched and yawned (the startlingly human yawn of little babies), raising her eyebrows with a comical caricature of world-weary lassitude. The young parents laughed uproariously and began to play with her, like two children with a toy. 'Doesn't she look too sweet for words in that pastel blue?' exclaimed Lottie, 'I do believe blue is going to be her colour, don't you, Ralph?'

'Supper's on the table,' said the grandmother, rather explosively. (Who was it who had found and put on that blue wrapper?)

The two young people looked at each other, and through their eyes Mrs. Bascomb saw herself once again as a dry, joyless Gorgon.

'S'e s'all come to supper too, so s'e s'all!' said Lottie, bringing the baby to the table with her.

They sat down, Lottie holding the baby on her lap and trying to eat with one hand. But it was impossible to take her tea in that manner.

'Gracious!' she exclaimed, as soon as she had tried to manage her cup, leaning out awkwardly over the baby's head. 'Gracious! I can't do this! I'd *never* get anything to eat.'

She pushed back her chair and carried the baby to the pillows on the couch. A wail immediately arose; and another, and another.

The grandmother half rose from her seat, laying her napkin down on the table. 'I'll hold her,' she said hastily.

'No, I don't want her to think she can always have her own way,' said Lottie peremptorily, 'she's got to learn to lie still. *She's* all right. It won't hurt her a bit to cry.' She looked at her mother-in-law hard and repeated in a measured voice, with little intervals between the words, 'I want her left right *there*.'

The baby screamed and screamed. Lottie raised her voice and talked volubly. She had had a letter from a married cousin whose husband worked in the Ford factory at Detroit. She said, 'Marie says that Tom's foreman is getting meaner and meaner, and she don't know but what Tom'll quit. His foreman's wife and Marie have had some kind of run-in, and Marie says she's one of the kind that's always looking for trouble and since her brother got to be something in the City Hall . . . no, I guess it wasn't her brother, it must have been her husband's brother. I know all about them, for they used to live next door to us for awhile. Wasn't it funny their moving out to Detroit too, same as Marie and Tom. I remember at school one time she went and told the teacher some of us were passing notes and kicked up the nastiest mess . . .'

The baby screamed and screamed. Mrs. Bascomb was not eating a mouthful. Ralph ate fast and nervously, his shoulders hunched.

'Just because,' said Lottie, 'none of the boys ever passed *her* any! But we got even with her all right, all right. One of the boys wrote her a fool note like he was dead gone on her, and when she answered that, he dropped her note where the teacher could get it and . . .'

The baby's shrieks rose in pitch.

'God Almighty! I can't stand this,' shouted Ralph. 'I'm going to take that child up.'

'All right, if you want to,' Lottie conceded it as a privilege she was willing to grant. 'But I don't see that you need to swear so about it.'

The baby, blinking and sniffling in her father's inexpert arms, rubbed her face sleepily with her fists, fell from one uncomfortable position to another, but did not cry, staring fixedly at the brightness of the electric drop-light. Ralph ate what he could over and around the baby and finished his meal at about the time Lottie finished her story. At last she interrupted herself to say, as the clock struck seven, 'My goodness, who'd have thought it was as late as that!'

Her accent was special. She waited expectantly.

After an instant of trying to say nothing, Ralph asked, 'Why, did you want to go anywhere this evening?'

Lottie burst out at him hotly, 'Well, what do you think? I guess you'd want to go somewhere or do something, if you'd been stuck in the house all day, working like a nigger and tending a baby, without a soul to speak to till you were just about *crazy!* What do you think I'm made of, anyway?'

Mrs. Bascomb rose and went hastily into the kitchen, but as she went, she heard, 'You and your mother have it easy! You dress up every morning and get out *with* folks all day long! You haven't any idea what it's *like,* here in the house. I should say I do want to go somewhere and do something! Why wouldn't I?'

In the kitchen her mother-in-law stood wiping her cold shaking hands on the roller towel, over and over, although they were quite dry. She held her under lip fast between her teeth, but her chin trembled so that it continually slipped out. 'I won't stand it. I won't stand it another minute!' she was saying to herself, rigid with anger.

She looked through the crumbled surface of the roller-towel, and saw the bright, pleasant lecture hall of the Community House, the comfortable seats filled with familiar forms, people like herself, middle-aged, nicely dressed, refined good citizens, interested as she was, in improving their minds. The lecture was to be on 'Moral Growth,' and Mr. Bancroft, the Y.M.C.A. Secretary of Harristown, was to speak. He was always so inspirational. And everybody she knew would be there.

From the dining-room came the sound of Lottie's crying, and Ralph's voice agitated, defiant, apologetic. His mother shuddered with contempt for his weakness, and with hatred for Lottie.

'I'll simply put on my things and *go!*' she told herself decisively, turning towards the door. 'I'll just leave them to stew in their own juice.'

She had not been aware that she knew such vulgar expressions as came constantly to her mind in these days.

Chapter 10

SHE had not taken a step away from the roller-towel, when everything in her mind was blotted out by a new idea . . . the baby's dirty clothes, and a way to get them clean. 'If I had the house to myself, I could wash and iron and put away all her little things before they get back from the movies. Lottie would probably never notice it, and if she did, she would be all over her resentment by the time I got home from school to-morrow.' Lottie never could keep her mind on anything, not even a grievance.

She could do it! Her imagination sprang forward . . . she saw the baby's round face above a fresh, clean-smelling white dress, such as she had not worn for days, her little feet in spotless pink socks, the small knit blanket which lay foul and evil-smelling in the drawer above, immaculate and fluffy, wrapped about the little body. She savoured the picture like something good to eat.

Yes, she could do it, if they would only leave her alone. She would have plenty of time. Ralph and Lottie were always late in coming in. Lottie liked to go around to a dance-hall and have a turn or two before coming home. There would be plenty of time. She felt warmed, supple, eager. She called from the kitchen to the dining-room, 'Don't stay at home on my account. I don't believe I feel like going to that lecture.'

The profoundness of the momentary silence told her that they were obliged to take an instant to remember what she was talking about. Oh, they had forgotten about her wanting to go to the lecture! Whatever the difficulty was about their going out, it had not been (as she had taken for granted) due to any thought of her. Here was another of the incessantly recurring stabs with which they showed her how entirely they disregarded her. But this one did not go through to the quivering quick as most of them did. She was hurt, but more dimly . . . she even felt a faint shade of astringent humour at her complete misunderstanding . . . the first amusement of that sort she had ever felt.

'There!' said Lottie to Ralph, recovering herself first. 'You see! That ought to settle it. If Momma doesn't need us here, I'll run up and get my things on. We'll be a little early. But we can go to Graham's for a soda.'

In the silence after her mounting the stairs, Mrs. Bascomb thought of them as she had often seen them during the first months after their marriage, sitting at one of the round marble-topped tables at the back of Graham's drug-store. Lottie made her soda last a long time, sipping it slowly through a straw, staring at people coming and going in the shop, giggling and whispering comments on the women's clothes into Ralph's ear. When a man stepped in and stood in front of the shop to take a soda or make a purchase, her manner changed. Her eyes examined him calculatingly. If he was young, alone and well-dressed, she looked at him till she caught his eye, and held it with her own till a certain spark came into his, a certain expression in his face as he stared impudently back at her. As soon as this happened, Lottie tossed her head and looked loftily away, or put her hand ostentatiously on Ralph's arm, sitting closer to him and beginning to talk to him with exaggerated animation. Sometimes at such moments, she could not restrain a strange little whinnying laugh of excited triumph. It was not in the least a laugh of amusement over an effect of comedy. It was not a real laugh at all. Whatever it was, it made every man in the shop turn his head to look at her, and then, for a moment, not look away.

Oh, yes, Mrs. Bascomb knew very well why Lottie liked to go early, and have a soda at Graham's. Everybody in town knew, too. She had seen the elderly principal of her school look at Lottie as all experienced teachers look at girls of a certain kind. She knew well enough what people thought of Lottie and Ralph, how the prestige which she had built up by years of faultless living had been dragged in the dust.

She heard Ralph start out towards the kitchen . . . and thought, 'How can he look me in the face after such a return as he has made to me for all my sacrifices for him!'

Ralph came in. The baby was still in his arms, still

70

awake, though deplorably tired, yawning, rubbing her flat nose back and forth with fitful movements of her unco-ordinated arm muscles, fretting uneasily, though too sleepy to cry aloud. In her father's awkward grasp, her boneless little body had settled heavily down into helpless discomfort. She could not sleep, tired though she was.

Mrs. Bascomb flew at him and snatched the baby from his arms. Her own back ached to see the way the baby's was bent and crooked. She could scarcely breathe, poor dear.

Her grandmother laid her over her shoulder and patted the little back. She felt the small cramped body stretch out and relax. She shared the exquisite sensation of relief. Just wait till the darling was clean from top to toe! Her grandmother could scarcely wait to begin.

Ralph was saying something to her. Oh, yes, about her giving up the lecture. She had forgotten the lecture.

Lottie came downstairs, her blue velvet picture-hat aslant rakishly. 'I expect after your teaching you feel too tired to go out,' she said amiably, through the door of the kitchen, to her mother-in-law.

Behind her stood the disordered dinner table. Before her stood the disordered kitchen.

'It'll probably do you good to have a nice quiet evening all by yourself,' she said, pulling out a curl on her forehead. 'Come along, Ralph! I'm crazy to get out of this house and see something going on.'

The front door closed behind them.

Mrs. Bascomb felt herself shaken by fury as if by the blasts of a tempest, sweeping upon her from every direction at once. 'A nice quiet evening . . .!'

The baby in her arms gave a squeaking gasp, and she found that her arms had tightened nervously so that the little thing could scarcely breathe. She was horrified! She had hurt her darling! She shifted the baby, bending over her remorsefully. With a long breath, the tiny, swathed cocoon straightened out in comfort; the blunt shapeless features smoothed themselves again into the tranquil Buddha-expression of repose.

Her grandmother looked down fixedly at the calm sleeping face; tiny atom of serenity in the howling of the tempest. She could not take her eyes away . . . the quiet of those lowered eyelids, the sweetness of the mouth folded shut like a flower bud, the little hands up-thrown, limp and soft. The beating gusts of her fury died down with the quieting of her pulses. She felt them slower and stronger . . . they became a deep rhythmical pulsation which came and went like a great tide through her and through the warm small body in her arms, as if they had been one. She stood at the very heart of quiet.

She had forgotten to breathe, and now drew in a long sigh, which lifted her breast flutteringly. The bright mist melted before her eyes. She blinked a little, stopped and kissed the baby's cheek with a touch like that of a butterfly's wing-tip.

Now she felt strong and eager for activity. Her plans for the evening rushed into her mind, bringing her a keen forward-looking pleasure. Yes, she remembered, she had planned to begin by washing all the little things first, and doing the housework afterwards, while they were drying.

She laid the baby down on the couch to sleep, and ran upstairs to the white chest of drawers, emptying its contents into a soiled sheet from the baby's crib. She stepped cautiously into the front room, averting her eyes from the phantom Lottie who always stood there in her vulgar triumph, and picked out here and there, bits of baby-gear adrift on the whirlpool of disorder. She looked into the bathroom and snatched up traces of the baby's passage there, wet soiled cloths thrown down in a lump, a nursing bottle with milk dried on the nipple. For Lottie was giving the baby several bottles of milk a day now, so that she could be free to go out in the evening and so that her night's rest might not be disturbed. The little crib still stood beside the grandmother's bed. It was the grandmother who woke at three in the morning to feed the baby.

Mrs. Bascomb glanced at the clock as she flew down the stairs. She had not an instant to lose. She flung up the lids of the stationary tubs, and set briskly about her washing as if in time to a stirring quick-step. She worked with one eye on the clock, rejoicing as she saw how rapidly she was progressing . . . those bits of garments were nothing

72

to wash! There! She had the white things ready to boil. Now for the flannels. At quarter to eight the flannels were finished. Only the blankets to do. Five minutes to eight – everything woollen done and hung up to dry.

The table to clear . . . a digression to swoop down on the sleeping baby with another butterfly kiss.

Eight o'clock – time to rinse and hang up the white things. Fine! The movies did not even begin till a quarter past. She flew in and out of the steaming kitchen with food, and with dishes, first dirty and then clean. Half-past eight – her quick-stepping feet paused while she planned her next moves. She would see to the furnace now, so that she would not be obliged to interrupt the baby's bath. Bring in the blankets airing on the line upstairs. Prepare the milk-bottle for the meal after the bath. Put towels on the radiator to warm.

Like a competent commanding officer, she issued this staccato series of orders to herself, ending with an inward 'Forward, *march!*' which sent her racing down the cellar stairs to the furnace.

She did not dally long over the evening bath, dearly as she loved that moment of the day. They had fallen into the habit of having the baby bathed at night because as Lottie said to visitors, 'Momma's so crazy about the baby it would be mean to bathe her in the morning when Momma can't be here.'

This had infuriated Mrs. Bascomb . . . was one of the thousand things which infuriated her. But she loved the bath in the evening too much to make any open comment.

To-night she had no time to play with the soft naked body as she often did. 'Into the tub with you, small darling, paddling feebly with your little feet, the soles still turned in with that simian gesture, the little hands grasping weakly at the bare arm under you . . .'

How huge and massive the grandmother's slender fore-arm looked beside that scrap of a body.

'Sputter over the soap? Never mind. That's a good girl. Out with you now. On the warm, dry towel on grandmother's lap. You little thing! You little, *little* thing! How foolishly you wave your arms about. Will those limp little fingers ever hold a book? A pen?'

A thought like a blow between the eyes . . . 'What *will* those little fingers do as they grow strong? With Lottie for a mother. The darling will soon no longer be a little plaything to hold safe on your knees. What will she see? What will she hear? What will she be?'

No time to-night to brood and shudder. Only time to be sure that grandmother will always be here. She will always find a way to protect her darling, to work for her as she is doing now, to fight for her.

Half-past nine. Is the bottle warm enough? Yes . . . there, little pig, darling, darling little pig . . . isn't that good?

Ten minutes of enforced quiet and thought while the baby takes her supper. How silly to call her still 'the baby.' Why don't they decide on a name and have her baptized like a Christian? Perhaps they are going to give the grandmother a sweet surprise by calling the baby after her, 'Mary.' Or 'Joanna' for her grandfather. How beautiful to have her called 'Joanna.' Every time her grandmother spoke to her, the name would be sweet on her tongue, would remind her of that first moment when their eyes met, and she had seen that the baby *was* Joanna.

There, the last drop of milk was gone. The baby was asleep. Joanna was asleep. How beautifully well she was! There was something magnificent about such health. You felt it radiating warmth on you, like sunshine. Into the little crib with her, beside grandmother's bed.

Now, quick, down to the kitchen. Were the irons hot?

Nearly ten. They would be back from the cinema at half-past or a little later. She wouldn't have time to iron the flannels as she had the cotton things. But they would be clean at least.

Half-past ten. All done. The drawers filled with clean, smoothed, carefully folded little garments. In the kitchen no sign of the evening activities save the odour of soap in the air. That was better than the smell usually in the air in that house.

But how her feet ached. The bottoms were like boils. She would take a hot bath and get to bed.

Oh, the bathroom! She picked her way in, sickened, raging . . . a black rim around the tub, damp towels flung down anywhere, talcum powder and twisted-up wisps of hair on the glass shelf over the grimy wash-basin, and, in the air, a stale smell of perspiration, perfume, and baby's diapers. How Mrs. Bascomb loathed Lottie!

Her loathing was like the crack of a whip across her face. She forgot her aching feet. She set the room in what order she could, as she drew the water for her bath.

Ten minutes later as she stepped into the hall, her wrapper over her night-gown, she heard the front door open. They were just coming in. If she stepped noiselessly, perhaps she could get to bed without needing to speak to them. But they had seen the light in the hall; Lottie's voice (her cheerful voice, the one she had after she had been out of an evening), '*Oh*, Momma! Still awake?'

Mrs. Bascomb did not answer, drifting on tiptoe to her open door.

'We've thought of a name for the baby,' Lottie went on, 'a regular beaut, too! It was the name of the heroine in the movies to-night. I always liked it. Gladys.'

No answer from above. 'Did she hear, do you suppose?' asked Lottie, turning to Ralph.

Ralph ran up the stairs. The upper hall was empty, and the door shut to the little room which had been his and was now his mother's. 'No one there,' he said, going down. 'She must have gone to bed and left the hall light on.'

'Well, we can tell her to-morrow morning just as well,' said Lottie, easy-going and good-natured. 'Wasn't that last dance a beaut!'

Inside the little room, the weary, weary feet were stretched to rest. But the sore angry heart still throbbed wearily on. . . . 'Gladys! I will never let that hideous name pass my lips.'

How desperately tired she was. Her eyelids fell shut as if they were of lead. Confused, incongruous thoughts whirled through her mind . . . but nothing could keep awake anyone as tired as she.

The incoherent thoughts came and went dimly, like things moving in a thick mist . . . with long intervals between, when she dozed. Gladys! What a name! What could you do with such a name! Gladys!

But the baby's clothes were all clean, anyhow.

Oh, damn! She had washed Lottie's dirty dishes again!

How heavenly good it seemed to lie down, to rest . . . it made one weep with relief. How good it must feel to die! But now she wouldn't dare to die. What would happen to her darling?

Had she said 'damn'? *She*, Mary Bascomb? Oh, well, it didn't matter. Nothing mattered. Nothing except . . . What was it that mattered? She could not remember. But there *was* something. Half-drowned in fatigue, less than half awake, she reached her arm out of bed and laid it across the little crib so that her hand rested against the baby's side. She felt the light, even, healthful breathing of the sleeping child. She took light, even breaths. She was asleep. She was sleeping now as soundly as the baby by her side.

Chapter 11

THE winter went slowly by, labouring like a water-logged raft with a load of shipwrecked mariners. Things already as bad as they could be, went steadily from bad to worse. Mrs. Bascomb knew now why Ralph did not like to 'go down town' with Lottie in the evening. It had nothing to do with his mother's welfare. It was not even because of his own deadly fatigue.

His mother learned why one afternoon in January, when she came into the house after school and found Lottie 'entertaining a man friend' as she put it later at the supper-table, when she told Ralph, making a great show of being perfectly open and natural about it, 'He's a dandy fellow, Ralph. Why, *you* know him! Don't you know, he was down at Hudson's Hall a few nights ago and I introduced you to him. The one with the diamond ring, you *must* have noticed his diamond ring. And the great line of talk. He's got a perfectly wonderful line. Just keeps a

person in one scream after another. Everybody says he
ought to be in vaudeville. He'd make his fortune all right.
But he says he'd rather stay poor but honest. His business
is selling mining stock. Aw, Ralph, go on, you must
remember him . . . he was the one that showed me that
swell new step in the hesitation.'

She had talked a great deal, rather too fast, and now
stopped and took a drink of water with ostentatious
coolness.

Ralph asked, 'How'd he happen to be around here?'

His mother did not recognize his voice. It was not
Ralph's voice at all. Another man's. Rough, hoarse,
strange.

In her usual role of disregarded, negligible spectator,
she looked at him hard, and recognized his expression as
little as his voice. He did not look like Ralph. Something
she had never seen was smouldering in his eyes as he fixed
them on Lottie.

'How'd he happen to come?' repeated Lottie airily. 'Oh,
he's got a "prospect" living somewhere up this street. An
old lady that's just lost her husband and has got his insurance money to invest. Mr. Bosch's brother works in an
insurance office and he lets him know on the quiet whenever
they have to pay a policy. And he . . . why, as he went
by, he just happened to see me through the window and
came in for a minute. He was crazy about Gladys. He's
crazy about kids, anyhow.'

Mrs. Bascomb had found the baby upstairs, strapped
in her crib, silently and happily playing with her rattle.
But she pressed her lips together. She would not demean
herself to tell tales on Lottie.

'Has he been here before?' asked Ralph.

Lottie hesitated the fraction of an instant, shot a glance
at her mother-in-law, and said emphatically, 'No, of course
he hasn't.'

The certainty that she had lied filled the room like an
odour.

'What have I done?' thought Mrs. Bascomb, sickened,
'to be forced into contact with this low-lived '. . .?'

'How'd you like it,' said Ralph, 'if I went around calling
on girls in the afternoon?'

Lottie opened her eyes very wide, with a childlike expression of astonishment. 'But Mr. Bosch isn't *married!*' she said.

'No, but you are,' said Ralph, pushing away from the table.

'Oh, well, if you're going to be so mean about every little thing,' said Lottie, but without her usual flare of defiance. She looked at Ralph curiously, and fell into silence for a time, as though she were thinking over what she saw in his face. Except that Lottie never thought over anything.

She did not ask to go out that evening, but bustled about the house in a large apron, in one of her fitful crises of housekeeping, which were even more disastrous than her periods of complete inertia. It took days to find anything after Lottie had had a 'spell of tending to things' as she put it. She hummed and whistled cheerfully, over and over, the 'Merry Widow Waltz,' then at the height of its popularity, talked cheerfully about the neighbourhood gossip in which she was an expert, and told one or two funny stories which she said she had 'read in the paper' that morning.

Ralph's grimness did not soften. He sat, lowering and silent, holding the evening paper up in front of his face, although he was interrupted from time to time by Lottie's coming to pat his head, or sit for a moment on his knee. Her expression as she looked at him was wary and cautious. The clock had not struck nine before she said, yawning widely, 'I don't know what's the matter with me. I'm just all in this evening. Come on, Ralph, let's go to bed. Momma won't mind for once giving the baby her last bottle, I know.' As they mounted the stairs, her arm was around Ralph's neck.

While Mrs. Bascomb was bathing the baby and putting her to bed, the house was as silent as if she had been alone in it as usual. But as she herself was undressing, she heard the murmur from the other room, the faintest breath now, broken by long pauses of silence. She turned her light out and laid herself stiffly down upon her bed. The house was black as well as silent. She lay there, tense, listening, trying not to hear.

78

Presently through the blackness came the sound of a laugh, Lottie's strange little laugh of excited triumph.

Mrs. Bascomb buried her head in one pillow and pulled the other over her ear to shut out sound. She heard nothing else. But that laugh rang in her dreams all night.

In the morning as she was getting breakfast, Ralph came downstairs. He was pale, his delicate features pinched, his lips colourless and withered. But the strange expression had gone from his eyes. He looked just like Ralph again, Ralph as he used to look as a little boy, when he wasn't very well, just beginning or just recovering from a sickness.

'Lottie's got a sort of headache this morning,' he said gruffly. 'I guess I'd better carry her breakfast up to her.'

Mrs. Bascomb, going to take up the baby after he had gone back with the tray, saw through the door he had left open, Lottie with the tray before her in bed, Lottie, perhaps a little weary looking, her cheeks creamier than usual, but prettier than usual too, with a bloomed-out brightness on her smooth lips, in her eyes.

Ralph was standing by her, looking down at her. As his mother passed, he stooped with a violent quickness. From her own room as she lifted the heavy baby from the crib, she heard the rattle of silver and china and Lottie's laughing, choked voice, 'You silly! Ralph . . . let go! I can't breathe. Where'd that orange go? You bad boy!'

Mrs. Bascomb, the baby in her arms, passed back before the open door, her face turned away. 'What have I done? What have I done to deserve this?' she was inwardly crying. She felt the phantom Lottie looking at her in mocking triumph.

During all the months past, she had given up reading the Bible before going to bed. But now, in the middle of that first period of Ralph's marriage, when things went from bad to worse, she once more opened the familiar, leather-covered, much worn book. She knew where to turn in it to find what she wanted. Oh, yes, she knew on which pages to find the right words. When she sat down in her room, exhausted, the baby sleeping near her, the house empty, the denunciatory splendour of the words she saw on the page seemed to flame out from her own lips.

'For the lips of a strange woman drop honey
And her mouth is smoother than oil
But in the end she is bitter as wormwood;
Sharp as a two-edged sword.

Her feet go down to death.
Her steps take hold on hell.'

The words filled, like the menacing growl of a wild
animal, the little room where Mary Bascomb sat.

'Now I will judge thee according to thy ways:
And I will bring upon thee all thine abominations
And mine eyes shall not spare thee, neither will
I have pity, but I will bring thy ways upon thee.'

Mrs. Bascomb's eyes burned, her hands trembled, her
heart pounded and knocked in thick, irregular throbs.

As the winter went on, in February, she suffered so much
from heart palpitations that she was sure she had some
serious organic trouble, and took one noon hour to go to
consult Dr. Dewey.

She told him her symptoms, terrible and alarming ones
they seemed to her, sudden onsets of furiously rapid pulses,
dizziness, a frightful sensation of smothering, and often,
almost constantly, the nervous tremor of her hands, which
she could not control. Was she on her way to palsy?
Was she likely to drop dead at her desk in school?

The rough old doctor listened attentively to all she said,
looking at her deeply, and at the end gave her a minute
and entirely silent examination, adding not a word to the
brief commands, 'Breathe deep.' 'Tell me if I hurt you.'
'Turn around.'

When he finished, he did not speak for a minute or two,
eyeing her reflectively. Was he trying for once, to think of
some gentle way to break fatal news to her, he who had
always blurted everything out?

He said, 'Nothing's the matter with your heart. Or any
other organ. You're all right. You must come from magnificent stock. You're all right . . . physically. *I* can't do
anything for you.'

'But, doctor,' she protested, shocked, 'you don't understand. I have such terrible fits of trembling, all over.
I can hardly hold anything in my hand. And there are
moments when my heart beats so fast I can hardly get
my breath.'

'Do you ever have those spells in school?' he asked.

Her answer came with a promptness which surprised
herself, 'No, oh, no.' It occurred to her now, for the first
time, that not since she had begun teaching had she done
her class work with so little fatigue, with so little tension.
Nothing about it bothered her, as it used to. She looked
forward to it every day. It actually seemed to rest her.
Now she thought of it, she was surprised.

The doctor dropped his eyes from hers and began fiddling
with a pen-holder. 'I guess you take things at home pretty
hard, Mrs. Bascomb,' he said. 'I imagine that's what ails
you. You'll have to learn not to get so excited. You
probably have what we call brainstorms, nervous spasms of
exasperation; and that drives the blood in from your outer
capillaries, and gives you those queer feelings in your heart.
You will just have to learn to take life easier.'

For the first time . . . the only time in all her life, she
spoke out. A little. Three words. 'How *can* I?' she cried,
bitterly, looking at him squarely, forcing his eyes up to
meet hers, insisting that he acknowledge things which he
understood very well without words.

'Yes, I know, I know,' he said hastily.

He hesitated, scratched his drawn-down upper lip with
his forefinger irresolutely, still looking at her, and finally
said, 'I think you're making a mistake, Mrs. Bascomb, in
trying to go on living with your son after his marriage.
It never works. A young couple always get on better by
themselves. I'll bet they are not enjoying it any more
than you are.'

She fell back in her chair, stupid with astonishment.
The phrase 'Go on living with your son,' shocked her like
an indecent joke. She opened her mouth to shout out,
'Go on living with them! Why, they are going on living
with me. It's *my* house! I'm paying most of the expenses.'

But the telephone bell on the doctor's desk rang sharply,
and in an instant he was miles away from her, absorbed,

intent, oblivious. She could not, it seemed, even for an instant, even when she paid cash for it, hold the centre of anyone's attention any more. She was always being shoved peremptorily off the stage.

The doctor was saying anxiously, in the receiver, 'When did the temperature begin to rise? An hour ago! Lord! What's his pulse? Why didn't you call me before. Start with the amyl nitrate at once. I'll be there in five minutes.'

He sprang from his seat, excused himself to Mrs. Bascomb with a rough, hurried gesture, reached for his coat, clapped on his hat and was gone.

She was left alone, as she always was nowadays, with no spectator to know or care what she did or what she felt or what became of her. She had had her moment of attention and now, unimportant, unconsidered, was dismissed and must pass on . . . nobody cared where. She fastened up her cloak with her shaking fingers, casting about her a vague glance as if she were looking for something forgotten, really looking for some way with which to round out the episode with a little dignity for herself.

Something about her action struck her. That helpless look around. It was familiar. Where had she seen it before? She had certainly never looked that way before, because never before had she been made to feel this slighted, helpless, rebuffed humiliation.

It came to her. That was the way the poorer, sadder mothers looked, when they had stood for their instant before her desk, when she had given them their moment of her attention, and then, with a look, with an emanation from her inner impatience, pushed them along, off the stage. Oh, was this how they *felt*? Was it out of such trouble as hers they had come to her, groping for help? Was it back into such bitterness and lonely misery as this which now overwhelmed her, that she pushed them with a look? Had they come to her, as she had gone to the doctor, hoping to receive more than they dared ask for, because their need was so great?

She was shamed and humiliated to feel herself in their position. She was ashamed too, as she remembered it, of the look with which she had pushed them away from her. The sympathy she felt now was not tender, it was angry, was hot and sore. It hurt her. Yes, it pierced far down to her quick, where it hurt her cruelly.

She had walked all along the street blindly, and was back at the door of the schoolhouse before she came to herself, as the saying goes (but she hardly knew in those days what 'herself' was), before she thought again of Lottie and Ralph and the fact, the screaming, thumping, monumental fact, on which everything turned, the fact which the doctor had so outrageously disregarded, the fact that *it was her house!* It belonged to *her!* She had bought it with her own money, with cash that she had earned by her own labour. She piled up in her mind all the mountain-high testimony to the fact that it belonged to her. Every one must know such an important fact as whom the house belonged to! How could anyone for an instant forget that, even if they did not know (as they could not, because she would not lower herself to tell anyone) that she paid the taxes and bought the coal and paid for the washings and settled the electric light bills and the gas-bills and paid for the weekly day of the cleaning-woman and did practically all the housework with her own hands. She heaped higher and higher all the rightness which was on her side. 'Go on living with your son indeed!' She bounded with indignation at the phrase.

She was entering her own classroom now, and the heavy hand of habit shut, with its nonchalant puissance, the door of the room where Mary Bascomb blazed with indignation over the way she was being treated, and opened the door of the room in which Teacher, with the easy adroitness of experience, reflected that it was about time to start a review of the French and Indian wars.

That afternoon, when she went home, she found Lottie once more entertaining Mr. Bosch in the living room. Lottie, her eyes repeatedly on her mother-in-law, said nothing about this at dinner. And neither did her mother-in-law.

Chapter 12

SHE said nothing about it because as always, she would not sink herself to Lottie's level, even for the purpose of making trouble for Lottie. The only thing which sustained her at all, was her never-shaken conviction that she was another order of being from Lottie.

But there was another reason for her silence; an unreasoning instinct rather than a reason, which during the next few months, kept her intensely silent about Lottie's actions. Through the silence there made its way to her, little by little, creeping and unavowed at first and then fiercely exultingly alive, the hope which lay behind her instinct.

By the coming of spring, it had become an accepted tradition that Ralph's mother did not care to go out in the evening, was getting too old, was too tired after her day's teaching, and preferred a 'nice, quiet evening at home' to any outside diversion. But she still went to church every Sunday morning. Lottie said to visitors, 'Momma thinks so much of her church, and it's about the only thing she does care anything about, so we always put ourselves out to fix things so she can get off Sunday mornings.'

Ralph and Lottie slept late Sunday mornings, and lay abed later still; and often, after nine, took the fed and dressed and cared-for baby into their bed to play with her.

The Reverend Mr. Bancroft thus saw Mrs. Bascomb as usual, devoutly joining in the 'Responsive Readings from the Scriptures.' He would have been astonished to know how her heart lifted as he read aloud, with his best Sunday intonation:

'Yea he hath conceived mischief and brought forth false-
    hood
He hath made a pit and digged it,'

Or, if he could have heard the passion in her voice, lost in the comfortable drone of the congregation as it answered him,

'He has fallen into the ditch which he made
His mischief shall return upon his own head.'

The minister reaching into his pocket for the paper with
notices of the meetings of the Ladies Aid Missionary
Society, read on,

'His violence shall come down upon his own pate.'

He did not hear the fury with which the middle-aged
woman cried out in answer,

'I will give thanks to Jehovah according to his righteousness.

Mr. Bosch came oftener to be entertained by Lottie.
At least it was in the afternoon that Mrs. Bascomb heard
him most often in the living-room as she entered the house
through the kitchen door and went directly upstairs to
her room. She usually found the baby there, sitting in her
little pen, with her playthings tumbled about her. She
was a strong, healthy child with an excellent digestion,
and hence a large fund of good nature, and she seldom
protested against this solitary imprisonment. It was an
exquisite moment in Mrs. Bascomb's day when she opened
the door gently and stood there. The baby lifted her eyes,
at first a neutral inquiry. To see that indifferent look of
inquiry change to joyful recognition that shone through
the little face like a lighted flame, to see her drop whatever
toy she had in her hand and stretch out her arms to her
grandmother, to hear her little voice, a human voice now,
shout out, 'Dannie! Dannie!' and then as she grew older,
'Gwannie! Gwannie!' There was never a day when
Mrs. Bascomb was so heart-sick that she did not leave all
the world behind her as she stepped into that room. It
was now the third room in her life, a room where she was
neither Mary Bascomb, raw and hurt and right and
aggrieved about the wrongs done her; nor Teacher, self-
possessed, active, impersonal, manipulating the tools of her
profession smoothly and deftly. As she took the baby into
her arms, those two women dropped from her memory.

85

She became Grannie, who lived in so small, so narrow a life that there was nothing in it but a baby too young to talk, so limitlessly great that Grannie's heart was often too small to hold it all.

Of late two of these women sometimes lived together in the same body, turning their eyes away from each other, as Grannie, holding the exuberant little body on her lap, tried to dress it for the daily outing; while Mrs. Bascomb listened grimly to the crackling laughter and loud jocular voices from downstairs.

It was Mrs. Bascomb who sat silent at the supper table while Lottie talked of everything except her caller; it was Mrs. Bascomb who sitting up in her narrow bed, in her high-necked, long-sleeved night-gown, read exultingly,

'He that goeth down to Hell shall come up no more,
He shall return no more to his house.
Neither shall his place know him any more.'

It was Grannie who, before she went to sleep, laid her arm cautiously across the crib, so that her fingers touched the baby and rose and fell with the light, even breathing which was now her only nightly prayer.

It was Teacher who listened with professional interest to the gossip at teachers' meetings, about the excitement over in Harristown, in the Warren Street School there. They were 'having trouble' there, one of those envenomed ingrowing quarrels which start from nothing and, in the airless world of a large, populous school building, grow to strange, mean, fierce, life-and-death battles.

It had begun (but by this time nobody ever thought of how it had begun) over a difference of opinion as to teaching geography in the third grade. But it was now a well-defined war, into which everybody contiguous had been drawn. Part of the teachers took sides with the principal, part with the school board. Into the seething cauldron of bad feeling, the Main Street teachers in the other, smaller town, looked with complacent interest. There had not been a really energetic faculty row in their building for years; not, in fact, since they had Mr. Kennedy for Principal – cool, elderly, cynical Mr. Kennedy, who

86

'managed' his subordinates so neatly through their weaknesses.

The progress of the Harristown battle was reported weekly by the seventh-grade teacher, whose family lived in Harristown, and who spent her week-ends there. All battles are absorbing spectacles, especially to those not menaced. This one was no exception. The bulletins from the front were circulated briskly among the Main Street School teachers, who had a professional interest in how things came out.

Things came out with a bang which startled them, for the explosion upheaved the ground under their own feet. In the midst of the row, the Harristown Principal received from a prosperous Pacific-Coast city an offer to start an advanced modern school there. It was an opulent, cash-freighted, Pacific-Coast offer; his acceptance of which, at the last meeting of the year, he flashed exuberantly before the noses of the niggardly, reactionary Eastern school board, 'handing them his resignation' with the triumphant gesture of a prize-fighter handing his opponent a knock-out blow. There was more to it than this. He took with him, at salaries far in excess of their Harristown pay, the six teachers who had sided with him. The seven made a simultaneous disappearance which had in it a quality of nose-thumbing insolence intolerable to the Harristown school board. They lost no time. They descended upon the smaller, poorer, neighbouring city, bearing gifts, and the Main Street teachers were startled to learn that Mr. Kennedy, their Mr. Kennedy upon whom they had counted as upon the recurrence of the seasons, had been offered so large a salary to take over and reorganize the shattered Harristown school that he had accepted.

'Mrs. Bascomb, could I see you for a moment at the noon hour?' Mr. Kennedy had said; and there she was in his office, the door shut, wondering what in the world he could have to say to her.

He said it with the remoteness of manner which had enabled him to steady and direct all those excitable women's natures. He put it to her as if she could consider it as calmly as he, as if it were not preposterous . . . but then of course, he had no notion of what she knew, of what she was hoping for, of what she was sure would happen, in one way or another. He invited her to leave her present position and her home and go with him to Harristown, along with four other of her present colleagues. He put the advantages before her, lucidly. 'The salary is five hundred dollars a year more, and the work lighter. Never more than twenty-five in a classroom, and all from well-to-do families. No working people's children at all, only those from the nicest homes.'

He paused here to let this sink in. Having observed Mrs. Bascomb for eleven years, he knew that this would have more weight than the money. But she said nothing, did not look impressed.

Well, he had other shot in his locker, two or three more.

'The living conditions are especially pleasant in that residential portion of Harristown,' he went on. 'Three doors from the school building is one of the nicest boarding-houses I ever saw, kept by a real gentlewoman, in her own fine old house. And you know what advantages Harristown has for anyone with your intellectual tastes; the finest lecture courses, the best things from the New York theatres, Sothern and Marlowe in Shakespeare, Sembrich in recitals. . .'

He was perplexed by Mrs. Bascomb's expression. He could not make it out. He could not see why she did not jump at the escape from the mess which her son's marriage had made for her at home. She had been looking like death all winter. Here was her chance to get out with dignity. He had counted on that.

She said quietly, 'Thanks for thinking of me, Mr. Kennedy. I appreciate it, but I couldn't think of accepting. I am needed at home.' (She had almost said, 'I will be needed at home.')

Mr. Kennedy could not have had a better opening for his last shot. 'Mrs. Bascomb,' he said, leaning forward, 'will you let me speak with the frankness of an old friend. Will you let me say, what of course you must know, yourself . . . that it is never a good plan for a mother to live with her married son? There is always unhappiness.

88

In your case, I know . . . we all know well enough . . . that the ah . . . unhappiness is no fault of yours. You . . . ah . . . have had our sympathy. But we have all felt . . . ah . . . if I may say so . . . that it is better for young married people to shoulder their own responsibilities. People who marry,' his voice became rotund, 'people who marry take on certain duties which they should . . .'

This was absurd, thought Mrs. Bascomb. The idea of his getting off these stale old generalities in her case! She would not stand it for a moment. She stood up to cut him short. And yet not resentfully. She was too sure of her ground to feel resentment. After all, Mr. Kennedy, not knowing what was taking place at home, the door of hope that was slowly opening before her, could not know how flat his little ready-made aphorisms sounded.

She said, 'There are sometimes special circumstances which . . . no, I think I will be needed at home too much to think of accepting a position elsewhere.' Nettled at his not knowing what she did not tell him, she ended with a little stiffness, 'I think I am as competent to judge my own affairs as . . . as other people.'

Mr. Kennedy did not acknowledge defeat. He really needed Mrs. Bascomb. He would have his hands quite full enough in Harristown, without breaking into the work an inexperienced young teacher who might or might not turn out well. So he said genially, ignoring her rebuke, 'Well, Mrs. Bascomb, think it over, think it over. I'll keep the place open for you a week. Nobody of sense can decide anything in less than a week. You come in next Wednesday and let me know your final decision.'

When she stepped into the kitchen that afternoon, there was no sound from the living-room. Apparently Mr. Bosch had not come. But as she went through into the hall, she heard a sudden startled stir on the other side of the portières, a chair grated, a step or two was hastily taken, and there were voices, rather breathless but fluent in the note of casual conversation. She paused irresolute. Lottie's voice said, 'That you, Momma? My! aren't you back early? Mr. Bosch and I were just saying how this lovely spring weather makes a person step along!'

Lottie stood there, pushing back the portière. Her mother-in-law leaned against the wall to take off her goloshes, keeping her eyes bent downward on them. She did not look once at Lottie. She murmured something about the baby and went upstairs.

Behind her she heard Lottie's voice, relieved. 'No, she didn't . . .' Lottie must think she was a fool. So much the better. She was saying to herself,

'They that hate thee shall be clothed in shame
And the tent of the wicked shall be no more.'

'Gwannie! Gwannie!' shouted the baby's voice. She was so clever, the darling. She knew just when to expect her grandmother and her longed-for daily outing. She recognized even the step on the stairs, now.

The door to the little bedroom was open. The baby was standing up, leaning over the railing of her little pen, stretching out her arms, stamping her cushiony feet with impatience. 'Gwannie! Gwannie! out do'! out do'!'

The light from the window, deflected from the white door, fell strongly across her splendid great brow, left her eyes in shadow and brought out, in an unusual relation, the line of her cheek and jaw. Her grandmother suppressed a cry, and clapped her hand to her heart, which had given a great leap. Why, it was John's very face, his very expression. He was there, looking at her from those loving, living eyes, welcoming. . . .

She snatched the child up into her arms, searching her face.

'Out do'! Out do'!' cried the little thing, bouncing impatiently, straightening her small, muscular back in the astonishingly vigorous leaps of a healthy baby. The thin, middle-aged woman could scarcely hold her. The grandmother, startled, moved, her heart still beating wildly with the shock of that likeness, had but one desire . . . to hold her close, close – to cover her with kisses, to feel her, to be felt by her.

But the baby had no such desire. What she wanted was to go out, to see the world, to breathe new air. What she wanted of her grandmother was to serve her.

Mrs. Bascomb loosened the hold of her arms which ached with longing, set the baby down, and turned to look for the little cap and cloak.

Chapter 13

LOTTIE was frightfully difficult to live with during the next few days. Her moods, always eddying about in gusts of feeling inexplicable to her mother-in-law, varied almost from moment to moment, instead of from hour to hour as usual. Whatever anyone did was wrong, whether it was to speak or keep silent, to take up the baby or to leave her alone, to suggest going out or staying at home. She went into a fit of anger because Mrs. Bascomb, thinking the weather had changed since morning, took off the heavy woollen sweater which Lottie had put on the baby and dressed her in a light-weight garment which was a recent purchase of her own.

'She's *my* baby!' Lottie had said furiously, snatching off the coat, flinging it upon the ground, and cramming the baby's arms back into the sweater sleeves.

She found out that Ralph had spent half an hour at the ball-game (the opening one of the season, the first one he had seen for more than a year) and shut herself into a sullen, swollen silence which Ralph apologetic, remorseful, exasperated, tried in vain to break down with long repeated explanations of how it happened, how he had not had time to telephone her, or to take her along, how the boss had come in half an hour before closing-time and had said, 'What say, Bascomb, shall we go to the game?' It made Mrs. Bascomb furious with Ralph to see how anxiously he kept his eyes on Lottie's face, how alarmed he was to see a shade of displeasure upon it, how uneasy he was until she allowed herself to relax and smile again. Lottie had only to look at him, she thought angrily, to rule him.

And yet it was in the middle of this period of storms and petulance and unreasonable fits of temper, that Mrs. Bascomb caught a glimpse of Lottie as she had never seen her before. She usually spent Saturday afternoon keeping the baby outdoors while Ralph and Lottie 'went somewhere and did something,' if it were only to attend the movie matinée. But Ralph was not free one Saturday afternoon in May. He had telephoned from the office that extra work (always welcome because it meant extra pay) would keep him all the afternoon. Lottie had dressed and gone down-town directly after lunch. Mrs. Bascomb had an appointment with the dentist at three o'clock. There was nothing for it but to take the baby with her, in the folding push-cart which she could get up and down steps alone.

She was exactly on time at the dentist's office – she was never late anywhere – but he was not ready for her. He never was. Usually as she sat there waiting, through his wrong, when she had taken the trouble to be on time, she consumed herself with revolt against the unfairness of the world. But that afternoon the injustice done to her promptness seemed to slip past her, did not penetrate and rankle. She could not put her mind on it. Queer. Perhaps it was because her attention was distracted by the baby, astonishingly interested in pictures, far before the usual age. Among the weary, limp, old periodicals on the dentist's table was a battered picture-book. It amazed the grandmother to see how deftly the little hands turned the pages, how attentively the bright eyes gazed at the gaudy pigs and horses and camels displayed.

'I never saw such a smart child in my life!' she thought proudly. And then with an impulse new in her, she smiled at herself with amusement. Why, she was just like any other doting grandmother.

It was the first time she had ever thought of herself as not being quite different from every other person.

She looked away from the baby for a moment, out into the street. The dentist's office was on the ground floor. The pavement was directly before his window. A group of working girls stood there, in the delicious idleness of Saturday afternoon, chattering lightly, like the flock of parrots their bright-coloured hats and dresses made them look. The shrill, uncultivated, care-free young voices came in through the open window in confused and disconnected bits of disarmingly foolish talk.

'I said to her, I said, "You'd better keep your own on straight," I said.'

'She told me, "pastel-pink's your colour and never you mind what anybody else tells you." '

'He started to be mad, but he couldn't keep himself from laughing right out.'

'The new step that she was showin' me . . .'

'A piping of black satin down the seams . . .'

'If you singe the ends . . .'

They giggled and put their heads together to whisper, and burst into fits of laughter, rocking on their high heels, their smooth white young throats thrown back like those of birds about to sing.

Mrs. Bascomb caught a glimpse of the face of one of them, framed for an instant in the curtains . . . a pretty, childish, foolish face, brimming with pleasure, the face of a school-child on the playground at recess time, filled with the delight of the precious ten minutes' reprieve from lessons.

The curtain blew back. The group of girls loitered along, their voices dying in the distance. That face had been familiar. Where had she seen it?

Why, it was Lottie!

'All ready, Mrs. Bascomb,' said the dentist, opening the door behind her, 'and very sorry to have kept you waiting.'

Knowing Mrs. Bascomb of old, he made his apology with apprehension, and was relieved when Mrs. Bascomb made no comment on his delay.

At the house that evening, Lottie was stranger and moodier than ever. Mrs. Bascomb, having bathed the baby, fed her and put her to bed, sat down as she rarely did at home, for half an hour with a book. She never went to sit in the living-room now of an evening. Her part of the house was reduced to the small bedroom which she shared with the baby. On this warm spring evening she left the window and door opened so that air would circulate, and sitting beside the drop-light, turned to shade the sleeping baby's eyes, she opened the book and began to read.

It was the report of a Committee appointed by the National Education Association to look up the so-called Austrian method of teaching subtraction. Mr. Kennedy had handed it to her and asked her to report her opinion on it at a teachers' meeting. That had been weeks ago, but she had been so distracted with her rigorously repressed anger, hope, and impatience that she had not been able to think of it. It was said to cut off three school weeks from the time necessary to give to subtraction, and to leave that much more for teaching the multiplication table. Such a saving was of course important.

As she sat there, trying to fix her attention on the lucid, logical presentation of the idea, she was dimly aware of Lottie, roaming restlessly about the house, going in and out of her room, in and out of the bathroom, shutting doors, opening drawers and slamming them shut. It was evident that she did not know what to do with herself. With all the work there was to do in the house!

This unquiet stir continuing, Mrs. Bascomb wondered if perhaps Ralph had gone out, for a wonder without Lottie. Presently, this idea rising closer to the top of her consciousness, she laid down her book and went downstairs ostensibly to get a drink of water. Ralph sat in the living-room, deep in the arm-chair, his arms spread open before him holding open the great pages of a New York newspaper, the one he always liked to read because of the 'snappy' sporting news. Mrs. Bascomb had seen him thus a thousand times, and the familiar picture was barely noticed by her. 'Why, yes,' she thought. 'Ralph was there all right. What had made her think he had gone out?'

The Austrian method of subtraction came back at once into her mind. She began thinking of certain children in her present class who found arithmetic hard. Would this system really be easier for them?

She was once more sitting by her drop-light, the book open before her. Lottie and her lazy, purposeless stirring about forgotten. Silence.

Was the concept of addition really easier than subtraction, more fundamental to the ordinary brain of the ordinary child? She cast her mind back over the teaching experience of her past years and considered this point intently.

In the midst of her weighing of evidence, she was startled

by the impression that someone was looking hard at her. She turned her head quickly and saw that Lottie was standing in the door. Mrs. Bascomb tipped down her head so that she could see over the top of her reading glasses to find out what it was that Lottie wanted.

'Did you ask me something, Lottie?' she said.

'I've been standing here wondering what book you are reading,' said Lottie unexpectedly.

She was dressed in a rumpled wrapper, and her face was not very clean. It was not for an evening at home that Lottie spent long hours before her mirror.

'What *I* was *reading?*' exclaimed Mrs. Bascomb, very much astonished, and wondering if she could have heard aright. She looked at Lottie. She looked down again at her book. 'Why, it's a report from the N. E. A. on the Austrian system of teaching subtraction,' she said.

Her plain statement of a plain fact had an unheard-of-effect on Lottie. She flung her arms up over her head. She cried out passionately, 'Oh God!' She burst out weeping and rushing back into her room slammed the door shut behind her.

Never had Mrs. Bascomb known such pure surprise, never had she been so utterly at a loss. It was as if she had added up four and four and, before her eyes, had seen them make fifteen. There was simply no use in trying to understand Lottie . . . to make anything out of her actions. It was like trying to understand a cat or a dog.

And soon there would be no more need to try!

Composed and disdainful, Mrs. Bascomb went on reading about the methods used in teaching subtraction in the Austrian schools.

Chapter 14

MRS. BASCOMB had often asked herself with anxiety what attitude would be the best for her to take if . . . when . . . She was afraid that she could not pretend to be astonished because she had thought so many times of all the possible ways it could happen, that no one of them could be unexpected to her. And Ralph would be sure to think it queer if she were not astonished.

But in the event, she found that she had no need to concern herself with the attention that Ralph would pay to her. She knew this from the moment when, on Monday afternoon, she opened the door and saw Ralph, the baby in his arms, his eyes blazing in his white face.

She was so startled by his expression, and indeed to see him there at that hour, that she cried out as though she did not know what his answer would be, 'Why, Ralph! What's happened?'

'Lottie's gone,' Ralph flung at her, in a hoarse voice. 'Run away. Gone with that Bosch who came here to see her once. She sent word to the office that I was to come home at once because the baby would be alone. And when I got here, there was a note from her.'

'Oh, *Ralph!*' cried his mother, her knees failing her. She sank into a chair, her eyes fixed intently on his face. How did he take it?

He thought her cry was of sympathy and cast it off roughly. 'Oh, I don't care,' he said savagely. 'You needn't think it's anything to me! *Let* her go!'

His mother's pale, startled face seemed to surprise him, to exasperate him. 'Good God, Mother,' he said angrily. 'You must have seen what a hell of a mistake it's been. What a fool, a perfectly damn fool idiot a man can be!'

His mother drank in his words like nectar. She felt her breast heave high. She began to take in what had happened. It was over! The incredible nightmare was finished. She had lived through it. And Ralph did not care. Had never cared. She had Ralph again. Her own Ralph. And she had the baby, John's granddaughter. The years opened before her with a clang of golden gates.

'Oh, Ralph,' she cried again, the tears running down her cheeks. 'My dear boy! my dear boy!'

He *was* her boy again, emerged from the dingy episode which had made him seem so despicable to her, which had cut them both off from decent people, decent ways of living. He could start all over again, the poor boy, live to be a credit to himself and her. She felt her old mother's love come back to her, as purely as she had ever felt it.

'My dear, dear boy,' she cried through her tears, going blindly towards him, 'Mother's right here. We'll live it down together. We'll forget it all. Everybody will soon forget it. And we have the baby. She has left us the baby.' She put her arms around him and the baby, holding them strained close to her. She loved him unspeakably for not caring about Lottie's going.

He stood rigid and unresponsive in her embrace and she felt . . . what did she feel? Something which the closeness of their bodies brought to her, something she had not seen in his face, nor heard in his voice, a message from his body to hers which did not go through the brain . . . something which an instant later she refused to acknowledge that she had felt. 'Give me the baby,' she said. 'You go upstairs and wash your face and hands. It will do you good.' For two burning tears had forced themselves from Ralph's eyes and streaked his white cheeks.

While he was gone she thought, 'He is simply beside himself with the immensity of his relief. Of course it is a nervous shock. Any great change is. I must get supper earlier. He needs food.'

When he came down she sent him out into the back yard with the baby who at that time was beginning to stand alone and take a step or two. She herself hurried about the kitchen and dining-room. Her feet did not seem to touch the floor. She felt as though with one bound she could have leaped over a chair or the table. Such a frenzy of relief was frightening. No wonder Ralph looked distraught. She must not let him talk too much about it, must lead him to quiet, cheerful thoughts of the future. . . .

'The future' . . . at the word, a trumpet rang out in her heart. She and Ralph and the baby. They could call her Joanna now, her real name. They would have her all to themselves to love, to bring up, to cultivate like the rich garden of possibilities which she was. All her own experience as an educator, as a mother, could be brought to bear on the dear child, John's granddaughter. . . .

'Come, Ralph,' she called, 'supper is on the table.'

That supper! To have a meal without a dispute, without gossip, without long involved recitals of the plot of the last movie, without nervous fears of inexplicable sudden anger, without endless incoherent tales of the doings of the unknown and detestably common people who inhabited Lottie's past. It was incredible, the pleasure Mrs. Bascomb felt in having the baby in her high-chair, eating peaceably the plain nourishing food before her, the victim neither of spasms of causeless foolish indulgence ('Here, Momma's 'ittle dirl s'all have a pickle if s'e wants one'), nor a causeless sudden severity ('Oh, you nasty little thing to get your bib so slobbered. It makes me sick to look at you. Sit up straight there, or I'll shake you. I never saw such a dirty kid').

Mrs. Bascomb tried her best to keep the talk in a quiet, unexcited tone, away from Lottie, on the baby's bright, funny little ways. She made the child say over and over all the words she knew, and hearing her put two words together to make a sentence, cried out on it as wonderful.

'Baby hot,' she said distinctly, as explanation of snatching from her mouth her first spoonful of soup. 'Why, Ralph,' said her grandmother, 'I don't know that I ever heard of a child so young, being able to . . .'

Ralph said thickly, 'Where could she have been meeting him, I wonder? Not down on the street anywhere. I'd have heard of that.'

As his mother looked at him apprehensively, he burst out at her furiously, 'Not that I *care!* If *he's* the kind she likes!'

'Look here, Ralph,' said his mother. 'Don't let's eat any dessert to-night. We neither of us have any appetite. You amuse the baby for a little while, will you, while I hurry and get the work done. Bed's the best place for us. We'll feel more like ourselves in the morning.'

But as she hurried about the kitchen she thought she would never feel more like herself than now. Yes, she was herself once more, after months of being a mere suffering bruise.

Wave after wave of exultation burst into the room drenching her, lifting her up. Lottie was gone! They would never see her again. Ralph was her own once more to mould into useful, creditable manhood just as

98

she had always planned. And she had the baby, too. *Her* baby now. John's own child.

'God moves in a mysterious way,' she sang silently in her heart, swallowing down the joyful tears. She was stricken with awe at the way in which God had after all arranged her reward for her. 'It's like the story of Job,' she thought reverently. 'God tried me to see if I could resist.'

She washed and hung up her dishcloths to dry, and turning out the light went through into the living-room. She had heard no sound from there for some time, and guessed that the baby was drowsy. She saw her fast asleep in her father's arms. Ralph sat upright in a straight-backed chair, looking fixedly over the baby's head at a spot on the wall. When his mother came in, he did not move for an instant. Then he started, looked at her strangely, almost expectantly as though he did not at first perceive who she was. When he recognized her, he said with a defiant shake of his head and shoulders, 'I was just sitting here, thinking what a good thing it is she's gone.' He spoke more loudly than was necessary in the small room, and went on in the same strident voice. 'We'd just have gone on rubbing each other raw. Gee! It's a relief to have it over.'

In his voice was an echo of that wordless message which had come to his mother when she had held him in her arms. She heard it with anxiety. She took the sleeping baby out of his arms and said, 'You'd better go to bed, Ralph. You must be all worn out with excitement.'

'Who?' Me?' said Ralph noisily. 'Not on your life. It's nothing to me. I tell you. She's gone with somebody of her own breed.'

'You'd better get to bed, Ralph,' said his mother uneasily.

'Well, maybe . . .' he said irresolutely.

They went up the stairs together. By half-past nine the house was dark and quiet as if every one within it were sleeping as soundly as the baby.

But Mary Bascomb was not sleeping. The moment was too priceless. Its potent savour was reward for the gall she had fed upon. 'Sweeter than honey and the honeycomb. . . .' She could not even lie upon her bed in the attitude of sleep. Those mid-ocean surges of excitement smothered her, unless she was upright to breast them. She sat up. But that was not enough. She stood up on the floor in the warm, early-summer night, and felt her room swirling full of the tides of passion. The night, all the long night would not be long enough for her absorption in this ecstasy, to make it part of herself.

Some new aspect of it continually struck her, a petty one, a mighty one, flung pell-mell together . . . the bath-room! She struck her hands together with the joy of thinking that she could now keep the bathroom decent again. She planned to rise at dawn and before she left for school to fling into the dust-bin every sickishly per-fumed toilet preparation, every pot and bottle and tube and red-smeared rag. Before Ralph could waken in the morning, she would have thrown away and burned up every trace of Lottie's passage through the house.

After that, she would have the house done up, the rooms repapered, the chairs recovered with new stuffs. New curtains. New pictures. Even if she had to take money from her small savings-bank account, she would have the house transformed, purified, ready for the new life . . . 'for lo! the winter is past, the rain is over and gone, and the time of singing is come.'

She went to the window and leaned her head against it, looking out into the blackness of the cloudy June night. She was thinking, 'If Ralph really did not wish to be a lawyer, he could choose some other profession of course. But he *had* wanted to, before Lottie seized on him and deformed him. He really *had*! No matter what he said now. And he would again. She knew she could bring him to it again. She knew how to manage Ralph, a little at a time, not driving him too hard. He never could resist steady pressure. He would want to be a lawyer again. The men of her family had always been lawyers. All the fabric of their life which she had so excellently planned, rose again from the ruins.

And the baby . . . little Joanna . . . with her young father to love her and play with her, and her grand-mother to care for her . . .!

Alone in the darkness of her room, Mrs. Bascomb felt the approach of another of those overwhelming tides of exultation. She caught at the window casing. Solemnly through the dark, it flooded over her. Lottie was gone!

'The wind passeth over it and it is gone and the place thereof shall know it no more.' Ralph was free and her own once more. And now she had the baby she had longed for all her life, John's child as Ralph had never been . . . and now her own baby as much as if she had physically borne her within her own body.

The tide sank slowly down from the intolerable crest of its wave. Littler things came to her: how lovely to have the house to herself again, to live decently and pleasantly to go out in the evening, to meet her friends without shrinking from their pity, to have Ralph beside her, a credit to her once more.

Over and over she saw it all as the exquisite hours ebbed by, each rich with its freight of vindication for her. Presently she lay down, her body trembling with fatigue, her mind feeding avidly on ambrosia. Her suffering of the past months sharpened her vision of the years to come to such an ecstasy as she had never before felt. Not even in her youth, not even in her early marriage had she known such strong vital forward-looking, such impatience for the dawn that she might rise with it and begin living.

It was so like a dream that she was not sure she had not slept, and lay listening to hear the clock strike. Presently it came. Two strokes. Yes, she must have slept a little. It was long past midnight. She rose and went to the baby's crib. She knelt down by it and put her forehead lightly against the little fingers. Words from the Bible came into her head.

'The Lord rewarded me according to my righteousness, according to the cleanness of my hands hath he recompensed me.'

She thought that these words were a prayer.

In the silent, empty street she heard footsteps, rapid, hurrying, uneven steps, half running. They turned in on the walk before the house. They hastened up the steps to the porch.

A key clicked in the front door.

Mrs. Bascomb sank back on her heels, her fingers straining around the wooden rail of the crib. She was dreaming. She was still in her bed asleep. Yes, this must be a nightmare, for she recognized the true nightmare quality of causeless terror, the nightmare inability to move.

The front door opened. And shut.

Cold sweat burst out on her, running down her cheeks, glueing her nightgown to her skin.

Quick steps ran up the stairs in the dark. To Ralph's room. That door opened. And shut.

Mrs. Bascomb sank wholly down upon the floor as if all the bones in her body had turned to water.

But in an instant she heard Ralph's voice, an angry bellow . . . as she had never heard any man's voice in her life . . . not like a man's. Like an animal's.

Its bestial fury was elixir to her.

She was on her knees again, strong, vital, praying. Oh, yes, this time really praying, clamouring for help, screaming out voicelessly to Ralph, flinging her will silently through the darkness to drive back the enemy.

She heard Lottie's voice now, weeping loudly . . . talking desperately. Ralph ought not to let her talk. *Don't let her talk, Ralph!* Oh, God, harden Ralph's heart. Ralph! She has only come back because the other man would not have her. Take her by the shoulders and thrust her out of the house. No, no, don't touch her! *Don't let her touch you!* Oh, God. I have trusted in the Lord, let Him not forsake me in the hour of death. Ralph, scream out again in that brutal, horrible voice. Strike her. Drive her away. Why are you silent?

For there was now no sound but Lottie's voice, sobbing, sobbing and talking. Why had Ralph not broken her neck before she opened her lips.

Lottie's voice sobbing . . . talking . . . imploring. . . .

Lottie's voice talking . . . imploring . . . coaxing. . . .

Lottie's voice murmuring. . . .

Silence. Silence.

On the floor in the darkness, Mrs. Bascomb lay like water poured out.

Silence. Silence. Endlessly silence.

Presently through the darkness, through the silence, a faint sound slid coldly through her flesh into her heart.

Lottie's little excited laugh.

Chapter 15

'YES, ma'am,' said the hollow-cheeked, fifteen-year-old boy in the filthy apron. 'Yes, Mis' Bascomb. Mr. Bascomb must be somewheres around.'

Mrs. Bascomb looked at him and recognized as she did almost everywhere in town, a boy who had been in her class in school. But she had not, this time, her usual professionally friendly phrase of greeting. Indeed, she looked at him so queerly that the boy thought she had not heard him, and raising his voice above the smashing and banging of the presses in the big loft behind him, he shouted, 'That there over there is his desk, and his hat is still on it, so he hain't gone out to lunch yet.'

'I'll wait here till he comes. If you see him, tell him his mother would like to see him for a few minutes.'

She had never before seen the background of Ralph's working hours. She did not look at it now. She sat down by the dusty, disordered desk in the dusty, disordered cubby-hole separated from the noise of the racketing press-room only by a vague partition, half of old boards, half of very dirty window-panes. It did not dull in the least the infernal din of the rattle-trap, out-of-date printing presses which crashed and slammed as discordantly as the thoughts in her head.

As she sat there, she caught sight of Ralph's back on the other side of the ugly room. He was standing, note-book in hand, talking to a bald-headed workman in inky overalls. She saw her dirty-faced messenger approach him. Ralph turned (she saw that his face was flushed), listened to what the boy said (she saw his face harden), and following the boy's gesture, looked across the press-room towards his desk. Above the banging, clattering confusion of the big machines, their eyes met, and exchanged a long gaze, before he turned and began to make his way back.

Mrs. Bascomb had not been able to imagine how he would look when she next saw him, how he could ever hold up his head to look her in the face again. To her astonishment, there had been in his expression rather anger with her, than shame before her, and being sure that she alone had . . . and that beyond measure . . . the right to anger, she felt her hands shake and her face flush. Of the two discordant emotions clashing within her, the cry of indignation rose the higher.

'But I will not quarrel with him,' she told herself, folding her hands together hard, 'no matter how outrageous he is, I will not speak one word of reproach to him for his sinful weakness in letting his bad wife whom he knows to be despicable, take him back through the flesh. I will never have angry words with my son. I will merely announce to him what I have told Mr. Kennedy and see how he will take it. I think he will come to his senses if he realizes that I am perfectly able to leave them to look out for themselves, that I am not the weak rag he thinks me, who will everlastingly go on letting them live off me, letting them treat me like a dog. I think he must know that last night's performance is beyond even my powers to endure.'

Her excitement grew as she saw him coming closer and closer, picking his way around the jagged masses of metal which clattered with their jaws and slammed themselves crazily open and shut. They looked like a picture of what was going on in her mind.

'I won't quarrel with him, but I'll have it out with him, once for all,' she said, tightening her hands against each other. 'We'll see what he has to say when he hears I have a notion to turn my back on them, to stop paying their bills and doing their housework and providing their shelter and taking all the care of their baby.'

At the thought of the baby her heart gave way. No, she mustn't be too hard on them, not even to make Ralph realize where he stood and how entirely he depended on her. She would relent as soon as Ralph had showed that he was frightened enough. For in spite of what she had told Mr. Kennedy that morning, she knew well enough that she never could leave the baby.

As soon as Ralph entered the hideous little hole in which he had spent most of his life for the past two years, she said steadily, in a self-controlled voice, 'Ralph, I didn't see you this morning before I left the house, so I couldn't speak to you about my plans for the future. Mr. Kennedy has offered me a very advantageous position with better pay in the Harristown schools, and this morning I went to tell him I have accepted. He wishes the teachers who are going with him to take courses in the Columbia Summer School this summer so I shall leave for New York in about ten days, as soon as my school work is over. I shall not, of course, return here after that, but go direct to Harristown in the fall. I wish you would telephone this to Lottie this afternoon so she will know it before I go back to the house.'

She recited this as if she had learned it by heart. As she had.

She had known that Ralph would be astonished to the limit of astonishment at the idea that she could uproot herself and disappear. And he was. An utter blankness took the place of the lowering, bull-like expression of his face. Evidently it had never occurred to him that it was a physical possibility for his mother to live elsewhere than in the setting he had always seen about her. Of all the things for which he had been bracing himself as he crossed the room, this was not one. It was so unexpected he could only gape upon his mother.

Mrs. Bascomb had expected this. And she had expected as confidently that Ralph's next expression would be of consternation. How could he manage the material problems of life if his mother withdrew her help and left them to his own poor resources? Who would get the meals, and keep the house clean and pay more than half the bills and take care of the baby? Where would they live, indeed, if not in her comfortable house?

But Ralph's next expression was not of consternation. It was of relief. He was glad she was going. Unmistakable relief. He had taken her at her word, had thought she meant what she said. And was glad of it.

More than this. He found his relief so natural, he made

no attempt to hide it. He even spoke of it in the first words which came to him. He said as he sat down heavily in the battered swivel-chair before his desk. '*Well!* . . . Well, I guess that'll be the best thing all round!'

From her own battered chair, his mother looked at him in an astonishment as great as his had been. Was this the man, the despairing boy who, less than twenty-four hours ago, had said that he never wished to see his worthless wife again? And had he no idea at all of what his mother had been doing for him all these months? She sat there, grey, silent, and felt her head swim.

He recognized with exasperation that he owed her some explanation of the change in him since he had last seen her, and said resentfully, blaming her for having been a witness to what now necessitated an awkward statement.

'That was all a mistake about her having . . . what she said in her note. She didn't mean it at all. She wasn't with . . . with anybody. She never intended to stay away. She just wanted to scare me . . . thought I didn't care about her any more. She's just a kid, and she'd got herself all worked up so she didn't know what she *was* doing. She's been having an awful fit of the blues, too. But she was crazy to get back to me and the baby . . . she'd never thought of anything else.'

His mother sat, granite-faced, in astounded silence. It was of course incredible that Ralph had been taken in by that trashy story. How shameless of him to repeat it to her, to try to make her think that he believed it, as a screen to his weak sensuality. He knew well enough what had really happened, of course. Anybody who knew Lottie would know instinctively that if she had come back it was only because that man would not have her.

As she kept this bitter silence, Ralph's resentment against her increased. He began to work himself up into a self-defensive anger. He said in a louder, rougher voice, his nostrils quivering, 'The fact is, Mother, you don't do much to make Lottie happy and that's the truth. I hadn't realized it until last night. Men don't take in those things, things between women at home. And she's been so game about it, keeping it to herself. I never realized what a hell on earth it's been to her. Poor kid! Made to feel that

106

every single thing she does or does not do is wrong. Living every minute of the time she's in the house in a regular hades of being disapproved of. I know how she feels. I've been there myself. You've made me infernally sore, too. I've been able to run away from it . . . lots of times, I've skinned out of the house, ever since I was big enough, down to the Public Library, down to a pool room, to hang around the street, anywhere to get where I wouldn't be frozen to death over some little thing I'd done or hadn't done. Lottie hasn't had a fair chance. She's been perfectly miserable. I never saw anybody feel so bad as she did last night. And it almost took a bust-up of everything, before I realized it. I've been awfully dumb. She's pretty sore too, about the way you try to take our baby away from us.'

He leaned towards her defiantly, blustering because (the teacher of many years knew this automatically) he was still half afraid of her. His face was crimson, his eyes bloodshot. As he talked more and more loudly, her ear had caught a thickness in his speech, and now, through the smell of printer's ink and machine-oil and dust, she caught another odour, sour, putrid, unmistakable, the breath of a man who has been drinking.

This was the crowning indignity, extravagantly beyond any limit she could have imagined. With his wife, his sense of decency and self-respect had succumbed to his sensuality and now, he had been stupefying himself with whiskey so that he would be able to insult his mother. Once more she had all the right on her side.

Sustained by this as by steel braces, she rose, all in one piece. She did not say a word, not one. She did not look at her son, any more than at any other sordid, dingy object in that sordid dingy lair. She turned her back on him and walked out of his life.

As she walked down the dark hall toward the street door, her mind was formulating one loud, definite statement after another, but she was so deafened by her agitation that she could not give them her attention, could not understand what had happened, what she was telling herself, 'Now I will *have* to leave. I will have to leave the baby. He has driven me away. How could he have thought I meant what I told Mr. Kennedy! My son has driven his own mother out of her house.'

At the word 'house' she thought sharply, 'He said nothing about getting out of the house. Whose does he think it is? I will sell it over their heads. I will burn it down with my own hands.' But she knew well enough she would never do this, that she could never bring herself to speak of it to them, to anyone. It would become another item in the vast indictment against them which they were heaping up, another element in the immensity of her rightness and their wrongness.

Even as she felt this, she was telling herself with another part of her brain, and not believing a word of it, 'This means that I am abandoning the baby to them. I shall not see the baby any more. They are driving me away from my darling.'

A working-man coming in from the street, opened the door and held it open for her to pass out. Standing there an instant, gazing palely upon the strangeness of the sun-shiny air as though she had come out upon another planet, she presented the usual decent, refined aspect of Mrs. Bascomb who taught the Fifth Grade in the Main Street School.

Her feet carried her out upon the pavement and turned automatically back towards the school building. Her eye noted by the clock in the steeple of the Congregational Church that it was a quarter to one. She would not be late to her class.

She stepped forward with a careful rigidity. Someone behind her called in a genial tone, 'Well met, Mrs. Bascomb! Wait a minute. I know you must be going my way.' It was Mr. Kennedy, sweeping his soft felt hat from his greying hair to greet her.

He was in an unusually expansive mood, pleased by her acceptance of his offer, and the consequent simplification of his own problems, pleased by the prospective increase in his salary, by the fineness of the weather, by the excellence of the lunch he had just eaten, by the fact that his son had won honours in his class at college . . . pleased a little, too, among other things (now that he saw Mrs. Bascomb had thought about it) by having helped an estimable woman and a good teacher out of a difficult position and into a most agreeable one. This last was, naturally, the item in his good humour which he now brought to the surface for expression, especially as he noted that her expression was rather sombre. 'She needs cheering up,' he thought good-naturedly. And began with confidence to cheer her up.

'I've just been talking about you to my wife, this noon, Mrs. Bascomb, and she is as pleased as I, that you are going to Harristown with us. She says she is writing her sister . . . did I mention to you that her sister is the wife of the postmaster? . . . to put your name up to be a member of the Fortnightly Club. That's the nicest woman's club in town. I know you'll enjoy the ladies very much. You never made a wiser decision. A change is good for all of us. For all of us, yes. You'll be surprised to see how you'll take a new lease of life in the new surroundings.'

He meditated a moment on how he might tactfully refer to the circumstances in her life which made the change especially welcome, and went on, 'You've always done so much, worked so hard, carried so much responsibility, it'll be a real holiday to you to have nobody but yourself to think of. And high time you had a vacation like that, too, high time you thought of yourself a little. You'll be able to do what'll be new for you, Mrs. Bascomb, *just what you like.* You'll be able to have things just as you want them.'

He thought this phrase so expressive of an ideal way of life, that he repeated it as they turned in together at the door of the school building.

'Yes, by George,' he told her enthusiastically, 'it ought to be just about perfect for you, for you'll have nobody but yourself to think of, and you can have things just as you want them.'

PART TWO

Chapter 16

In the three years which followed the exodus to Harristown, Mr. Kennedy often remarked with satisfaction to his wife, that it did his heart good to consider the case of Mrs. Bascomb. 'The change has turned out pretty well for all of us. But, by George, it's wonderful what it's done for that woman! You couldn't imagine a pleasanter life than she has. Well, I can take some of the credit of it. I told her she'd be making the mistake of her life if she didn't come. Here in Harristown, she's got things just as she wants them.'

Yes, Mrs. Bascomb had things just the way she had always wanted them. Her liberal salary (with only the expenses of one to be taken out of it now) enabled her to have the best room in the best boarding-house in town, the delightful old family home where the decayed gentlewoman took in paying guests. It was a large front room, on the second floor, facing south, with a sunny bay-window just the place for the house-plants she always liked to have about her. She had a bathroom of her own, too, an old bedroom transformed into a bathroom and hence twice the usual size, with a wide, bright window, a deep cupboard, and room for a pretty dressing-table, as well as the wash-basin with its glass shelf and bevelled mirror. It was, of course, always exquisitely clean and in order, well-aired, fresh, smelling faintly of the most expensive kind of imported scentless soap with perhaps a whiff of lavender . . . the perfect expression of what Mrs. Bascomb had always thought desirable. She told herself loudly, many times, that it was 'like living' to have a decent bathroom once more.

And her room, nothing could be pleasanter than her room, with chintz-covered chairs, with a few pieces of good old mahogany dating from the day when the gentlewoman had not been decayed, with fine net curtains at the clear, shining windows, and a pretty drop-light on the convenient desk. The bed was of the sort which folds into a davenport, so that Mrs. Bascomb's room was, with the help of the bathroom dressing-room, a most agreeable sitting-room. 'All one woman could possibly use,' she often said to visitors, as they looked about them admiringly, envious of her well-arranged life.

For she had visitors. Her social life was as much to her taste . . . what her taste had alway been . . . as her bathroom. Her circle was made up of just the sort of people she liked: refined, well-dressed mothers of nice, growing-up families, serious-minded women of good education who belonged to the Parents-Teachers Association, to the Women's City Club, to the Civic-League, to the Women's Suffrage Association (this was in the last days of the fight for Votes for Women), to the Fortnightly Club (a literary, exclusive organization with that essential proof of club success, a long waiting list) and in the church, to the Women's Friendly Society, and the Missionary Society. In due time, Mrs. Bascomb, too, belonged to all these, having been recognized at once as the right material for them. To do her school work, to accept in turn the invitations to dinner of the well-to-do parents of the children in her classroom, and to attend the meetings of all those organizations, gave Mrs. Bascomb ample occupation of the kind she had always liked, the kind which involved wearing one's dressiest clothes, looking one's best, and meeting nice people.

She was put on committees, of course, who met in her room, and to whom, after the meeting, she served tea in a pretty pink-and-white porcelain service which harmonized with the pink in her chintz hangings. And as they rose to go, settling their excellent fur wraps over their tailored suits, they always said, 'We've had *such* a pleasant time, haven't we, ladies? We certainly owe Mrs. Bascomb a vote of thanks.'

On alternate Saturdays she met with these same kindly well-dressed people in the church parlours to sew for the poor; she sat beside them twice a day in church on Sundays; on Thursday evenings she saw them at prayer meeting; and rustled beside them out of the lecture-room in the Community House, saying to them and hearing them say, 'Wasn't it a splendid talk?'

Yes, there was nothing lacking to the realization of Mr. Kennedy's prophecy of her life. She had nobody but herself to think of, and things were just as she wanted them. By the end of the first year, people told her, 'It doesn't seem possible you are a newcomer to our town. You have fitted in so wonderfully.'

And by the end of the third year they had forgotten that she had not always been on committees with them.

The summers of those three years she spent in New York at the Columbia Summer School. Together with three of her teaching colleagues, she lived in 118th Street, just across the Street from Columbia, in a furnished apartment belonging to a member of the Teachers College faculty, who went to the country for the summer. There she found again a background of her own sort, with photographs of English cathedrals and Italian madonnas on the walls and the right kind of rugs on the floor. The four teaching women had the most agreeable summers imaginable, full of instructive courses of lectures, coloured richly with culture. They saw Shakespeare played out of doors on the campus, listened to the best of music executed with sufficient competence, and heard lectures on every possible subject delivered by people whose names were often seen in print. They turned on the taps of the Pierian springs and held their cups up under the resultant gush with every appearance of satisfaction.

Mrs. Bascomb, with, relatively speaking, plenty of money, better dressed than she had ever been, slim, pale, well-preserved, needed little volition to direct her life, as she was washed about and up and down by these well-ordered tides of her existence. Good manager as she was, with only one person to look out for, and no expense for the upkeep of a house, she was saving money at last and saw before her, by the help of an annuity, a self-sufficient and comfortable old age. As she came and went along the well-trodden paths of her life, up and down the corridors of the school building, in and out of her pleasant boarding house, people said of her, 'What a nice-looking woman that Mrs. Bascomb is. So refined.'

Once in a while somebody asked idly, 'Don't you think she's a little silent and absent-minded?'

But such a comment was always put down by a chorus of the less observant with, 'Why, no! what an idea! She's just as chatty! Always has a friendly word of greeting for everybody.'

Occasionally some one asked vaguely, 'Didn't she have some trouble with her son about his marriage? Seems as though I'd heard something of the sort.'

But there was always someone else, informed and positive, to announce with conviction, 'Not at all. I know all about her. Her son married somebody not her kind, rather common they say. The kind you get along better with if you don't see them too often, if you follow me. So Mrs. Bascomb very sensibly doesn't try to live with them. They've just agreed to disagree, that's all. No break or anything like that. Her son often comes to Harristown on business, and I've seen him taking lunch with his mother lots of times. They're on perfectly good terms.'

But once, one of the younger teachers, a girl about to leave her profession to be married, insisted obstinately, 'Well, there's something funny about her. She looks to me like a person that's walking in her sleep.'

Chapter 17

MRS. BASCOMB could have given her another reason for the absent look which was often on her face. It came from an expectancy, quite causeless . . . what was there for her to expect beyond what she had? Apparently, it never quite left her, for at the least slackening of the current of external events she was painfully aware of it. She found this sensation of waiting very troubling and tiring. It was as if she were perpetually in the listening, taut mood of someone who has forgotten a well-known name, who has set his subconscious self to think of it, and

114

who expects at any moment to have it rise, with a click, into his mind.

But Mrs. Bascomb felt there was nothing that she had forgotten. She could not have set her subconscious self to look for anything because she was sure that there was nothing for her to find. And yet, at every pause in her agreeable life, she felt herself straining her ears for the something which seemed almost there, if she could only remember it, only think of it.

It was singularly fatiguing, that groping search in the dark. But it did not in the least fade and die away in the day-by-day passage of time, as to her great astonishment, the rages and indignations of the last year burned out and died down. On the contrary, this feeble groping and fumbling grew from a vague feeling of uneasiness, easily drowned by outward activity, into a steady pain which became a futile bitter longing as, out of the twilight of the half-conscious, the object of her search loomed up . . . alas! the wholly unattainable object.

For months and months of the first year it was obscured by the blaze of her righteous wrath. Even after those smoking flames began to die down from lack of new grievances, they leaped up hurriedly to hide this dim longing whenever it drew near. Even after she knew that what she was thus awaiting, in spite of herself, was some possibility to go on serving her darling, her helpless darling, abandoned by the only one who could help her, this knowledge was darkened by the hasty flaring up of the old angry cries, 'Abandoned! The idea! Driven away! Cruelly driven away! Forbidden to return.'

A self-protective rush of her old certainties clashed and clattered their unanswerable reasons, and drowned out the entirely unreasonable murmur of her heart. 'No use thinking of the impossible!' said logic to her clearly and decisively. 'That is a closed chapter. You tried everything possible and more. You endured more and did more than any other woman would have dreamed of doing, and you accomplished absolutely nothing, beyond embittering every one. That was a perfectly conclusive experiment. There is not one faintest possibility which you did not explore.'

With a flourish, logic handed her on to self-interest and self-admiration which bade her look around her at the useful, pleasant and highly esteemed life which she now led. 'What more can any woman want? You are enjoying now the reward of your lifetime of intelligence and right doing. There is no more respected citizen in this town. Put the one unfortunate episode out of your life. It's nothing compared to what many women around you have to forget. And unlike them, you have nothing to reproach yourself with – quite the contrary. You have perfectly done your woman's task. Now live, as men live, for themselves and their work. Put those intimate personal relationships out of your head as men do. Not only is that the sensible thing to do, it is the only possible thing to do. Aren't you letting Lottie and Ralph have the use of your own home without a word of protest? What other mother-in-law would be so generous?'

She had many comforters like these, among them public opinion on which she had always leaned so heavily. It did not fail her now. It told her, 'There is nothing unusual about your position. It is as common almost as being married. It is an axiom that mothers of sons cannot get on with their daughters-in-law. All around you, the nicest sort of women are in your position. Do they complain because they are no longer forced into that old woman's world of narrow, pressing personal relations? No, they are relieved. They turn to other forms of activity. They are emancipated from the narrowness of womanish personalities. And everybody admires them for it. Everybody admires you, too. Everybody.'

Yes, everything was all right, or as nearly so as it could be in this world. And even if it were not all right, there was nothing she could do about it. Over and over she learned this fact, each time thinking it was once and for all. Again and again, she settled herself anew, permanently she thought, in her pleasant, useful, satisfactory life. She made much of the idea of living like a man of her age, or she thought men of her age lived . . . for themselves and for their work, with much external activity and no inner personal life at all. For herself she procured anything she could think of, for which she had ever felt a liking, however vague; pretty, lace-trimmed underwear, silk stockings, delicacies of diet which had always seemed too self-indulgent and expensive. She made regular appointments at a 'beauty parlour' to have her hair treated and her hands manicured. She bought new clothes exactly in the prevailing fashion. But she found little savour in all this, often forgetting to eat the expensive delicacies till they dried up; and being bored and depressed by the hours spent under the hands of the coiffeur.

It was easier for her to concentrate her attention on her work. She had always liked her profession; it had been more to her than she had realized, and it stood by her throughout her life as nothing else did. No teacher was more constant in her attendance at teachers' meetings, and at Educational Conventions. No one thought more on the problem of teaching, discipline, administration, was more ready to do committee-work; none more faithfully read educational magazines, and 'kept herself abreast of the times' more conscientiously. This concentration on her profession gave her many hours, sometimes whole days, when she seemed to have won at last to what she conceived the attitude of a middle-aged man to be, when the important things in life seemed honestly to her to be how widely or how intensively geography was taught at the Fifth-Grade age, or how much all these modern notions of personal initiative among the children could be applied, as a matter of actual practice, in an American state school supported by taxes.

She piled such conceptions higher and higher over the ache in her heart, and thought she had it hidden. But it required incessant effort to keep the pile in place. At any pause – a sleepless night, a two-days' illness, an hour's waiting for a train – she felt a wind rise from some remote corner of life and blow softly and steadily upon all those impersonal interests. Before it, like a heap of shifting sand, they sank down to nothing, leaving her trouble stark and bare, and greater than when she had faced it last.

New York it was, perhaps, which gave her the greatest temporary relief. She used it as sore-hearted humanity, starving for happiness, has always used great multitudes, as an opiate to drug a hunger. Those myriads and myriads of men and women, the flood of them always renewed from some vast, never-failing reservoir, plunging past her with their Niagara-like roar . . . they stunned her sense of proportion. With such countless throngs of men and women and children, what did one more or less matter? Of what consequence was it that one little girl was, perhaps, not having her fair chance at becoming what she might be? This huge, yelling, scurrying rush of humanity would be neither better nor worse off because of what one middle-aged school-teacher did with herself. Nothing that any one person did was of the slightest importance. Nobody noticed, nobody cared, nobody was in any way affected. The thing to do was to yell and scurry and rush with the others, and grab as much as you could of what you wanted.

Yes, summers in New York brought to Mrs. Bascomb more forgetfulness than she found elsewhere.

But so frail a forgetfulness! At the mercy of one quiet hour of silence. Like a smoke-screen, at the least failure of fuel, it began to eddy off, to grow thin, and Mrs. Bascomb became aware by the leaden heaviness of her heart that back of the screen, her slow, futile, hopeless search still dragged itself about in the dark.

She had always been so constant a Bible-reader that thoughts, even those quite her own, often came to her clad in some familiar Scriptural phrase. At this time as she went from one edifying occupation to another, she was tormented by the recurrence of the words, 'Thou art careful and troubled about many things. But one thing is needful.'

Little by little there emerged from the ruins of her old life the one thing needful for it – it was the survival of the living spirit which had come to live in her son's child. Compared to this what were little, gritty, angular, impersonal 'interests'? Heap them as high as she might, they were never any the less dead. She had had something living in her life, something living and precious and helpless which needed her, which no one else saw, or loved, or served. She had turned her back on it.

All over again her suffering from this thought began as though it were quite new to her. It reminded her of the slow torture of the years after John's death, so long ago, when she had not been able to believe him gone, when night after night, she had started up from her sleep, thinking she heard his step on the stairs. It was now as if John had died to her a second time.

It was worse. For now it was as if John were not dead, but alive, living only a few miles from her, desperately in need of her. As if she had left him, had known that he needed her, and had turned her back on him. With a sulphureous flare, up blazed righteous anger to cry out the sharp correction, 'Turned your back! What an idea! You were driven away. Driven cruelly away. Through no fault of yours!'

And with that came the return to whatever reality lay about her . . . the well-lighted lecture-room with a suave or earnest speaker; or perhaps her own classroom with the rows of pretty, well-dressed, leisure-class children, their rosy, clean faces bent docilely on the lessons she taught with the half-absent ease of practised experience.

She saw Ralph once in a while. When he came to Harristown on business, he sometimes took lunch with his mother as if nothing had happened. Well, nothing had happened. She was about as close to Ralph as she had ever been, she thought. They had kept the shell of decent family relationship, had managed her departure with an outward correctness. After all, why not? There was nothing unusual about a teacher's accepting a better position in another town. When she had left them, she had shaken hands with Lottie and Ralph, had kissed the baby . . . that had been a hideous moment often lived over in her dreams afterwards . . . and they had gone to the door to see her drive off. A neighbour happened to be out on his front lawn, seeing which, Lottie had called after her, 'Hope you have a grand time in little old New York.' And Ralph had said, 'Good luck to you!'

But they neither had said anything about her coming back. To her own house!

She did not, as time went by, cry out that last phrase with such intensity. The piercingness of the feeling that it was hers was one of the many things which had drifted off into the distance as she went staggering forward. It did not seem to matter as it had, whose house it was. Many things did not seem so much to matter.

She looked forward to and dreaded Ralph's occasional duty visits. They talked quietly enough, asked each other if everything was all right, and assured each other that it was. Yes, Ralph said, the baby was fine. Getting to be a big girl. She couldn't pronounce her own name very well, and had made a funny little nickname of it, 'Dids.' They had picked it up from her. Everybody called her that now. Funny, how she'd ever got that out of 'Gladys.' Lottie didn't like it very well, thought it sounded queer, and how could you tell whether it stood for a girl or a boy. But he thought it just fitted the little tyke. Anyhow, that was what she was always called. It had stuck.

His mother said the name over to herself, 'Dids.' It was a humorous flight. Yes, it sounded funny. John would have liked it. John who always had some whimsical turn to put into what was solemn or matter-of-fact to other people. 'Dids.' Yes, she liked it. It sounded like one of those sudden smiles of John's, after his long attentive look.

'Does she like to joke, Ralph?'

'Who? Dids? Oh, yes, she's a lively little kid. What I see of her. But I don't see much, of course. I'm almost never at home, daytimes. She's asleep mostly, soon after I get back at night.'

'Oh yes, of course.'

Sometimes he made an effort to remember something more definite about her to tell her grandmother. 'She's a smart little tyke. Everybody thinks so. Always has something to say. A queer little thing some ways. Doesn't look a bit like Lottie or me. She's got the funniest little trick of looking at you from under her eyebrows . . . I don't know if you ever noticed her eyes, set rather deep they are and they look so serious they make you feel awfully queer when she keeps them on you for awhile. And then, all of a sudden, she'll smile, quick! It makes her look like somebody else, the complete change in her face.'

Mrs. Bascomb had little to say to such casual bits of

description of her granddaughter. She usually dropped her eyes and folded her lips together to stop their trembling.

She always asked with ceremony after Lottie's health which was not, it seemed, especially vigorous.

'Nothing to brag of,' Ralph told her with more and more frequency. 'I guess Dids' birth was pretty hard on her. She says she hasn't felt just right ever since. Oh no, nothing serious. First one thing and then another. She's trying electric treatments now. Gosh! How they cost!' He turned the subject abruptly. 'Everything all right with you?'

'Oh, yes, everything's all right with me.'

'You're certainly fixed up comfortably,' giving to his mother's tasteful, well-ordered room the admiring glance which every visitor bestowed on it.

No, except for that one moment in the printing room, she and Ralph had never 'had words.' And on that terrible occasion, as she often told herself, the words had all been Ralph's. At first, she had taken great satisfaction in this fact. But later it began to fade out, and like other things, not to seem so important.

He never brought Dids with him and his mother never asked him to. She took for granted that Lottie would not allow it.

She was wild with uneasiness if too long a time chanced to pass between his casual visits. But she always had a bad night after he had been there, waking suddenly and before her defences were up, saying to herself, 'You have turned your back on the best that life has ever shown you, on the only human being who needs you.'

The outrageous injustice of this accusation stung her wide awake to cry out the more than sufficient defence, 'Turned my back! I was driven away. I would not be allowed to go back. I am not wanted. There is nothing I can do. Nothing.'

There were nights, when, after this, she lay awake till dawn, bitter tears forcing themselves out from between her closed lids. She was worn out, crushed by the monstrous falsity of that wicked accusation. It was too much, to have suffered as she had . . . and now to be blamed for

not doing what no human being could do. In what strange
corner of her heart did it lurk, this enemy of her peace?
She knew it of old. This was the old uneasiness which
the memory of John's attentive eyes had always brought
to her. Why? Why?

But now it was terribly more than uneasiness. It was
like a consciousness of guilt. And she so guiltless.

She could not even longingly reach out her arms in the
dark towards those well-remembered living eyes of her
darling, because she saw reproach in them, and
blame.

How could there be blame, she cried passionately.
When she knew so well that she was blameless, had always
been blameless.

Chapter 18

She marvelled, from the first, at the difference in her life
that was made by only a few miles of distance. Less than
an hour by train from her old existence, she could not
more completely have changed everything if she had gone
half around the world. She felt during the first days and
months as though she had stepped from the maddening
clatter of Ralph's press-room, had slammed the door
behind her and found herself in a sound-proof cell. Or
as if, like a child frantic with anger, she had been shut into
an empty room to 'cry it out.' Her ears rang loudly in the
silence.

It took her a long time to adjust her inner life to the
absence of strife and misery and recurrent anger, which
had half-crazed her during the year after Ralph's marriage; and by the time she had lived herself into her new
world, into the inner vacancy of her new life, many
curious changes had taken place in her. She became conscious of an inner shifting of values, very disconcerting
and troubling to her, but which seemed to go on with no
volition on her part. It was not that she thought of things
differently, but that she felt them differently. Over this
slow change of feeling she seemed to have no control. It

went on like a natural process, like the inevitable burning out to ashes of a fire no longer fed.

It had burned hotly for a long time, the fire of her well-founded indignation. For months after her arrival in Harristown, she went on warming her hands at the knowledge that she had been outrageously treated; and at the conviction that this was of the highest importance. But with no new occasions to rekindle those blazing resentments, they burned lower; smouldered; and finally died down to ashes. She still had no doubts that she had always been in the right. But this certainty now brought no comforting heat. After all, what if she had? At the mere glimpsed-at guess that this might not be so important as she had always felt it, a cold dreariness settled down upon her. If being in the right had lost its warmth, at what vital fire could she warm herself? Was this perhaps the beginning of apathetic old age? Had she lived through all the emotion of which she was capable?

During this three-year pause, elements in her inner life which had seemed at the very core of her existence dropped from her soundlessly, as if of their own weight; as, on a windless autumn day the old leaves fall silently from a tree about to enter another season. Shivering and helpless she watched them fall, and could think of nothing that would be left her when they were quite gone.

From the moment she had read Ralph's letter announcing his marriage, she had been wholly occupied by the erection of her indictment against Ralph and Lottie. She had not lacked material. She had but to stoop and pick it up from the heaps about her. Every day had brought her a new grievance, a new stone to add to the great cairn which marked the blood-feud between them. There had been a furious excitement in piling it up higher and higher. Now it was complete, a finished monument to their wrongness and her rightness. Not a grievance was lacking to its huge bulk.

There it stood, towering high. In the breathless hush of her new life, she contemplated it at her leisure. But what could she do with it? Day by day sifted down upon it the fine, invisible dust of the passage of time. It began to lose the harsh sharpness of its outlines; the sinister jaggedness of the different wrongs composing it became blurred, try as she might to feel them with the voluptuous pain they had once caused her.

She did not understand what was happening to her and this frightened her. She felt old and horribly lonely. The instinctive turning to her husband came oftener to her, and was harder to fight off with the manifold trifling occupations which had been her protection against this longing. She dreamed of him again, as she had not for years. And now in her dreams his little granddaughter stood beside him. They both bent on her from their dark deep-set eyes that attentive look of waiting for her to do something else than what she was doing, which wrought her to such a pitch of bewildered misery that she frequently woke herself up, trembling, her hands outstretched to protect herself from their gaze. What did they expect her to do? What else could she do? What else could she ever have done?

She caught desperately to herself all the many occupations of the Harristown routine. They were like those she had always had; even better, more to what had always been her taste. Always before they had been enough. Why was it that now they seemed to be so pitiably small in the brooding hush which fell about her in every vacant hour?

She grew afraid of a question which asked itself of her, like a far-away half-heard voice, in moments when her mind was not intent on active thoughts. It asked her, 'What is the use of being so right, and others being so wrong, if it does not help you to serve the one human being who needs you?'

Chapter 19

ONE afternoon in late June, of the third year Mrs. Bascomb had spent in Harristown, she went down to the shopping street to buy some odds and ends of sewing materials for her travelling sewing-kit. The ebb and flow of the tide which washed her up and down and back and

124

forth had brought her once more to the time for the Columbia summer-school. Her usual summer companions were making their usual preparations to start, and automatically, she began to make hers.

As she turned the corner by the drug-store, she saw a large battered automobile draw up to the kerb in front, and heard from it the bird-like chattering which announced a 'joy-ride' of young people. Her ear, practised in all the intonations of the region, classified this group as made up of not very nice young people, the kind who shriek and laugh in public even more loudly and shrilly than those supposed to be a social class or two above them. She remembered it was Saturday afternoon, and that the spinning-mills and collar factories had begun their summer practice of giving their 'hands' a half-day weekly holiday. These were probably factory boys and girls.

Sure enough, she recognized them, as the brightly dressed girls and the roughly dressed boys in the car began noisily to uncoil themselves from the heaps in the tonneau of the old car. They were from her own old town, Gilmanville boys and girls who had spent a year in her classroom not so long ago as people of her age reckon time. They were the set who, as soon as they pass the compulsory school age, hurry into the shops and factories to earn the good wages which they spend light-heartedly on the frightful clothes they love. They were not, she saw, the tough set, who as their fibre hardens and sets, drift into reformatories, ward-politics, and prisons. They were only the common set, who as life took hold of them, would drift into smeary marriages . . . often enforced . . . or waiting on tables in cheaper restaurants, or the poor blind-alley jobs in the factories.

She knew them, she now saw, not only collectively but individually, as they jumped and fell and scrambled out of the car. With her teacher's memory she even knew their names . . . Gertie Baumann, Budd Stone, Pete Daugherty, Mamie and Minnie Flacker, Gladys Wood, Bill Weismann, Mike Connelly, Flora Johnson . . . it was like the roll-call of one of her classes. She knew what poor past lay back of them, and what poor future lay before them. Like any experienced public-school teacher, she knew all this in the glance she gave them, as she turned the corner on her way to buy her needles and thread and hooks and eyes.

They knew her, too, as every one in Gilmanville did. 'Oh, hallo, Mrs. Bascomb,' they cried out at her, with their loud, promiscuous good-nature. 'Looks like home to see you around.' But they did not think of stopping her to talk further. They had not at all been the sort of schoolchildren who were Mrs. Bascomb's favourites, and they were not now in the least the sort of ex-students to whom Mrs. Bascomb ever paid much attention.

It was Mrs. Bascomb herself who stopped short, looking past them at someone left in the car, at a pale little girl, just tall enough for her deep-set, dark eyes to show over the arm of the seat.

The lively young people, trooping past the school-teacher on their way to ice-cream sodas, were startled by the sudden whiteness of Mrs. Bascomb's face. They turned their heads hurriedly, saw, understood and began to exclaim, all talking at once.

'Why, yes! Say! We got the little Bascomb kid with us!'

'And here's her Gramma.'

'What do you think of that?'

'Can you beat it?'

'We never thought of that!'

What they knew about the relations between Mrs. Bascomb and her son's family now came tardily into their minds. They stopped short, ill at ease and looked at each other. One of the girls cast about her with an awkward goodwill to find some way out of the embarrassment. 'I bet you haven't seen her for ever so long, Mrs. Bascomb. We hardly ever see you over our way. She's the cutest kid on our block. Our gang calls her our mascot. Look here, Dids. Look'y here, say how-do to Gramma.'

They bore Mrs. Bascomb back towards the car in a chattering rush, and flowed around her and the little girl for an instant of quickly-lost interest in the meeting between the two. Then one of the girls said, 'Let's leave her with Mrs. Bascomb while we get our sodas. Mom told me Dids hadn't ought to have any to-day. She's been having one of her sick spells lately, and her stummick ain't just right yet. And it'd come hard for her to see us having something she couldn't. You'd just as soon stay with her a minute, wouldn't you, Mrs. Bascomb?'

'Yes, I'll stay,' said Mrs. Bascomb, opening the car door and getting in beside the little girl, who had been staring at her in a graceless silence.

As the noisy young people trooped away, she said to the child, gently, 'How do you do, dear?'

'*I'm* all wight,' said the child, instantly, with a startling pert self-possession. She did not take her eyes from the grey-haired woman with the eye-glasses, whose gloved hands were shaking so queerly on her lap.

Mrs. Bascomb stripped off her gloves now, and took the child's hands into hers, thin, grimy little hands, with black finger-nails. The little girl did not draw them away. But they did not respond to the gentle pressure of the shaking white fingers. They lay passive, as if the child did now know what to make of the gesture. She did not seem shy, only watchful, attentive, on her guard.

'Isn't it fun to go riding in automobiles?' said Mrs. Bascomb. 'I'd love to go. But I don't often get a chance.'

'I'm doing to det to do widing every Saturday afternoon this summer,' said the little girl. 'Mamie and Gertie told me so. And I'm doing to det taken to the movies, too. That's what we're doing to do this afternoon – do to the movies. Bill says it's a humdinger dandy one, too.'

'Does your mother let you go to the movies?' asked Mrs. Bascomb in spite of herself.

'Oh, Mom don't know about me being here at all,' said the child proudly. 'The bunch came and dot me after she went down-town, and they'll take me back before she dets to Baumann's house. She won't never know I've been, 'tall.'

Mrs. Bascomb could not follow this. But she did not venture to ask too many questions. She sat silent for a moment looking down at the child, who had not taken her eyes from her since she had entered the car.

The little girl was dressed in a pink silk dress, the short skirt rounded into scallops at the hem. The binding of the scallops had been hastily sewn, and raw edges stuck out raggedly at intervals. The front of the badly-fitting dress, flat over the child's meagre body, was spotted with chocolate which had been wiped off, but never cleaned. At the back, a missing hook showed dingy underwear. Coarse white cotton stockings wrinkled around the thin legs at the end of which swung dirty white shoes.

'I'm all d'essed up to-day,' said the little girl. 'Mamie sneaked my d'ess-up clothes over without Mom's knowing.'

'I see,' said Mrs. Bascomb. 'It's a very pretty dress.' The little girl looked down at her dress, stroked its soiled folds lovingly, and returned to her searching gaze up into the eyes bent on her. What they were saying in words was only a small part of what was passing between them. The child now moved over a little closer to the new-comer, and laid one arm across her lap.

'Would you like to see what I have in my hand-bag?' asked Mrs. Bascomb, opening it. 'Sometimes little girls like to play with the things in it.'

'You bet your life I would,' said the child eagerly. 'Mom'll never let me look in hers. She says I'd break something.'

Mrs. Bascomb passed the bag over on the pink-silk lap, and sat looking at the little girl as, with brows drawn together, she rummaged in the contents. She pulled out a key-ring, a spool of adhesive tape and a small penknife and began to examine them, bending her head low over them. She had magnificent hair, thick, dark, long. It hung in straight, unbrushed witch-locks over her shoulders, and was tied back from her forehead with a dark-red ribbon. 'What movie are you going to, dear?' asked Mrs. Bascomb. 'Do you know the name?'

'Sure I know the name,' said the child smartly. 'Wild Love's the name.' She held out the spool of adhesive tape. 'What do you use this for?' she asked.

'To mend broken things. See, this side's sticky, and that side's very strong cloth. It'll mend almost anything that's broken.'

'Can I 'tick something with it?'

'I don't see anything here,' said Mrs. Bascomb, looking about the car, 'but there are always plenty of broken things that need to be mended. If you'll come home with me for awhile, I could find lots of things to stick together. We would have a good time. I love to play with paper dolls, and I know a lot of stories. Do you know the story about the good giant and the little boy with leather breeches?'

'What's a giant?'

'Oh, you know, a very, very big man, as big as a house. Like the giant in the story of Jack the Giant-Killer.'

'What's Jack the Giant-Killer?'

'Why, didn't you ever hear the story of Jack? Well, I'll tell you that one, too.'

Ice-cream sodas were finished by now. The shouting mob surged out of the drug store and spread in a pool on the side-walk, chattering, laughing, staring at passers-by, pushing each other around, squealing and handling each other, pretending not to know that they were being looked at and listened to . . . in short, enjoying an afternoon off. Mamie Flacker caught sight of the two in the car, and went towards them with a good-natured smile, 'Well, you two seem to have hit it off together all right,' she said, leaning over the edge of the car, and trying to tickle the little girl, who drew away from her closer to Mrs. Bascomb.

'Ain't she the cute kid?' Mamie went on, making no effort not to be heard by the child. 'Momma says she's a perfect wonder for her age. Her mother brings her over to our house lots, and leaves her with my mother while she goes down-town. Dids' father is kind of foolish and fussy about her mother going down-town much, so she don't let him know. If he gets home before she does, she tells him she's been over to our house to do some sewing with Momma. There's lots of ways of getting around men that are too fussy.' She laughed and laid her hand kindly on the little girl's rough hair. 'Dids is such a funny little scooter, she tickles Momma most to death with her cute tricks. You never know what she's going to say next. We just love to have her around. She's a good little girl, too. She wouldn't ever tell on her mother, never, would you, Dids?'

'Nope,' said the child, trying to see how the keys came off the key-ring.

'She can keep a secret as good as a grown person,' said Mamie warmly. 'You can bank on her for that. You wouldn't believe it, but this is the third time we've took her off with us, and she's never let on to her Momma but what she's been right at our house all the time. The boys like to have her along. She answers back so cute, no matter how they josh her. Keeps us all laughing, don't you, Dids? And it just serves her mother right, when it comes to that, for not taking her along when she goes off for a good time. If her mother can fool her father, I guess Dids can fool her mother, can't you, Dids?'

'Yep,' said the child, absent-mindedly, jingling the keys on the key-ring.

'See here, Mamie,' said Mrs. Bascomb, 'why don't you let Dids come back with me for the afternoon. She'd only be in the way with you young people at the movies. Let me keep her, and you stop to get her when you're ready to go back. I'm boarding at the big white house with tall columns next door but one to the central school building.'

'All right, ma'am,' said Mamie easily. 'If Dids wants to, she can. Which'd you rather do, Dids? Go with us, or go with your Gramma?'

The child did not answer. She hung down her head, looking for the first time a little shy.

'Well, honey, which'll it be?' asked Mamie, stooping over her. 'Go with Gramma?'

The child seemed almost imperceptibly to shake her head.

'She says she'd rather go to the movies,' translated Mamie, straightening her back, and looking apologetically at Mrs. Bascomb, 'and we promised her we would . . .'

Mrs. Bascomb murmured some half-heard acceptance of this decision, kissed the child, and descending from the automobile, turned away. At the corner of the street she heard a light patter behind her and felt a small, bony hand thrust into hers.

'She's changed her mind, I guess,' called Mamie, laughing. 'All right, Dids. You're the doctor.'

Mrs. Bascomb went back a step or two, holding the little thin, dirty hand closely in hers. 'You'll remember, Mamie, it's the next house but one to the school building,' she repeated.

Something crossed Mamie's mind now, as she looked from the child to her old teacher, formidably immaculate in her iron-grey tailored suit and spotless linen collar. A recollection of her school-days came to her and made her laugh. 'Look-y here, Mrs. Bascomb, I know you. Don't go cleaning her up or anything, or her mamma'll get wise.

I don't want her folks to get on to our taking her off with us. You leave her just the way she is. I've got her old dress and shoes with me and we'll put them back on her as we get into Gilmanville. Now you leave her good and sticky, so she'll look natural or we'll have trouble. Lottie's good-natured enough, but she flies off the handle awful easy and when she gets going . . . believe *me*. . . .'

'I won't touch her,' promised Mrs. Bascomb, looking down at the little thing.

As they started off together, she asked, in a cheerful voice, 'Would you like to have me tell you a story right now, as we walk along? I know a nice one about a little tailor who killed seven flies with one blow on his piece of bread and butter, and then had such exciting things happen to him afterwards.'

The little girl nodded and tilted back her head to look up into her grandmother's face as she talked.

They finished that story by the time they reached Mrs. Bascomb's room, and as she sat down and took the child in her lap, she asked, '*Now*, what story would you like?'

'Oh, I don't know,' said the little girl, vaguely, with a long drawn breath of satisfaction. She slipped one arm about Mrs. Bascomb's neck and leaned against her.

'What kind of stories do you like best?' asked Mrs. Bascomb. 'Fairy stories? Or real stories about real children?'

'What's fairy 'tories?' asked the child.

Mrs. Bascomb was silent for a moment. 'Didn't you ever hear of fairies, dear?' she asked gently.

The little girl shook her head, her face very sober as if she felt herself at fault. 'I never heard *any* 'tories before,' she said, 'except Mrs. Flacker told me once about how her little boy got his hand most burned off.'

Their eyes were meeting again in that long, deep gaze.

Mrs. Bascomb murmured at random, 'Well, do you think you like stories?'

The child nodded and murmured, 'Yes.' But they were neither of them thinking of the words they were uttering. The child's eyes opened wider and wider. Her sensitively cut mouth quivered, and all at once she burst out into loud sobs, the tears splashing down her pale, grimy cheeks. As she wept she tightened her arm about Mrs. Bascomb's neck.

Her grandmother did not seem at all surprised. She did not ask the child what the matter was, or try to check her sobbing. With the helplessly absurd gesture of middle-aged emotion, she snatched off her glasses, behind which her own eyes were brimming, laid them hastily down on the table and put both arms around the child, holding her close in a tender clasp.

The little girl, crying apparently with all her might, nestled her face into her grandmother's bosom and burrowed closer into the arms about her.

Over her head, Mrs. Bascomb's face was distorted grotesquely with the grimace of restrained weeping. But she did not weep. She sat quietly holding the child till her own quiet had flowed into the little body in her arms.

The child stopped crying as suddenly as she had begun, and sat up, screwing her fists into her eyes. 'You said you'd let me 'tick some broked things together,' she said in a comforted tone of familiarity and assurance.

She looked up into her grandmother's face and smiled. It was the first time she had smiled.

Mrs. Bascomb caught her breath in a loud, audible gasp. But she said at once, in a steady, cheerful voice, 'So I did. Well, I will too. We'll mend a lot of broken things, together.'

At five o'clock Mrs. Bascomb stood looking after the automobile, waving her handkerchief in answer to the flutter of a tiny hand. She felt more at peace than she had since she had come to Harristown, since Ralph's marriage .... perhaps since the day of her birth. And yet there was nothing in her consciousness but a certainty that a turning point in her life had come, and that before her lay a new road, leading to she knew not what.

Her reason rose in panic and snatched at her to pluck her back from the folly of attempting what she knew to be impossible. But she had seen too much of the helplessness of reason. There was another solvent to the questions which harassed reason could not answer. Strange that she had not thought of it before.

She turned her back on reason, and set out resolutely along the new path.

PART THREE

Chapter 20

But in spite of this new certainty her knees were weak under her as she once more turned up the walk leading to her own house. It looked dingy and battered, one shutter was hanging by a broken hinge, the paint was peeling off from the attacks of the same summer suns which had parched the bit of lawn in front to a brown tangle of weeds. She saw these things but they seemed to her of the last insignificance. What would happen in the next hour? That was significant.

She went up the unpainted steps to the porch, dusty and ill-kept, with rickety wicker-chairs leaning sidewise upon their feeble legs. She rang the bell and listened, as well as the loud thumping of her heart would let her, to see whose footsteps would approach. Through the screen door she could see her own hall and living-room, the rooms where she had stood when she read Ralph's letter, where she had seen the ragged jute tassel. She perceived now vaguely that it all looked like the tassel, shabby, sordid, the pictures awry, the floors dusty, a litter of newspapers, odd clothing, and children's toys in the corners. But this made no impression whatever on her mind. Someone had opened the kitchen door and was looking cautiously around the corner to see who had rung.

'Why, *Mother!*' said Ralph's startled voice. He stepped out into the hall and stood facing her for an instant. He was in his shirt-sleeves (not a very clean shirt), a soiled kitchen towel in his hand, his bagging trousers slipped rather low down on his slender hips. His face was pale and a little puffy as if he had not slept well; his collar was off because of the heat, and his dry hair was rumpled into hay-like wisps. Of the brilliance of his radiant youth, there was, for the moment, not a trace left. He looked frowsy and weak and shabby, the sort of man for whom Mrs. Bascomb had always felt a scornful distaste.

133

His mother looking at her son through the screen-door, against the dreariness of the room behind him, saw nothing but the expression on his face, and felt herself pierced with sorrow and pity. She abased herself to the dust with the thought, 'My poor boy! My poor boy! I have never loved Ralph till this moment.'

She said with a resolute matter-of-factness, 'I thought I'd like to come to see you and Lottie, Ralph, dear.' She expected Lottie to appear at any moment.

Ralph came to himself, hastened to open the screen door and held it open while she entered. 'That's a good idea,' he said with an odd intonation. 'Come on in.' He looked at his mother strangely, she thought, but though all her senses were sharpened to a desperate acuteness, she could perceive nothing in his expression beyond uncertainty and astonishment.

He added, 'Lottie isn't here just now. I guess she and Dids are over at the Flackers. Lottie goes over there a good deal, with her sewing, to have company.'

A sharp smell of hot metal came out brusquely into the hall from the kitchen.

'Oh, gee whiz!' cried Ralph, making a dive through the door. 'I left . . .'

Following him she saw him snatch a deep saucepan from the gas-stove (forgetting to use a holder), give a yell at the hotness of the handle, and drop it with a banging clatter on the floor.

The action, his gesture, and his look upon her as he blew on his scorched fingers, laughing ruefully at his foolishness, were so like the boy he had been, that his mother forgot the frowsy, unkempt man he had looked at the door. She laughed too, a little hysterically, and Ralph's eyes, doubtful and on their guard till then, brightened at the sound.

'Great little old cook, I am,' he said, stooping to pick up the saucepan.

'What were you going to do with it?' asked his mother, taking it out of his hand.

'Oh, I thought I'd get some potatoes on to boil so there'd be something started for a hot meal when Lottie and Dids get back. She stays rather late some afternoons, over at the Flackers. And the doctor says Dids ought to have cooked food. Her digestion isn't very good, and cold food isn't good for her.'

Mrs. Bascomb's ear and eye, sharpened as they were by the crucial nature of the moment, saw in his averted look, heard in his accent, that he knew perfectly well that Lottie was not at the Flackers but that, out of moral fatigue, he pretended that he did not know. Had Lottie beaten him down to such a point? But she knew very well he had not by nature very much capacity for resistance.

At this, the acuteness of her desperation unexpectedly turned traitor to her, and drove home the sharp-edged realization that she had carefully trained him to have as little resistance as possible, had herself beaten down by a look every beginning of it in him. He had never been able to withstand her and now he was incapable of withstanding Lottie.

The thought took her breath away. She turned from it sharply. 'Here, let me put the potatoes on now I'm here.'

'Far be it from me to fight with anybody for the privilege of cooking potatoes,' Ralph assured her, still with that momentary return of the gay lightness of his boyhood.

The clatter of the falling kettle, and his mother's laugh had broken something that had stood between them. They looked at each other naturally now, the wary alertness of suspicion for a moment laid aside.

Mrs. Bascomb seized the moment . . . it might not come again . . . and crowding down her heart-sick apprehension of what Ralph would answer, she said in as even and steady a voice as she could manage, 'Ralph, I've been thinking lately about giving up the Harristown position. I find there is a position I could have at the Baker Street School, here in Gilmanville, right near the house. I've just been there to see about it. And then we could all live together again. I find I get rather homesick for you and Dids.'

She was filling the kettle at the tap as she spoke and now said over her shoulder, 'You're . . . you're all I've got, you know.' She turned off the water, took her courage in her two hands and faced about to see how Ralph took it.

She had known he would be surprised . . . he had heard her say a hundred times that nothing would induce her to teach in that slum-district Baker Street School, filled as it was with all the children from the dump-heap. Yes, she had known he would be surprised, but she had not expected what she saw . . . Ralph was looking at her, too astounded by the unexpectedness of her news to hide the emotion it caused him. And the emotion it caused him was relief . . . oh, an almost dreadful relief, like that of a child, struggling forlornly alone with a task too great for it, who sees it taken from him by competent adult hands.

'Why, *Mother* . . .' he cried in a high, quavering voice.

Two impulses reached Mrs. Bascomb almost at the same instant and battled to possess her; one a sulphureous gust of an old instinct – a quick perception that he had thrown himself open by that cry of relief, and a fencer's lunging reflex to take advantage of the opening, to profit by his surprise and emotion to wring from him an explicit admission that she was sacrificing herself for him. She opened her lips to ask him definitely, mercilessly, 'Oh, you do want me back, then? You *have* missed me? You have come to appreciate a little more all that I did for you?'

Yes, all this had passed through her mind. But from her heart poured up such a rush of loving compassion for him, that she found the water in her eyes as she looked at him silently, smiling with lips that trembled. She nodded her head, she bit her shaking under lip, and said humbly, 'I think I could do better now, dear.'

She was horrified by the almost wild surprise in Ralph's deeply moved look upon her. It came to her that if, till now, she had never really loved Ralph, that this was also perhaps, the first moment of real love for her which Ralph had ever felt. 'Oh, *Mother* . . .' he said protestingly, and then to her humility he granted impulsively the vindication she refused to ask of him. 'Why, Mother . . . *you* weren't to . . . it . . . it wasn't *your* fault,' he murmured huskily in a low voice.

She let this pass as though she had not heard it. The startled gratitude in Ralph's eyes shamed her. He had never looked at his mother like that before. She bestirred herself now not to take advantage of it. She must protect him from saying something which ought not to be articulate between them.

'I'd better get the potatoes on,' she said quietly. 'Where are they kept?'

'Oh, Lord knows,' said Ralph vaguely. 'Somewhere around.'

They found them in a paper bag, standing on the floor in a corner together with some scorched and greasy dish towels. Mrs. Bascomb went to wash them at the sink, piled high with dirty dishes, thinking that there was yet one more chasm to cross. There was something else to be spoken of, and yet which must not be mentioned. She could not imagine what words would be possible to use for the question which must not be asked. Finally she took the baldest and the shortest words. At that, she had no need to use them at all. She had said only, 'Will Lottie? . . .' when Ralph took her up abruptly as though it had been he who had spoken first.

'Damned if I know,' he said in a depressed tone, addressing the wall. He added sombrely, 'It depends.'

Mrs. Bascomb's sharpened senses told her that he meant it depended on how Lottie happened to feel when she came in.

He stirred, looking at the clock and said, 'They'll surely be here before long. Maybe we might as well get the table set.'

They went together into the dining-room, where the spotted table-cloth lay askew on the table. Mrs. Bascomb took it off to shake it, noticing automatically which one it was, the fine damask she had bought at the Bassett auction, observing that it had fruit stains indelibly boiled into it, and that it had been laid on the table without a felt under it. This was evidently the custom of the house, for the fine mahogany of the old table was covered with blistered white spots where hot dishes had been set. She felt that Ralph saw her looking at it, and glanced up at him. His anxious expression shocked her because she remembered it as his look when he feared that Lottie was in a bad humour. The two-edged sword of awakened observation turned again in her hand. That was not only his look of sensitive fear of brutality from Lottie, that was also the look Ralph had often turned upon her when he had been a sensitive little boy, helpless before his mother. The thrust was so unexpected and went so deep that it made her feel sick. She tried to think of some words with which to make Ralph feel how little to her now were spots on her table. And she realized there were no words which he could believe, in the face of his years of knowledge of her. It would need the passage of many other different years before he could believe her.

He said now, uneasily, as if it caused him intense discomfort to speak and yet as if he dared not be silent, 'I've just thought of something . . . I don't know . . . it's about bedroom space.'

She looked at him surprised.

'You see the baby is so big now, she's outgrown her crib. She sleeps in the bed now, in the other bedroom, in my old bed.'

Mrs. Bascomb was for an instant struck dumb by this obstacle.

'Maybe we could set up a cot-bed for her in our room?' suggested Ralph uneasily.

From this idea his mother recoiled with a rush. 'Oh, no! Oh, no!' she said hastily. 'Not that!' She cast about for a cloak to cover her meaning and said, 'She's old enough to have a room by herself that she can learn to keep in order. Every child ought to have that, of course.'

She thought for an instant, focusing on the obstacle the clean hot wholeness of her selfless purpose and felt the obstacle melt away to nothing as she had known all obstacles would vanish now that she herself no longer stood blocking the path. 'How about the attic room? You slept up there when Dids was born. That'd be all right for me.'

'The attic room!' he looked at her in amazement.

'Yes, why not?' she said briskly, trying to pick enough knives and forks to set the table from the criss-cross jack-straw confusion in the silver drawer. 'There are all sorts of pleasant cosy arrangements to be made with an attic-room. Some plaster-board and pretty wall-paper and fresh curtains at the windows, and some nice new furniture, the right size . . . you'll be surprised when you see what can be done with it. I'll have the nicest room in the house out of it.'

She saw another opening and went on negligently, 'I

have plenty of money just now, you know. I've been saving quite a little, and it's high time I spent a little of it on the house. I've neglected it of late. I ought to have taken care of the necessary repairs long ago; I imagine every room in the house needs fresh paper. I know Lottie will enjoy choosing it. And the floors ought to be done over, too. I've let it go too long. And that's always a mistake with a house.'

No, she felt she had overdone that. She must learn to have a lighter, more discreet touch. Well, she would learn that, would learn everything that had to be learned.

'What else were you planning for supper?' she asked to change the subject.

'Oh, I don't know,' said Ralph, 'sometimes we have canned tomatoes.'

'How do you cook them?'

'We don't cook them. They're cooked already when you buy them. We put them in little sauce-dishes and dip our bread in them.'

'How'd you like to make a tomato bisque soup instead?' asked his mother. 'I saw a bottle of milk in the ice-box.' It had been his favourite soup.

'What's your guess as to how I'd like it?' he said laughingly. 'I'd hate it, wouldn't I?'

'Well, you run over and ask Mrs. Baumann for a couple of heads of lettuce from her garden, and we'll have some salad, too,' she said, and as he went out of the back door she took off her hat, went into the howling desolation of the kitchen and set to work.

It was a good deal later when she saw Lottie and Dids descend from the tram at the corner, and come slowly up the street towards the house, wearily dragging their feet.

'Lottie feels the heat so,' said Ralph, looking at her through the window. Already at the mere sight of Lottie in the distance, there was the apologetic, explanatory, excusing, fatigued note which his mother remembered so well. Her heart sank like lead. Ralph could not be counted on for any help in the encounter which was before her. She said, 'I'll go and begin serving things, and make the iced-tea.'

'Oh, iced-tea!' cried Ralph with a childish accent of

pleasure. He hesitated, 'I guess I'll go out and meet them,' he suggested, looking at her.

'That's a good idea,' she said, returning to the kitchen.

Her knees were shaking under her again, as she went back and forth from the kitchen to the dining-room with the soup plates and the tall, clinking pitcher of iced-tea.

'It depends,' Ralph had said. It depended, among other things, on whether she could smother down to invisibility the loathing which the distant sight of Lottie had brought up like a horrible taste in her mouth, like the smell of a horrible drug in her nostrils. To be again dependent on Lottie's whims for any peace . . . the revolt from those whims shook her in a well-remembered spasm. Come, come, she must keep her head. She must be self-possessed and quiet so that she would know how to say the right things, how to make it apparent that she claimed nothing, offered everything, would make herself small, small . . . because she had a purpose beside which herself was nothing, and that, once and for all, she would let Lottie have all the right on her side.

She saw through the window that Ralph had gone out to meet Lottie to tell her the news. They were standing at the front walk, talking together. Lottie's silhouette, in spite of her heat-fatigue, was modish and smart as it always was when she was dressed for the street. Would Ralph know how to say the right things? Would he remember to say what she had been telling him to say . . . that she would be humble, expect nothing for herself, would give all she had, that she would gladly occupy the attic room, that she asked nothing better than the chance to do the housework again, that she did not mind at all how her furniture had been treated, that she had money to spend and would let Lottie spend it on the house, that . . . above all, a sudden divination told Mrs. Bascomb that this last would have more weight with Lottie than anything else . . . above all, that she had a good supper ready this hot afternoon, so that Lottie had only to sit down to eat it.

Looking out at them she saw the child who had been dragging heavily on her mother's hand, look up quickly at her father as though she had caught something he said. She turned her head towards the house then, and pulling her hand away, started unnoticed up the walk at a trotting run. She pushed open the screen-door and stood stricken with shyness, looking at her grandmother with bright dark eyes from under her bent brows.

'Hallo there, little Dids,' said Mrs. Bascomb, holding out her hand towards the child.

At the sound of her voice, the little girl's intent face broke into a sudden radiance, her grandfather's flashing smile.

Mrs. Bascomb's heart cried out. She longed to rush at the child, to strain her wildly into her arms, to cover her with kisses, to weep aloud.

She said cheerfully, 'Aren't you hungry? Come along and have some red soup. I've put yours in the plate that has the elephant on it.'

Dids let the door shut behind her, and went up to her grandmother.

'Will you tell me 'nother 'tory?' she asked.

'Oh, all you like,' said Mrs. Bascomb, picking her up in her arms. 'I'm just made of stories.'

The child profited by being in her arms, on a level with her face, to lean forward and say in her ear, 'I didn't tell 'em I sawn you. I never said a word to anybody.'

The whisper turned Mrs. Bascomb cold. She clasped the little girl tightly and said in a broken shaking voice, 'God help me! God help me!'

'What did you say?' asked Dids.

Her grandmother did not answer. She had seen through the window that Lottie and Ralph were now coming towards the house. She put the child down hastily and moved away to be at a little distance from her.

Through the screen-door she saw Lottie coming up the porch steps which shook under her. Lottie was much stouter than she had been. Her rounded plumpness was now frankly superfluous flesh and her corset strings were rather tightly pulled. Her dress was blue silk with large white dots on it, and she wore a smart, small cheap straw hat.

'Well, Lottie,' said Mrs. Bascomb in a friendly tone, coming forward to open the door, 'you see I can't keep away. Has Ralph been telling you that I'm homesick for my own folks and perhaps will leave my job in Harristown and come back here – if you'll take me in.'

On seeing her, Lottie had hastened her steps and now with a little rush, opened her arms widely and put them around her neck. Mrs. Bascomb felt once more on her lips the well-remembered melting softness of Lottie's.

Lottie kissed her energetically, and then, holding her off at arm's length said in the grand manner, 'Our home will never be shut to our mother. No matter what comes, you will always have a welcome in your son's house.'

'Oh, Lottie, how *kind* of you to say that,' said Mrs. Bascomb appreciatively.

That evening she sat in the bathroom on the same chair where she had first seen her grandchild's eyes looking up into hers. She was leaning over the bath-tub now, where little Dids sat in foamy suds, plunging up and down in the water a new celluloid duck, while her grandmother washed her bony little back, sticky with sweat and dust. She turned away from the bath-tub now for an instant to reach for the soap, saying over her shoulder, 'And just then Sinbad saw a great shadow, and lo, and behold, it was the roc again, spreading its wide, wide wings over the valley.'

'I bet Sinbad dets away this time,' remarked Dids, reaching behind her for the duck, which had bobbed itself out of her hands. She reached too far, lost her balance and slipping suddenly in the soapy water, fell on her back with a splash, the water dashing up into her startled little face.

Mrs. Bascomb had no idea how the child took small accidents, and dreading an explosion of anger or fear, snatched her up, sputtering and kicking, and said hastily to divert her attention, 'Well, that was a regular swim for a little froggie.'

The child was still gasping for breath, but she said instantly, 'Frogs haven't dot *hair*. I'm a swan!' And with the drollery, she slid so sly and humorous a glance at her grandmother from the corners of her bright dark eyes that Mrs. Bascomb burst out into an astonished ha! ha! which rang through the house.

Hearing her grandmother laugh, the little thing laughed with her, and then they went on laughing idiotically at their own mirth, with the delicious silly hilarity known only to little laughing children and those who care for them lovingly.

'For mercy's sakes, what can anybody find to laugh at, this frightful hot night!' said Lottie's voice from the hall.

She came to stand droopingly in the door. The iridescent bubble of their causeless mirth broke at once. Mrs. Bascomb reached again for the soap. Dids set her duck carefully afloat in the land-locked harbour between her bent knees and her lean little body.

'Gracious, I should think you'd be too tired to bathe Dids to-night,' said Lottie. 'I'm just killed by this heat. I can't *breathe*. I should think you'd be tired to death.'

The word struck sharply on Mrs. Bascomb's ear. Tired? What was it to be tired? Had she ever been tired?

Glancing up at her daughter-in-law she caught sight of herself in the mirror. She scarcely recognized her own face. She looked from those shining eyes and curved lips up into Lottie's moody face.

'No,' she said moderately and discreetly, 'no, I don't seem to feel specially tired.'

'Well, goodness knows, *I* do,' said Lottie, turning away heavily.

Chapter 21

'YES, she shall have all the bananas she wants, Momma's little girl shall. Bananas are *good* for children. I always ate them, lots of them. Dr. Dewey makes such a fuss about her being underweight! Everybody knows bananas are very fattening; it's one of the things they don't let people eat when they're reducing.'

When, the next morning, Dids woke with deeply flushed cheeks and heavy eyes, 'It's scarlet fever, I know it is !' cried her mother, snatching her from Mrs. Bascomb's lap, where she sat limply, drooping her head against her grandmother's breast. 'It's scarlet fever! Mrs. Flacker says there's a lot of it on Warren Street, and I bet the children in your school have it! I don't think it's *safe* your coming and going, from all those children that may have goodness knows what!'

'Perhaps we'd better take her temperature,' suggested Mrs. Bascomb, looking for her clinical thermometer.

'I was just going to say that,' said Lottie.

But the feverish child, fretful and weary, pushed the little glass tube away, petulantly, 'No, no!' she said, turning her head from one side to the other.

'But, little Dids darling,' said her grandmother, holding it off for a moment, 'it won't hurt you. It hasn't any taste at all, and it's just as smooth as smooth. It's a magic stick, did you know it, that can feel around under your tongue, and then tell us just what's the best thing to do for a little sick girl.'

Dids' heavy eyes looked faintly interested. Mrs. Bascomb came a step nearer, and held out the thermometer for Dids to look at. 'See, it hasn't any eyes, and yet it can know the minute it touches your. . . .'

Dids turned her head away again, with a momentary return of her doubt, and her mother cried, clasping her closely, 'Poor little sing! They s'ant pester her with nassy sings in her poor mouth. No, Momma won't let 'em bozzer poor Dids.'

To her mother-in-law she said over Dids' head, 'I never could stand those things either. They make me wild with nerves. And Dids is just like me. She's very nervous. I don't believe in all the fuss they make over thermometers either. Folks got along all right before there were any.'

Mrs. Bascomb put the instrument back at once in its little case, saying in neutral tones, 'Well, shall we have the doctor come to look at Dids?'

'I suppose so,' said Lottie. 'But I wish to goodness we had a decent doctor to call in. That old Dr. Dewey makes me tired. He's a regular rough-neck. No gentleman at all. And I don't believe he knows a thing about his business. He's certainly never been able to help *me* a bit.'

'Don't want Doctor,' cried Dids suddenly, shrilly. 'Don't *want* wuff-neck doctor.' She began to cry and struggle in her mother's arms.

'Well, I don't blame her a bit,' said Lottie to Mrs. Bascomb, adding reluctantly, 'But I suppose we'll have to have him. You'd better go and 'phone him to come.'

When he came, in answer to his questions, 'No, Doctor, no,' said Dids' mother with wide candid eyes. 'No, Dids hasn't had anything different to eat but what she has every day. And I'm always *very* careful about her food. I think what they eat is very important for children, don't you, doctor?'

As the doctor turned his old lion's head to look again at Dids' crimson face on the pillow, Dids' mother shot a warning look at the child and put her finger to her lips. Dids immediately shut her eyes and assumed a blank expression. No effort was made to hide this exchange of looks from Mrs. Bascomb standing in the doorway, who now turned away, her hands clenched tightly together.

'I guess she needs a dose of castor-oil, that's all, probably,' said the doctor's voice from inside the room.

'Oh, doctor, I can't give her that nasty stuff. I just can't make her take it. She always cries and screams and struggles so, I can't get it down her.'

'Maybe she wouldn't if you didn't tell her beforehand that's what you expect her to do,' said the doctor roughly. 'Here, I'll give it to her myself. I can do it all right.'

Horrid sounds from the bedroom . . . choking shrieks and screams from Dids, shrill tearful protestations from Lottie, a bass rumble from the doctor of, 'Let go my hand, Mrs. Bascomb. *Let go my hand!* There, now, little girl, down with it. There! It's nothing! Everybody has to have it. *All* over! There you are.'

Out on the landing, Mrs. Bascomb rigid, her teeth ground together, restraining herself with an effort from beating her head against the wall.

Exit of the doctor, striding past the grandmother, calling over his shoulder to the mother, 'Keep her quiet, and don't let her have a single thing to eat till to-morrow morning, and she'll be all right.'

Inside the bedroom, sobs of ardent self-pity from Dids, and indignant sympathizing exclamations from her mother. 'Nassy mean old doctor to treat poor baby so. Momma'll drive old doctor away if he tries to tum and make poor Dids take nassy medicine. . . .'

'Not a thing to eat for her till to-morrow, remember,' the doctor's voice called up from the hall below.

That night, when, after the day-long absence at school, Mrs. Bascomb was sponging off the hot little body, she found the bed full of cake-crumbs.

At the supper table (one of the good days).

As Ralph was serving the beefsteak, Mrs. Bascomb said, 'Dids, you ought to have heard the story that Nellie McIntosh told my class to-day, about her little brother when he was four and a half years old, just your age. She said that last summer he was playing around in their yard, and saw a baby robin fall out of the nest. He trotted over to look at it, and saw the neighbour's cat came streaking it up. The brave little fellow knew just what to do. He held the baby bird as high over his head as his little arms could reach. The big cat must have been very hungry, or else wild with the idea of catching a live bird, for she jumped up on the little boy, and clawed at him and scared him; but he kicked at her with all his might and held the bird more tightly and shouted for help. A man driving a grocery cart heard him and went to see what the matter was. Of course he climbed up the tree and put the bird back in the nest all safe. Nellie said they were all so proud of her little brother.'

Ralph commented warmly, 'Pretty smart kid, I'll say.'

Lottie nodded her head. 'There was an old tree in our front yard,' she began, 'when we lived next door to the Works that the birds used to put their nests in and a mean low-down Polish boy used to climb up and poke the little birds' eyes out with a nail till Poppa caught him at it one day and got after him with a stick. He was the limit anyhow, that Shrevensky kid. I guess there was something the matter with his mind, kind of idiot maybe, for he'd think of the terriblest things to do. I saw him once, a crowd of us girls did, holding a cat over a fire he'd built on a vacant lot. My! It makes me sick to think of it. He'd got her tied up so she couldn't scratch, but she could yell all right, and that was what made us look through the knot-hole to see what was happening. We hollered at him to stop, and he turned around and made the awfullest face at us, enough to scare us to death. He was a fierce-looking thing, anyhow, one of the kind that their mouth hangs open all the time, and his eyes were sort of goggling too. He didn't have any forehead either, not to speak of, his hair grew right down to his eyebrows almost. They took him off to the Feebleminded Home, I guess, after he got so big it was dangerous to have him around with girls. Why, he'd got so that he'd run after us girls if we went out on the street after dark, if it wasn't but just to go to the next house, and he'd try to grab us and holler out the awfullest . . .'

Crash! Mrs. Bascomb in reaching for the bread-plate had swept her arm sideways. Her gesture had sent Ralph's glass of water flying across his plate, splashing the water and startling Dids who had been gazing at her mother.

'Mercy! How clumsy I am,' she said apologetically, springing up to repair the damage. It was quite a little undertaking, to brush up the bits of broken glass, to spread down a dry napkin over the soaked place on the cloth, to get Ralph a clean plate.

As she took her place again, she remarked to Lottie, 'What a pretty blouse that is. That white trimming on the blue looks so fresh and dainty!'

Lottie said good-naturedly, looking down at it, pleased, 'I got it down at Clarke's removal sale this morning, and it was the only rag there that I'd wear if I was paid to do it. They'd got out the fiercest lot of old duds for their "sale." But they couldn't work them off on me. I shop around too much. It's the only way you can keep ahead of them, shopping around, first one and then the other. And they know it too, and that's the reason the sales girls are so snippy to customers that don't buy. They're told to be. The store-keepers don't want you to know too much about prices and things. They pass the word around to the girls to be as nasty as they can to ladies who come looking, so they can fool them with their "sales" and "end-of-the-season clearances," and all the rest of their guff. But they don't get ahead of me. I know my rights and I know how to stand up for them. I think it's a person's duty to keep posted so you get the good of your money. No matter how miserable I feel, and goodness knows those pains in my side and arm make me feel miserable enough to lie down and die lots of times, I always feel I must get out to keep up with things.'

She was talking so fast that she could not take the time to eat the piece of biscuit in her hand, continually presenting it to her lips and constantly snatching it away to continue her flow of words.

'They can't scare me off with their snippy ways, the girls can't. When one of them tries to get funny with me, she gets hers all right. This morning when I was at Simmons' there was a smart kid tried to show off. "Moddam," she says with her chin in the air, "Moddom, I've showed you every piece of blue silk in my stock," she said, "and if it's only half a yard you want, why don't you step over to the remnant counter and see if you can't find something." "No, you don't, young lady," I says to her. "No, you don't come any such game on me. There's too many standing around here waiting for you to wait on them," I said. "I'd never get waited on again at this counter, if I moved away, and whether it's half a yard or not is nothing to you," I told her. "You're paid to show me goods," I said, "and you'll stay right on the job," I said, "till . . ." '

Mrs. Bascomb said in a low tone, 'Ralph, are you ready for your dessert? Because if you are, I'll clear off.'

'*I'm* not,' said Lottie. 'Mercy, how can you people eat so fast! Don't you know it's bad for you to gobble down your food without chewing it good. A woman I saw to-day, down-town, was telling me about her husband, what a stomach he'd got on him by eating so fast. The doctor said. . . .'

The supper table (one of the bad days).

Lottie, furiously: 'Those brand-new patent-leather shoes I paid five dollars for at Curtis' store have cracked right across. I don't believe I've worn them three times yet. I wore them down to Curtis' and just raised the roof. They started to answer back, but I said I'd see the old man or nobody, and they went to get Mr. Curtis himself, and we had it hot and heavy I tell you. Didn't he have the impudence to say that his clerk had told me when I bought them that they were too small for me, and anyhow he had it printed all over his store that they didn't guarantee patent-leather goods. I said to him, "Don't you suppose I know what size shoe I wear better than any shoe clerk does." I said, and he . . .'

Mrs. Bascomb, resolutely: 'Is your tea quite right, Lottie? I'm afraid I made it rather strong this evening, without thinking, and you know the doctor says you oughtn't to take strong tea because you're so high strung nervously. I'm sorry if it's not right.'

Lottie, stirring it, 'Oh, it's all right, I guess. I'm just as nervous as I can be anyhow. What was I talking about?'

Mrs. Bascomb: 'I saw something interesting in the paper to-day about Mr. Burbank. It seems he is working with cactus, trying to breed a variety that won't have thorns on it. It'd be splendid if he could. This Mr. Burbank, Dids dear, is just like a magician in the *Arabian Nights*. Only he really does do the wonderful things — there is no trick about it. He can take a plant with thorns, and keep working away with its children and grandchildren till by and by they haven't any thorns at all, and lots better fruit. He learned how to do it by watching how that had happened already. Did you know that our nice big red apples, so sweet and juicy, used to be little and dry and hard, like the red haws on the rose bush I showed you yesterday, and the apple trees used to be set thick with thorns, like the rose bush too. But people have trained them till. . . .'

Ralph, laughing: 'The way we try to train you, Dids, to put on your napkin, and take small mouthfuls, and not lose your temper. You're like a little thorny wild bush, and we want to turn you into. . . .'

Lottie: 'Oh, *I* know what it was I was talking about . . . those shoes! Well, what do you think? That mean old Curtis says he won't take them back. "But, Mr. Curtis," I said, "I can't do anything with them." And he said, "Well, madam, what do you think *we* can do with them?" The nerve of him! But I'll get even with him, if I have to stand at the door of his old store and tell everybody that goes in that . . . .'

Ralph: 'Oh, hold on there, Lottie. He'll get the law on you if you start. . . .'

Lottie, flaring up, her lips trembling, her face flushing,

'That's all you care about what happens to me. You never pay the least attention to what I say except always to take the other people's side against me. You *like* to have people wipe their feet on me! And me feeling ready to fly with nerves. That pain in my side. . . .'

Ralph: 'Oh, I listen to what you say all right. I'm sorry about those shoes. But Great Scott, nobody's had a chance to get a word in edgeways.'

Lottie: 'You've had plenty of time to get in a lot of words about some old cactus or other that nobody cares anything about.'

Ralph, shortly: 'What do you *want* me to do? Spend the whole time talking about those damn shoes?'

(Dids' quick intelligent eyes going from one to the other. Mrs. Bascomb's eyes on Dids).

Lottie, bursting into sobs: 'I want you to show a little decent . . . I'm just perfectly miserable, anyhow. Nobody cares a cent about me. I wish I was dead and . . . I don't know what makes everybody so mean to me.'

Ralph, bringing his fist down on the table: 'Oh, God Almighty, let up on. . . .'

Mrs. Bascomb, abruptly: 'Oh, did you hear that the Baumann house was broken into last night?'

Lottie, astonished and thrilled: 'No, for heaven's *sakes!* Right next door.'

Mrs. Bascomb: 'You know that little side window in their basement?'

Lottie: 'The one on the left as you go up the front steps? Yes, I've *often* thought somebody'd get in there. I've had it on the tip of my tongue dozens of times to tell Mrs. Baumann she ought to . . . .'

Mrs. Bascomb: 'Well, you were quite right, for that's the way the house was entered.'

Lottie: '*Did* they get Mamie's new furs? Wasn't old Aunty Rader scared?'

Mrs. Bascomb: 'They weren't any of them home last night, it seems. Maude Baumann Whitman told me they thought it was just a tramp looking for a place to sleep out of the cold and snow. He hadn't gone upstairs into the house at all, she said, just slept on some old rags in the furnace cellar.'

Lottie, disappointed: 'Oh, just a tramp. When we lived out at the end of Fuller Street, that was when I was seven years old . . . no, I must have been eight because I remember that was the year that. . . .'

A little before Christmas, Mrs. Bascomb's class was taken off one afternoon to the assembly-room of the school, to practise carols for the Christmas entertainment. They were to be dismissed from there, which freed the grade teachers from routine earlier than usual. Mrs. Bascomb decided to use the unexpected hour for shopping. She had given so little thought of late to her wardrobe that it needed replenishing.

She bought quickly what she needed in stockings and underwear in one shop and was on her way to the shoe-store for goloshes when, passing a drug-store, she remembered that there was no tooth-paste at the house and stepped in through a side-door to buy some. Ralph and Lottie had insensibly slid back to the old habit of allowing her to keep up the household supplies of such standard articles. From the condition of Dids' teeth, she gathered that during her absence the supply had not been kept up.

At the far end of the drug-store before the soda fountain counter, she saw Lottie and Dids, having what in Lottie's vocabulary was called a 'high old time' with the white-jacketed, gleaming-haired clerk.

'You're going to marry me, when you grow up, aren't you, Dids?' said the lively young man, leaning over the counter and putting his arm around the little girl's neck.

'You tell him you're going to catch a handsomer fellow than he is,' cried Lottie, laughing.

'I'm doin' to det a feller with lots and lots of *money*,' announced Dids unexpectedly, with the foolish, self-conscious look of a child who has said something sure to be laughed at.

Lottie and the young man were convulsed, looking into each other's eyes as they laughed.

'So you're going to catch a feller with lots of money, eh?' said the gay young man. He called out to another clerk, 'Here's a young lady beginning early. She says she's going to pick out her feller with plenty of dough.'

Dids looked around at her audience, her baby face

shining with satisfied vanity, 'Yep, you bet your life I am,' she affirmed.

'But you want him good-looking, too,' the soda clerk told her, pouring deep into her dewy eyes the soiled knowingness of his own gaze. 'You wouldn't want to kiss a feller that wasn't good-looking, would you?'

'Won't kiss him 'tall,' said Dids pertly. 'Won't kiss him 'tall. Just marry him.'

At this the hilarity of Lottie and the young man became uncontrollable. They smeared over Dids their shouted conviction that she was the smartest kid in the country, and greedily gloating over her innocence, they repeated again and again, 'Won't kiss him 'tall. Just marry him.'

Lottie said fondly. 'She's getting to the age when it's real fun to have her along. Kids are an awful nuisance when they're little . . . seems as though you could hardly live *through* it. But when they get smart enough to take notice of what's going on, you can get some comfort in them. I tell you one thing, I'm going to keep her home from school for company for me just as long as I can . . . till she's eight or nine anyways. It's better for her. They learn more. Don't you suppose but what she learns more going around with me and hearing people talk, than she would shut up in a horrid schoolroom with a bossy old maid ordering her around.'

'Sure, she learns more,' said the young man, rubbing his hand over the satin-smooth skin of Did's neck and slipping his fingers below the collar of her dress. 'Sure, she learns a lot more.'

'Bossy old maid,' said Dids, anxious not to be left out.

'And I always pity a girl that's been to school too much,' went on Lottie. 'It makes them sort of school-teachery themselves. Men haven't any use for a woman who knows too much.'

'Oh, I guess the men will always like any daughter of *yours*,' said the clerk in a low tone with a special accent, his eyes on Lottie's.

It was at this point that Dids, screwing herself around and around on her stool, discovered Mrs. Bascomb at the other end of the shop buying tooth-paste. 'Hallo, Granny!' she shouted.

Lottie's face clouded with annoyance and embarrassment. She was visibly lost at once in a calculation of the distance between them, in wondering what, if anything, her mother-in-law had heard. But Mrs. Bascomb was touched almost to tears to see that Dids' expression did not change in the least. She was merely pleased to have a new spectator for her cleverness, and searched her grandmother's eyes for praise as naturally and fearlessly as those of the clerk, with exactly the same clarity and unconsciousness.

She was such a little, *little* girl still.

Mrs. Bascomb knew that a word or a look of criticism of Lottie would bring down an avalanche of morose bad humour, so she made herself very small and quiet, saying in a friendly tone, 'Oh, there you are, Lottie?' and 'Hallo there, Dids darling, do you like tooth-paste best in red tubes or in blue ones?'

The avalanche remained poised a perilous moment but did not fall.

'Hallo, there, Momma,' said Lottie, good-natured at not being made to feel at fault. 'I thought this was school-time for you. 'Tisn't four o'clock.' She paid her reckoning and went to join Mrs. Bascomb glancing sideways at her reflection in the mirrors of the shop and re-arranging the angle of her hat. She studied herself with complacency, and yet with apprehension. When she turned sideways her silhouette was thickening alarmingly. 'I'm really getting too fat,' she murmured, 'I'll simply have to diet.'

She said this almost every day now.

'How much is that candy?' she asked the clerk who was wrapping up Mrs. Bascomb's tooth-paste. 'Is it real fresh? The last I had from here was as old as the hills,' and then, 'Well, I'll try it again. Wrap me up a couple of pounds, will you?'

She added, 'Oh, say, Momma, just pay for that along with what you've bought, will you? I forgot that I've spent nearly all I have with me. I'll pay you back as soon as we get home.'

In the tram on the way home there were not many seats left, and their little party was separated. Mrs. Bascomb sat down near the door with Dids on her lap. Lottie was in the front, the candy box already opened on her lap.

'Oh, say, Granny,' said Dids, nestling closer to her. 'Couldn't you go on with that 'tory? You left off in a terribly 'citing place.'

'Yes, so I could,' said Mrs. Bascomb, looking down into the dark eyes, clear and deep under the nobly modelled brow. 'We were at the place, weren't we, where Beauty had found the Beast, just ready to die, lying on the grass in the park of the palace?'

'Yes, yes,' said Dids eagerly, 'what happened?'

'Well, when she saw how sadly he gazed at her, and how dreadfully sick and weak he was, she forgot all about his looking hairy and rough and awful, and only remembered how good he'd been to her father and to her, how kind and gentle and sad . . . never asking anything for himself. And now she had killed him!'

Dids' eyes were fixed on the story-teller. She was evidently leaning over the dying Beast herself. She sat perfectly motionless, a beautiful expression of pity on her face. She was far from the tram, from the soda-water fountain. She was such a *little* girl, still.

'Beauty ran up to where he lay, and knelt down by him, and put her arms around his neck and whispered, "Oh, dear, dear Beast, don't die! Don't die! I love you! I want to make you happy."

'And what do you think happened?'

Dids' eyes widened and her lips dropped apart a little.

'The words weren't out of her mouth when the Beast's hairy, rough, queer outside looks all went away . . . between two winks of your eyes, that was all gone, and there before her stood a beautiful young prince holding her hand and looking at her with the gentle eyes of the Beast, only they were not sad but very happy. He had been shut up in the Beast all the time, enchanted, and now she'd broken the enchantment by loving him, and that let him go free.'

'Oh,' said Dids, with a long breath of relief. 'Gracious! I was so afraid he'd die. Oh, I'm so glad she got him out all right!' She smiled up brilliantly at her grandmother, the beautiful smile which had come down to her from another beautiful and strong spirit.

She was such a darling little girl still.

But she would not be a little girl much longer!

Mrs. Bascomb took the tiny mittened hand in hers and sat quiet, her heart overflowing with love and pain.

One evening a few days later, Mrs. Bascomb, left with Dids while Ralph and Lottie went to the movies, was brushing up the dining-room floor, while in the next room Dids put her dolls to bed on the couch. She was chattering volubly to them as she undressed them. 'You've been bad to-day, 'Tildy, and I've half a notion to tell your Poppa on you and have him give it to you good.' The doll apparently said something audible to her ear, to which she answered, indulgently, 'Oh, well, I won't then this time, but if you don't be gooder to-morrow, I'll take you to the hospital and the nurse'll whip you and strap you into a bed and not give you anything to eat except the awfullest medicine for hundreds of years.'

'Oh, Dids darling, you mustn't tell your babies such stories. The nurses in the hospitals are ever so good to little sick children.'

'That's what Momma told me,' said Dids, raising her clear eyes to her grandmother. 'She told me when she was mad at me yesterday.'

'Had you been bad?' asked Mrs. Bascomb.

'Yep, but I didn't know any better. Mrs. Flacker asked me if Momma'd been down to Hargreave's Drug-store yesterday and I said, "Yes, we went there 'most every day." I didn't *know* Momma didn't want Mrs. Flacker to know. Momma says Mrs. Flacker is mad because Minnie Flacker used to go with the soda clerk and he's gone back on her now. I told Momma I wouldn't again, and she didn't slap me or anything.'

'Oh,' said Mrs. Bascomb, sweeping the dust carefully into the dustpan.

Dids went back to her dolls.

'Marfa Ann,' she pronounced clearly, 'you got to sit up prettier than that if you're ever going to catch a felleh when you grow up. You've got to know how to wink at them the right way, before they pay any attention to you, you know.'

Then taking the night-gowned doll into her arms tenderly, she murmured, 'But Momma loves you just the same, darlin' Marfa. Momma's going to sing you to s'eepy-bye-bye, and rock you nice.'

The small sweet voice filled the silent room with its crooning. This was the lullaby she sang:

'I should worry, I should care,
I should marry a millionaire.
He should die, and I should cry,
And I should marry another guy.'

When the baby was asleep, she laid her down very gently and took up 'Tildy. 'Do you want me to tell you a poem Granny told me, 'Tildy?' she asked her, murmuring.

Mrs. Bascomb stood still listening.

'Simple Simon went a-fishing
For to catch a whale,
And all the water that he had
Was in his mother's pail, and he caught a lovely
big fish and his mother broke it open, and cooked
it, and they had it for supper that night.'

She looked up a little uneasily at her grandmother, and said, 'I know that wasn't just the way you told it to me, but I thought 'Tildy would like it better that way. I know she'd feel so bad for poor Simon if he didn't catch *any*thing.'

There was again the beautiful expression of pity on her face.

Chapter 22

An unusual treat had been promised the town of Gilman-ville for New Year's Day of 1913, six months after Mrs. Bascomb's return from Harristown. The local paper had been full of it; a Winter Carnival Procession arranged by the new Board of Trade, part of their more or less secret campaign against the mail-order houses. Each of the leading stores was to provide a float. Two handsome prizes were offered by the Board of Trade, one for the handsomest float and one for the most amusing. There were to be, so people heard, floats representing 'Winter' and 'Old King Cole' and 'The Triumph of American Ideals' and 'Washington Crossing the Delaware' and others; among which was a comic one, arranged with a floor covered with real ice, on which people, some of them dressed like clowns, slid about, tripping each other up and falling down. Somebody had told Lottie, she said, that one of the well-known lively young men about town took part in this, dressed up to kill as an old maid, with bonnet and corkscrew curls, and every time he fell down he sprawled out his legs so that his skirts flew up and showed his underwear, a perfect scream, white panties with Hamburg edging, enough to kill you laughing. Lottie said she bet that float would get the prize offered by the Board of Trade all right. She could hardly wait, she said, for the day to come. The papers announced that in order not to interfere with morning church-going, the procession would start at precisely two o'clock in the afternoon, from the corner of Prescott and Main Street.

Although the sun rose clear in an exquisite pale blue winter sky, the day did not start auspiciously – it was one of the fated occasions dreaded by the family when a malign destiny descended on Lottie, and when her hair 'would *not* go up decent.' She struggled against fate with all her energy, dressing her hair with religious care, walking around the house afterwards uneasily looking at herself in every mirror to get the effect afresh, and finally snatching it down about her shoulders again with a cry of desolation. Ralph, home for the holiday, took Dids out of doors early to help her make a snow-house, and Mrs. Bascomb kept herself in the kitchen, cooking the gala dinner. There was no mirror in the kitchen.

At half-past twelve they sat down to the table, eating the excellent dinner cautiously as it were, making wary talk which skirted far from any topic likely not to be well received. Mrs. Bascomb was sickened as she often was by the spiritless cowardice they all showed, even Dids . . . yes, Dids most of all . . . in accepting eagerly any conversational lead offered by Lottie, in showing the keenest interest in any story she related, in agreeing ardently with any opinion she chanced to let fall, in sympathizing warmly with all of the many grievances she had against life, especially with the wandering pains which were once more sharp as carving knives, darting over her from her shoulder to her heart, or down her arm. On this day they followed those pains with a condoling interest which they did not always show. They were so hoping on that sunny holiday to create a little enjoyment-in-common! And as one of the means to it they went through the motions of cheerful table talk, their eyes bent placatingly on Lottie's clouded face.

But, luckily when she came to put on her hat, the big black velvet 'Picture hat' with the sweeping white ostrich feather plumes, Destiny relented and the very coil of her hair which had been obstinately out of place proved to have the happiest effect under the dashingly upturned brim of the hat. Lottie was enchanted with it, turning her head this way and that before the mirror to admire it. Her face cleared, and the lowering, threatening sky over their heads lifted and lightened.

She looked extremely pretty and very striking, as she nearly always looked when in her own language she was 'all dolled up for a killing.' Consequently her bright eyes shone with good-nature. Lottie had really beautiful eyes, the lustrous liquid opaque dark eyes which often accompany a trivial conception of happiness. Under her long furred winter cloak, her growing tendency to stoutness did not show as plainly as in thin summer dresses. To the vivid youthful colouring of her face there was now added the conscious brilliance of physical maturity. Her flesh had the luscious pulpy firmness of a completely ripe fruit, and brought water to the mouth of the beholder. Mrs. Bascomb saw it come into Ralph's mouth as he looked at his wife.

He, too, dressed carefully for the outing, reassured by Lottie's high spirits, stimulated to desire for her by her appetizing aspect, enjoying in advance the admiration other men would feel for her, was looking bright and young. Under the brilliant January sunshine, they were a handsome couple as they walked down the street together towards the tram. Behind them, flat-chested and school-teacherish in her plain dark street suit, walked Mrs. Bascomb, holding the little girl by the hand, like a middle-aged nursemaid. But no disembodied spirit could have been more unconscious of her looks and of what anyone might be thinking of her. She had passed beyond all that. There was now no room within her for more than one great question, beating away like a heavy pulse. 'What is the way out? What is the way out?'

In the tram, she and Dids found places opposite to and some distance away from Ralph and Lottie, who talked together with animation. Presently Mrs. Bascomb was aware that Dids was saying something to her. She stooped to listen. 'Momma looks like wed velvet, doesn't she?' said the child.

Mrs. Bascomb looked at her in the astonishment which Dids often caused her by a speech which seemed to her grandmother to show an extraordinary accuracy of observation and expression. What capacities lay dormant in the child! She had never known a child of her age, of any age for that matter, to say such things, to think such things. John's granddaughter! John's acuteness and intelligence struggling towards life. The question hammering inside her head quickened its pulse. 'How can I find a way out for her?'

'Here we are,' said Lottie, standing up, glistening as though anointed by the consciousness that all the men in the car were looking at her.

They found the fringe of spectators already gathering along the paths. Everybody looked at Lottie, and she looked back at everybody, laughing loudly at all Ralph said to her. Mrs. Bascomb noticed that, as sometimes happened, she had forgotten to brush her teeth that morning, perhaps for several mornings. A furry coating of whity-grey matter on her gums was visible as she laughed.

'Why, we're 'way ahead of time,' said Ralph, looking at the clock in the tower of the Congregational Church.

'A half an hour!' cried Lottie. 'Oh, I wonder would I have time to run around to Flackers' and get my muff I left there.'

'No, you'd never do it,' said Ralph. 'But I'll go and get it for you if you want it.'

Lottie flashed a quick, suspicious look at him and answered, 'No, you wouldn't know where to look for it.'

There spread about her like an odour, plainly perceptible to Ralph and his mother, the fact that it was not for her muff that she wanted to go to the Flackers'. Mrs. Bascomb had been startled so many times by Dids' precocious perception of things, that she now glanced apprehensively at the child. But for once Dids was only her age, absorbed in watching some little boys across the street who were 'showing off' for her benefit. 'But it will be only a short time before she too . . .' thought her grandmother, a black pool of despair welling up coldly in her heart.

Ralph and Lottie were exchanging irritated looks. 'You can't do it,' said Ralph imperatively. 'What do you want your muff for, anyhow? Why don't you put your gloves on if your hands are cold?'

In the intervals of her hair-dressing, Lottie had spent the morning in polishing her finger-nails. Ralph knew perfectly well why she did not put on her gloves. Lottie took the question as it was meant, for a taunt. Her stubborn look came into her face. 'I guess I know what I can do,' she said. 'If *you* could do it, I'd like to know what's to hinder me from doing it. I've got more than half an hour. It's not far. I'm going.'

'You'll miss the show,' Ralph called after her, although he did not in the least think such a catastrophe was likely.

But half an hour later it began to loom as a terrifying possibility. The floats were assembling and Lottie had not returned. The three in their excellent places on the street corner, paid little attention to the glittering circus-parade splendour before them. Their eyes anxiously turned back up the street along which Lottie had disappeared. 'Where can she be?' said Ralph in a nervous tone. 'I bet the Flackers' clock is 'way late again, and that's fooled her.'

'Gwannie, why don't Momma *come?*' cried Dids, pulling at her grandmother's hand.

'She'll be here in a minute,' said Mrs. Bascomb soothingly to both children. But she herself was taut with apprehension. It would be too awful to think of, if Lottie missed seeing that procession!

'She'll be late. She won't see it. She'll be awful mad!' said the child, her voice trembling, her eyes turned up toward her grandmother.

'Here, you take Dids. I'm going after her,' said Ralph desperately, pushing his way back through the crowd on the path back of them. 'Maybe I can hurry her up. I bet it's that clock of the Flackers'.'

Mrs. Bascomb knew that he had little hope of meeting her, but that he had not been able to endure the suspense.

A bugle rang out merrily, now, 'Ta *ta!* Ta ti *ta!*' its clear voice like an echo from the silver-shining radiance of the winter day, its gaiety like that in the faces of the well-dressed, well-fed people on the paths. They were laughing aloud now, for the comic float chanced to stand just in front of Mrs. Bascomb and Dids. It was quite as comic as had been predicted. Upon it, amateur clowns, dressed like Charlie Chaplin and Fatty Arbuckle, slid with grotesque gestures of alarmed uncertainty, and the gigantic old maid continually fell down, showing the Hamburg embroidery of her white drawers and squalling in prudish horror. Printed in large letters on the white cloth draped over the wheels of the float were the words:

DEARDORP'S AND GRUENBERG'S STORE SELLS THE CHEAPEST!

COMPARE OUR CARPET SWEEPERS WITH ANY OTHER!

'Why don't Momma come?' wailed Dids, beginning to snivel and wiping her nose with her mittened hand. 'They'll be gone!'

As a matter of fact they now did begin to move. The clock in the tower of the Court House struck two, the bugle blared out its bright laughing, 'Ha *ha!* Ha ha *ha!*' The band at the head of the procession struck up 'Alexander's Ragtime Band,' the old maid clutched a clown to her flat, masculine bosom, shrieking coyly in a bass voice, 'Oh, catch me, mister, before I fall,' and to a chorus of appreciative laughter and applause, the wonderfully successful first Winter Carnival procession of the Gilmanville Board of Trade started on its way.

Dids turned about from it, hiding her face in her grandmother's skirts and sobbing loudly.

The crowd about them stirred and began to trail after the procession, straggling out into the street, the little boys capering to the music, the men's voices chiming in with the refrain. Presently the procession turned the corner and disappeared.

Mrs. Bascomb picked up the sobbing child and turning, saw Lottie bearing down on them from one direction, her face rigid with incredulous horror, and Ralph racing up from the other direction. Lottie had time only to fling out 'The Flackers' clock . . .' when Ralph was upon her, one long arm stretched out to seize her hand. 'Quick, quick,' he panted. 'A man just told me they are going to go along Simmons Street and up Hargreave Hill and if we cut through the back way. . . .'

Hope came to them like a reprieve. Lottie gathered up her long full skirt and ran off beside Ralph, tottering on her high heels as they dashed into a badly-paved alley-way, her ankles turning under her weight, one hand clutching at her great hat careering from one side of her head to the other. Dids wriggled down from her grandmother's arms and bounded over the ground like a scared rabbit.

'Hurry,' panted Ralph, 'hurry!'

They ran insanely, as though they were trying to head off a passenger train from a broken bridge, as though they were escaping from a flood. Dids' short legs soon gave out, quiveringly though they strove to keep up. 'You and Lottie go on,' Mrs. Bascomb gasped to Ralph, 'I'll stay with Dids.'

Ralph nodded without speaking, and putting his arm around Lottie's waist, doubled a corner and was out of sight.

Dids stopped at once (it was evident that it was not at all to see the procession herself that she had been killing herself with haste). 'Goody! Goody! Goody!' she said. 'I'm *so* glad Momma's going to see it.'

The two walked along silently at random, getting back their breath and presently came out on a side street at the far end of which they perceived the procession passing by, the dissonances of the band's unskilful brass softened by the distance to a clear faint sweetness.

'But that isn't the way Poppa and Momma went,' cried Dids, horrified.

162

The same idea had thrust itself into Mrs. Bascomb's head with the same horror. They stood silent and motionless, crushed by the new blow. And now they saw Lottie and Ralph coming towards them and heard the sound of Lottie's voice . . . 'You always get everything wrong! What made you *think* it was going this way? We'd have had plenty of time to catch up with it if we'd gone over by Pelham Avenue. You never get anything straight, never! Almost killing me, hurrying me so, for nothing. I ache from head to foot. You never think of *me!* You'd just as soon I . . .' And then in a clamour against fate, 'That's the way it always goes for *me!* Nothing ever goes right. Here I've looked forward for weeks and weeks in this darned old stick-in-the-mud town, where nothing ever happens . . .' There were real tears glistening in her eyes, rolling down her cheeks.

Once more they trod the glittering snow in the silver winter sunshine, the young couple in front, the grandmother and the little child behind. The air was like sparkling wine, dry and cold. From the million facets of the immaculate snow-crystals, the sun flashed into their eyes a fairy-like splendour. With every breath they drew misery into their lungs and breathed out wretchedness.

Presently the raging voice ahead fell silent, a rancorous silence which lasted the rest of the day and which was worse than any outcries. Ralph walked heavily, his shoulders hunched together, his half-buttoned overcoat dragging and falling into uncouth folds.

When they returned to the house he buried himself at once in the sporting pages of his New York newspaper, a be-damned-to-everything expression on his face. Lottie went upstairs to her room and shut the door loudly behind her.

Mrs. Bascomb looked at Dids, standing disregarded in the hall, her wraps still on, her mittened hands hanging limply at her sides, a stunned expression on her face.

She knelt to unbutton the child's cloak. 'See here, darling, I'm going into the kitchen to do up the dishes. How would you like to come along and blow soap-bubbles? I have a clay pipe for that all saved up for you in the cupboard.'

As she worked at the sink, she cast frequent glances at the

163

child, longing to see the cloud lift from her sensitive face. But although Dids played quietly for an hour or so, her hands in the warm soapy water, she met her grandmother's eyes with an unsmiling gravity, whenever Mrs. Bascomb tried to make cheerful talk with her.

Later in the afternoon, just before she rang the bell for supper, Mrs. Bascomb missed Dids and went about the house quietly, looking for her. The child was nowhere to be seen, until her grandmother, searching more systematically every possible corner, opened the door to her own cupboard up in her attic room. There was Dids, her face very white, squatting down in a heap on the floor.

She looked up at the opening door, a terrible expression of hysteric fear on her face. Her eyes lightened a little when she saw her grandmother. 'Don't tell Momma! Don't tell Momma!' she said in a loud whisper. Mrs. Bascomb was frightened by her aspect. She stepped to the door of her room, closed it, locked it and came back to the child, stooping over her. 'What's the matter, darling?' she said in a quiet tone. 'Perhaps Grannie can make it all right for you.'

The child clutching at her arm with fingers as stiff as bird claws, only repeated, 'Don't tell Momma. Don't tell Momma.'

Mrs. Bascomb lifted her up and saw what the trouble was, a large jagged tear in the front of the child's dress.

'Oh,' she said, looking at it, 'how'd you do that, Dids?' She knew the dress only too well, its cost having been the occasion of an explosion between Lottie and Ralph.

Dids said, her white lips moving stiffly, 'Momma said she'd get the p'liceman to put me in jail if I spoiled this dress. But I didn't mean to. Honest! I never knew, all of a sudden, I heard it tear, and when I . . .'

'I'll fix you up all right,' said Mrs. Bascomb, laying the child down on her bed and slipping off the torn dress. 'I'll get you another one, and mend this one to-night. I can manage it all right.'

'You won't let Momma know? She's so mad already. She feels so *bad* because she missed the procession.'

'No, I won't let her know,' said Mrs. Bascomb steadily.

'You won't let the p'liceman get me?'

'No, I won't let him get you.'

The child's face relaxed, and her head fell back on the pillow.

Mrs. Bascomb went downstairs, encountering Lottie emerging from the bathroom. She looked soddenly at her mother-in-law. The will-to-please had gone out of her face, and with it all her physical charm. She looked as gelatinously unappetizing as a dead fish. Mrs. Bascomb remarked to her, warily, that she thought it might snow some more, received no answer, and watched the door slam shut after her as she went again into her own room.

From the white chest of drawers in Dids' room, Mrs. Bascomb took another little dress, and hiding it on her arm, under a couple of clean towels, in case Lottie might emerge suddenly and ask what she had, she went back upstairs.

The exhausted child on the bed had already fallen asleep. She lay as limp and still as if she were dead, her delicate features pale, her sensitive mouth a little open, a bluish shadow under the heavy shut eyelids.

Her grandmother looking down on her silently, heard in her heart: 'Wherefore I praised the dead which are already dead, more than the living which are yet alive. Yea, better is he than both they, which hath not yet been, who hath not seen the evil work that is done under the sun.'

Chapter 23

YES, there were times when Mrs. Bascomb went to bed feeling – not with her old passionate violence, but in all soberness of measured thought – that the best thing she could do for little Dids was to clasp her close and leap with her into the river where it ran deepest, foam-flecked and swirling, under the Pelham Avenue bridge.

But she did not always feel this. The human soul has as many different ways of laying down its burden, as there are nights in a human life. She often dreaded to go at night-time up to her little attic room, where she felt all the motions of the day gathering in a black cloud to await her entrance; and yet there were other evenings when as she undressed, she wondered at herself for taking things so tragically, told herself she was foolishly impressionable, hysterically so, decided that with less nervous tension and more plain bluff good-nature on her part, the situation would have nothing so tragic in it. 'What ails me to lie down and give up so? Where is my will-power? And my courage? I certainly amount to as much as *Lottie!* I know exactly what I want and I am willing to pay any price for it. Of course I can get it. Now, to-morrow I shall start all over again and this time it shall be *my* moral atmosphere and not Lottie's which shall fill the house. One good laugh will clear the air more than all the good intentions in the world.'

But time after time she made the discovery that Lottie's moral atmosphere was like the perfume she used, far more penetrating and clinging than any mere fresh air could be. Perhaps one good laugh would have cleared the air. The difficulty was to draw a breath free enough for even the shortest laugh.

Shortly after her return she had thought with a cold calculating energy, very different from her old raging frenzies of resentment, 'There is only one thing to do – to resist Lottie with her own weapons, to be as violent as she, and more so. To oppose an instant, active opposition to her tyranny.'

Until she gave up this method, the days which followed were the worst of all, days of loud angry voices, of 'scenes,' of recriminations, of bald, hideous words such as Mrs. Bascomb had sincerely believed impossible for one human being to say aloud to another, of quarrels in which Mrs. Bascomb, to her incredulous horror, lost all her impersonal calculation of effect, lost her head entirely, and found herself capable of wrangling as fiercely and as vulgarly as Lottie.

At the beginning, little Dids had been tragically responsive to the fury of the two women. But at other times, especially after a longer experience of domestic storms the child showed a cynical callousness to their emotion, watching their faces with cool eyes, and beginning shrewdly to play off one against the other. Mrs. Bascomb never forgot one showery April afternoon when as she and Lottie were

166

sitting in the front porch, she had met one of Lottie's flashes of bad temper by a hotter flash of her own. With the gunpowder quickness of all their explosions, it had instantly become a tempest of recriminations, into which Dids had presently emerged from the house, passing their angry voices indifferently, and holding out one tiny palm to the weather as she looked up inquiringly into the sky. "Tain't waining 'tall,' she announced to herself with a quiet satisfaction, turning to take her dolls out for a walk.

Mrs. Bascomb did not know which was the most horrifying to her, the child's suffering from their quarrels or her indifference to them, or the canny slyness she began to show in arranging a little hidden life of her own, in spite of them.

As for Ralph, he took frankly the traditional, masculine attitude of half-amused, half-alarmed and wholly contemptuous aloofness from the disputes of his women folk. Whenever voices were raised, he jumped up, clapped on his hat and disappeared, presumably to a pool-parlour or some other such male refuge, leaving his mother and his wife to fight it out. These were the evenings when Mrs. Bascomb laid herself down on her bed, humiliated to the last fibre of her being.

How long it took her to understand anything! Weeks and weeks had passed before she saw what was, as soon as she had thought of it, perfectly plain to her, that she could never succeed by violence, because violence and anger hurt nothing which Lottie prized, but were fatal to exactly what Dids' grandmother was striving to secure. In fact Lottie rather enjoyed that period of lively dispute. It made a welcome break in the monotony of her inner life. A quarrel with angry words flung about like poisoned arrows followed by a moist, sentimental scene of reconciliation (Dids being called upon dramatically to witness both phases) – such a storm was to Lottie what a rousing good thunderstorm is to a sultry day.

It was finally borne in on Mrs. Bascomb that she could no more protect Dids by fighting about her, than she could protect a garden-plot of delicate young plants by engaging in a wrestling match all over it. No matter who won, the tender young shoots were broken off and trodden under foot into the dirt. She was doing infinitely more harm than good. She would better have stayed away than darken Dids' life as she was doing now.

She paused breathless, and reflected deeply. If not by violent resistance, how?

She must find a way soon or it would be too late, for Dids was taking to herself with the avidity of healthy youth all the life-stuff which was offered to her, so much of which was deadly. It was far worse now than in that first year which she had found so intolerable. Then it had been a mere question of keeping Dids' defenceless little body clean and well-fed. What had caused the misery of that year had been Mrs. Bascomb's resentment at what was happening to her! The Mrs. Bascomb of the present looked back on that resentment in incredulous astonishment. How could it have seemed important to her? She had been like a woman caring for a child at death's door, and troubled about the colour of a ribbon, or the hang of a sleeve.

But even now that she was long past caring for such trifles, now that she could scarcely remember when she had ever cared about them, she seemed to be quite as helpless, because now the peril was so much more acute. She saw herself and Dids as at the bottom of a sand-pit, the sides of which were slowly sliding down to engulf them. Every move she made to put the child in safety brought down the smothering masses upon them with a more deadly rapidity. They kept their unstable equilibrium only when she stood breathlessly still and did nothing at all.

But she had not come back from Harristown to Gilman-ville to do nothing at all. Nothing at all was what had been done during the four years of Dids' conscious life; and the child was half-buried already. With every fresh, coolly executed lie from the little girl, with every vulgar intonation copied with exactitude, with every outbreak of hysteric fatigue or excitement, with every revelation of a new raw spot of secret, sick terrors in the child's inner life, Dids' grandmother felt a spasm of panic. She cast about her for help, more and more hurriedly, more and more recklessly . . . and found no help.

At the end of six months, she told herself that her return had accomplished nothing but that Dids now had more

baths and as a rule ate more reasonable food and went to
bed more regularly. She did not know whether to rage or
weep over the fact that this slight, merely physical amelior-
ation in the child's life had wrought such wonders for her.
The sickly, hollow-eyed little girl, with her days of inexplicable low fevers had disappeared. With the astonishing
vigour of a completely robust constitution, the child reacted to the new conditions. Her very step was different.
She did not walk now, that dragging, grown-up gait ab-
horrent to normal little children, she skipped and hopped
and ran on her tiptoes like a sparrow. Dr. Dewey meeting
her occasionally on the street with her grandmother, gave
her a brief inspection like that of a benevolent ogre, taking
her up in his arms to pull down her lower eyelid, and look
at the colour of her ear-lobes, and examine her tongue and
feel her arms and legs. He professed himself as much
astonished as he was pleased by the change in her. 'I'd got
to thinking of her as a delicate young one,' he told Mrs.
Bascomb, 'but she seems to have pulled right out of that.
I bet a nickel she's getting more decent food and sleep and
fewer movies.' He set her down, told her to trot ahead to
look in at a shop-window of toys, and added to her grandmother, 'And maybe she's not being told so often that the
bogie-man'll get her. Gee! That kid must have the constitution of a horse to have survived what she had there for a
while.' He added with the disillusioned resignation of an
old doctor, 'But then, Lord! that's what most kids have to
survive.'

When in her desperation, Mrs. Bascomb finally tried to
enlist Ralph's help, she found that he shared the doctor's
conviction that their life was about the usual one, and that
Dids' chances were about those of most children . . . 'good
enough, good's the average' was his phrase. Although he
evidently did not understand a word his mother was saying
to him, he was not irritated or impatient when she tried to
talk to him about the situation. She had been struck by
the fact that, since she had renounced any notion of 'what
she had a right to expect' from Ralph, he gave her a great
deal more than ever before of good-nature and natural easy
kindness. Whatever it had been between them which had
made them 'rub each other the wrong way' at every

contact, it had disappeared along with many other elements of the old life.

Looking up at her now from where he lay, relaxed and at ease on the couch, his newspaper in his hand, he listened to her trembling, anxious words with tolerance, but with a very sincere surprise.

'But, Gosh! Mother, what's the matter with you? We're getting along fine now, since you've come back to run the commissary and sort of hold things together here at the house. It was surely fierce there for a while. Lottie's no cook and never pretended to be one. But now, what's the matter? Why, look at Dids. She's as rugged as a bob-sled.'

When his mother tried, hesitating and shamefaced, to say out in words what they lived through every day, he was even more uncomprehending. 'Oh, shucks! We get along all right. Except when you and Lottie get to pulling hair! You're a funny person, I must say, to object to differences of opinion. You hold your end up, all right, I notice. I never dreamed you could quarrel as you do sometimes. Our little squalls, Lottie's and mine, don't amount to anything. We get along the way everybody does, with ups and downs. What do you expect? We're just humans, aren't we? I lose my temper a good deal, I know. And so does Lottie, but what of it? Folks have to get used to that. It's good enough, good's the average. You can't expect a good-looker like Lottie to stick around the house all the time. And she adores Dids. You know how crazy she is when Dids is sick. You take things too *hard*, Mother. You always did. Dids'll scramble along and grow up, the way everybody else does. *She'll* be all right.'

He paused to see if he had talked his mother into a state of mind which would allow him to return with comfort to his newspaper; and saw to his annoyance that, far from that, she was looking even more overwrought and intense than ever. 'Great Scott, women are the limit!' he thought, sitting up on the couch and putting his hand on her shoulder, as a man passes a calming, masterful hand over a high-strung horse, fretting and quivering over nothing. 'Now, Mother,' he expostulated, 'just cool off. There isn't a single thing the matter if you don't expect too much. You've lost your sense of proportion, that's all. Dids is a nice little kid, and a smart one . . . gee whiz! I think rather a lot of Dids myself. But the universe doesn't revolve around her for all that. She's no heaven-born genius, or she wouldn't be in our family. She'll grow up just like everybody else, you know she will, children always do. What's the use of throwing fits all over the block in the meantime?'

His mother caught at his hand, as women do, to feel at least a physical nearness. 'Don't talk like that, Ralph!' she cried. 'I can't bear to hear you.' Her voice was out from her control, high and shaking, as she knew Ralph disliked to hear it. 'You can't be thinking of what I'm talking about. It's not because I think Dids is going to be a genius . . . it's because she is right now, a child . . . entirely dependent on us . . . helpless. If we only give her second best . . . third best . . . whatever isn't too much trouble . . . she ought to have the best chance we can get her . . . not because she's Dids . . . *any* child! It's the principle of the thing! If we don't at least *try* to give them the best we . . . the least we can do is to *try* . . . it's wicked to be satisfied with . . .'

How could she be coherent? How could she finish her sentences when she saw, half-way through each one, that it was not reaching Ralph, that it found no lodging place in his mind. She cast each one away hurriedly, and tried another, vainly. All that Ralph heard was her incoherence, which allowed him to think her negligible; all that he saw was that she was in an uncomfortable, disquieting mood when he wanted to read his newspaper.

He broke in on her now, patting her hand, 'There, there, Mother, take it easy! Take it easy!' (He spoke in the tone he would have used to say, 'So, girl! Gentle now! Gentle!') 'Now, mother, you've gone and got yourself all worked up and can't . . . *was that the telephone?*'

He sprang up with one bound, as if he had been waiting for the bell. His mother followed him out into the hall, and stood behind him, waiting to go on with her appeal. He had not begun to understand yet, had not even begun to listen. She *must* reach him.

She heard him say in a startled, horrified voice, 'Great Scott, man! Thirty-four to eight! For the love of Mike, what happened to our team?'

'Did Gubleman play guard?'

'Well, in the name of thunder, why not?'
'Hell! That's no reason!' The back of his neck became suffused with red.

'The big stiff! What is it to him?' Ralph's free hand, clenched, was shaken furiously in the air to emphasize this.

The thin distant voice which Mrs. Bascomb heard issuing from the telephone squeaked along volubly for some instants now, in a long statement, to which Ralph's entire body became attentive, like that of a hunting animal on the alert

When the voice stopped, it was as if the hunting animal had sprung.

'Look here, Hack, this thing has got to *stop!*' cried Ralph, banging his fist on the wall. 'Something's got to be *done*. What'll happen when the Pitt and Killingworth team comes along will be aplenty. We've got to get busy before that. Listen, where are you telephoning from?'

'Well, listen, you wait right there till I come. I won't be ten minutes. And we'll turn right in and clean this thing up if it . . .'

'Oh, yes, we *can!* We can just raise merry hell till Gubleman is put back on the team and Laville is playing centre again.'

'Oh, dry up, you make me tired. Take it hard? Sure, I do. Why wouldn't I?'

'Shucks! You listen to me . . . nobody ever got anywhere by lying down on the job.'

And then with the true, dauntless Anglo-Saxon note, 'If folks aren't ready to put up a *fight* to have things the way they ought to be . . . why, they get what's coming to them . . . and that's a bum team. We've just got to buck up, I tell you!'

Mrs. Bascomb turned away silently and mounted the stairs to her attic room.

Chapter 24

No suffering which Mrs. Bascomb had ever known bore any
relation to the blackness which hung lower and lower over
her as she began to conceive the possibility that she might
fail, that an idle and inexorable destiny might not in the
least take into account that sacrifice of all herself on which
she had so counted, with a certainty that now seemed so
foolish and naïve. She had given up any attempt to nurse,
or even to keep alive her own ego, set up ferociously as it had
been, its protecting shell broken to bits. She had loyally
made the supreme gesture of renunciation, she had buried
it in its grave, her mind radiant with the divination that its
death and burial were but a planting to new life.

But nothing had happened. Nothing was changed. No
new, miraculous, transfiguring strength sprang up from that
grave. Perhaps it was a lie, the old pious fable that in renunciation was a living germ sure to spring into irresistible
life.

She had been brought up and had brought others up on
those assorted maxims of optimism so much beloved by
Americans, which presuppose (if they do what they consider
to be their duty) the inevitable triumph of what they consider
to be the right. She had never told any child the original
story of Little Red Riding Hood, because it seemed to her
wrong to suggest to children so wicked an idea as that wolves
ever could eat nice little girls. She had used the version,
widely spread by an evangelical organization, in which the
little girl's father, passing by the hut at the right moment,
rushed in and killed the bad wolf and took the child back to
her mother without so much as a spot on her pretty little
hooded cloak. Every year up to Ralph's marriage, she had
made herself a block calendar, much admired and copied by
her acquaintances, on every page of which was a reminder of
the fact that even if the snail was on the thorn, God was in
His Heaven. A good many of these quotations were culled
from the pages of a 'New Thought' publication, of which,
although a consistent church-member, she quite approved.
She had shrunk away from authors whose works seemed to

doubt the certainty of this triumph of the right, or to indicate that there might be any uncertainty as to where the right lay. Such writers had never seemed important to her, rather disagreeable and insincere than frightening, because she had never believed a single word of what they said. She had turned her eyes away from them with the mere distaste she felt for rough words, uttered by unrefined men.

Now it seemed to her that wherever she looked, she saw that all but a fortunate few of the children of the world were being devoured by wolves and that nobody cared, or lifted a finger to save them. No matter what book she picked up, her eyes fell on some black saying of despair. And such sayings no longer lay passive and unreal upon the page, helpless before her disapproval, to be shut up within the covers of the book and forgotten. They screamed aloud at her, piercingly, as if they were the living voices of other human beings like herself. They shrieked in horror as they saw themselves doomed to defeat . . . just as she felt herself doomed . . . defeated by that casual, indifferent evil genius of things in which she had never believed, which she had always thought would slink away from one vigorous gesture of her righteous hand. It mocked at her cynically now, it did not care in the least that she had sacrificed her all.

> 'We shall be winnowed with so rough a wind
> That even our corn shall seem as light as chaff,
> And good from bad find no partition.'

It roared upon her, that rough wind; it burst into her prosaic desk-encumbered classroom, sweeping heedlessly from nothingness to nothingness, carrying with it . . . all alike chaff . . . Ralph, Lottie, and herself . . . indistinguishable motes in the headlong blackness. She could not open her Bible without meeting the lustreless eye of some other human being who had given up, as she felt that she soon must give up, 'For I said in my heart, "that which befalleth the sons of men, befalleth beasts; even one thing befalleth them. As the one dieth, so dieth the other."

' "So doth a little folly outweigh wisdom and honour."

' "The heart of the sons of men is full of evil, and madness is in their heart while they live. And after that, they go to the dead, and the dead know not anything, neither have they any more a reward, for the memory of them is forgotten. Their loves, their hatred, and their envy is perished long ago." '

Upon the middle-aged school-teacher, correcting spelling papers and assigning arithmetic lessons, was poured out all the age-old corrosion of despair. Her poor little recipes for tidy moral house-keeping were scattered like straws in the chaos of her darkling plain. The universe which had been for her a pleasant, smallish room, designed for the comfort of people who tried their best to be nice, now revealed itself to her as a huge, malign conspiracy against any attempt to make sense of it; against any attempt to be nice; above all with a special hostility to any effort towards what she wanted for Dids, the development of the best and not the worst in her. Now she saw that the real world wanted Lotties, and threw its huge weight on their side – 'There is nothing better for a man than that he should eat and drink. A man hath no pre-eminence above a beast; for all is vanity.'

All that was mortal in her sickened and died before the onslaught of these powers of darkness.

But there was something in her now which was not mortal. Her passionate longing to protect Dids stood up straight and strong in the blackness, shining with the unshakable permanence of the divine. It never failed her. It never faltered. She set her back against it and defied the powers of darkness.

So there was no meaning in human life? Yes, there was, her love for Dids was a meaning in itself.

So all was vanity. No, it was not. When one human being could feel for another the undemanding love she had for Dids, there was one thing which was not vanity.

She had never been able to imagine what Heaven would be like, and among the many unavowed distastes of her life had been a secret dislike for the pictures of Heaven she had tried to imagine from what was said of it in sermons and hymns. This had been one among innumerable small hypocrisies which had fatigued and depressed her. Now it seemed to her that she could guess, a little, what a Heaven could be. It might be to feel always what she felt for Dids in those gusts of flame-like love.

But the very violence of this desire to have the best for Dids brought her to the lowest ebb in the moments when she realized that apparently Dids had no chance even for the second best. When she felt this fear, beating its black way about in the corners of her consciousness, she always aroused herself fiercely to fight it. But there were days of low vitality when this defiance sank to a mere, unlovely, snarling refusal to let go the hope she knew was not for her.

She *could* not let it go. She came of fighting stock. Not one of all the throng of her ancestors had seen any beauty in resignation or submission. To admit defeat, to accept it (even when it was certain) had seemed to every one of her fathers as unclean an action as to trail the flag in the mud. Many were the days when this inheritance of idiotic, reasonless resistance was all that stood between her and the black pit. To her intelligence telling her lucidly that she was already beaten, that there was not in all the indifferent universe one single element on her side, she could only gasp out fiercely a 'No! no! no!' as a cornered rat gnashes its teeth.

Chapter 25

LOTTIE's increasing weight fatigued her. Her feet ached often, after she had been in her tight, patent-leather shoes especially now that warm spring weather had come. The family heard a great deal about the intense pain they caused her. Someone in the Baumann family had a story to tell about a cousin who 'had trouble with *her* feet, and it turned out to be some of the bones shoved out of place, and she had to have treatment for it.' Lottie then remembered that on the day of the Winter Carnival when Ralph had so roughly and inconsiderately forced her to race over those badly paved alley-ways, she had felt something give way in both her feet . . . 'the funniest feeling like something sort of cracking, right *there*. First in one foot, and then in the other.'

For a time this theory was fruitful of peace in the house. It provided Lottie with the new topic of talk which was so indispensable for her. But Dr. Dewey, on being consulted, took an X-ray photograph of her feet and reported them completely normal. He suggested wider soles and lower heels and a size larger.

'He didn't half try,' said Lottie indignantly. 'He never pays the least attention to me anyhow. He's never helped me a bit, miserable as I've been ever since Dids was born. He just hates me. I don't care what he says. You could tell the way he talked, right from the first, he'd made up his mind before he ever took his old X-rays. I can *feel* the bones spreading out, as I step on them, right *there*.'

They tried friction with liniment, Ralph and his mother taking turns in rubbing the poor disfigured feet, with their overlapping deformed toes, and their reddened joints, scarred with the results of the innumerable varieties of 'corn cures' which Lottie had tried with fresh faith in each one. That relieved the pain for the time being, if they rubbed long enough; but it was just as bad when Lottie again tried to walk out in her dress-up shoes.

She and Ralph had noisy disputes over her shoes, Ralph contemptuous of their foolish shape and refusing to grant her sympathy for her suffering as long as she clung to them; Lottie volubly convinced that they had nothing whatever to do with the pain, and indignantly claiming as her right, sympathy for her very real suffering. 'I can't wear those horrible Health-Form shoes!' (Health-Forms were what Mrs. Bascomb always wore). 'My feet just aren't shaped like those ugly hygienic shoes. I've always worn shoes like this, and they never hurt me a bit till now, so it can't be the shape. My arch is too high to wear those dreadful, sensible things. I've got a very high arch, naturally.'

She not only insisted on wearing such shoes as she preferred. ('For Heaven's sakes!' she exclaimed in astonished self-defence. 'If a person isn't going to be allowed to pick out her own *shoes*, what next? Somebody'll be cutting up my food for me, I suppose.') But she insisted no less on picking out the shoes worn by Dids, claiming it as a right quite as elementary, 'Who's her mother, anyhow?'

On each of Dids' feet was now a tiny corn, pearl-coloured in the morning after a night's rest, red and angry at night when the pretty, stylish little patent-leather strapped slippers were taken off.

'Those aren't *corns!*' said Lottie defiantly. 'Anybody's likely to have a red spot or two on their feet.' She looked with a bewildered resentment from her mother-in-law to her husband, although neither of them had said a word, and Ralph had only silently taken the child on his lap to look at her feet. 'For the land of love!' Lottie cried out, her voice shaking. 'I never *saw* such a fuss made over nothing!'

They still did not say a word, but to their surprise, Lottie now began to cry as though her heart were broken. 'It's too mean,' she sobbed. 'I don't want anything bad. I just want to have things nice, the way anybody does. And you jump on me for it. You jump on me for everything. It's just fight, fight, fight, all the time if I'm allowed to have a decent thing for me and Dids.'

She went on weeping wretchedly, her head on her arms, her shoulders shaking. 'I like pretty things!' she cried brokenly. 'And you just seem to hate them. I get so tired fighting all the time. I wish I could have a good time, just *once*, and not have everybody down on me for it. I've never been happy a single day in all my life.'

With a practised gesture, Ralph reached unobtrusively for his hat and slid quietly out of the door. His mother had noticed in the evening paper that the basket-ball team from the Pitt and Killingworth ironworks was to play the local team that evening.

Left alone with Lottie, Mrs. Bascomb sat for a moment, struck by the misery in those broken sobs. She whipped up her scorn sharply. She said to herself, looking fixedly at Lottie's broad back, and trying to steel herself against that lamentable weeping, 'It's ridiculous to cry, ridiculous and unreasonable like everything you do. If you weren't so lazy and greedy you wouldn't get so fat, and you could wear the same shoes you used to, without killing yourself.'

But there was a stirring of something else in her mind, which, quite against her desire, fluttered with each of those forlorn sobs. To feel any sympathy for Lottie in this pre-posterous grievance of hers . . . how ridiculous! As ridicu-lous as Lottie was.

She would prove to herself how ridiculous it was. Rising

178

with an effort, for she herself was very tired at the end of the day, she went upstairs and brought down a foot-bath, filled it with warm water in the kitchen and kneeling by Lottie began to struggle with the fastenings of the straps which had fairly embedded themselves in the soft flesh of the instep. She finally slipped them off, pulled off the silk-stockings (Lottie submitting with no comment but an occasional sniffle), and set the puffy swollen feet into the warm water.

Behind the mask of her quiet face, she indulged herself in an exhilarating draught of contempt, as she saw the extravagant relief in Lottie's face.

'Oh, my! that feels good!' she said with a long breath, a beatific comfort coming into her eyes.

'You'd better sit there and soak them a while,' said Mrs. Bascomb, 'while I put Dids to bed. Here's the coloured supplement from yesterday's paper.'

Upstairs as she lovingly washed Dids' beautiful little body, Mrs. Bascomb was calling up all her defences against that uneasiness which had stirred in her heart when Lottie began to sob. She brought out her strongest vitriol to burn away this passing streak of sentimentalism. 'Hurt feelings! Nonsense! Lottie hasn't any feelings. Hurt corns, that's all it was. With her feet in hot water and the last Mutt and Jeff to look at, hurt feelings won't bother her much.'

She splashed the water about Dids in the bath-tub, to drown out those pitiable sobs; and later as she gently rubbed cold-cream into Dids' reddened, maltreated little feet, she told herself savagely. 'Pretending to have her feelings hurt! The minute her feet stopped aching she looked about as hurt as a cat in the cream.'

But all this, like everything else mortal, dropped from her mind as she knelt beside the child's bed, her arms about her.

'Good night, Grannie,' murmured the sleepy child drowsily.

'Good night, dear little girl,' said her grandmother, her prayer for the child's welfare burning up like a flame.

Late that evening she heard Ralph come in and as he

came and went between the bathroom and his bedroom, washing and undressing, she heard Lottie's aggrieved voice, complaining of his lateness and of her own dull evening. Then the bedroom door closed on the two discordant voices, and shortly there was silence.

Mrs. Bascomb thought, as she thought every night before falling asleep, 'If Ralph could only be physically separated from her, even for a short time, she might lose her power over him. It is like an evil spell. Every day he escapes from her. Every night, she takes him back. And every day he is a little commoner, more blunted, more unashamed of himself. How *can* he . . . when he knows Lottie so well! And despises her so!'

She could never get over her stupefaction to see Ralph's eyes, often as contemptuous of Lottie as her own, glisten in the old greed, when he came unexpectedly on his wife in her corset and petticoat, her opulent bosom bare above the dubious lace and ribbons of her corset-cover. Back he fell, into her grasp, each time a little lower.

Mrs. Bascomb had given up any idea that Ralph could ever save himself, turn of his own accord, from this sagging lower, and climb upward. Indeed, at any notion of it, he would probably say, with the new, hard look which sat so strangely on his face, still unripe and boyish, 'Save myself? What sort of "come-to-Jesus" nonsense is that? I'm just in love with my wife, the way men *are* in love. What else do you expect?'

But his mother now made a guess that the bond which held him to Lottie was dependent on ever-renewed freshness of physical contact. 'It's stronger than he. Perhaps it's stronger than any man,' surmised the middle-aged widow, lying on her narrow bed and thinking intently in the darkness. 'But maybe it's strong only as a habit is strong. Perhaps it is more a habit than anything else, now.'

But of course there was no chance of breaking the habit.

The next morning after this, Lottie elected to stay in bed for an hour or so, because her feet were still painful. Breakfasts when Lottie stayed in bed were bright occasions, for which Mrs. Bascomb joyfully paid by the extra work of carrying up a tray.

What fun they had, the three of them at table, relieved from the pressure of Lottie's eyes, light-hearted with their certainty that none of their cheerful pleasantries would be taken literally and amiss.

Ralph was smiling as he kissed them all around and went off to work. Dids' face was bright as she ran out in the yard to play. Mrs. Bascomb began hastily to clear off the table. As she worked, she thought, 'Oh, if Lottie could only take *all* her meals in bed!'

And with the thought, so naturally, so lightly, so almost casually formulated, she naturally, lightly, almost casually slid from one half of her life to the other.

PART FOUR

Chapter 26

LIKE many another dynamic thought, its first appearance was not dramatic. It sank beneath the surface of the conscious to commune in the darkness with a thousand other strong, living, and disavowed elements in Mrs. Bascomb's life. Hurrying to finish the morning work before starting off to school, she was scarcely conscious that it had passed through her mind.

Nor did it show its head during the next week or so, during which Lottie, impatient of Dr. Dewey, was 'trying treatments' given by a 'lady-doctor,' a Chiro practor, whose office was in the wing of her own home on their street. Lottie had very little opinion of lady doctors and Mrs. Bascomb none at all of chiropractors, but Lottie felt that anything was worth trying, and Mrs. Bascomb welcomed anything harmless which gave Lottie something new to think about and provided an innocuous place for Dids to frequent. And, like most of Lottie's trials of new medical methods this did not last long. The lady doctor ended by repeating with unfeeling bluntness just what Dr. Dewey had said, and Lottie left her indignantly.

Her feet continued to hurt her more and more as she thought about them, and the hurt, so she said dolefully, was 'running up into her hip now.' She began to say that she just bet she had sprained a bone in her back that time Ralph had dragged her around so. Ralph remarked one morning at breakfast casually, that he didn't think it could be anything serious. 'Mother used to complain of pains like that running up into her hip. Or was it down into your heart?' he asked. 'Anyhow, you see, she's got all over them now. You never hear her say a thing about an ache or a pain.'

Mrs. Bascomb experienced something of the same surprise she had felt a few days before, at learning through a casual comment of a fellow-teacher that her hair was white, had turned without her noticing it. Why, yes, she remembered dimly that she had been troubled with just such pains as Lottie had now . . . vague, always in a new place, unsympathized with by the doctor.

'I'll bet she never had anything like the pain that goes shooting up my leg into my hip, like a red-hot darning needle,' said Lottie resentfully. 'I wish I could get a decent doctor who would do me some good. You have to have a broken bone before they take any interest in you.'

It sounded exactly like the talk at breakfast on any morning. How could Mrs. Bascomb know that she had already stepped over an invisible line and was already treading a new path?

Nor was there any warning of a change when that afternoon she turned into the front yard and noticed that the hyacinths were in bloom, shaking their clear scalloped bells in the spring air. Mrs. Bascomb wondered . . . her first thought always . . . whether Dids had noticed the arrivals of the new blooms in the flower-beds. One of the many joys Dids gave her was the child's delight in flowers. The expression on Dids' face as she stooped above a newly opened blossom made a lump come into her grandmother's throat.

Mrs. Bascomb stood for a moment looking down on the strong living beauty of the many coloured petals miraculously sprung from out of mud and a brown root. They made her think of Dids. Nearly everything made her think of Dids, but flowers especially. She bent her stiff precisely-clad body to sniff their perfume with the same loving impulse which made her put her arm around Dids whenever the child was near her.

As she stepped up on the porch she noted that although she had had the floor painted last summer, it needed another coat after the winter's storms. She pushed open the door and stepped into the hall, where for an instant at each fresh entry, she always saw hanging a bright green shiny straw hat and a jute tassel pretentiously covered with artificial silk fibres.

She heard voices from the living-room. Lottie's voice, with a new note in it, eager and respectful. 'Yes, doctor, just exactly like you say, a perfectly turrible pain that goes all the way up my back the minute I bear my weight on my feet.'

Mrs. Bascomb thought satirically, 'So it's got to her back! It was only as far as her hip this morning.' She stepped to the door of the living-room to see what foolishness Lottie was up to now.

Dids was sitting on her mother's lap with that intent receptive look on her sensitive face which made Mrs. Bascomb so wretched when it was her mother to whom Dids was listening. Lottie was on the couch talking in her usual pauseless flow. Installed in the arm-chair was a tall, ugly, handsomely dressed man who looked about forty years old. The room was scented with the odour of expensive cigars and high-priced eau-de-Cologne.

His broad, swarthy, rather battered face was bent upon Lottie in an expression of attention as keen as that of Dids. For once Lottie was being listened to as intently as she could have wished. He was looking at everything about Lottie, her pretty plump powdered face, her exuberantly curved body, her glistening nails and slightly dingy hands, her cushiony feet rising between the straps of her patent-leather shoes in little mounds of flesh, over which was drawn tautly the transparent fabric of her silk stockings. To Mrs. Bascomb's surprise in spite of the man's coarse face, there was in this attentive survey nothing of the covetous animality which Mrs. Bascomb so detested in the look bent on Lottie by most men. And yet it made her uneasy. There was in it a cool shrewdness like that of some one mentally adding up figures to see where his profit lay. He was looking Lottie over calculatingly, as if his gaze were sucking out of every detail of her appearance facts which might be to his purpose. Before he caught sight of the newcomer standing in the door, Mrs. Bascomb saw him run a swift glance over the room, which had in it the same sort of suction, as though he were drawing out from each object what there was in it for him.

The instant he saw Mrs. Bascomb looking at him, another expression flashed into his face. It came and went before Mrs. Bascomb could make out what it had been.

Lottie followed the direction of his eyes, saw her mother-in-law, and rose, a little embarrassed as she often was over some small detail of formality in daily life. Although she bought many books on etiquette, she had never learned to perform an introduction smoothly, without looking ill at ease and breathing hard. She said now, 'Oh . . . Dr. Pell, this is my mother-in-law, Mrs. – '

He interrupted her, coming forward cordially to meet Mrs. Bascomb with outstretched hand, into which Mrs. Bascomb's sank as she told herself, 'as if into a feather bed.'

He said in a rich deep voice with acquired inflexions like those of a politician, 'Oh, I know Mrs. Bascomb very well. I passed two years of my childhood in her classroom, in the dear old Main Street School building. I have never forgotten the inspiration it was to come in contact with such a marvellous personality as that of my teacher.' He paused and repeated richly with a grave nod of his head, 'Inspiration. Marvellous personality.'

Seeing that Mrs. Bascomb did not recognize him, he added briskly, in his natural voice, 'From 1892, to '94, it was.'

Up through the years came memory, rising rocket-like and exact, half amused, half horrified . . . why, it was that frightful little guttersnipe of a Maurice Pell, the one who had become the quack doctor.

Her practice in keeping over her real face the quiet mask of school-teacher dignity served her well now. The slight start she gave and the flash of recognition which came into her eyes might have been mere recollection.

'Oh, yes, Dr. Pell. I remember you very well now,' she said, sitting down, her hands in her lap, on her guard, suppressing a laugh at the solemn pretentiousness of his manner. 'Inspiration! Personality!' When she remembered the incessant warfare between them during the two years he had afflicted her schoolroom!

Lottie explained volubly. 'Mrs. Flacker told me that her cousin's wife had been just wonderfully helped by Dr. Pell's treatments.'

Dr. Pell deprecated praise with a white smooth hand which Mrs. Bascomb remembered as grimy, chapped, and given to appropriating what did not belong to it

'And this afternoon as I walked along with Mamie,

didn't she see Dr. Pell coming out of the Williston House
. . . he's treating Elizabeth Williston's spine, she fell on the
ice it seems more than a year ago. I hadn't heard a thing
about it but Gertie told me that it seems she was coming
out of their back door with some water for the hens and
there was some ice on the back steps and. . .'

Mrs. Bascomb did not like the profound scrutiny which
Dr. Pell was giving to Lottie as she talked. It made her
nervous for anybody to examine Lottie so closely. Why did
he think it worth his while? She broke in, cutting Lottie
short – no conversation could proceed without interrupting
Lottie. 'What do you think, Dr. Pell, about the trouble my
daughter has been having with her feet?' She was really
curious to see how he would carry sail in a medical conversation.

A grave expression came into his eyes, which were black
and set slightly close together, with streaks of yellow in the
white. But before he opened his mouth to speak, he turned
to look at Mrs. Bascomb. She had been startled by the
intentness of his look upon Lottie; she was much more
startled by the searching glance with which for an instant
he probed into her own eyes. People never looked at her
any more. She had grown used to the almost complete
invisibility of the useful middle-aged woman. Not for years
had she encountered an eye sufficiently interested in her
to make it hard to keep her mask in place. It was nothing
to anyone what sort of woman she was becoming.

But apparently it was something to Maurice Pell. He
had almost penetrated to her real feeling for him, before
she could thicken to opacity her usual expression of effaced
quiet and look back at him with an expression in which
there was nothing but expectation of what he was about to
say.

But still he sat as if meditating in a baffled silence, his
eyes on hers. 'What's he up to?' wondered Mrs. Bascomb.
It was Lottie, surprised by his silence, who spoke first.
'Why, it's perfectly wonderful how the doctor has put his
finger right off on what's the trouble with me, and none
of those other doctors came anywhere near it. It's just
what I've been telling you and Ralph from the first. I felt
it the very day Ralph was dragging me around so rough. I

slipped on the ice, sort of. I can see the very spot now, as we went around the corner of the alley between Fulton and Melton Street, I think it was, or maybe it was Fulton and Grant, because I remember there was the back door of the Pelman House there – yes, I guess it was Fulton and Grant, and when I slipped, I felt something give way in my back, right here.' She put her hand on the small of her back. 'Just as plain. The doctor asked me if it didn't feel like a string stretching, and it did, exactly like that. And it seemed, so Dr. Pell says, I must of slipped one little corner of a bone past another or something. The doctor says it's a perfect wonder I've been able to get around at all. He says any other woman would of been flat on her back in bed long ago. But I told him I never was one to give up to things. I *will* keep going, you know, no matter how bad I feel. And there is so much to *do*. I didn't feel I ought to give up to it. You know how it is with housekeeping, doctor, a woman never sees the time when she can really take a rest. And it seems, the doctor says, that all that turrible pain in my feet comes from the nerves running down the backbone. I can feel them when I step on my foot. You know this mórning how I was saying to you and Ralph, how when I bear my weight on my foot it shoots up perfectly awful into my back.'

She went on and on as she did when no one stopped her.

Neither Mrs. Bascomb nor the doctor stopped her. The doctor kept his eyes watchfully on the face of his old teacher. Mrs. Bascomb's eyes were bent fixedly on her hands in her lap.

Of all that Lottie said, one phrase only had meaning in it for Mrs. Bascomb. 'Flat on her back in bed.'

The phrase had burst with a shout in her mind. Poised there on the vast dusky surface of forgotten and rejected thoughts, it was excitedly peering and fumbling about for another idea which belonged with it, which was its pre-destined mate, its other half. What was it? What was the submerged thought which Lottie's phrase had grazed? Mrs. Bascomb sent down her grappling irons deep; she felt its heavy weight, there below the surface. With a blind pull she had it almost up to the top where she could see it

. . . her attention wavered an instant . . . it was gone. There was nothing but Lottie talking.

She whipped herself to the effort again, but in spite of the strain she put upon herself she could feel her flagging memory letting slip that faint recollection which had stirred sluggishly at the casual touch of Lottie's phrase.

She was aware too that Dr. Pell was waiting for her to make a comment, to show her hand before he showed his. She must really say something soon.

Dids had one of her dolls in her arms and bored with the talk had been amusing herself by seeing how far she could let 'Tildy slide down her mother's knees and still recover her. Growing careless now she did not make her rescuing grab quickly enough, and 'Tildy fell from Lottie's lap to the floor, her wooden head making a clicking knock as it struck.

At the sharp unexpected rap, Mrs. Bascomb gave a nervous start . . . and as if she had with it suddenly pulled from the depths that nebulous idea, there it was, as clear as when she had casually formulated it, weeks before, but grown to monstrous proportions since the day she had let it sink into her mind. It towered above her now like a djinn let out of the bottle. She looked up at it horrified. It seemed to bear no relation to her, so changed from her original idea was it. Yet she knew that every atom of its vast bulk came from her own heart.

And yes, yes, yes, it was the predestined other half of Lottie's phrase. Like chemical elements, the two leaped together, uniting with a Day-of-Judgment flare. And instantly they became something else, which neither of them had been before. What they had become . . . what they were now . . . made Mrs. Bascomb's heart stand still, frozen.

When the doll had dropped, Dr. Pell hastened to pick it up, caressed the battered wooden curls, smiling hard at Dids, and said in a playful tone, 'Poor dolly! Doctor'll make her cracked head all right. There! Doctor'll rub some liniment on it. *Now*, she's all right again,' and returned the toy to the pleased and flattered little girl.

This had taken perhaps a moment, perhaps two. When he once more leaned back in his chair with his appraising

189

look on Mrs. Bascomb, she was ready to speak, although her breath came quickly and her voice was uncertain.

Was it *her* voice? Was it really she who was saying those words? Where did they come from so fluently?

She said earnestly: 'Why, doctor! Really something the matter with her spine! That's awfully serious, always, isn't it? My poor daughter! How she must have suffered! And none of us with any idea it was anything alarming. How could we have imagined it was just some little trouble with her feet!'

Lottie's breath was taken away by this unexpected personal triumph. At the compunction and sympathy in her mother-in-law's voice, her eyes filled with tears. 'I kept *telling* everybody it was something perfectly turrible,' she said, blowing her nose and looking comforted. 'But nobody'd believe me. They thought it was just foolishness. That's why I've been keeping up so. I'd have given up long ago only I knew everybody would think it was laziness.'

'Well, it was certainly providential you happened to find Dr. Pell,' said Mrs. Bascomb, wondering if those could possibly be the familiar tones of her own voice. 'We'll do just as he says, of course; follow any treatment he prescribes. So you think, doctor, that she ought to give the spine absolute rest, lie in bed for a time?'

At this Lottie drew back, looking a little alarmed, but Mrs. Bascomb heard her own voice saying urgently, 'Yes, yes, Lottie. No sacrifice is too great if it is for your health. We can manage it. We can get some one to come in day-times to stay with you, till my school is out for the summer – it won't be long now till vacation.' She turned back to the doctor, 'My daughter is so afraid of making trouble, but of course nothing ought to stand in the way of her health.'

She turned back to Lottie. 'You mustn't think,' she said, 'that you would need to go to the doctor's office for his treatments. They bring even the X-ray instruments to the patient's house, now, don't they, doctor? I'm sure the doctor could manage your daily treatments right here, without wearing you out to go and come.' She turned back to the doctor, afraid that she was talking too fast, saying too much, but not daring to stop for fear she had not said enough. 'What *is* your treatment for this sort of trouble, Dr. Pell?' she inquired. 'Violet rays? Or manual manipulation?'

Now, at last, she stopped, her heart fluttering.

Now, at last, Dr. Pell spoke, his reassured eye going from one woman to another, his rich voice rising and falling with preacher-like flourishes at the end of his phrases. He paused after each of his long sentences, looked magnetically from one pair of candid eyes to the other and repeated with a grave nod of his head the word he considered the most important, or the one they would be least likely to recognize without repetition. 'Homolateral flexion,' he said as a priest says 'In sæcula Sæcularium' and 'Afferent neurones,' and 'Brachial plexus.'

The three women folk listened, docilely, respectfully until Dids dropped off to sleep, 'Tildy in her arms.

When Lottie began to look a little frightened, Mrs. Bascomb slid her chair nearer and took Lottie's soft hand in hers. It was the first time she had ever made a motherly gesture towards Lottie. It did not seem to her now that she had really made it, any more than that she had really said all that she had to the doctor. But reality reached her for an instant when she felt Lottie's moist, clinging fingers close gratefully on hers. At this a mortal horror of herself slid its poisoned dart far down below the numbed unreal person acting in her place, far down to what she quite recognized as herself, responsible for what she was doing. What *was* she doing? What was she doing?

What she was actually, materially doing was to murmur respectfully at intervals, 'Yes, doctor. Yes, doctor,' as she sat there in her dark tailored suit, a look of estimable dignity on her middle-aged face. Presently she heard herself saying, 'Of course we want to do whatever is best for my son's wife,' and crowded down the writhing sickness in her heart.

As he looked at the two women, the doctor's yellow-streaked, close-set eyes glistened. He threw out his chest, pulled down his waistcoat, put the tips of his fingers together, deepened his voice, 'Pervascular cell-infiltration,' he said rotundly, and 'pathological changes in the cerebro-spinal fluid,' and 'scattered analgesis.'

'Oh, I do believe you understand my case!' said Lottie, weeping a little with relief and satisfaction.

That evening as Ralph opened the front door, his mother was just coming out from the kitchen door, a dish in her hand, on the way to the dining-room. The hall light fell full on her face, and little as Ralph noticed the alterations in his mother's expression, he was shocked by her aspect. 'Great Scott, Mother!' he cried. 'What's the matter? Anything happened to Dids?'

No, he saw Dids there, rosy and calm, putting 'Tildy to bed.

Lottie however was not visible. Where was Lottie?

So awful was his mother's pallor – it was more than pallor – that there passed like a lightning flash of insanity through Ralph's mind the notion, 'Mother looks as though she had killed Lottie.'

'Where's Lottie?' he asked loudly.

'Upstairs in bed,' said his mother in a grave voice.

With the dish still in her hand, she told him, standing there in the hall, that a new doctor had come to see Lottie who understood her case and, sure enough just as she had always thought, she had some real trouble with her spine, which might be due to an accident unperceived at the time, or might (after examination he had been unable to say which was the cause), which might have come from trouble at the time of Dids' birth. 'You know,' said Mrs. Bascomb, 'Lottie has never been quite strong since then!' She went on to tell him that Lottie was to give her spinal cord absolute rest, perfect immobility in bed, which the doctor hoped, together with daily treatments, might help her.

Ralph was sympathetic. 'Why, poor old Lottie,' he said. 'And I was so sure it was those fool shoes she wore. Funny, only to-day at lunch a man was telling me about his wife, how she had such trouble for years after childbirth. I remember Lottie had some symptoms of this before. She used to have electric treatments for them, but they didn't help her much.'

Following helplessly along a familiar brain-channel into which this had led him, he went on to say, 'Gosh, how those treatments did . . .' and stopped abashed.

Mrs. Bascomb remembered too. 'That's another thing I want to tell you, Ralph,' she said. 'I want you to let me bear the expense of this treatment. It's always hard for a young man just starting in life to have sickness in the family. I have plenty of money for the present, and I'll be *glad* to take care of this.'

Ralph was deeply touched, and in a gesture rare with him, put his cheek up against hers, and kissed her. 'That's awfully good of you, Mother,' he said gratefully.

Mrs. Bascomb crushed down the mortal sickness which rose in her and turned back into the kitchen. But she paused and putting one hand up against the side of the door and leaning her head against her arm as though she were tired, she added, 'Oh, one more thing, Ralph. The doctor says that Lottie ought to have the bed to herself. So for the present, I've moved your things into Dids' room, and made up the bed for you.'

Ralph was startled. 'As bad as that?' he said (but his mother saw nothing in his face beyond surprise). 'But where'll Dids sleep?'

'I've set up a cot in the other end of the attic for her. That would make,' said Mrs. Bascomb, dropping her arms and going on into the kitchen, 'that would make a nice little bedroom with a dormer window on each side. We might have a carpenter fix it this summer.'

'Great Scott, Mother, Lottie's going to be up and around before this *summer*, isn't she?' cried Ralph.

His mother hastened to reassure him, 'Oh, I suppose so, yes.' But a moment later she remarked over her shoulder, 'Still it would be handy to have another bedroom available. And the view from that south window in the attic is lovely.'

After dinner, Ralph and his mother went upstairs together to see how Lottie was. The light from the hall shone in through the open door of her bedroom so that after standing on the threshold for a moment till their eyes grew used to the twilight, they could see Lottie lying sweetly and soundly asleep, one hand under her pretty rounded cheek.

At least that is what Ralph saw. When he glanced at his mother, he perceived that her eyes were directed to quite another part of the room as if someone were standing there. Surprised, he looked back into the room. There was nothing at all in the place where his mother was gazing.

'What are you looking at so?' he asked her in a whisper, startled by the strangeness of her expression.

She turned away instantly. 'Nothing,' she said.

There was something so unrestful in the air of the house that evening that Ralph felt uneasy and awkward. He tip-toed around like a man in a house in which an operation is being performed, who is afraid that he will not seem to highly-tuned feminine nerves sufficiently stricken and apprehensive.

He longed to sit down in his arm-chair and read at his leisure the report of an important prize-fight that had taken place in Montana the evening before, but thought it would not 'look well' if he did. After fidgeting about he stepped out into the kitchen to offer to help his mother with her evening work.

'No, no,' she told him quietly, in her usual formula, 'after your day's work you need a quiet evening.'

She was washing her hands as she spoke, brushing them very hard with the stiff brush used for cleaning vegetables. As he stood there shifting his weight from one foot to the other, she finished, rinsed them thoroughly, dried them on the roller towel, and immediately plunged them into the dishpan full of soapy water. 'What a funny thing for Mother to do,' he thought. 'She's getting to be a regular old crank about clean hands.'

He said, 'Why, Mother, what's the matter with you? What'd you stop to wash your hands for, right in the middle of washing dishes?'

'What did you say?' she asked him over her shoulder in a tone of surprise, and in the face she turned him he read that she had not known till then that she had been washing her hands.

He repeated queerly what he had said, and after a silence she answered in a low tone, 'Oh, I don't know, I get absent-minded sometimes.' She added, 'There is something you can do for me. Carry the garbage pail out to the back porch.'

It occurred to Ralph as he stepped outside with the pail

194

that since he was to sleep by himself he could seem to go to bed early and lying there comfortably with the drop light beside him could read in peace the account of the prize-fight. He had always enjoyed reading himself to sleep, but of course since his marriage he had fallen out of the way of it. It gave him pleasure to feel it possible again.

'I'm pretty tired, Mother, that's a fact,' he said, coming in from the back porch. 'And I believe I'd better tuck myself up early.'

With the paper under his arm folded small and with a furtive backward look to see that his mother did not chance to see it, he bounded up the stairs two steps at a time, and into his own old boy's room, closing the door behind him with a feeling of liberation from womankind. The bunch down at the office had been saying that the third round of the fight had been a corker.

Presently having read himself into a delicious state of drowsiness, he put out the light and went sweetly to sleep. He did not take this latest upset of Lottie's at all seriously. Women were always doing that sort of thing. Lottie'd clamber out of bed all right and step as lively as the next one the first time a Douglas Fairbanks movie came to town.

In the night he awoke to see the light streaming in through the cracks around the door. Mother must have left the hall light on. He rolled out sleepily and opened the door.

There, in her nightgown, her white hair in curl-papers, her thin withered face bent over the wash-bowl, stood his mother washing her hands.

Ralph was neither timid nor imaginative, but he distinctly felt a little cold chill trickle down his back.

'For Heaven's sake, Mother!' he shouted, reassuring himself by the loudness of his voice.

She started, snatching her hands out of the water, and began hastily to wipe them dry.

'What do you think you're doing anyhow?' he asked her, his manner rough because he felt shaken.

She smiled at him wanly. 'I . . .' she began to sidle past his door on her way to the attic stairs. 'I think I must have

195

had a dream,' she proffered, putting out the hall light and going on up the steps.

Ralph went back to bed thinking, 'Why, Mother's getting positively *queer!*'

And later on as he turned over in his bed, he thought, 'Notions. She's got real notions!'

And then, 'Folks do get queer as they grow older. Seems though Mother was hardly old enough for that, though. How old *is* she? Let's see . . .' Never having had any head for people's ages, and less than no interest in past family history, Ralph found it hard to get a starting point for his calculations. 'Let's see, when were she and Father married? I was born in '87 . . .' (That was one date he was sure of). 'They must have been married in '86 or '85. I don't believe they'd been married so very long. Well, now suppose it was '85, and she was twenty-three or four when she was married – it's 1914 now, how long ago is '85 . . . or did I say '86?'

But now he was asleep again.

In the morning, he remembered his unfinished calculations and having a boyhood recollection that his mother's wedding date was engraved on the locket she always wore about her neck, he asked casually at the breakfast table, 'Oh, Mother, let me see that photograph of my father in your locket, will you? Old Mr. Watson spoke to me the other day about how much Dids' eyes are like. . .'

He stopped, looking at his mother's face in alarm, fearing that, as a man so often unwittingly does, he had stepped into one of those feminine storm-centres, which it was the aim of his life to avoid. His mother had flung up her head with so distraught an expression that he feared a detested emotional scene.

But to his astonishment and relief, his mother said nothing at all for a moment, and then in a quiet tone, 'I'm not wearing that any more.'

He was surprised. He had never seen her without it. 'Why, you had me fix the chain only last Sunday,' he said.

'Yes, I know. I know. I . . . I only took it off last night,' she said.

Ralph backed hastily away from thin ice, incurious of

how it came to be thin, only thankful that he had not broken through. 'It's no matter. I just happened to remember what Mr. Watson said.' He looked at his watch. 'Great Scott! It's half-past eight a'ready. I must beat it.'

Chapter 27

THE Baumanns were surprised to see their neighbour, Mrs. Bascomb, coming across the fresh grass of her well-kept little lawn, before breakfast.

'For goodness' sakes, world without end!' called Gertie, who was doing up her hair in great hurry, her boss requiring inhuman promptness, 'what's old Mrs. Bascomb doing this way so early?'

'Coming *here?*' said Mrs. Baumann, putting down the coffee-pot to go to the window.

'Maybe they're out of something, sugar or coffee, and she's coming to borrow it,' suggested Mrs. Rader, Mrs. Baumann's old aunt.

Her remark met with the scoffing contradiction which was the usual fate of her comments on life, when they received any notice at all. 'Old Mrs. Bascomb *borrowing!*' said Gertie. 'She never borrowed so much as a pin in all her life. Lottie's the little old borrower of that family.'

'Land, yes,' said Mrs. Baumann. 'It's a good thing for us that Mrs. Bascomb come back to keep house for them. We wouldn't have had a thing left in the house that Lottie hadn't taken the new off of.'

Mrs. Bascomb was now in their front porch, knocking at the door. The three women within took various attitudes of unconsciousness and called neutrally, in answer to her knock, as if that were the first indication they had had of her presence, 'Come right in.'

She didn't look so very well, they thought, as they nodded to her with the respect they felt for a woman who was one of Gertie's old teachers, a good church member, and who used better English than they did.

With her first words they saw why she looked so poorly. She'd had a bad night, it seemed. Lottie was sick. She

197

must be really sick this time, if old Mrs. Bascomb paid any attention to it. Trouble with her *spine!* What do you think about that? They were thrilled, savouring the excitement of hearing such important news so early in the morning. Dr. Pell had been there. Oh, the Dr. Pell that there was so much talk about. It *must* be serious. They dropped everything to gather round her, fascinated by hearing of 'symptoms.' Mrs. Bascomb went into detail, too, just as they liked when sickness was being talked of.

'My!' said old Mrs. Rader with relish, 'my!'

'For goodness' sakes!' said Mrs. Baumann, 'you don't say so!'

Although Gertie had never till that moment thought of Lottie's spine, she could not now resist the natural human impulse to cry out, 'I've kept *telling* Lottie she'd have trouble with her back yet,' and having said this she believed it. They had not been so much interested since the McDonald family down at the end of the street had typhoid fever, and the health officer had found a dead hen rotting in their well and made them seal it up and use city water, and pay for it too.

They would have liked to hear about Lottie's sickness all over again, and for Mrs. Bascomb to go into yet more detail of what the doctor had said, and what Lottie had said, and what she had said; to have the opportunity to say again that they had noticed Lottie hadn't been feeling real good lately. But Mrs. Bascomb had no time to spare. 'I must hurry back and finish getting breakfast,' she said. 'I just came over to see if Mrs. Rader couldn't help us out till Lottie is better, or till my school is out, when I can be with her at the house all the time.'

They looked at each other in astonishment to have their queer, negligible old aunt's name mentioned by anyone For many years she had been an unconsidered member of their family, and no one had ever turned to her for anything. She was lame, past sixty, not very bright, rather lazy, and not at all self-assertive, so that she herself had come to disregard her existence as completely as the others, and never dreamed of salvaging from life anything more than three rather grudgingly provided meals a day, and the old clothes nobody else would wear. At Mrs.

Bascomb's suggestion that she might be useful to someone, she looked as bewildered as if she had been asked to run a locomotive.

Mrs. Bascomb explained, 'I don't mean to do any of the housework. I can manage that by getting my charwoman to come twice or three times a week, instead of once. And you wouldn't have Dids to look out for, either, because I can take her to school with me. She's almost of legal school age, as it is, and I know Miss Sterns in the first grade will take her in for a while. They have a sand table in there and lots of picture books. Dids will be all right.'

'But I thought Lottie wouldn't let Dids go to school so young,' said Gertie.

'Oh, it wouldn't be what you'd really call "going to school." And it wouldn't be for the sake of having Dids *learn* anything. Just to keep her from bothering her mother. Lottie must have perfect quiet about her.'

'Well, of course, you wouldn't want a kid racketing around,' admitted Gertie.

Mrs. Bascomb turned again to old Mrs. Rader, whose mouth was hanging open in amazement. 'You see it won't be hard. I just want you to sit over there instead of here, so that Lottie won't be alone in the house. Just to have somebody there, to take her any little thing she wants, like a glass of water, or an orange, or the newspaper when it comes. And I wouldn't expect you to put yourself out so for nothing. It would be a great help to me, and worth two or three dollars a week. More, if you would be willing to keep the fire going in the range, and about half-past eleven to put on some potatoes, or macaroni, or something like that to cook, so I'd find it done when I got back at noon. I'd buy chops or steak on my way home, and I could have lunch ready in no time.'

Mrs. Baumann looked at Gertie. She did get awfully tired of having doddering old Aunt Agnes around under foot every single minute of the day. Wouldn't it be great to have her out of the house for a while. And if she were making money like that, she could be made to pay for her own shoes. Henry always grumbled so about having to buy Aunt Agnes' shoes.

Mrs. Rader looked dazzled. Two or three dollars a

week, maybe more. She hadn't seen real money like that for years.

'I would need you from ten minutes to nine to ten minutes past twelve, and from half-past one to a little after four,' explained Mrs. Bascomb.

She looked anxiously at Mrs. Rader whose mouth was now closed firmly.

'Well, I might,' said the old woman reluctantly, with the accent of one hard pushed to an unwelcome proposition.

'She could *try*, I suppose,' said Mrs. Baumann dubiously, as if conferring a favour.

'Thank you so much,' said Mrs. Bascomb appreciatively. 'And do drop in as often as you can, won't you, to visit with Lottie. She'll want to hear all the news. Tell the Flacker girls to come over the first time you see them. They'll do Lottie good. She ought to have lots of cheerful conversation.'

'Yes, sure I will,' said Gertie, delighted at the thought of having such interesting news to tell.

At a quarter-past four, Mrs. Bascomb and Dids, hurrying along the path, saw a car drive up beside them. 'I'm on my way to your son's house,' said Dr. Pell, throwing away his cigar and opening the door. 'Can't I take you two ladies along?'

Mrs. Bascomb stepped in and took Dids on her lap. 'Thank you, doctor, I'll be glad to save the time. And I wanted to have a talk with you too.'

'About our patient,' said Dr. Pell. 'Yes. Yes, indeed. About our patient.' He bowed his head to her with the air of a man about to deliver a compliment and said, 'I am glad to see you too, before I see her. What you report would have great weight with me. I can see that I am going to depend greatly on your judgment in this case, on your judgment, yes.' He spoke in the grossly cajoling tone a man uses to someone he thinks slow of understanding.

Mrs. Bascomb opened her hand-bag and took her handkerchief. 'She had a very bad night, doctor. I was up half a dozen times, hearing her turn and toss, and although she was not actually awake, she was moaning in her sleep.

And this morning she looked badly. Such a strange grey colour.'

'That's one of the well-known symptoms,' said Dr. Pell magisterially, 'that colour is. Well-known symptom.'

('Yes,' thought Mrs. Bascomb with relief, 'he takes me for an imbecile.') Aloud she said, 'And she seemed so weak. I felt she ought to have something to keep up her strength, and I insisted on her eating a hearty breakfast, although she said she didn't feel like eating anything at all.'

'Yes, that's quite right,' said Dr. Pell, 'we must keep her strength up. Keep her strength up.'

'And at noon, doctor, I took her up a tray of good nourishing food. There's no dieting necessary in spinal trouble, is there?'

'None whatever. Let her have what she feels like,' said Dr. Pell generously.

Mrs. Bascomb opened her bag, put her handkerchief back in and snapped it shut, immediately thereafter opening it once more and taking out her handkerchief. 'Doctor, of course you with all your experience . . . you must foresee . . . My son's wife is young and full of life. It may be hard to keep her quiet enough. She may not realize how serious spinal trouble is. Do you . . . ?' Keeping her eyes on the doctor's face, she fumblingly undid her bag, put the hand-kerchief back in and shut the bag with a click.

The doctor told her that of course, as she had thought, he had out of his long experience foreseen just this difficulty; but the same wide experience had taught him, he said, that it was not a serious one, that to keep people quiet was much easier than she thought. 'I've had so many cases I know. It's all in getting used to it. I've noticed it with many patients, especially women. The beginning is the only time that is hard for them. If they only stay quietly in bed for a few weeks – not the least bit of trouble after that. Why, Mrs. Bascomb, many people who aren't in pain, actually come to enjoy staying in bed, enjoy it. It's positively,' said Dr. Pell, drawing up to the path in front of Mrs. Bascomb's house and opening the car door politely for her to descend, 'it's positively often hard to persuade them to get up again. They seem to get the habit. And of course a person like you with your experience of human nature and your intimate knowledge of her likes **and** dislikes, you can be a great help to me in keeping **our** patient quiet and contented.'

'I'm sure I want to do everything I *can*,' murmured Mrs. Bascomb, nervously getting out her handkerchief again.

Chapter 28

'THERE,' said Mrs. Bascomb cheerfully, setting the tray down on a stand, and moving the handsome new bedside table in front of Lottie, propped up on her pillows, 'I do hope I have thought of something to tempt your appetite.'

'That tray would make a stone image sit up and whet his teeth,' called Ralph from the bathroom. He came to the door wiping his hands, his nostrils dilating at the delectable blend of odours; freshly made coffee, crackling sausage, browned toast, raspberry jam. 'We never have such spreads as you, Lottie,' he added as he turned away. 'Mother spoils you for fair.'

'Poor Lottie,' said Mrs. Bascomb. 'It's the least we can do for her, to get her good things to eat. And if I didn't make a special effort, she wouldn't eat enough to keep a bird alive. The doctor says she must eat, to keep her strength up.'

'Here goes for keeping up mine,' called Ralph over his shoulder, as he disappeared down the stairs. 'Come on, Dids. *Breakfast!*'

On another morning. 'I've a surprise for you, Lottie,' said Mrs. Bascomb, lifting the emptied and lightened tray. 'I bought a sofa yesterday at Dustin and Westover's – they're having a sale, and they delivered it last night. It occurred to me all of a sudden, that it would make such a nice change for you every day, to be moved over to it, from the bed. We can set it next the window, and you could look up and down the street ever so far.'

'I'd *love* that,' said Lottie eagerly. 'I believe I could see as far as the tram in Elm Street from that south window.'

Mrs. Bascomb had another idea. 'Oh, I know. I'll go and get those old field-glasses my father used in the Civil War. They're quite strong. I believe they'd bring Elm Street and the tram as near your eyes as the Baumann house is now.'

Lottie's face brightened. 'Say, wouldn't that be great!' she said. 'I could see everybody that got on or got off the tram, and they'd never know anybody was looking at them.'

'But do you suppose you could bear your weight on your feet that far?' asked Mrs. Bascomb, measuring with her eyes the distance between the bed and the window. 'You know how it hurt the last time you tried. And Dr. Pell's orders are so strict.'

Lottie looked ready to cry with disappointment. 'I don't believe but what I could,' she said. 'How do my feet look this morning?' She thrust out of bed for inspection one white rounded foot. 'Are the bottoms as bad as ever?'

Mrs. Bascomb looked at the sole, touching with her finger the flesh from which the naturally thickened skin was now peeling off in large, yellow-white flakes. It was almost as soft to the touch as the flabby calf of the leg, jelly-like in its pendulous white skin.

'They look pretty queer,' she said dubiously, and then with a sudden inspiration, 'Oh, how stupid of me. We can push the sofa right beside your bed every morning. Ralph can roll you over on it, and then push it over to the window after you're on it.'

'Why, of course,' said Lottie, relieved.

Summoned, Ralph went through the programme laid out for him. As he heaved Lottie over on the sofa, he said, laughing, 'Gosh A'mighty, girl, you're no feather, do you know it? I bet you've put on twenty pounds this month you've been in bed. And you weren't the champion light-weight before.'

'That's nothing,' said Mrs. Bascomb, 'everybody who has to stay in bed for awhile puts on extra flesh. But it goes right off. Lottie'll run it off quick enough once she gets up.' She added, 'Now, Ralph, push the sofa over there by the window,' and followed after him with the bed-side table. 'I must beat it,' said Ralph. 'Lottie, you can watch me get on the tram and see if I do it right.'

Mrs. Bascomb hurried to get the field-glasses and Lottie adjusted them in haste, crying out delightedly, 'Oh, I can see everything, just as *plain*. I can see the buttons on Ralph's coat. It's wonderful. I can see who's getting into the tram with him, just as if I were there. Oh, if I turn it, I can see Schuster's grocery store. I can see what vegetables they've got out in front. Why, I can see Emery's drug store! There's a lady going in. It's Min Flacker's sister-in-law. She's had that blue suit of hers re-modelled.' She gave a long sigh of content, and turned the screw slightly to make the focus better. 'This is certainly *great!*' she said.

Mrs. Bascomb moved rapidly along Main Street between the plate-glass show windows with the roving eye of a hunter in the woods. In front of the Curtis shoe store it fell on a pair of crimson velvet slippers trimmed with swansdown. 'Ah,' said Mrs. Bascomb to herself and turned into the store.

Emerging later with a package under her arm, she encountered a loitering young lady, dressed in crackling taffeta silk of a bright blue, ornamented with many rows of slightly tarnished gilt braid. On her head was a lavishly flower-and-fruit trimmed hat; on her feet were many-buttoned black velvet shoes, the heels of which were a little run over, the toes of which were rather worn.

'Oh, Minnie, how do you do?' said Mrs. Bascomb cordially. 'I was just hoping I would run into one of you girls, and get you to go home with me. I try to get some of Lottie's friends to drop in every day. She's always so interested in all the news.'

Although Mrs. Bascomb's cordiality no longer threw Miss Flacker into the acute bewilderment it had caused her at first, she could not, she told herself, 'make it seem natural to be walking along so easy and sociable with old Mrs. Bascomb.' Miss Flacker would not have admitted for an instant that she wasn't as good as Mrs. Bascomb or anyone else in town, but she had always felt, helplessly, a social difference between them, which had been rigorously though silently marked. And she enjoyed the absence of it now. She didn't mind a bit being seen with somebody to whom all the important people of town nodded and said

'Good afternoon,' with respect – the president of the bank, the editor of the newspaper, the wife of the proprietor of Clarke's Dry Goods Store, and the ministers. Yes, she was quite willing to go to see Lottie as often as she met Mrs. Bascomb to suggest it.

Even without this agreeable preliminary, it was fun to go to see Lottie. There were lots of other things she liked about those visits, that all Lottie's gang liked – mostly things to eat. Mrs. Bascomb surely did lay herself out when Lottie's friends came. She always made lemonade or fruit punch, or chocolate with whipped cream (none of them would have liked tea except as an accompaniment to the evening meal) and she always had more kinds of cake than you could shake a stick at; angel-food, with eleven egg-whites in the recipe, or rich chocolate cake, or nut cake with thick gooey marshmallow filling, or coconut cake with a creamy frosting almost as thick as the layers of the cake. Mrs. Bascomb was sure a grand cook! There was candy too. Always a box of it opened, by Lottie's sofa, a new kind every time you went, the kinds with well-known trade marks, not the cheaper kinds sold in bulk in the local candy stores. And there were always the latest jig-saw puzzles too; and Lottie had all the newest records for the gramophone Ralph's mother had bought her, all the popular screams from the Broadway shows. And a detective story, and a Harold Bell Wright novel and all the illustrated magazines in the world lying around.

Lottie's visitors often told Lottie that she hadn't got anything to grumble at, even though her back might be pretty bad. (She told them it didn't hurt her hardly at all as long as she lay perfectly still). They went back rather wistfully to their daily grind after having spent an hour in the bright room where Lottie lay enthroned in gorgeous silk *négligés* (such as they hadn't supposed anybody but the wax models in the department stores ever really *wore*), doing just as she pleased all day long, with somebody to wait on her and to order around, for it was scandalous how she ordered them all around, even Mrs. Bascomb herself. As they trudged back to their early rising and incessant wage-earning, or their kitchens and exciting husbands and turbulent children, they sometimes said it seemed funny how things happened to some folks so they got just what suited them best. There was Lottie, always had been the laziest thing in creation, could lie around doing nothing for longer than anybody on earth; and now things were arranged so that was all she *had* to do. And get sympathized with into the bargain. Although of course, they hastened to add (using the phrase exorcisingly as Sicilian women would have fingered their pronged fork of coral) of *course*, they knew what a perfectly terrible thing it was to have spinal trouble.

They spoke perhaps more often and more enviously than of any other one detail in Lottie's life, of how perfectly elegant her hands were nowadays. With all the time in the world to manicure them, and never any work to harden or soil them, Lottie's hands attained in their eyes an unearthly beauty. They hung over her wax-white fingers and rose-red nails with cries of admiration which brought a happy smile to Lottie's lips, especially when one of them laid her own firmly muscled, strongly marked lean working hand beside the fine-textured, pink-and-white skin of the invalid's. To her friends, Lottie's hands were an ideal visibly realized. They often said, 'You just can't imagine anything more *perfect* than Lottie's hands are. They actually don't look as if they'd ever done a single lick of work in all their life.'

Chapter 29

DR. PELL came to see the invalid three times a week: Tuesdays, Thursdays, and Saturdays. Those days did not seem to Lottie like other days of the week. They did not even seem like each other, for the doctor had a different treatment for each one, so that when Lottie woke up on Tuesdays, her first thought was that this was the day for her electric rays; and on Thursdays, that she would have her vibration; while the very air of Saturday morning was coloured with the expectation of her weekly massage.

Dr. Pell did not call the Saturday treatment 'massage,' and he did not like at all for anyone else to use that name. But the explanations he gave of his own nomenclature of 'psycho-manual manipulation' were so complicated that no matter how many times Lottie heard them, she never could repeat them in the report which she gave to her friends of all the doctor did and said to her. She always spoke of it as a 'massage,' adding hastily and guiltily, 'though that's not *really* what it is at all. It's *much* more than just massage.'

It was what she liked best of the three treatments, although she enjoyed every detail of the ritual which surrounded them all. Tuesdays had their special significance, because they came three days after the last visit of the doctor, instead of two, so that she had a little forgotten the sound of his step, the rich dignified odour of cigars and eau-de-Cologne which preceded him up the stairs, and the ring of his wonderful voice as, followed respectfully by Ralph's mother, he came into the sick-room, rubbing his beautiful white hands and inquiring solicitously how she had lived through the days since he had been there last.

Lottie was filled to astonished gratitude that there was somebody who went right on caring such a lot about how she felt. Her feelings were rather an old story now to the 'girls,' her visitors; they listened, of course, when she told them about changes in her symptoms, but they no longer listened very hard, and the moment she stopped they began callously to tell her about their own symptoms. Ralph frankly would no longer go through the motions of listening. And Ralph's mother, being always there, knew how Lottie felt without Lottie's having a chance to tell her.

But Dr. Pell really cared; you could feel that from every expression in his eyes and voice. The first part of every visit was a detailed report of everything that had happened to her since he had been there before; how she felt after each meal, what had agreed with her digestion, and what had seemed to 'lie heavy'; how she had slept; and every wandering sensation up and down that delicate spine of hers. He often took notes on these reports, listening intently, and interrupting her for an instant to write something down in a leather-bound note-book, the beautiful smell of which was part of his aroma.

It gave Lottie occupation to store up items for the report

to Dr. Pell. After every meal she bore in mind that she must know how those particular viands had affected her, so that she could tell the doctor; and always after sitting up against her pillows for an hour or so, she stopped whatever she was doing to take serious thought as to the sensations in her spine and legs.

Sometimes she had the most curious and interesting things to report – a numb place, all of a sudden, right *there*. Or needle-like pains suddenly radiating from a spot which had never before given her any trouble.

'Where was that?' the doctor would ask eagerly, as if that gave him a clue, and when she showed him the spot on her back or thigh, he would tap all around it with his finger, pressing hard from time to time and asking her if it hurt more there, or here. He always wrote her answers down in his note-book.

She knew when the interrogation was over, because the doctor closed his note-book, snapped an elastic band over it, and rising said something like this, 'Well, well, we'll have to see what our rays will do' (or 'vibration' or 'psycho-manipulation'). 'We'll soon have you out of here, doing the family washing and scrubbing the floors as good as new.'

Lottie felt an alarmed fatigue, almost a faintness, at the brutal mention of those frightfully energetic tasks of active life. When it was such an exertion for her to hold her arms up long enough for her to do her hair, however could anybody stand up for hours, washing dishes and making beds and lifting mattresses! At the very idea she shrank back and lay more heavily upon her soft pillows.

But she had great faith in the doctor's treatments, which certainly did make her feel perfectly elegant. On Tuesdays he brought with him a large, handsomely finished velvet-lined box, from which he extracted shining nickel and red rubber tubes and a strangely shaped hollow glass utensil. This last, after he had fastened the complicated apparatus together and connected it with the electric current, suddenly glowed intensely with a bodeful blue flame, and gave off a low roaring noise, of which Lottie felt the vibration in her diaphragm. He pulled down the blinds before he summoned this unearthly blue fire so that it was the only light in the room, lighting up weirdly the doctor's serious swarthy face and the elderly pallor of Ralph's mother.

Then Lottie turned on her side and the doctor applied the diabolical glass tube (astonishingly enough, it was only comfortably warm) up and down her back in long sweeping strokes. 'Do you feel the rays penetrating the flesh?' he would ask after a time. 'Because I can make them a little stronger if you can bear it.'

Thinking hard about whether she felt them penetrate her flesh, Lottie became aware of various odd sensations which she hastened to report. 'It feels like somebody sort of tearing silk up and down my spine,' she would say, over her shoulder.

'Ah!' said the doctor, 'I'll reduce the current a little. We don't want to overdo the matter.'

Yes, Tuesdays were a little awesome and exciting to Lottie. She liked them but she was rather glad when they were safely over.

Thursdays were different. That was vibration day. The doctor brought along another expensive velvet-lined case, out of which he took another apparatus, culminating in a thing like a hammer, with a rounded head of hard rubber. When he turned on the electric current, the hammer began to vibrate a great many things to the minute (the doctor told her how many, but she could never remember it, repeating it to her visitors as, 'forty times a minute . . . or was it four hundred?'). With this, Dr. Pell proceeded to strike her back millions and millions of little soft blows only stopping when she became quite breathless and implored him for a respite. 'You must stand all you can,' he told her, pressing its viciously hammering head up and down the broad expanse of her back which he pushed and pulled about with a dry, professional indifference to its smooth whiteness. ('I suppose he sees so many,' thought Mrs. Bascomb to herself, noting the absent coldness of his eye on Lottie).

What Lottie liked best was his Saturday massage. For Lottie, that was the pivot of her week. Everything sloped up to it and died away from it. It took her all that day and part of the next fully to emerge from the hypnotic peace into which she was plunged by the incessant passage over her back of the doctor's strong firm hands, oiled to satin smoothness by the creamy ointment which he rubbed into his palms.

That ointment was the doctor's special secret and invention. It was compounded of many rare elements, he explained, one of which had a pungent spicy smell, entirely different from any other odour that ever came into Lottie's life. She had great faith in the ointment, and began to feel relaxed at the first whiff of it when the doctor unscrewed the silver top of the crystal receptacle in which he kept it. He always lowered the window blinds before beginning the treatment, and lowered his voice too.

'Psychic calm is an essential part of the "cure,"' he explained. The low hushed voice he used on Saturday mornings was for Lottie as much part of the treatment as the strange, delicious odour of the ointment, and the sliding, thousand-time repeated pressure of the doctor's wonderful hands up and down her spine. 'Now you are going to relax and be utterly at peace,' he told her quietly and masterfully, over and over, in a murmuring voice. 'This is taking away all the pain and restlessness, away, away, entirely out of your body, and leaving you filled with quietness. Soon you will feel a great repose stealing over you; you will soon be at rest. At rest . . . Quite at rest. . . .' Towards the end, as his hands moved more slowly, his voice died to a mere inarticulate murmur, which was like a part of the twilight in the room, the silence in the house.

When he had finished, he turned her passive body gently, till she lay on her side, and then with a final, silent nod of leave-taking, melted from the room, closing the door behind him so quietly that not the faintest click broke the hush which brooded over Lottie as she lay floating in a lassitude which seemed to her like peace.

By the doctor's orders no one was allowed to enter the room until she called for food. Sometimes she lay thus entranced for many hours of half-consciousness.

It was certainly not longing to be up on her feet, rushing around, washing dishes and sweeping floors, which filled Lottie's mind on Saturdays.

Mrs. Bascomb took care always to be on hand during the doctor's visits. Not continually in the room, although often stepping in and out. But always in the house. She let him in when he came, taking his coat and hat like a well-trained maid, and when he descended the stairs after his visit, she was always there to let him out of the house. He paid less and less attention to her as time went on and as his tri-weekly visits became a deeply grooved habit for all of them. At first he did not notice that his monthly cheque was made out by old Mrs. Bascomb, instead of by the husband of his young patient, but Dr. Pell was not very fastidious about who made out his cheques; and little by little as the years went on, that monthly cheque came to look to him like a dividend from an investment, as regular, as impersonal.

Mrs. Bascomb, however, did not by any means acquire such matter-of-fact acquiescence in Dr. Pell. The days when he had been there, she could not eat, sitting at the table serving Dids and Ralph and trying to conceal the fact that she herself was taking nothing. Generally they did not notice this, but sometimes Ralph said, 'Now, Mother, you haven't taken a thing but your cup of tea. What's the matter with you?'

'I don't seem to feel very hungry to-night,' was her usual murmur as she hastily began to cut up something on her plate, 'but I feel perfectly *well.*'

Once in awhile Ralph insisted still further, saying with a rough affection, 'Gee whiz! Mother, you'll blow away if you don't eat more.'

Once or twice she had not been able to control the spasm of revulsion which contracted her throat as he pressed food upon her.

'Leave me alone, Ralph,' she had cried, with a heat which startled him into silence, 'I couldn't choke down a mouthful if my life depended on it!'

Chapter 30

THERE is no human relationship more intimate than that of nurse and patient, none in which the essentials of character are more rawly revealed. Mrs. Bascomb had not taken care of Lottie for two months before she discovered that she had had several total misconceptions as to Lottie's nature.

One of them was of vital importance. Mrs. Bascomb had feared that of all the elements in her active life, Lottie would miss most acutely the covetous masculine admiration of the men with whom she joked and laughed on the street corners, the physical proximity of men who desired her, the excitement of Ralph's infatuation for her. To Mrs. Bascomb this had seemed the logical, the only deduction to be made from Lottie's actions – that she was 'crazy about men.' Here was a lack which would be hard for Mrs. Bascomb to supply.

But Lottie revealed herself quite otherwise in the interminable tales to which Mrs. Bascomb now lent an anxiously attentive ear. Never before had she even tried to listen as Lottie wandered on through her incoherent and tedious reminiscences. But now, needing desperately every hint she could get as to the springs of action in her patient, she not only listened, she asked questions, she drew Lottie out. She learned a great deal about Lottie, learned far more than, for the time, she knew what to do with. Many of the facts thus revealed were not relevant to her purpose. These she thought she flung to one side and discarded. But as no one can ever fling quite aside anything once heard and understood, all this information about Lottie and Lottie's life sank into the cup of her consciousness where it slowly dissolved and added its colours to what it already found there.

For the present, Mrs. Bascomb, hard driven by an urgent need, pounced only upon facts which would guide her through her immediate difficulties. The most important of these facts was Lottie's attitude towards men. Mrs. Bascomb's astonishment was so great as to be grotesque when she discovered that, far from having an obessed need for the proximity of men, Lottie did not like men as much as she herself did; that, as a matter of fact, Lottie hated men and feared and despised them. And for very good reasons. Many and sickening were her grievances against them from her little girlhood up, which now came out in the wandering recital of her life. Bitter and resentful was the philosophy which Lottie had constructed for herself out of her first-hand experience. Ruthlessly and justifiably predatory was her creed about them, 'No matter how soft they talk, they only want one thing out of you. And they want to get that for nothing.'

Of Mrs. Bascomb's own feeling about men, the one she had taken for granted was universal with mature, experienced women, there was not a trace in Lottie. Mrs. Bascomb had supposed that women who had worked beside men in wage-earning occupations, or who had lived with men as with other human beings in a family, felt towards them, as a matter of course, a natural human mixture of friendliness and exasperation. But Lottie's feeling had no friendliness in it; and although she felt plenty of exasperation, she thought it expedient to hide this warily from men, because if you ever showed them anything you really felt, they took advantage of it. For Lottie, men were simple creatures who exploited women if women did not do the exploiting first.

Very early Lottie had found that it was profitable to tantalize men, that she could obtain from them by playing on their senses and not gratifying them, a number of desirable things which she saw no other way of obtaining – candy, for instance, as established and tyrannical a habit for Lottie as opium or morphine for an addict, and pretty clothes such as she had forced from Ralph by alternations of exciting and denying him; and opportunity to indulge her great natural indolence of body; and admiration . . . but she really enjoyed women's admiration more, thinking it harder to secure and more discriminating. Above all she had extracted from this fencing with men (and from no other source) the element in life which she most craved and was most helpless to create for herself – the sensation of what she called 'something doing,' of some stir in the air to combat the terrible ennui which dropped, stifling as poison gas and quite as terrifying to Lottie, upon her every unoccupied moment.

Looking at Lottie from the outside, Mrs. Bascomb had naturally supposed as a logical conclusion of what she saw that Lottie had a strongly sensual nature, exigent in its demands on her. But as the outlines of what Lottie really was began slowly to emerge from her cloudy loquacity, Mrs. Bascomb seemed to discover that what she had seen leaping up in Lottie's eyes to answer the look of awakened animality in men's, was not hunger of the senses in the least, but deadly helpless boredom, craving anything to break its killing monotony, and finding nothing available but this easily kindled spark in men's eyes.

It was not until she had been beaten almost sodden by the iteration of Lottie's talk that Mrs. Bascomb perceived that Lottie herself was beaten sodden by the bareness and emptiness of life as it had been open to her. She looked back now on incidents of the past and held the key to what had been baffling mystifications – for instance, Lottie's insane disappointment at missing that preposterous winter-carnival; her aimless gloomy pacing about the house on the few stormy evenings when no outside event had been planned for her; her moodiness and discontent, her grasping at any external event, no matter what, as material for talk.

Bringing before her again the hideous day of the winter-carnival, Mrs. Bascomb saw for the first time that those had been tears of real despair which had furrowed the powder on Lottie's cheeks.

Such childishness was of course beneath contempt, but she was quite aware that it was grist to her mill. She realized that she had taken a long step forward when she thus learned the necessity of keeping boredom out of Lottie's sick-room, as nobody had ever kept it out of her life, and she saw as a tool in her own hand, Lottie's helplessness to keep herself diverted even in her own way.

She was making progress every day in discovering what Lottie's own way really was; and every discovery was a surprise because she found nothing strong and sinister to deal with, as she had taken for granted, but an incoherent triviality which went beyond her powers to imagine. What Lottie wanted was, after all, what everybody wants, 'something to happen.' And because nothing ever happened inside Lottie, every break in the ghastly monotony of her life must come from the outside. But in that outside world the only human beings who ever had any interest in Lottie were the men whose senses were pleased by her appetizing aspect. Step by step, Mrs. Bascomb's logic led her around to a wholly new reading of her daughter-in-law.

Sitting hour after hour, 'helping' Lottie with her jig-saw puzzles (which she loved but had not continuity enough of purpose to finish) and listening to the flow of Lottie's talk, Mrs. Bascomb discovered that Lottie was not only not strongly sensual, but that she had the essential un-imaginative coldness of puerility. Indeed to the normal woman beside her, who had known happy love in marriage, Lottie seemed actually lacking in ordinary human feeling towards the sensual side of life; never apparently conceiving of it as anything she might share and enjoy, always speaking of it cynically, as a rather disagreeable but serviceable tool which fate had placed in the hands of women – their only one. But Mrs. Bascomb gathered, Lottie would have preferred to secure her candy and pretty clothes and admiration and 'something doing' without having to bother so much with this inexplicable, convenient, but tiresome desire of men, 'always to be pawing at you,' as she said with her unstudied spontaneous vulgarity of phrase which constantly made Mrs. Bascomb's gorge rise.

Such was life as Lottie had found it. Nothing but playing on that masculine desire had as she said, 'ever got *her* anything.' Mrs. Bascomb felt a naïve amazement to find that Lottie reciprocated heartily the secret contempt which men felt for her and her kind. 'Men are such nasty things,' was an expression which often fell from her lips in a matter-of-fact tone as if that summed them up. That this was all there was to say on the subject seemed her honest conviction. Apparently in their contacts with her they had consistently, sooner or later, lived up to this conception.

This feeling seemed to go back as far as Lottie could remember. The unprotected childhood and girlhood, revealed in her rambling stories, showed her as too early and too harshly initiated into the physical realities of life, ever to have any romantic feeling for men or boys, even to have had a natural human liking for one. She had apparently found out before she could remember that it was too dangerous a game 'liking' a man – if indeed she had ever seen one to like. In Lottie's experience you did not like men or enjoy them; you 'worked them' for whatever you could get out of them . . . expensive treats if they had money, excitement that made you forget the dullness of life, if they were inflammable; and you were never to go far from a safe and swift road of retreat from them, or they'd work you, instead of you them. 'Poppa's doing night-work at the mill and having to sleep most of the day, and Momma's dying when I was a kid, I tell *you*, I had to learn to look out for myself,' she often said, recounting some episode in the long campaign of her self-defence. She often added aggressively, 'I'd been engaged lots of times, but I was a good girl till Ralph came along, though the Lord knows how I managed. They began picking on me and bothering the life out of me before I was out of the Grades . . . I was so big for my age and all.'

In all the millions of words to which Mrs. Bascomb listened, as Lottie meandered her way back through the narrative of her life, there was never one which told of ordinary, disinterested human treatment from any man. 'I used to think it was because the nice ones wouldn't have anything to do with poor girls,' Lottie said, 'and I used to feel awful bad about being poor. But now I guess they're all pretty much of a muchness when you come to know them. I often look at a minister, talking so proper, or at the picture of the President of the United States that everybody thinks so much of, and say to myself, "Oh, shucks, you can't fool me. I know what you're like inside, I bet."'

Little by little it came to Mrs. Bascomb with a final shock of absolute surprise, that Ralph was the occasion of this last grinding bareness of disillusion. 'I did sort of use to think,' said Lottie, 'that Ralph was different. When he first came along he seemed so refined compared to some of the roughnecks you see, kind of like what you read about in novels. I thought Ralph was in love with me *nice*, like he pretended to be. And I certainly was crazy about

Ralph. He's the only man I ever really fell for, honest, the the only one. But it's turned out just like all the married girls tell you. There's only one way to hold your husband, and that's by keeping your good looks, and wearing fancy underwear, and making him keep on *wanting* you. And I tell you, you get pretty sick of it, especially when you see him other times, looking at you like you was the dirt under his feet. Ralph never talks to me nice, you know about *things* . . . the way you would to anybody you really thought anything of, that you thought had any sense. And when I try to talk to him, it nearly kills him, he's so bored. He'd rather go to a ball-game any day than stay with me an hour. And he makes no bones of showing me he would. And yet, any time he happens to feel like making love to somebody again, he expects me to be just as crazy about it as ever. That's the man of it! But of course, it's up to a wife to hold her husband's love, or people think she's fallen down on her job. Everybody is always sure it's *her* fault. You have to play the game the way men like it. It's just another example of what us women are up against.'

Once as if running on with the impetus of her unchecked talk, further than she meant to go, she said something which gave Mrs. Bascomb a glimpse back into an episode of which she had always had quite a different interpretation. 'There was a while there, I was about crazy when I found out Ralph didn't have any real use for me. I thought I'd die if somebody didn't want me . . . more than just to make love to. I was frantic. I didn't care *what* happened if only somebody would like me nice, like in a book. But I soon found out how horrid men are! Ralph's a gentleman, if he *is* a man.'

Mrs. Bascomb found herself contemplating with stupe-faction the possibility that the story told Ralph by Lottie on the horrible night so long ago might in its general outlines be somewhere near the truth . . . that it was of Lottie's own accord that she had drawn back, and come racing panic-struck back to Ralph and Dids.

Mrs. Bascomb had more than enough to think of every evening up in her attic room, as brushing her thinning grey hair, she took account of stock, set in order the impressions of the day and turned anxiously over and over the strangely rearranged elements in her life. She often felt bewilderment shut down thick about her like a cloud, over the dim and crooked path which she must somehow find and follow. But she continually struggled out of this by telling herself sternly that she must keep her head clear, not think of anything but how to get through the next day, or she would lose her way in the welter of every day's confusion. Little by little as she concentrated thus upon only those elements of the situation which were vital to her at that moment, some things began to show clearer outlines. She began to know on what she could count.

The first summer of Lottie's invalidism was not passed before she was saying to herself, 'Now, I've put my mind on the things Lottie wants, I miss my guess if I can't get more of them for her than she ever got for herself.' She looked at herself in the mirror, flat and old-womanish, in her long, plain, high-necked night-gown and found that among the crude ugly anxieties and calculations which clashed together in her mind, there was again room for that harsh humour which was so new an element in her life. 'I may not look like a hair-oiled stock salesman,' she reflected ironically. 'But I bet I can beat anyone of them at the job of satisfying Lottie . . . because I can do what no man ever can, I can keep my mind on it.'

She was often half frightened by such grim unlovely pleasantries, gazing darkly at the hard woman in the glass, secret as a hidden well. Who was this strong unscrupulous woman now living in her body?

She thought during this period that she permitted to enter her mind of Lottie's endless confidences, only what would help her to understand and dominate the present situation; but the mass of her new information had already coloured her plans for Dids. Before she fell into the death-like sleep of physical exhaustion her last thought was, very often, 'Dids must have plenty of interests, plenty to do, plenty of fun . . . no loiterings, no empty hours . . . no boredom, no idleness.'

She thought that her mind was filled by the discovery, 'Lottie wants from man no more than I can give her.'

Chapter 31

ALTHOUGH this fact had seemed all-important and decisive to her, she found as time went on that it by no means assured Lottie's acquiescence in the *status quo*. Vary Lottie's life as ingeniously as she might, fill every day full, hour by hour, of things which Lottie liked and had never before had in sufficiency, there were stormy hours when Lottie 'hated everything,' her invalidism included.

'I'm sick and tired of all this nonsense,' she would say, gloomily, pushing away the candy and the easy fancy-work, and the detective story, and the newspaper with the long account of the latest murder, and the gramophone records and all the other playthings. 'I don't believe that old doctor understands my case a bit. I believe I could get right up this minute and walk off as good as ever I did.'

Sometimes Mrs. Bascomb tried to divert her attention. 'Wouldn't you like me to brush your hair? The High-School girls in our building have a new way of doing it up, with a roll back from the . . .' Sometimes this would be accepted, more often savagely rejected. 'No, I don't want you to *touch* my hair,' Lottie would burst out rudely, 'I'm tired of having my hair done. I want to get up and get dressed and go down-town and have a soda, and I don't believe but what I *could*.'

From the first Mrs. Bascomb had had an intuition never to oppose Lottie in anything, and never did so. 'Well, suppose you try,' she would say. 'Maybe the doctor *is* wrong when he says it would strain something in your back. They don't know everything, doctors don't. I had a cousin once, with a bad back, that the doctors bothered her about, and she got right up and walked around, just as she liked in spite of them.'

'Did it hurt her any?' asked Lottie.

'Well, she ended by being a paralytic, but I'm sure I don't know that her getting up had anything to do with it. It mightn't have, you know.'

'I've a good notion to try, anyhow,' Lottie returned moodily, but on a less energetic note.

'I won't tell the doctor if you do,' said Mrs. Bascomb, 'and if it does make you any worse we needn't let him know the reason.'

'I bet I *could*,' Lottie repeated, adding as she often did, 'First thing I know, I'll get the habit of laying down all the time.'

'Oh, you'll soon be up and around,' Mrs. Bascomb always reassured her. 'The doctor thinks his treatments are having such a good effect. But if you don't feel you can wait any longer, why don't you try to stand up, just for a minute, and take a step or two. Here, I'll help you.'

Many times in that first year, they went through the same manœuvres; Lottie sweeping the bright silk quilt from her prettily shod feet (for Mrs. Bascomb always bought her just the sort of foot-gear she loved, high-heeled, pointed, narrow-soled), Mrs. Bascomb solicitous, acquiescing, slipping her arm under Lottie's armpits to help her to rise, telling her, 'Now the minute those shooting pains in your legs begin, lean on me, just as heavily as you like.' Lottie, her mind full of the recently mentioned shooting pains, slowly bearing the weight of her obese body on the strengthless flabby white flesh of her leg muscles. Sometimes she gave up at once, sinking back on the sofa with a groan. Sometimes she persisted in trying to take a step or two, only to find the connections between her will and her nerves rusty and creaking. 'Why . . . goodness me! I can't lift my foot at all. You don't suppose I'm paralysed now, do you? I can't budge it! There! I've pushed it out a little way . . . oh! OW! how it hurts! I can feel something giving way in my back! Quick! Quick! Let me down before it breaks!'

Then a long storm of despairing tears and laments. 'I'll never get well! Oh, I did want to go down-town and have a soda! Why don't the doctor help me! I might as well be dead as the way I am! I wish I *was* dead! I'm just as good as laid out in my coffin this minute.'

She often clung to Mrs. Bascomb, as she thus sobbed, her arms around the older woman's neck, her head buried in her mother-in-law's bosom, like a weeping child.

Over the shining dark head, Mrs. Bascomb looked straight before her, her face grey and grim.

PART FIVE

Chapter 32

D IDS had always loved her home, of course, from as far back as she could remember it, the way everybody likes his own home, but there was no part of it so dear to her as something that wasn't in it at all, and that was the view from the window of her bedroom in the third story. Being up high, of course, it would have had a nice view, no matter how the ground around the house had been; but as it was, with the back yard sloping away so steeply, it was beautiful. The tips of the tallest trees down there at the bottom of the ravine were below the level of her window-sill. You looked out across them, feathery, always stirring in the wind, over to the far other side of the wide ravine, where the distant railway trains ran like toys against the sky. Then your eyes swept up along the open curve of the sky, back safe to your own little room, to your own little self. But you'd been quite a journey; and you knew that you could always take it again with one sweep of your eye out of the window. Dids liked that feeling of a free circling swoop off far, far, and yet with a safe solid shelter to come back to.

Dids was glad her room had always been up there. Not really always of course, for Granny had told her (Granny liked to talk about old times as old people do) that when she was a baby she had slept in what was Father's room now. There hadn't been any Dids' room then at all. It had been only a part of the attic and nobody had ever thought of looking out of the window, down, across, and then up, up, up. It was all hers. Nobody else had ever had it any more than anybody else had ever had her hands and feet before.

Dids always felt in the back of her mind the airy, lofty quiet up there, as she skipped and hopped about the rest of the house, coming and going to school, helping Granny with the housework, or sitting in Mother's lovely, flower-filled room playing cards with her or helping her with a jig-saw puzzle. Dids liked all the rooms in the house, the way you do rooms you've had good times in, and every room seemed like a different person to her. But her room was herself, and she loved to get back to it, after one of her good long days of play and work.

The hall was sort of middle-aged and quiet, not specially handsome of course, but friendly and peaceable looking, and when you opened the door and came in from the big world, it seemed to say 'Hallo there! Glad to see you back.' Of course, Dids supposed, everybody's front hall looked like that to them, when they got back home. That's what it meant to have a home. There was usually something of Father's hanging up on the hat-rack, and perhaps, if Granny had come in before you, one of those Granny-hats that you could tell were Granny's a mile away.

Beyond the hall, the living-room positively smiled at you as you took off your things and hung them up (Granny was terribly particular about hanging things up the minute you came in). Perhaps it seemed to smile because the piano was open with all its white teeth, waiting for you to sit down to make it sing. And Father's arm-chair with the floor lamp standing near it looked comfy too. You'd seen Father so often sitting there, the big sheets of the newspaper strewed around him, having such a good time reading the paper. The living-room always seemed full of the good times they had had in it . . . quiet evenings with a bunch of other little girls that Granny'd invited in, all sewing on doll's clothes and chattering, with Granny coming and going from Mother's room to show them how to manage the button-holes and the hard places. Or maybe, if Father was at home in the evening so he could take Granny's place to read aloud to Mother or play cards with her, the little girls had livelier evenings, with Granny at the piano and all the kids crowded around singing and sky-larking. Or almost better, evenings when 'Home work' was dispatched in one fierce pounce (Granny helping with the hardest arithmetic problems) which left Dids free to curl up on the couch, deep, head over heels, in a book that Granny had brought from the library for her. The living-room was as full of the book-people Dids had met there, as of the actual children

222

who had romped about in it. Yes, she *liked* the living-room!

If the hall looked middle-aged to her, the dining-room looked positively old to Dids, heavy and dark and aged, and rather interesting though of course you wouldn't want to sit down in it except to eat a meal. It seemed old because of all the dark old furniture in it, furniture that had belonged to . . . there! Who *had* it belonged to? Dids had forgotten again whether it was Mother's grandmother, or Granny's. Or were they the same person? Granny was always telling her about those old people of the family, but Dids never could keep them straight. She couldn't see why Granny made such a fuss about them anyhow. Dids had no head for relationships and didn't see what difference they made. All those people had been born and died long before Dids had appeared, so how could it be very important which came after or before which?

The kitchen was a nice room too, Granny being so particular how it was kept. It was just as sweet to look at as any other room in the house, and often sweeter, when Granny was cooking spicy gingerbread in it, or letting Dids and her friends mess around in it on rainy Saturdays, popping corn or making toffee or learning how to make biscuits. Granny was a terrible old fuss about having the kitchen cleaned up, all the time, but when Dids went with her playmates into their homes and saw their kitchens, she was always very well pleased to come back to her own. To have a kitchen like that made a nice clean feeling in the back of your mind, very much like the sweet secret cleanness you felt when you'd just had a bath and washed your hair and had put on everything fresh from the skin out. Nobody knew you were any cleaner, but the cleanness of it made a difference in the back of your mind. Dids had a great assortment of back-of-her-mind feelings, and the way she took life depended a great deal on things being right back there.

Of course poor Mother's room was *lovely*, the loveliest in the house with the prettiest things in it. It ought to be, shut up in it as she was. Granny often told her that nothing they could do for Mother would be enough to make up to her for being an invalid and a shut-in.

One of the far-past memories Dids could faintly bring to mind was the time when there were carpenters coming and going, and Granny bossing them around, making the many-windowed sun-parlour that hung out from the house like a big upstairs porch, where Mother spent so much of her time. And yet, though Dids could remember the noise of the hammering and sawing, and the long yellow boards up-ended against the house outside, and the very look of an old workman who had given her a beautiful darkly shining knot to play with, still, it seemed like a picture she had seen in a book and nothing real, because she couldn't in the least remember how Mother's room had looked before the sun-parlour was there.

It was certainly scrumptious now. Dids was always proud of it and of Mother, when Granny thought Mother was well enough for her to take in a little schoolmate for a few minutes. Some of the other girls had invalid Mothers, to be sure, but none who looked so like a picture as Mother did, a bright silk quilt drawn up over her, dressed in one of those delicate ruffled and puffed *négligés* which Granny was always making for her, lying back on snowy-white lace-trimmed pillows, her beautiful black hair gleaming and glistening in the coils and braids which Granny knew so well how to make. The other little girls always said she looked just like somebody in the movies, and she did, without a line in her pretty smooth face . . . of course her face was really rather too round and when she held her head down there was a big roll of flesh under her chin, but as Granny said, the reason why Mother didn't have any wrinkles in her face was just because she was so fleshy. It might have been a bother to her if she'd had to be up and dressed, but you never noticed it except for her double chin when you saw her always lying down as she was, on the bed or sofa, with loose clothes on. And it did keep her face young-looking. Very different from Granny's, which was awfully old and wrinkled, the skin hanging loose and flapping under her jaw in folds that Dids hated to look at. But of course that was natural, Granny being very old . . . sixty-five her last birthday . . . or was it fifty-five? Dids never could remember people's ages when they got up so high as that. They always sounded alike to her, the way a billion doesn't sound different from a trillion. Once you were past thirty what difference did it make?

What Dids liked best in Mother's room were the flowers. The sun-parlour was like a green-house . . . no, how stupid of her to say that! It was lots better than a green-house, it was like a fairy palace in the sky. Whenever Granny let her go in to see Mother, Dids waited a minute outside the door, before she opened it, to remember how it looked. And then it was always much better than she remembered because she couldn't get into her head to stay the brightness of the long gold sun-rays nor the smoothness of the flower petals. Dids loved the beauty of the texture of flower petals so intensely that it made her ache. She used to hang over them, staring and staring, till her eyes couldn't see anything but that satiny perfection. And to think that it was alive! That idea always moved Dids' imagination more than anything else. To think that that lovely, lovely, *'squisite* thing was just as she was, with a life-current running up and down those finely carved flower veins, just as her own blood ran up and down and around in her own veins. Dids always felt like a coarse, stub-fingered giantess after she had been staring at a flower-petal for a long time. It made her want to speak more softly, step more lightly, to handle everything more delicately; it made her feel almost as though she could see the air, the bright transparent air that would be so much lovelier than anything else to see, if you only could. Sometimes if she had been gazing at a flower before she went to bed, Dids dreamed that she could see the air, and it was better than going to Heaven, lots!

Flowers were mostly what they talked about, she and Mother, when they talked at all (for mostly they did puzzles together, or played cards), flowers and what was happening to them. For Granny managed so that there was always something happening – a narcissus opening out its crinkled white flowers so fast you could see it, if you held your breath as you looked; or a tulip shooting up its strong green lances so fast that Mother said she could see a difference from one half-hour to the next, or maybe an oxalis, keeping house tidily and silently, withering up and dropping down the brownish, oldish flowers, and unfolding new silky bright pink ones to keep the little feathery bush bright and gay.

225

When a plant got dull and uninteresting and was just living along any old way, Granny took it away from Mother's room and kept it in the kitchen or the living-room, tending it till it was ready to do something to amuse Mother. Granny said they ought to try as hard as they could to have something interesting happen for Mother every single day, shut in as she was.

Well, she was certainly good at managing things to happen, Granny was. Not a day that she didn't bring Mother a new book from the library, or finish up something pretty for her to wear, or bring in a new plant to watch, or a box of candy. Dids didn't think it was really quite fair that Mother was allowed to have all the candy she *wanted* when she, Dids, could only have one piece after a meal; but Granny explained that Mother's sickness was nervous, and hadn't got anything to do with her digestion, and it would be wrong not to let her have the comfort of candy. Granny was always discovering some new kind of fancy-work for Mother to do, too, the easy kind with long stitches that made a quick showing such as Mother liked; and when Mother grew tired of it, Granny always took it off and finished it up and never said a word when Mother showed it to visitors as sometimes she had done, and they said, 'Oh, what lovely work you do, Lottie!' Sometimes it was something new from the drug store, a new cold cream or manicure polish. Mother spent lots of time on her nails and they always looked lovely too. Sometimes it was a new card game. Mother loved solitaire. Or Granny thought of a brand-new way to do up Mother's hair; that always interested Mother for ever so long, and gave visitors something to talk about.

It was wonderful how Granny could always think of something new for Mother. But after all it was natural, wasn't Mother her own daughter . . . or was it Father who was Granny's son? Dids never could remember about relationships. And what difference did it make after all, the grown-ups of the family all being related in one way or another.

Chapter 33

Dids liked to skate, and Granny approving of any active outdoor play, time on the ice was always provided for her. Granny had found out that one of the young ladies in charge of the Harristown Y.W.C.A. knew how to skate very well, and as long as the ice held, she came over to Gilmanville twice a week to give Dids and a bunch of her schoolmates skating lessons. It was the greatest fun! Dids loved winter because of the skating. But she loved summer and spring and fall too, because there were so many kinds of good times in all of them. Dids really had not hours enough in the days for all the good times there were to be had.

But perhaps she liked skating best of all. It was almost as good as flying, she thought; at least a thousand times better than walking, stub, stub, stub, one foot planted jerkily in front of the other . . . such hard work . . . and a millions steps to take before you got anywhere. Rather different from that poor hobbling along was the effortless glide off on one skate, in a dream-like sweep which you could change into a cleanly-drawn circle just by throwing your weight to one side, around you came like a bird dipping, and there you were where you started from. Really you didn't know what it was that so strongly and swiftly pushed you over to the far side of the ice pond and back again. It just seemed to happen of itself.

Dids sometimes thought of her days as if they were such circles. When you got out of bed, you seemed to glide off and away you went, sweeping around, apparently so far, and yet, when night came, there you were safe and sound, back in the place where you started, taking off the clothes you had put on, ready to get back into the same comfortable bed you had climbed out of.

Granny had a circle too, a very different one from Dids, around which she swung every day. And Mother too, although hers was small. But it was just as well-marked and Dids knew all its smooth curves just as well as her own.

It began the first thing in the morning when Granny went to shut Mother's window and light the fire. A year or so ago when Dids had been eight or nine, Granny had had a fireplace built because (she said) an open fire is so cheerful for an invalid. Mother loved to turn over in bed and watch the bright flames and hear the lively snapping of the wood. When the room was warmed a little later, Granny called up the stairs to Dids that it was her turn now; for as Dids grew older, Granny let her do more things for Mother. Dids was so sorry for poor Mother she liked to wait on her. When Granny called her, she slipped on her wrapper and slippers, ran down the stairs to the second floor, poured some warm water in Mother's pretty pink wash-basin, and got the soap and towel all ready. Then feeling important, she stood by the bed to hand things to Mother as she needed them, and to hold the hand mirror so that Mother could set her lace-trimmed morning cap straight. While this was going on, Granny was getting breakfast.

Then Dids went back upstairs to her own room to dress and do her hair (for Granny had taught her to take care of herself while she was still a little thing, and by the time she was twelve, she could do her hair better than anyone else). She always knew by the smell of the good things to eat when Granny brought up Mother's tray, and this made her hurry down to her own breakfast. After breakfast, Granny got Mother ready for the day, sort of half dressed her in loose silky things and pretty little slippers. Granny was extravagant about Mother's slippers. She kept buying new ones all the time. It seemed to Dids she had dozens of pairs; blue shiny ones of leather, black velvet ones, fur-trimmed ones, tassel-trimmed ones, and all with the highest heels and pointedest toes. Mother liked them that way and Granny said since she never walked on her feet, it couldn't hurt them to wear the kind of shoes she wanted. Mother took such comfort in her pretty slippers. She always pulled up a fold of her *négligé*, so that one foot showed, and no wonder! They were just as pretty as the silk-stockinged wax feet in the windows of the shoe stores.

Then Granny and Father put Mother on her sofa and rolled that out into the sun-parlour, and Granny brought her the pretty red lacquered box, all full of little pots and tubes and brushes and sticks, Mother's toilet box. There was everything in it you could imagine; four or five kinds

228

of cold cream, vanishing, astringent, skin-food, anti-double-chin; and eyebrow tonic; and more than forty 'leven things to do to your hands and nails. Mother always looked so happy and interested as she began to set out on the sick-bed table all the little 'do-funnies' as Dids' Father called them. About now at a quarter to nine was the time when old Mrs. Rader came to wait on Mother if she needed it, when Father went off to his work, and when Dids and Granny put on their things to go to school.

It took Mother, she used to tell them, till half-past ten every morning really to finish her toilet. You just couldn't do it in less time and do it right, she said, *nobody* could! By that time she was pretty tired with smoothing and rubbing and polishing and trimming. It was so hard for Mother to hold her arms up for long at a time. She often used to tell them that she had to lay down the nail-file fifteen or twenty times to rest her arms, before she could get through the morning's manicuring. Mother liked to keep track of things like that – how often the telephone had rung during the morning, or how many cars had gone down the street between eleven and twelve. Of course if was even harder for her to lift her arms to take care of her hair, and she was often just worn out, she said, when she finally finished all she had to do. Poor Mother, she had no strength at all, as she said. The least little effort was too much for her.

So, by half-past ten or eleven she was usually ready to rest and doze for an hour, unless the morning mail had brought a newspaper with something especially exciting in it for her to read. Granny subscribed to three New York newspapers for Mother, the ones that had the most coloured pictures and 'special features;' and yet she would hardly let Dids look at one of them. She never actually said Dids mustn't, but she just managed so she didn't. She had the funniest ideas, Granny had. Dids was all out of patience with her lots of times.

And yet, there was no use talking, Dids enjoyed those lunches with Granny, after Mother's tray had been carried up to her. She wasn't such a bad old scout, Granny wasn't, even if she had fussy ways as old people do. Dids wished once in a while that Granny would pay a little more attention to her clothes. She never had anything new, just the same old tailored suit. It pretty nearly had holes in it before she'd see about buying a new one. And her hats! Mother said sometimes she couldn't imagine what Granny *did* with her money . . . she had savings in the bank and got a better salary than Father did, and had nobody but herself to spend it on. Mother said it did *seem* as if she might loosen up a little and afford to have a little style.

Still, Dids didn't really care how Granny dressed. What difference did it make for such an old person. She wouldn't have looked to Dids like Granny if she didn't wear one of those dark, plain Granny-hats. And anyhow, she liked Granny, she really did. The other girls didn't believe her, but she liked to stick around with Granny. Old as she was, and fussy as she was, Dids liked being with her a good deal. They actually had lots of fun together at lunch. Whatever Dids happened to be interested in just then . . . stamp-collecting, or different cuts to bobbed hair, or skating, or conundrums, or the spelling match at school, or the latest volume of Dickens Dids was reading . . . no matter what it was, Granny was just as interested as Dids. She always had some idea about it too. Dids never let on to Granny, but she often used to wait till she heard what Granny said about something, before making up her own mind. Not that she always agreed with Granny. Indeed, she often made a point not to seem to agree – if only about some little detail. But all the same Dids always felt she needed to know what Granny thought about things before she felt sure of what she thought – at least, up to now when she was twelve years old.

Granny knew more conundrums than anybody and could say lots of poetry right out of her head and had all kinds of funny stories to tell about old-time doings when she was a little girl. The two of them never lacked things to talk about. Their tongues click-clacked every minute, and how they laughed! Granny laughed like a man . . . right out ha! ha! ha! so that you couldn't help laughing with her. And Dids adored laughing.

And of course from talking so much together, Granny knew all about everything that was happening to Dids, so that she could start right in the middle of a story, and not have to explain the beginning as she did with Father. She would have had to explain even more with Mother, only Mother not knowing anything about what went on in Dids' life, it seemed hardly worth while to start to tell her anything and Dids never did. Mother wasn't well enough anyhow to take much interest in what happened outside her sick-room. Father *said* he wanted to hear about things in Dids' school life, but he always had to lay down his paper to ask, 'Who *is* this Miss Drummond?' although he'd heard you talk millions of times about the music-teacher at school. Or, 'Hold on, what rehearsal?' And that slowed things up so, and took Dids so long to explain that by the time she got back to telling what it was that happened, she had lost her interest in it. Father never had such a lot of interest to begin with! They didn't get very far.

But with Granny, you could always start right in, 'That play the Eighth Grade is giving, well, Lorina Sheldon is not going to be Rowena in it after all.' Or, 'Down by the lake, that same big dog came up and played with us again.' Granny knew who Lorina Sheldon was, and all about the lovely big dog who played with them as they skated. Yes, lunches with Granny were quite fun.

In the afternoon, either old Mrs. Rader came back or it was one of the three days a week the charwoman was there, so Mother wasn't left alone when Dids and Granny walked back to school together. They did not often come home from school together, at half-past three, although Dids on her free afternoons usually went round to Granny's classroom to see if Granny were ready to start. If there were only a few people waiting, Dids sat down to wait. But lots of times there was such a gang around Granny's desk that she gave it up. Sometimes it was rather interesting to sit there and listen, but mostly Dids found it very tiresome and couldn't understand how in the world Granny endured those queer-looking women, who never had any style to their clothes and usually a dirty-faced baby with them. They always had some hardluck rigamarole to tell Granny, it seemed to Dids, and Granny'd listen, just as interested! You'd think they were her best friends. And mercy! how they did talk things over and *over*. Dids was yawning her head off by the time Granny just seemed starting in. It was one of Granny's tiresome ways. None of the other teachers put up with the dumb-bells among the mothers the way Granny did. Dids often wished Granny'd learn to turn 'em out, one a minute, the way Miss Slocum, her own teacher in the Seventh Grade did. Miss Slocum often argued with Granny about it. She said mercy! she'd earned her pay when she'd taught all day without being cheated out of what little fun she could have after four o'clock on the blessed days when there wasn't any teachers' meeting. She said she didn't see why she had to add hours to her working day just because Mrs. Wienerschnitzel couldn't get on with Mr. Wienerschnitzel. What was it to *her*, Miss Slocum used to ask Granny. Not to speak of Granny's taking care of all the plants in the building out of hours. 'Yours are always all right,' Miss Slocum told her. 'Why don't you let it go at that? Why bother with other people's? *Let* their old ferns curl up and die, if the other teachers don't water them.' Granny was apt to answer to this that she liked to fuss with plants, and couldn't bear to see them droopy just because she knew what to do for them.

'That's all the thanks you get for it!' said Miss Slocum, snapping her fingers. 'The other teachers take the credit. Nobody even knows you do it!'

Granny never seemed to have any special answer to this. But she always went right on taking care of the plants. Of course, Dids reflected, Granny never having what you could really call fun or a good time, anyhow, on account of being so old, perhaps, didn't miss anything by extra hours of work, the way young and pretty Miss Slocum did. Maybe Granny even liked it. You never could tell about grown-ups, they liked such queer things, especially old grown-ups. If indeed, they liked anything at all, the way Dids liked things. Come to think about it, it must be that Granny liked having everybody in creation pile on her back, or she wouldn't let them.

Perhaps they hung on to her because she never seemed too tired to listen. It was queer about that – her face often looked awfully old and grey and full of wrinkles, and some days her shoulders stooped so that she was all bowed over; but when she looked at you, Granny's eyes never looked tired. Not nearly as tired as Miss Slocum's often did.

Although she grumbled so about other people bothering the life out of Granny, Dids was not surprised at it. She herself always made one rush for Granny when there was anything the matter. Everybody in the building set right out, hot foot, for Mrs. Bascomb when there was trouble, and so did her granddaughter. It was very handy, Dids often thought, having an old person in the family, so old that nothing surprised her, or scared her, or was too much for her. Dids supposed it came from Granny's being so old that what happened to her didn't matter any more. Anyhow it gave Dids a very solid feeling, of having something to hold on to, if she needed it. Though mostly, of course, she didn't need it a bit, rushing through her busy, jolly days without a thought of Granny, except to groan over her fussiness about finger-nails and teeth.

On the many afternoons when she had something definite to do after school was over, Dids did not even look into Granny's room, but went straight off to whatever it was . . . a piano lesson, or a rehearsal of the school-chorus, or a game of hockey on the athletic fields; or maybe it was the afternoon for the dancing class Granny had put her in, now she was a big girl of twelve.

Saturday mornings as like as not, a bunch of her gang of seventh-graders would go over to Harristown on the tram and have a high old time in the Y.W.C.A. tank with the swimming teacher. Granny made some special arrangement so they were allowed in, although they were Gilmanville girls and not from Harristown. Dids seemed to remember hearing that Granny had lived in Harristown for a while, and probably had her pull with the Y.W.C.A. from that. Granny's pull was very handy at times.

Always, as regularly as the clock ticked, Dids must have her hour's practice at the piano, half an hour before supper and half an hour afterwards. And always she must go in and play cards with Mother before she went to bed. And always Granny arranged it so she could have a half-hour before she went to sleep, free to read just whatever she liked, and go to sleep, her mind full of the pleasure of a favourite book.

Yes, by the time Dids closed her eyes at night, a full day lay behind her; she had swept smoothly around a wide

233

circle of school, and music, and good things to eat at meals, and fun, and taking care of Mother, and reading and lots of games – really Dids didn't know what it was that so strongly and swiftly pushed her around it.

It just seemed to happen of itself.

Chapter 34

WHEN Dids was between fifteen and sixteen, she suddenly 'took a start up,' and grew so fast there was no keeping the hems of her skirts let down. It was not only in inches she grew. In September as she sometimes said to herself, she had been just a kid, for all she was starting her Junior year in the high school. She trotted around with the other kids, not at all above playing hide-and-seek, and interested in boys only as playmates. By February, looking back on herself, she could hardly remember when she had ever been such a mere child. Hide-and-seek! Now, she would as soon play with dolls, or suck her thumb. Her body was almost two inches taller. She herself was another person.

Had she been a pretty child? She had never thought about being pretty enough to know, having always played and studied too hard to have any time left over. But now, she knew little else than that she was a pretty girl. Whatever part of her mind was not occupied by this knowledge was filled by the exciting discovery that she was more than pretty, that she was attractive to boys.

She found that walking along the street with one of the big boys, she had only to look at him in a certain way . . . she really didn't know just what way it was, but when she felt full of electricity she could always do it . . . and in a minute or two, no matter how hard he was talking about baseball, he'd stop, and look back at her in a certain way, and walk closer to her so that they touched each other as they stepped. Then they'd both be tingling from head to foot, and laughing a great deal over nothing, and not really know what they were saying, at all. It was *frightfully* interesting.

And it made everything else that had been in her life seem flat and stupid and insipid. Lessons! Basket-ball! Granny!

234

Piano practice! Skating! Poetry books! Dids could hardly
remember when she had been such a child as to put her mind
on such things. Clothes! That was something worth thinking about! The shortest skirts, the thinnest waists, the film-
iest stockings (although tyrannical old Granny wouldn't get
them as thin as lots of the girls wore them), the exact position
of every hair on her sleek, closely bobbed head, her finger-
nails, and the right sort of scanty underwear . . . Dids fell
asleep thinking of these things, and woke up with her mind
full of them. And of Tug Warner.

For she and Tug had paired off definitely now. He was
her 'fellow' (although Granny hadn't seen it yet). She was
'going with him' just as she had seen older girls 'go with
fellows.' He 'took her to places,' all the places Granny would
allow her to go, and some she didn't know about. For instance, Tug took her two or three times a week after school,
into Peter's Drug Store and gave her anything she wanted,
even those expensive mixed-up sundaes to which she had
never aspired that cost twenty-five and thirty-five cents.
Tug's father ran the hotel in Gilmanville, so Tug had plenty
of money always and knew all the latest jokes the commercial
travellers told.

Perched on the high stools before the marble counter, the
two Juniors in the high school consumed as slowly as they
could the mixture of ice-cream and powdered nuts and can-
died fruits and thick rich syrups and melted marshmallows;
watching themselves in the big mirrors behind the silvertaps;
turning their heads this way and that; admiring themselves;
meeting each other's mirrored eyes provocatively; laughing
loudly and jostling each other. Sometimes they welcomed
the joking of the soda clerk, sometimes when he got too gay
they tried vainly to snub him. Dids knew that everybody
who came and went in the shop was looking at them and
listening to them. This gave her a giddy excited feeling which
she thought was pleasure. It was the same sort of feeling she
had when she looked deep into Tug's eyes when afterwards
they walked along together, their swinging hands occasionally brushing each other.

Sometimes after she was at home in her own room, with
her own well-worn books looking at her; or sitting before the
piano with some well-remembered silver phrase singing out

under her fingers; or lying very quiet, drowsy and at peace in her little room after the light was turned out – sometimes the remembered syrupy taste of all those sweets made her feel rather sick; and so did the recollection of the expression in the eyes of the men customers loitering about the store who had been looking at her, and laughing at her goings-on. But this was only fleeting. She was always ready to begin again, if for no other reason, because she felt the other girls' envy of her, warm and delicious.

She never mentioned any of this to Granny, who did not pass Peter's Drug Store on her way home from school.

She had never let Tug kiss her yet, but she supposed he would some day. She had read a great deal about kisses in novels, and what a wonderful feeling that gave a girl; and at the occasional movie which was all that Granny would let her see, when the hero and heroine exchanged a long, clinging movie-kiss, Dids shivered from head to foot. Yes, it must be *wonderful*.

When she looked at Tug, which she did a great many times a day, she did not see him; she saw the pale chiselled features and professionally burning eyes of the last movie hero she had seen. But although she did not see Tug himself, it was Tug whom she felt when he pressed closer to her. That warmth, that vibration, came from no shadow on a screen, but from a living flesh-and-blood boy. It was frightfully exciting.

Miss Mann, the teacher of English Literature, and Mr. Leonard, the aged professor of Math. who must be forty at least, were alarmed about Dids' suddenly poor recitations and inattention in class, Dids who had always stood so well. When they took her to task seriously, Dids gazed dreamily at them, seeing something which was a mixture of pale chiselled features and troubling young flesh-and-blood. How dry and petty her lessons seemed! What interest could she take in Lit. class, occupied in reading a play written hundreds of years ago; all about witchcraft and fairies and impossible things that nobody could believe . . . a man with a donkey's head! As if there could be such a thing. And a fairy queen who was such an idiot she fell in love with him.

Miss Mann read with careful intonation,

'Come, sit thee down upon this flowery bed,
While I thy amiable cheeks do coy,
And stick musk-roses in thy sleek smooth head,
And kiss thy fair large ears, my gentle joy.'

She broke off to look at Dids with irritation and say, 'Miss Bascomb, you're not listening again! Can't you *feel* the humour and irony of that passage?'

No, frankly, Dids couldn't see that it was anything to her, all that rigmarole. Once, bothered by Miss Mann's insistence that she should give her mind to the foolish story, she roused herself to protest, 'Honestly, Miss Mann, it sounds like nonsense to me. Nobody believes in charms and casting spells and that sort of thing nowadays. How can you take stock enough in the story to keep your mind on it? It's so improbable! She *must* have seen he had a donkey's head.'

Miss Mann was pleased to have stirred to discussion the girl who had formerly been her most brilliant student. 'She did *see* it,' she said eagerly. 'Titania did see it, but she was bewitched so that she thought it was handsomer than a man's head.'

'Oh, she couldn't have!' said Dids. 'Nobody could. That's just what I mean. You can't believe it, it's so improbable. And then to stop liking his donkey's head all of a sudden, without any reason except that some herb-juice had been squeezed in her eyes. Honest, now, Miss Mann, it's perfectly ridiculous!'

'I suppose you consider yourself perfectly qualified to judge,' said Miss Mann in a cutting tone. She was not long out of college, and frequently used personal remarks of a severely sarcastic nature as a means of inculcating a love for the beauties of literature.

Dids didn't care *what* she said, having fallen back into her dreamy langour. Let them have their own way. After this in Lit. class, to all that Miss Mann said, she professed entire acquiescence. 'Yes, Miss Mann,' she murmured compliantly, a thousand miles away.

And 'yes, Mr. Leonard,' in a mild tone, looking at his wrinkles and greying hair and wondering if he had ever been young and thrilling to touch as he walked beside you.

Following the tradition of the school, on Lincoln's birthday they had 'exercises' – music and a speaker from out of town. At ten o'clock in the morning the students filed into the assembly room, from the first-graders, trotting eagerly on their little feet, excited by being out of their own room in class time, up to the tall high schoolboys lounging in, their hands in their pockets, bored in advance by more talky-talk.

The music teacher had prepared several special 'music numbers' and the school chorus sat down in the front rows, quite interested in spite of their blasé air by having an important part of the programme. They had forgotten whose birthday they were celebrating. There was in fact at the moment nothing in their minds but the hope that the sopranos would hit the high notes a little better than they had at last rehearsal.

Mr. Elliott, principal of the school, general in command of their world, marched upon the platform, bringing with him a tall old man, very straight, very imposing, beautifully dressed as nobody ever dressed in Gilmanville. The way he stood there with his white head held high, made him look like somebody out of a history book. He gazed with curiosity and interest into the faces of the four hundred children as, in answer to a signal from Mr. Elliott they rose to show the respect for him which they did not in the least feel, for although they had been told ten days before by Mr. Elliott who the speaker was to be, the only impression made at that time on their minds had been that on February 12, there would be no recitations from ten to eleven. That was important, almost worth the bother of going to 'exercises.' Now as they received a very direct look out of a pair of very penetrating steel-coloured eyes, they sat up straighter and tried to remember what Mr. Elliott had said about the speaker.

Dids had been quite startled by the vivid glance she had received. It was as if the speaker had really seen her, really noticed her. Who was he, anyway? Had Mr. Elliott said he was president of some college? Or was it a famous chemist? Or a Judge of the Supreme Court? When they sat down she whispered to Florence King, 'Who did Mr. Elliott say . . . ?'

At her first word, Florence raised her eyebrows and shoulders to signify that she too had not the least idea. The exercises began.

Dids *liked* singing in a chorus. When she sat down after letting herself out in the alto part of 'Olaf Trygvasson,' she felt like a different person. Music always swept through Dids and filled her full of itself. It drove out everything else in her mind, so that when it stopped, she felt quite emptied and open to the next feeling that came along.

· The next feeling that came her way was the voice of the speaker. It was like the deep notes of a pipe organ. Gilmanville people never had that sort of voice, any more than they had that sort of clothes. Everybody in the assembly room sat very still listening to that voice; and a few of them listened to what it said. They did not cough or shuffle their feet as they usually did during an address, nor look around to see who it was coming in late at the back. Dids listened intently with the others, and although like most of the children, she could not have told exactly what that sonorous, civilized voice had been saying to her, she felt that it had been saying a good deal. Apparently they all felt that for, as they filed out of the assembly room, at the end of the exercises, the little children trotted softly, and the faces of the older children were dreamy.

Dids and the rest of the chorus on the front seats were obliged to wait for their own signal to rise and march, till the lower classes had left the aisles. To her surprise, just as they finally stood up to go, Mr. Elliott, who had been talking to the splendid old speaker, turned towards her and leaning over the edge of the platform, called to her, 'Just a minute, will you? Dr. Levering would like to speak with you.'

'With *me?*' asked Dids, looking over her shoulder to make sure that Mr. Elliott was not speaking to some one back of her.

'Yes, come around by the side stairs,' said Mr. Elliott, 'so that I can introduce you.'

So it happened that the last of the high school boys and girls, turning their heads as they went out into the hall, saw to their surprise that Dids Bascomb was on the platform shaking hands with the man who had just made the speech of the day. 'Well, what do you know about that?' their lifted eyebrows asked each other as they marched off to their different recitation rooms.

Dids herself was astonished to the limit of astonishment.

It was very exciting to be standing there beside the Principal and a celebrated man from out of town, whose tall person was to Dids' eyes stately with the prestige of being for the moment the centre of her world. What on earth could he have to say to her?

Mr. Elliott, called from the platform by a beckoning janitor, left the schoolgirl and the old man alone.

Now that they stood face to face she felt a vivid emanation of power from him. Her heart began to beat fast. She looked at him fixedly out of startled, very wide-open eyes. He bent his white head to bring it closer to her blooming face and said gently, 'I was so much struck by your resemblance to a very dear friend of my youth, whom I loved from childhood, with whom I lived in college that I inquired your name. It is the same as his.'

He paused, seemed to hesitate as though he feared to put the question, and asked, in a deep voice, 'Are you by any chance the granddaughter of John Bascomb?' He pronounced the name with a special intonation as though it were like no other name for him.

For the moment he addressed himself to her, Dids had been shaken to the core by the mere impact of the old man's finished and magnetic personality upon her own, rawly, helplessly impressionable, unhardened by experience as she was. She was now so startled by his question, by his pronouncing in that tone of sacramental affection a familiar name out of her own life, that she could not speak. She nodded dumbly, her eyes fixed on his, receiving from them with the avid haste of youth seeking its own, more vital material for the construction of her House of Life, than in weeks of ordinary life. It poured in on her, this unknown, instantly recognised stuff of life, her own come to find her. There was a place in her heart, unknown to her, which had been empty – waiting for just this golden flood . . . the recognition of depths, of greatness. . . . It could never be empty any more.

She had no idea what was happening to her. She only knew she felt like crying and knew she mustn't.

The tall old man looked down on her as if from a great distance and smiled as if he had always known her. Dids' eyes clung to his. When she nodded, his gaze on her deepened. He took her hand in his, a strong, warm clasp. He said, 'I can hope for nothing better for you than to grow to be such a woman as he was a man.'

It sounded to Dids like a prayer. She wanted even more to cry. She bit her lip and nodded silently, as if again assenting to what he said, although at the time she heard nothing but the deep feeling in his voice. It was hours afterwards before she really heard his words.

The time gong in the halls clamoured noisily. Mr. Elliott hastily reappeared. 'Oh, there's her class bell!' he said nervously. *'We mustn't make her late for class!'*

It was a class in English Literature and the recitation had already begun. Florence King scribbled on a piece of paper and passed it to Dids, 'What under the sun did he want of you?'

Dids wrote back, 'He used to know my grandfather.'

Florence nodded, her curiosity appeased, all her interest immediately gone. She passed Dids' explanation along to the others in the same row, and they all nodded, disappointment in their faces over such a prosaic undramatic reason for an episode which had promised interest.

Anton Zaleska was standing up, reading aloud in the surly hangdog accent which was the accepted one in school for correcting the foolishness of poetry . . .

> "For meeting her of late behind the wood
> I did upbraid her and fall out with her:
> For she his hairy temples then had rounded
> With coronet of fresh and fragrant flowers:

When he sat down the nearest person to him with a practised slyness passed him Dids' note, and he too nodded, with a slightly disappointed expression.

No one ever spoke to her about it again. It dropped instantly from everyone's mind.

At noon as usual Dids walked to and from school with Granny. Although she knew that Granny had not seen the incident because she had left the hall with her fifth grade among the first, and, although she was sure that Granny would be greatly interested in it, she could not seem to speak about it. Why not? Shyness? An inability to think of the right words? Perhaps she did not yet know what she felt about it herself nor with what intonation to mention it. She felt that she needed to keep it to herself for a while, till it had settled down, till it seemed less strangely unlike everything else that had ever happened to her. Several times she opened her mouth to tell Granny about it, but she always ended by speaking about something else. She couldn't think how to begin.

It was so steadily in her mind, however, that she was surprised when supper-time had arrived and the day gone. Her thoughts had been so turned inward that she couldn't remember what she had been doing. But she knew that she really must tell Granny and now it did not seem so hard. Just as she thought it would, it had sunk down a little more to the level of other impressions. As they were washing the dishes in the evening she said, 'Granny, that Dr. Levering who spoke to-day called me up on the platform to ask me if I were John Bascomb's granddaughter. And when I said I was he said he used to know my grandfather in college.'

She had known that Granny would be interested. But she had not dreamed she would look like this . . . pale and wild, her hands frozen on the plate she happened to be holding. She turned her head slowly.

'What did you say, Dids?' she asked as if she could not believe her ears.

As Dids repeated what she had said, Granny was hastily wiping her hands. The instant Dids finished, she flew to the telephone. Dids heard her talking, evidently to Mr. Elliott. She was breathing fast as if she had been running. 'The 8.30 train? On his way to the station now? I'd have time to see him a moment then? Yes, I'll hurry.' She hung the receiver up, called to Dids, 'Quick! Quick! Get your things on,' and began flinging on her own wraps.

In a moment they were out of the house, running towards the tram, and ten minutes later they were getting down from it, in front of the railway station.

Dids was startled by all this, and alarmed by her grandmother's expression. Granny looked as though she did not know there were any other people in the world. She kept swallowing hard and opening and shutting her hands. She looked *queer*. Dids was afraid she would do something queer that would make people stare at her. She looked as though she might cry at any moment. But of course, Dids supposed, people as old as Granny couldn't cry. She had never seen Granny shed a tear or even seem to feel like it. It had never before occurred to Dids that Granny could feel anyway in particular – like crying, or not like crying. Without thinking anything about it, Dids had always taken it for granted that Granny's *feelings* were all over, ages ago. It made her uncomfortable to sit opposite her in the tram and watch strange waves of excitement flood over the familiar face she had always seen so quiet and smiling and steady. She *did* hope Granny wasn't going to cry in public. What would people think if she should? They would stare, like everything. They would stare now, if they happened to look at Granny's face, for all she sat so straight and still. What on earth was the matter with her? Grandfather had been dead for ages and ages. Dids had always supposed that Granny never thought of him any more.

They did not see Dr. Levering in the waiting-room of the station. The clock showed twenty minutes after eight. Ten minutes before train time. Granny looked around the room, once, twice, three times, her eyes leaping from one person to another. She went to the ticket window and Dids heard her asking about a tall, elderly man. The ticket man thought the old gentleman had gone right out of doors to the platform as if he wanted to smoke.

Granny walked rapidly across the room, full of people who nodded and said, 'Good evening, Mrs. Bascomb,' but whom she did not seem to see, and went out of the door with Dids. A string of electric bulbs cast a cold white glare into the cold black midwinter night. Only a few people braved the frosty air, a couple of porters with a truck full of trunks, a lady with a little dog walking up and down. No Dr. Levering . . . oh, yes, off there at the dusky far end of the platform, a tall, dim form.

Granny walked so fast toward him that she was almost running. Dids followed along, horribly embarrassed and ashamed of Granny. What would a distinguished, famous man like Dr. Levering think of them, crowding themselves in on him like this? And Granny so old and plainly dressed,

243

with one of her most awful hats on. Dids wished earnestly that she had not come along, that she could disassociate herself from Granny and not share in the awkwardness which was before them.

He saw Granny coming towards him, turned, and as she came closer, lifted his hat partly from his white hair, looking surprised, and Dids thought very stand-offish and superior.

Granny did not begin by something polite like, 'How do you do?' or 'Good evening,' or 'Excuse me,' or anything. She said in a very low tone as though she hadn't any breath left, 'Is it true that you knew my husband? That you knew John Bascomb?'

Dr. Levering's face changed so that he looked like entirely another person. He took his hat off, put his hand out to Granny, and said in the same organ-like voice which had been throbbing in Dids' memory all that day, 'Is this John Bascomb's widow? Is this the woman John Bascomb loved?'

And then, just as Dids had feared, Granny began to cry, to cry so hard she could not speak, her whole body shaking; but she did not cover her face with her hands. She kept her eyes on Dr. Levering's face. Dids was very glad they were off in the dark where nobody could see them. It made her feel terribly upset for Granny to cry like that, for her not to cover from sight the tears flowing down her face, distorted by her sobs. She tried to speak now, but all Dids could make out was that she was saying brokenly over and over, 'You knew John. You knew John. It is so long. . . . So long . . . somebody who knew John.'

Dr. Levering had her hand in both his now. He, too, was trying to say something, but although he was not crying, his voice was unsteady. Dids heard him say, 'So you are John Bascomb's widow,' and draw a long breath. He went on, 'I have been living with him in memory all this day, because I saw his spirit look out of his granddaughter's . . .' He put out a hand to draw Dids closer . . . 'I was thinking about that clear, deep look of his. Wonderful to find it still living in a new human being.'

He turned back to Granny, who was continually, with a rough gesture, dashing the tears from her eyes, so that she could see him. 'At the moment you came up to me, I was thinking of him and asking myself if I had lived so that I would not fear, now, to look once more into John Bascomb's eyes.'

As though his words had struck her a physical blow, Mrs. Bascomb gave a wail which made Dids' heart shrink together. 'No . . . oh, no! Oh, misery!' she cried, putting out her hands as if to defend herself.

Dids was frightened. Granny looked so strange. It did not seem possible that this could be her own quiet Granny . . . this distraught old woman, who stood there in the dusk, her twisted white face glistening with her tears.

Down the track they saw the distant glare of the head-light. The tracks by which they stood began to hum faintly.

Dr. Levering said, 'Why, Mrs. Bascomb, *you* certainly would be proud to look into his eyes, with such a splendid girl as you are bringing up to inherit his spirit. I have been hearing to-day about what a leader she is, about your devotion to her.'

The murmur of the train grew louder. Granny caught at his hand. She said wildly, 'Yes, yes . . . that is all I have tried . . . I have tried . . . it was for her . . .'

The car-wheels came banging in over the switches of the yards, the head-light glared fiercely on them. 'She *will* be like him, won't she?' called Granny through the rattle of the approaching train . . . or that was what Dids seemed to hear her say, as the station woke to sudden clamour, someone raucously bawling out an announcement of the train, the doors bursting open before the rush of travellers from the waiting-room.

Dids saw Dr. Levering turn from Granny and look down at her; she saw him lean towards her; she felt him kiss her on the forehead. She saw him look back at Granny, saw his lips move, but the train was now thundering past them and she could hear only, 'Yes, she will . . .'

And then he was gone; people with suitcases were crowding around them, banging into them, pushing and calling to each other. She and Granny shrank back, away from the crowd, into a dark corner, so dark that they could not see each other at all.

But she felt Granny cling to her as though fearing to fall. She closed her arms in a tight embrace, stiffened herself to strength, and felt, heavy on her young vigour, the weight of Granny's thin, shaking old body.

How Granny clung to her! Or was that the tight clasp of her own arms about Granny? They were like one. She felt tears wet on her cheeks. Were they hers? Or Granny's? Why should she be crying?

So this was what it meant . . . to love.

She was glad they were in the dark where no one could see them, till Granny was more quiet. Already she was shaking less, leaning heavily against Dids, her head on Dids' shoulder.

Soft and cool on her forehead, the girl felt the kiss of the gaunt old man who had loved her grandfather, who had said as he gave her that consecrating kiss that she would be like the friend he had cherished. What did a kiss make her think of? She could not remember.

How strange it seemed to have Granny leaning on *her*.

It was too cold here for Granny. Her own feet were like ice.

'Come, Granny,' she said gently, 'perhaps we'd better be starting . . .'

'Yes, yes, darling,' said Granny submissively, 'we'd better be going home now.'

The next morning as she and Granny separated inside the front door of the school-building, Dids saw coming along the hall towards her with a proprietary smile, a tall, pimpled boy. She looked at him and saw him, cruelly saw everything about him, the showy ring on one of his dingy fingers, the absurd cut of the Norfolk suit which hung gracelessly over his flat chest, his expression, half of rustic awkwardness, half of fatuous self-admiration, his shambling step, the greed and coarseness in his eyes.

This was Tug Warner. It had been a kiss from those pale, loose lips, which she had . . . she shuddered at the idea. She violently blamed the boy for his shamelessness in continuing to exist.

From fierce young eyes, she shot a scornful look at him and turned loftily away.

His face altered ludicrously from its complacent self-assurance. His mouth dropped open, 'What's the matter with you, Dids?' he asked.

'Nothing,' she said dryly.

'I was going to make an appointment with you to go to Peters' this afternoon and have a Red-and-Gold sundae,' he proffered.

'No, thank you,' she said viciously. 'I'm tired of those sickish old sundaes.'

'But, Dids . . .' he said sentimentally, lowering his voice and using a certain tone which she recognized. She looked at him unwillingly. In his eyes was an expression familiar to her, and she saw that he was edging closer to her.

Dids boiled. How *dared* he? 'Oh, get away and don't bother me!' she said with robust brutality.

He was stricken. 'Why, Dids . . .' he faltered, astonished pain wiping from his face the foolishness and coarseness, and leaving him looking pathetically like a hurt little boy.

Dids would not drop another look upon him. With a terrible indifference she said negligently, with finality, jerking her shoulder, 'Oh, you give me the fidgets. I don't feel like going with you any more . . . nor with any other boy!'

She walked down the hall briskly, with a light step. At the door of the study-hall she saw a group of girls and boys, her own old gang of comrades in sports and hikes. They were waiting for her. Dids hastened her step to a skip and a hop and joined them with a rush. They looked good to her. She took possession of them again and knew that they liked it. So did she. 'You look awfully up in the air,' she said breezily, 'what's the matter?' In her tone was her old-time energetic implication that whatever it was that was the matter she was the girl who could mend it.

Florence King fell on her neck dramatically, wailing, 'We're going to have an exam. in English Literature to-day, and the mean old thing never told us.'

One of the boys said glumly, 'I've never even *read* lots of that darned old play yet, have you?' 'Have you read that last act yet?' asked another.

Dids did not lose her head or waste time in laments. 'No, I haven't,' she said coolly, 'but the exam. isn't till three this afternoon.' She looked at the clock and with flying fingers began to undo her strapped package of books. 'We've got fifteen minutes right now, before assembly bell.

And we can take turns reading to each other in the lunch-room. I'll stay here for lunch to-day. And after that we can take turns reading while . . .' Evidently she saw her campaign clear before her. She nodded confidently. The girls looked relieved. Dids would bring them out all right. She always did. One of them called over her shoulder to a new-comer, 'Come on, Retta! Dids is going to help us cram for that exam. in English Lit.'

'Where'd we leave off?' asked Dids, fluttering the leaves of the book.

'" And then I will her charmèd eyes release
    From monster's view, and all things shall be peace."

'Was it there? No, I remember, it was lots further along . . .

'"And think no more of this night's accidents
    But as the fierce vexation of a dream.
    Be, as thou wast wont to be;
    See as thou wast wont to see;
    Dian's bud o'er Cupid's flower
    Hath such force and blessèd power.
    Now, my Titania! Wake you, my sweet queen."'

'Say, Dids,' said Florence King, interrupting her, 'when you come to a line that you think is real good, let me know and I'll learn it off. One of the questions in the exam. is sure to be to pick out a line you specially like, and I *never* know what to say when they ask that. I think it's one of the meanest things they do in English exams.'

'Sure thing,' said Dids. 'I'll find you lots. Here, here's something scrumptious, peaches and cream in your mouth . . .

'"More strange than true; I never may believe
    Those antique fables nor these fairy toys."'

'But there are *two* lines there,' protested Florence. 'Which one shall I say?'

Dids never had the least idea why she had so suddenly hated the sight of Tug.

Mrs. Bascomb never had the least idea that she had ever been drawn to him and his kind.

248

PART SIX

Chapter 35

THE bright decade of years which had seemed so long and varied to Dids, which indeed summed up about all the life the fifteen-year-old girl could remember, had had for Mrs. Bascomb a very different colour. As far as she herself was concerned, those years had swept past her like a dream. She had been so little conscious of herself during that period that she seemed scarcely to have lived, personally, at all. But Ralph and Dids had lived and changed. When she looked at them, she realized that ten years had really passed by since that April in 1914 when Lottie had taken to her bed.

At that time, Ralph had been twenty-seven years old and had been married six years. He was still working in the printing-establishment where he had chanced to find a position on leaving college, and he was by no means making a brilliant success of his work. 'Gosh, how I hate it!' he said occasionally, as he hauled his overcoat on in the morning. But the exclamation was rather of resignation than of revolt. The treadmill exacted from him imperiously one straining step after another. He had no vitality left him for revolt. He had never been much of a rebel, and his life after his marriage had deadened what little gift in that direction he had originally. A man with a wife and six-year-old child . . . and now a bed-ridden wife . . . how could he afford to revolt? At twenty-seven, Ralph's face had had the dulled, blurred look of a coin stamped out of metal too soft to resist the battering usage it had received. The only time his face ever cleared and took on its old bright animation was on Saturday afternoons, at ballgames. But of that his mother and family saw only a faint reflection when he came in to supper, stepping lightly, hoarse, dishevelled, good-natured. That first year of Lottie's invalidism had been for Mrs. Bascomb a period of such intolerable care, shame, and strain that she gave almost no thought to Ralph beyond seeing that his meals were on time, his shirts and collars sent regularly to the laundry and his buttons sewed on. Long practice in these matters had increased her natural competence so that she managed such details automatically, without taking her eyes from the incredible complications of the course she was steering.

It was during the first year of Lottie's invalidism that she had slid from her forty-ninth to her fiftieth year and from what was left of her physical youth into the beginning of her old age, as unconscious of her body, of her health, of her personality, as the driver of a war-ambulance over a shell-swept road. As little as he, did she really expect to win through to the end, alive, and with motive power enough to continue. Like him she clutched the wheel, peering blindly ahead into a darkness which was lighted only by terrifying explosions; and from one alarming moment to the next could only try to hold out yet a little longer, and to steer around one more of the chasms in the road which continually yawned before her. Every morning, the instant she woke, she sprang from bed, too conscious of all that needed to be done to know whether or not she was tired or even ill. And every evening as, exhausted, she sank into bed, her only feeling was of astonishment that, for yet another day, she had held their life together.

But by the second summer in 1915, when Dids was seven years old, there came a slackening. Like every one who does not fail entirely in a new undertaking, she had created a technique for her task so that she was no longer forced to the strain of incessant improvisation. Most of the things that were going to happen to Lottie or to Dids had happened, many of them very often. When Mrs. Bascomb saw them coming she no longer summed up all her resources to cope with them, not knowing what she might need. With something of the experienced certainty with which she selected the right one among the familiar tools of her trade in teaching, she now reached for the right method of handling each particular difficulty at home. She knew about what Lottie would do in about all the circumstances which were likely to come up; she had taken Dr. Pell's measure with as close an accuracy as she needed; she had found out about how much and how little Lottie could be left alone with her various playthings; with about what sort of talk to fill in the hours she sat with the invalid; and with what games and other devices to provide Ralph in the time he spent in the sick-room.

It had taken her about a year to pull the material organization of things up out of the chaos with which at first she had barely been able to cope, and that with frantic efforts. Dids had a bright, gay little room, finished off at the other end of the attic; the glass-covered sun-porch addition to Lottie's room was completed and filled with flowering plants (and yet of the three thousand dollars which had been in her saving-bank account when she left Harristown, she still had left almost half); and although she had found it as impossible as any other Gilmanville housekeeper to secure a competent servant, she had arranged a passable division of the work between a charwoman, old Mrs. Rader, a visiting sewing-woman, and the widowed mother of one of her pupils; a woman who was kept at home with a crippled child and needed money. She was a fair cook, and sent into the Bascomb house late in every afternoon the principal dish and dessert for dinner. The period had passed in which Mrs. Bascomb laboured far into the night, doing the work for which she had not found a free instant during the desperate daytime hours.

Yes, when the summer of 1915 had begun and the first year of Lottie's invalidism was behind her, Mrs. Bascomb found herself with the almost forgotten feeling of vacation. Not, to be sure, with an hour of leisure . . . leisure and self-respect she was never to know again . . . but with hours filled only with sixty minutes of occupation. She had the sensation of drawing a long breath, and ventured to take her eyes from the road to see what had been happening to the other people travelling with her along to their unknown destination.

She did not need thus to look at Dids. The little girl had been, as always, the centre of Mrs. Bascomb's scene. She knew much more about what had been happening to Dids in that first decisive year, than about what had happened to herself. The thought of the child was a part of every breath she drew, and the change in Dids during that year shed a clear glory over the loathing of herself and her angry self-justifying blame of Lottie, which were the only personal emotions which Mrs. Bascomb knew at that period. The transformation of the child was, to her grandmother, like the sun rising to a new day and casting its innocent morning rays over a troubled sea writhing in the aftermath of a tornado.

Dids had now passed her seventh birthday, was very tall for her age, very strong, radiated vitality. She had finished the first grade at school, walking sturdily to and fro with her grandmother four times a day. Her active mind had pounced as greedily on all the new life-stuff offered to it in the schoolroom as it always had on any new material presented to it. Experienced teacher as Mrs. Bascomb was, she shared the natural astonishment of Miss Sterns, the first grade teacher, over the little girl's zestful gusto. 'Why, she just *loves* to learn things!' cried Miss Sterns incredulously, amazed at such a phenomenon among children sent to school. 'You don't have to *teach* her! She fairly grabs it off of you.'

What Dids specially wanted to grab (once she had guessed what lay inside book-covers) was the ability to read. Into the attack on that art she flung herself shouting, like a soldier dashing forward to a charge. Long before she could really read, she spelled out everything printed that came before her eyes, from the advertisements in the trams to the directions on the baking-powder cans. She stumbled over the longer words, she made ludicrous guesses, she tripped, she fell, she picked herself up laughing, and rushed on again, her face on fire with eagerness. At the time her mother had become bedridden, she had not learned her letters. The summer after, she was reading – any book she pleased.

Mrs. Bascomb had shared the excitement of that conquest, and she shared also the child's glowing satisfaction in the enchanted world into which she had valiantly fought her way. She and her little granddaughter became familiar sights in the Public Library from this time on. What book to give Dids next was one of the always present thoughts in Mrs. Bascomb's mind, in which there were now so many thoughts, always clashing together in disharmony. Strange-

252

ly mingled with her shame and hatred of herself and of Lottie, was her exultation at seeing the little girl's eager spirit feeding on strong, sweet, marrowy food . . . all sorts of food, for Mrs. Bascomb saw to it that she had first-hand experience of life, as well as that in books, gathering the children of the neighbourhood into her own yard under her own eye, around swings and sand-piles and other bait for children. Dids had never before played with other children (their noise and turbulence had made Lottie nervous), but she found her place at once in this new communal life. From the first she was the leader of her group . . . gay, inventive, good-humoured, masterful, and as bold as a lion in all the crises of little-girl life: – the passage of a panting dog heralded as mad by the shrieks of the neigh-bouring women, the breaking of a limb in the tree they were climbing, the cutting of an artery in a playmate's arm by a fall on broken glass. On such occasions, Dids took command instinctively, white-faced and tense, but collected and cool. She adored play, flinging herself into it with all her energetic might. But she adored no less the hours she spent in reading. As the sun sucks up the dew, she sucked up the contents of the books which Mrs. Bascomb artfully kept lying about the house; Greek myths and Celtic fairy tales; Indian stories and galloping ballads; Grimm and Andersen and Lagerlöf and Lang; Mark Twain and Lewis Carroll (how Dids loved to laugh!); Dickens and Louisa Alcott; historical stories and accounts of how to make things – all was grist to the mill which turned around and around, true on its axis, inside Dids' shining dark head. She shot up tall and strong, morally and intellectually, as she had shot up physically ever since she had sleep and food and quiet. Looking at her face, clear and bright, her grandmother often thought she looked like a nasturtium flower in full sunlight.

But there were times when that clear olive-skinned face was dreamy and quiet, the dark eyes wide, when poetry itself looked out from it, and when Mrs. Bascomb felt falling in her heart the tears she now never allowed herself to shed.

One evening in August of that second summer, looking for Dids at bedtime she went around into the back yard. It was a still, warm, moonlit night, with white mist rising

253

from the ravine back of the house. Near the edge of this creeping white vapour she caught sight of the little girl. She was standing with a long slim stick in her hand, waving it rhythmically, and waving her head slowly from one side to the other. Mrs. Bascomb stood for a moment to watch her, startled by the beauty of the child's face, filled by the loveliness and mystery of the night. She caught a word or two of what the little voice was murmuring,

'The moon like a flower
In Heaven's high bower . . .'

Finally, very gently, 'What are you doing, my darling?' asked the grandmother.

The little girl started and looked around to see who was there. Then, as if she were coming to herself from another world, she gave her sudden brilliant smile, the smile which stabbed her grandmother's heart with pain and joy. 'Oh, I was just magicking a little,' she explained readily, coming to slip her hand into her grandmother's and looking up at her, no shade of self-consciousness in her clear eyes.

Mrs. Bascomb thought of the little girl with the soda-water clerk.

Every day she was finding how strangely resisting and enduring is a human heart, and how infinitely spacious! How could hers carry about such a vast freight of utter misery and bitterness...and yet have room for such utter joy!

As she put the little girl quietly to bed that night, she was squaring her shoulders anew under the heavy, heavy load of her shame . . . and at the same time, trying to cast it off upon Lottie's. This she did forty times a day. Lottie was the one to blame, she told herself. It was Lottie's fault that she herself had become despicable.

And then with Dids' good night kiss, that struggle ended as it always did, by her thrusting both ideas out of her mind as of no consequence. It was no matter that, from being blameless, she had become despicable. If she were to blame for it – why, she was strong enough to carry that burden, to carry any burden, as long as she could see Dids racing free and light-footed before her, up the path which led to the little girl's true life.

Chapter 36

YES, Dids had changed, was wholly transformed during that first year, but Mrs. Bascomb had watched every phase of the change and was perfectly familiar with the child Dids was growing to be. It was when she looked at Ralph that she perceived that a change had taken place without her knowledge during that struggling year of absorption in her own problems. It was a change not only in Ralph but in that part of herself which was touched by Ralph. The relation between them was altered. A barrier between them seemed gradually melting away.

She had not known it was there (or perhaps she had felt it as inevitable between parent and child as the difference in their ages). It was only when she felt it disappearing that she knew she had always lived with it separating her son from her. She had not realized that whenever, after a silence, she said, 'Oh, Ralph . . .' something in him sprang up watchfully and suspiciously on guard. But now that he looked at her with nothing in his eyes but a natural, human consideration of what she said, she remembered the other look of half-defiant, half-alarmed distrust.

It was extraordinary how the absence of the unavowed tension between them sweetened the small, commonplace contacts of every day, gave to their life-in-common a serenity she had never known before. She was surprised to find how comforted she was that she and Ralph could talk together easily and casually on whatever they needed to mention, without considering every meeting as one more skirmish in a hidden duel for supremacy.

After a time, she began to see that this change was not only in Ralph but quite as much in herself. It was true that Ralph was no longer instantly on his guard when she spoke to him; but it was also true that when she spoke to him she no longer had a secret intention of carrying out through him some plan of her own, of influencing him to some action which would be acceptable to her. Having given up her own hopes and desires for him, she no longer felt a vexed disappointment with him.

255

To her astonishment, the absence of this disapproval did more for her than merely to quiet her relations with Ralph. It seemed to sharpen and deepen her vision of him beyond anything she had ever dreamed possible. Ralph was no longer an opaque and resistant mystery to her. When she looked at him, she understood what she saw. She shared what he was feeling because at last she understood it. Or was it the other way around?

The first thing she saw with this new clarity was that Ralph was unhappy. Not merely bored and disappointed and irritated and tired. Really unhappy. She saw now that never before since Ralph's childhood had she known what he was feeling below the surface.

Presently, after more living together on these new terms, she saw that he felt her eyes upon his unhappiness. Then she trembled. Always before, he had shown a hot resentment of any attempt on her part to enter his real life. She scarcely dared believe it when she saw that he now felt no distrustful impulse to hide his unhappiness from her. He did not mind having her eyes rest on him with sympathy and concern. He did not hunch his shoulders irritably, and look away from her, to show that he wished she had not seen. He did not hasten to thrust down to deeper invisibility what he was feeling. He looked back at his mother, and did not hide the trouble in his eyes. They communicated this to each other with no words . . . by the surer language of the intonations in their voices, by the way they looked into each other's eyes when Ralph occasionally kissed her good night, by the touch of his mother's hand on his shoulder as they stood sometimes on the porch before he started off to his distasteful work.

As never before in their lives, Mrs. Bascomb had said to her son, 'I love you. And I share in your trouble,' before she knew what the trouble was.

One afternoon in October, coming home from an errand down town, she saw Ralph, who in the dusk did not see her, emerge abruptly from the door of his office and intercept a slim, tall girl who had passed Mrs. Bascomb a moment before.

The girl stopped at once. 'Oh, how do you do, Mr.

Bascomb?' she called in a gay, friendly tone, which left no doubt of her surprise at seeing him.

The street light glared its cruel revelatory beam into Ralph's face as, stepping rapidly close to the girl and raising his hat eagerly, he answered her salutation. His mother stopped short, terrified at what she saw in his face.

The two young people stood by an instant full in Mrs. Bascomb's line of vision and then, as the girl turned her head, she caught sight of her. 'Oh, good-evening, Mrs. Bascomb,' she said with a natural accent of easy familiarity, 'All the Bascombs out this evening.'

Mrs. Bascomb knew her perfectly, had always known her. She was the youngest daughter of Dr. Dewey, her father's favourite, a bluff, fresh-cheeked, athletic girl at whom everybody smiled as she swung her friendly way through life.

If, the day before, Mrs. Bascomb had been asked how old Mildred Dewey was, she would have said fifteen at the most, possibly seventeen. Now, standing there, her heart beating hard, she made a rapid calculation . . . why, Mildred was twenty-one on her last birthday . . . a grown woman.

Not a beautiful one in spite of her youth and the high-spirited good humour which shone brightly from her blue eyes. As she chatted, she looked from Ralph to his mother and back again, with the same expression for them both. Not a rare woman in any way, but an honest one, and strong and brave . . . she was all that Lottie was not.

Ralph leaned toward her like an ardent boy, his eyes fixed on her hungrily, as though there was nothing in the world to hear but her voice.

She was saying ' . . . the coach took me off in a corner after the first half and said there was nothing to it, I'd have to play guard. I was scared to pieces. But it was fun all the same – corking! I wish you could have seen us rip them up – 17 – 8, you heard? I wish you'd been there.'

'I couldn't get to that Friday night game,' Ralph explained. 'I was detained.'

Mrs. Bascomb remembered. She had asked him to stay at home that evening to play poker with Lottie so that she could take Dids to a historical moving-picture.

The tall girl said heartily, 'Well, we missed you, all right.' She explained to his mother, 'Mr. Bascomb is the greatest old rooter for our team. He surely is one Gilmanville fan all right. He's our mascot, sort of. We don't think we can win a game unless he's in the front row.'

A newsboy passed them, damp, fresh papers over his arm. 'Great Allied Victory on the Russian Front!' he shouted. Neither Mrs. Bascomb nor Ralph paid the least attention to his cry. The war had been going on for more than a year and none of its cries had reached their ears. They had quite other and more pressing things to think of.

'Well, I'll come to the next game sure,' said Ralph. He could not take his eyes from the girl's honest, smiling face. He looked at her with so starved a craving that his mother was startled and glanced back at Mildred. But in that open, unsubtle face there was not a trace of consciousness. Was not Mr. Bascomb a married man? She looked at him with a cruel, impersonal liking, as if he had been a safe old man. 'We'll be looking out for you,' she said gaily, and nodding to them both, she turned away with an elastic step to buy a newspaper. Her father liked to keep track of what was happening in Europe, she remembered.

Mrs. Bascomb and Ralph walked onward side by side in the hideous glare of the electric signs on Main Street. Mrs. Bascomb hoped that no one in the crowds jostling along on the sidewalks would look at Ralph's face. The mother and son did not speak to each other, but Mrs. Bascomb's heart contracted in a painful joy when, after a moment, Ralph passed his arm through hers and took her hand. The moment they turned into the deserted darkness of their own side street, their silence fell from them like a cloak no longer needed.

'Oh, Mother . . .' groaned Ralph.

'My dear, dear boy,' she murmured. Through her pain she felt an astounded pleasure that Ralph did not shut her out, that he allowed her to share his misery.

More than that! To help him! To revolt as he never would. Her old fighting spirit rose with a tigerish, womanish bound. The poor boy should have *one* thing in life,

258

though the Heavens fell! He had been punished enough. It was simple idiocy on the part of society to call the connection between Ralph and Lottie a 'marriage,' to hold him to it with sanctimonious aphorisms of something 'sacred' in it, when it had been in essence something infamous from the beginning on.

Her heart seemed breaking in her breast as she remembered the hungry craving in his boyish face as he had looked at that strong, good, simple girl, his natural mate. She had never dared admit to herself that Ralph was weak, because she knew she felt contempt for weakness. But now she cried it out to herself – Ralph had always been weak, could not master fate, was beaten by life, but she loved him and she was strong and now having no longer anything to hope for for herself had nothing left to fear.

'See here, Ralph,' she said fiercely, '*I* can take care of Lottie and Dids, without you. You could . . . you could go away . . . far away . . . and never be heard of by Gilmanville people again . . . you and . . .'

Her hot, crazy words flashed jaggedly like lightning in the cold darkness.

Ralph was so startled that he stopped short, peering at her through the dusk, to see if she could possibly have meant what she said.

Her eyes left no doubt of that.

'Why, Mother . . . !' he said, open-mouthed.

And then, very strangely from him to his mother, he asked hesitantly, almost blankly, 'Would that be right?'

She blazed out, 'I haven't the least idea any more about what's right and wrong. I don't know that *anything* is right or wrong. But if it's wrong, I'll take it on myself. I'll take the blame. I'll manage so that people will hold me to blame. *You'd* never know.'

Ralph stood facing her, stupefaction on his face. As this passed, a new expression came into his eyes, one that his mother had never seen before, an enduring look, a strong look, a man's look. As she gazed at him, his boyishness faded from his face. She never saw it there again.

He said slowly, with a pause between the words, 'You make me so *sick* of myself!'

He drew her arm again under his roughly and started

259

forward. 'I guess it's time I bucked up and took a brace, that's all,' he told her sternly.

He added in a lower tone, pressing her arm against his side. 'You make me feel like . . . *I* never used to *realize* you were such a . . . Good God! Mother, I guess I can stick it out if you can.'

His voice changed to bitterness. 'It's *my* shooting match, not yours. I'm only getting what's coming to me. There's nothing to do anyhow, *but* to stick it out. Anything else . . . to drag anybody else into the mess. It'd be a crime for me even to think about. Who am *I* to expect anybody to . . .'

He broke off to say with a savage laugh, 'I'll tell you who I am – the biggest damn fool in the world, that's who I am.'

He added severely, 'But I've got a few faint sparks of ordinary sense left, if I am a fool . . . more than you have, apparently. Enough to know that it's up to me to take my own medicine. What do you take me for, anyhow, Mother?'

He spoke as if with indignation, as if he were putting her down brutally, but as they walked forward, he still held her hand tightly, and she felt as she had not felt since he had grown up, that he was glad to have his mother with him. The knowledge of this gave her a joy almost more than she could bear. She was proud of his roughness, of the violence with which he had repelled her so passionately proffered suggestion. She had been mistaken. Ralph was not weaker than she. She felt, with pride, his strength resisting hers and casting her off to one side as he pressed forward.

They walked in silence now, saying through the straining closeness of their handclasp something for which they knew no words. When they came before their own house, they stopped, dreading to go into the light, back into life. They stood there, invisible even to each other in the darkness, looking at the lighted windows of the house which had sheltered their fumbling incomprehensible lives . . . the house in which Ralph had been born, and his child born, and his father had died. It was almost as though they were disembodied souls, looking strangely from afar upon their material bodies.

The wave of feeling within them rose to its crest and broke.

Ralph put both hands on his mother's shoulders and shook her to and fro, as he was shaken by his bewildered pain. 'Oh, Mother! Mother! What's it all about?' he asked her in a loud, passionate whisper.

She had no word to answer him, but through the darkness he saw her eyes shining upon him, and flinging his arms around her neck he burst into sobs.

That she had survived till then – to be there for her son to lean upon, what more, Mary Bascomb asked herself, could any woman wish for?

Chapter 37

ON the day Mrs. Bascomb had taken off the locket, she had stopped reading her Bible and saying her prayers before going to bed; but at night after she turned out her light, she often lay awake for a long time, her mind filled with wide formless conceptions like no thought she ever knew in her busy daylight hours. Soaked in Bible reading as she had always been, it seemed natural to her that through these periods of almost blank contemplation, there often floated a Scriptural phrase, frequently some obscure paradoxical saying of the New Testament which she had never understood but which through repetition from her childhood had become as familiar to her as a memory jingle.

She did not understand them now, not as she understood other ideas. But in those spacious moments of contemplation in the dark she was no longer troubled and bewildered because she could not see the precise meaning of those close-shut hard sayings. Perhaps the part of her that really understood ideas had gone to sleep, worn out with the day's work. The part of her that was left awake seemed to gaze from an immense distance at the events of the day, and at a strange glow, shed upon her inexplicably from a group of words as puzzling and unmeaning to her intelligence as an incantation; but which, her intelligence being passive, shone upon her like sunshine.

'But if it die, it beareth much fruit.'

'He that is least among you all, the same is great.'

'He that loveth his life, loseth it.'

That night after she had known the ineffable sweetness of feeling Ralph lean upon her, she lay in her bed, thinking of that joy, living it over again. She was very tired, she was always very tired at night, and drowsiness soon crept over her exhausted body. With the dulling of part of her consciousness, it was as if a veil had been withdrawn from before her eyes. And yet her physical eyes were shut, leaden with fatigue.

She felt on-coming sleep blur the clear sharp edges of her thoughts; and with this blurring, another veil before her understanding dropped. Her shut eyes saw more clearly.

They saw that she had once more fallen back into loving her life.

How long it took her to learn! She was as sentimental and complacent as ever. She had taken for mother-love her enjoyment of Ralph's leaning on her. As if these later, savagely admonitory years and her love for Dids had not taught her that a mother is not a person to lean upon, but a person to make leaning unnecessary.

This kind of evil spirit is driven not out but by prayer and fasting.

She gave a long sigh that was half a groan, half a *sursum corda*, and the tears ran out of her shut eyes, although now she did not know whether she were awake or dreaming, so profoundly asleep was her tired body, old before its time.

And then through the cold blackness of her room, her alarm-clock was ringing sternly, and it was time to get up. Yes, she had been asleep, it seemed.

A day or so after this, she and Ralph sat alone for a few moments at the supper table, the meal being finished and Dids having gone upstairs to her usual evening duty of helping her mother prepare for the night. Mrs. Bascomb said, 'Ralph, you've never liked the business you're in, have you?'

'Like it?' said Ralph, astonished at the idea.

'I've been thinking,' she continued, 'and I believe I have an idea. I want to tell you about it now, and you must promise to listen to me, clear through, before you say a single word. It won't hurt you to listen to it, even though you think it's foolish . . . at first.'

'Shoot,' said Ralph apathetically.

He listened in silence while she unfolded her idea, looking at her with the smothering, ironical gaze with which some men look at women unfolding plans, sure before the first word was spoken that the whole thing was impractical. She fought wordlessly against this silent hamstringing of her imaginative effort, of the creative thrust upward which had come to her as a reward for intense, impersonal concentration. With difficulty she kept the last of her explanation to the level of hopeful certainty with which she had begun.

When she finished, Ralph said nothing, looked nothing.

'Well?' she asked.

'I didn't know whether I had leave to speak yet,' he said. 'Do you really want to know how it strikes me?'

'Of course,' she told him, nettled in spite of herself, her old quick temper rising.

He got up from his chair and came around the table to her. 'I think it's the craziest idea I ever heard of in my life, bar one,' he said dryly, stooping to soften his words with a caress of her cheek.

She persisted, 'But I told you that Willie Crane said that good sporting editors are hard to find, and are worth money when you find them.'

'So are good presidents of transcontinental railroads hard to find and worth money when you find them,' he said, laughing. 'Why don't you suggest that I start out for one of *those* plums? It'd be just as reasonable.'

She pulled him around in front of her and looked at

him squarely, all the force of her personality in her eyes. 'No, it would not be just as reasonable, and *you know it*,' she said crisply. Then, as twenty years ago she would not have been capable of doing, she let it go at that.

Ralph tried to go on talking and pooh-poohing the idea, 'I never heard such a wild notion in my life. . . . I never wrote a line – not since my daily themes at the University . . . who ever heard of . . .'

But she stopped him with, 'No, don't discuss it now. There's no use, till you've had time to think it over.'

'Discuss it!' Ralph cried out, half laughing, half outraged. 'I'm not discussing it. I'm telling you how insane it is.'

'Isn't once enough to tell me that?' she remarked, and left him shut in with her idea.

A day or so later she met again Wi'lie Crane, as she still continued to call the man who twenty-five years ago had been in her fifth grade, and who having inherited the Harristown *Daily Herald* from his mother's father, had come back from his position on a big Cleveland daily and was struggling to make over the old sheet on new lines.

'Say, Mrs. Bascomb,' he said, overhauling her from behind, 'Say, do you know, I've been thinking about that idea of yours, the other day, and I believe there's something in it. I bet you a nickel Ralph could do it. Lord knows I need him if he can.'

She stopped, looking at him calmly. 'Oh, he could do it all right, there's no doubt,' she said with the authoritative accent of one whose conviction is so firm that he feels no need to shout about it. 'But he won't consider it. I mentioned it to him the other evening, just as a possibility. And he went right through the roof. Said it was a crazy idea.'

'Maybe that's just because you took him by surprise so,' suggested the other.

'Maybe,' she said, letting him have the credit of that idea.

'I can't find anybody around the office who has enough pep to get out of his chair,' complained the new editor. 'Grandfather may have run a good paper back in George

Washington's day, but ever since the war of 1812 he's been accumulating mummies. I'd *like* to have somebody fresh and new on the staff. But of course for Ralph, it'd be leaving a sure thing for an uncertainty . . . and with a sick wife. . . .'

'Oh, I'd be right there to help out with the sick wife,' said Mrs. Bascomb, 'and he could always get another job if this didn't pan out right.'

'He knows more about sporting events than any other man in this town,' reflected Mr. Crane aloud.

'He certainly hasn't missed any since he was in trousers,' said his mother mildly.

Willie Crane laughed, and recalled by her irony to her personal existence, he looked at her with the liking (a reflection of the tenderness they feel for their own past) which some men have for their old nurses, or cooks, or school teachers . . . sometimes even for their mothers. 'Would *you* like him to make the change?' he asked with a special intonation which made her answer of importance in the matter.

She saw the friendliness in his eyes, and watching him closely, put on it as much weight as she thought it would bear. 'Yes, I would, Willie, very much indeed,' she said with feeling. 'You know what a hard time Ralph has had, all along. He never liked this printing business where he is now. He only fell into it because he had to do something right away . . . or because we thought he did. He'd do ever so much better in work he really cared something about. And I believe that this proposition we're talking about would suit him. I've known him for twenty-nine years now, and I've seen that the thing he has continued really to care about, right along, through thick and thin, has been athletic sports. I used to think he'd outgrow it. But it seems to mean more and more to him. It's his religion. Why wouldn't he make a good job of telling other people about what he loves, about what is all he really cares about?'

The warmth of her conviction struck a spark from her listener. 'By George, I believe he could,' said the new editor of the *Herald*.

'Well, *he* doesn't seem to think so,' said Mrs. Bascomb,

and having dropped this oil upon the fire she was kindling she walked on; once more leaving an achieved effect unspoiled by one stroke too many.

An evening or so after this, she saw Ralph eyeing her half-humorously across the table, and knew that Willie Crane had been talking to him.

'He started it,' she said boldly guessing. 'He came up behind me and I couldn't head him off.'

'A whole lot you tried to!' said Ralph. But he did not speak heavily or resentfully. Holding his tone in her ear and taking it slowly to pieces afterwards, Mrs. Bascomb thought there was in it a certain involuntary lightness. She was encouraged. 'I always did like Willie Crane,' she said to herself, although as a matter of fact she had, for years, till his reappearance, forgotten that such a person existed.

A period followed when to save Ralph's face, she looked the other way assiduously and saw nothing of what he was doing.

'He won't let go the job he's got till he's tried himself out a little at the other,' Willie Crane told her, on one of their casual street corner encounters, some weeks later. 'He's trying his hand at reporting the basket-ball games (the men's teams, he says he can't bother going to the girls'). Not for publication . . . just to see what he can do.'

'How *does* he do?' asked his mother eagerly, and yet annoyed to be forced to ask this of an outsider.

'Not so awfully well,' said Willie uncompromisingly. 'Gets, pretty well booked at times. No punch to most of it. Kind of soggy. But he's got an idea about how to do it, his way. That's something. If he can get hold of it by the right end, maybe he can fetch her loose.'

It was hard for Mrs. Bascomb's pride to have thus her only information about what was going on in Ralph come from another; to have him in a struggle, once more shut himself away from her. She had not, she sometimes thought sadly, deserved this from Ralph.

But the discipline of her later years had not encouraged her to brood over what she did or did not deserve to receive. Uncomplainingly and silent, from a distance, she watched Ralph as she sat across the table from his abstracted, deeply concentrated face, or stepped about her housework, while on the other side of the door to his room, he sat late wrestling with pencil and paper. Lottie complained that Ralph was less and less company for her every day, so that Ralph's mother was more and more occupied in filling his place, and had little time to let even her silent sympathy weigh upon her son.

For in one of those wide, vacant, brooding moments before she fell asleep, she had seen that even her sympathy now was an intrusion, that there was a reason for Ralph's shutting her out, that now was a moment when Ralph must stand alone, or not at all; that now was a time for his mother as well as all other outside helps to be non-existent.

She was touched, she was astonished at the tenacity with which Ralph laboured. Judging him by what she had seen of him, she had thought that of all his qualities tenacity of purpose was precisely the one of which he was most incapable. She perceived now that she had never seen him before directing his effort to anything that seemed really worth while to him. That it should be *games!* The serious-minded elderly woman was lost in wonder at it. And yet how she missed seeing it before? All these years, it had been crying out to her eyes. She had not wished to see it, that was why she had missed it, she told herself. She had not been able till her son was thirty years old, really to admit the possibility that he might be quite a different person from herself.

'He's going strong,' said Willie Crane, in mid-summer, with a humorous conspiratorial air. 'That peach of a report of the ball-game between the Harristown boys and our team was his. He's got his teeth in it all right, I guess.'

At the emotional feminine pleasure which showed in Mrs. Bascomb's face, a decent business man's caution sprang to life, alarmed. 'Of course, you must understand,' he said, anxious to tone down her expectations, 'a little two-for-a-cent sheet like mine can't ever pay big city salaries. It'd be pretty lean pickings for a time, probably; and at first he'd have to do other reporting . . . cover all sorts of things, fires and police courts and burglaries. But there's a chance for him if he really gets on. There's room for a man's whole time on a sports sheet. That's what the men, every mother's son of them, buy a paper for. That's the page you see 'em reading on the trams. Of course I'll have to keep on buying the syndicated big league sporting-page stuff. But that doesn't do a thing to put the *Herald* out in front. A reader can get that in any wide-awake daily in the county. What I want Ralph to work up is the same sort of line about our local teams all over this section. Not one of our readers in a hundred has ever seen a big league game. That doesn't keep them from liking to read snappy personals about Walter Johnson or Ty Cobb. Doesn't it stand to reason they'd lick up the same line about the men they really see play? I can get any cub to work out fielding averages . . . so can all the other papers, but if Ralph can put personality into it . . . that would put the *Herald* on every news-stand in the county. We've got a great little sporting territory. It ought to go big. But of course if he falls down there'll be nothing in it, and fixed as he is with a sick wife and an eight-year-old kid, it'd be a crime to let him gamble too much.'

She opened her lips to say, 'He couldn't earn much less than he's making now,' but a shrewd reading of the man before her shunted her off from this avowal to saying with emphasis, 'If he enjoys the work, he'll probably do it well, and soon be worth more.' Willie Crane had never been a boy, she remembered, to let anybody beat him on a trade of marbles.

When, several months later, the change was really made, although Ralph's mind was filled to overflowing by the excitement and interest of his struggle, past and to come, still he made an effort to give his mother an explicit verbal acknowledgment of her part in what meant so much to him. As part of his announcement and explanation of the new work, he told her generously, 'Do you know, I don't believe I'd ever have thought of it, except for you.'

She needed no effort to restrain a smile of amusement at this, for she scarcely heard his words, so loudly did the brightness of his eager, life-filled face speak to her heart.

268

'This is his true-love,' she said to herself, and reflected that if he had all but forgotten her existence, he had also evidently all but forgotten Mildred Dewey as he had forgotten Margaret Hill years ago; as Lottie had dropped from his real life. Now he was a free man, freed from his mother as from other women.

'A newspaper reporter!' commented Lottie, surprised. 'A sporting events reporter. For goodness sakes, what a funny sort of business! What salary are you going to get?'

Chapter 38

RALPH had been in newspaper work for eight years before there came slowly, almost furtively, into Mrs. Bascomb's mind some thought of the possibility that after all she might yet salvage for herself a few years of life, that it might not be out of the question for her to know a few hours of leisure, with no one expecting anything from her. During those eight years of reporting, Ralph's earning capacity had constantly risen. He had a good salary on the Harristown *Herald*, and he had built up as a vivid reporter of games a reputation which went outside their own part of the State. This meant occasional orders for extra articles for the Sunday editions of the larger Cleveland and Buffalo papers, and extra assignments to cover more important athletic events all around that section of the country. Such work, although irregular, was very well paid, and for their quiet scale of living made considerable additions to their income. Ralph loyally considered all these extra earnings as additions to the family income, not to his own. He spent little on himself and evidently one of the heartiest of the many new pleasures in his life was having money to bring home for his mother to spend on his wife and his little girl. He was very good to them all, his three women folk; very fond of Dids, very proud of her being in the basket-ball and swimming teams; always generous and kind and good-natured; a great bestower of gifts. But of course he saw little of them, coming and going at irregular hours, to and from Harristown, often out late at night and sleeping late the next day. Even when he was physically at home, eating at the same table with them, he was often far away, listening with a pleasant smile and not too obviously wandering an eye to their home-talk, but given to springing up in the middle of one of their sentences to rush to the telephone.

They knew as little of the life represented by these telephone conversations as he did of theirs. When he came back, he often said conscientiously, 'Excuse me, Mother (or Dids, or Lottie), what was that you were saying? I didn't mean to interrupt you, but I just remembered that I hadn't told Ferguson I'd cover that automobile race in Rochester.' (Or the prize-fight in Oneonta, or the football game in Columbus). But the lopped-off conversation seldom renewed itself. He did not notice this. After a time no one else did (except his mother). His relations to his family were, after all, just those of all the other good providers on the same street to their families.

The Bascombs had at last dropped into the accepted mould, and their Gilmanville neighbours stopped commenting on them in any but a casual way. It was luck for Ralph Bascomb, people said (only now they began to call him Mr. Bascomb), that he had his mother with him to do the housekeeping and take care of his invalid wife; and on the other hand, of course, it was a good thing for Mrs. Bascomb, because that arrangement made a nice home for her. Except for that, she'd be all alone in the world and entirely dependent on herself, which was always hard for a woman as everybody knew.

And what a smart girl Dids Bascomb was growing up to be, her neighbours remarked, as they saw her marching by, her sleek, well-brushed dark head held high. She was president of her class in the high school, the first girl ever to be elected president of the senior class. Gilmanville gossip had enjoyed talking over the rough-house started by some of the meaner boys because they wouldn't stand for a girl's being president. They had said they were going to break up the first class meeting Dids presided over, and the townspeople repeated to each other with amusement and respect the story of how Dids had put the amount of

business with one hand tied behind her back, so to speak
– how energetically the day before the meeting she had
organized and prepared those boys who were on her side
and all the girls; and how fearlessly she had jumped on the
ringleaders of the opposition the minute they started trouble.
She had had them put out of the meeting before they could
catch their breath and then, as cool as a cucumber, jollied
along all the rest of the crowd, putting the regular business
right through the mill like a practised old hand. The whole
thing was over and adjourned before her opponents could
really get together. She was a snappy one all right, Dids
Bascomb was. Gilmanville people were proud of the tall
girl, who had a lively, good-natured word for everybody,
for there was not a shy hair in her head, and she knew
everybody in town, black and white, big and little. No
nonsense about her. The real thing. A good sport if there
ever was one. Half the girls in town tried to copy her style.
You could see Dids Bascomb's clean middy blouses, low-
heeled shoes, and thick woollen stockings on every street
corner, worn by girls who were trying to look like her.
But none of them, Gilmanville men used to say, could copy
the way she looked at you, straight in the eye, bing! And
nobody had Dids' smile, that broke through her clear
straight look like a streak of sunshine. Everybody fell for
Dids when she smiled. Just wait till Dids got into the State
University, Gilmanville people said, and she'd show them
a thing or two. She'd prove that a small town can turn out
girls who are leaders as well as cities can. But she'd
make a hole in Gilmanville, all right, when she went
away. The little kids would miss her. Everybody would
miss her.

For Dids was counting, of course, on going away to the
State University. Mrs. Bascomb too was counting on her
going away as an element in her own release. She was now
far in the background of Dids' life (as of Ralph's) and she
knew that, along with the rest of Gilmanville life, she would
recede to invisibility after Dids went away to the bigger
world. There was nothing more she could do for Dids.
Nor for Ralph. And now that Ralph had money he
could hire somebody to do for Lottie all that she had done.
A good nurse, accustomed to chronic invalidism (for

271

Lottie was genuinely and helplessly a bedridden invalid by this time), would take care of Lottie better than she could. And if she paid Dids' expenses at college, Ralph would have enough money to pay for a nurse easily.

At the thought of laying down her burden, she felt dizzy. It was no pretty, envy-provoking installation, she now longed for, with a fine bathroom and a correctly æsthetic sitting-room in which to pour tea for committees. What she dreamed of now was silence . . . and an emptiness about her. A little hall bedroom (she would never even know how it was furnished, provided it had a bed) into which she could plod when her school hours were over, where she could sink down for hours of blessed emptiness of all that had so long irked her. Nobody to call on her; nothing to decide for anyone else; no need to look up responsive to someone else's mood; no need to master the million-times renewed problems of material life; no need to be sure that the intonations of her voice did not betray her deadly weariness; no need to pour out interest and sympathy and attention and care from her almost exhausted reservoir. For she felt that her heart was parched to dustiness with fatigue. The mere possibility of winning through to a period of peace made her feel weak and faint with relief.

She spoke of it to Ralph and found him, as he always was now, very kind, very willing to let her make any arrangement she liked, and at an incalculable distance from her. 'Would you really like to go off that way by yourself, Mother, in a little room in a boarding-house in Harristown?' he asked, with the reasonable tone of a patient adult trying to bring home to a child the impractical aspect of one of its half-baked ideas. 'You know,' he told her warningly, 'you got pretty lonesome when you tried that once, years ago.'

She could think of no answer to this, beyond murmuring, 'Well, I'm a good deal older now, sixty, my next birthday.' This had no bearing on the matter, but she knew that for his inattentive eye it would pass muster as an answer to his statement.

'Well, of course, Mother, whatever *you* want to do,' he said indulgently. 'I don't see why it wouldn't be all right to have a nurse take care of Lottie. As you say, her condition changes so little. Goodness knows, I haven't anything better to spend my money on than on you and Lottie and Dids.'

'You're a good boy,' she told him gently.

She added after a moment's thought, 'We'd better not say anything to Dids about it till we're a little surer. There's no point in talking of plans that aren't settled.'

'Just as *you* say,' he agreed with his usual, easy, pre-occupied willingness to leave it all to her.

But when she spoke to Lottie . . .

She had thought that any surprises that Lottie could give were in the past. For years now, their relations had run more and more smoothly as, around Lottie's life, the granite walls of habit rose, day by day, in ever-higher massiveness. Lottie had seemed quite contented to think about nothing but the little ebb and flow of sickroom events – her meals, the doctor's visits, the variation in her appetite and sleep, her small invalid occupations, the arrival or non-arrival of visitors, the developments in the latest burglary, murder, or divorce in the New York newspapers, the newest cut in house-dresses. There was nothing in this well-established routine which a good nurse could not provide for her as well as her mother-in-law, and this was what Mrs. Bascomb explained to her, carefully and re-peatedly, on the day when she first broached the subject of her own retiring from the family life.

Nothing gave Mrs. Bascomb the slightest warning of the storm which broke when Lottie finally understood what was being planned. None of Lottie's old outbreaks had been as violent as the hysterical tempest which over-whelmed her now. She wept so terribly, she talked so wildly about wishing she could die on the instant, she threatened so passionately to 'do something awful' if she were left 'all alone,' that Mrs. Bascomb, helpless before her own granite-like habit of keeping Lottie quiet at all costs, could think of nothing to do except to pat Lottie's hand when she could get hold of it in the intervals of Lottie's frantic gesticulations, and to smooth back the silk covers which Lottie thrust aside, as she threatened to drag herself to the window and cast herself down.

'There! There! we won't talk about it now,' murmured Mrs. Bascomb distractedly. 'We'll think about something else.'

Stronger than anything else in her mind was her astonishment. What could be the matter with Lottie? What made her act so? It must be that she had not really understood that she would have a nurse all to herself, to wait on her all the time, to read to her and serve her . . . that she would never be alone as she often was now.

Mrs. Bascomb decided that she would wait until Lottie was calmer, had had time to take in the idea more clearly, before she tried again to talk to her about it. For she had not the slightest idea of giving up the plan. Why should she?

But every time she tried again, Lottie dissolved in tears. She did not let Mrs. Bascomb get past the first words of her explanation before bursting into sobs. She did not cry wildly now, or threaten. She merely wept as though Mrs. Bascomb were breaking her heart with every word she said.

Against those silent tears, Mrs. Bascomb brought out all her invincibly logical explanations of how agreeable the change would be to Lottie, how much more attention she would have, and how pleasant it would be for her to have a trained attendant who would know how to bathe her with professional skill, and who would have all the time in the world to read to her, and play cards with her.

Lottie refuted these irrefutable arguments by the simple method of not paying the least attention to them. She only wept steadily till her handkerchief was a wet rag, and Mrs. Bascomb had to bring her another.

The two women were in a deadlock, and there they stayed for weeks (quite unnoticed by Ralph and Dids, coming and going cheerfully). And then with one thrust, Lottie reduced all Mrs. Bascomb's fabric to dust. One day out of a silence, she said, keeping her eyes on her mother-in-law's face, 'If you go away, Dids has got to stay with me. She ought to. I sacrificed my health for her when she was little, and it's time she did something for me. I ought to have some of my own family with me. It's selfish for her to go off to the University, if I'm going to be alone. What does she want with any more education, anyhow? She

274

ought to stay with her sick mother. If she had any proper feeling, she would. It's her duty to. *And I'm going to tell her so.*'

Mrs. Bascomb staggered under the blow, for she knew it was one she could not parry. After she had drawn one or two long breaths, so that her heart had stopped leaping wildly, she said, 'Oh, wait a while, Lottie. Nothing's decided yet.'

But it was decided from that moment, and she knew it. It was almost more than she could endure. To stay there and alone with Lottie! With Dids gone! Yet it was inevitable. She saw it now. How could she not have seen before that she had been carefully preparing, during all those years, a deadly danger for Dids? She had loved seeing Dids gallantly swing into whatever action she thought was right, never counting the cost, springing to the defence of weakness, warm-heartedly shouldering burdens too heavy for others. But the very thought of the girl's high-hearted magnanimity now terrified her. For it was a trait which would leave her quite helpless before such a claim as Lottie would know how to voice. She thought of the silent, effaced, young-old spinsters she had known, withered without having bloomed, who had 'devoted their lives to their invalid mothers.' Good Heavens! Suppose she herself should die . . . before Lottie did . . . or at least before Dids had grown to her full stature! In her panic at this new possibility, she forgot her own tragic disappointment.

She added this new terror to her other burdens and squaring her shoulders under a pack which twenty years before would have crushed her, she stepped forward steadily. She could not go away and rest? Very well, she would never think of it again. And she would not die, since she must not. She had learned many things about what there is room for in the human heart. She was learning now, something of the limitless endurance of the same heart. It can endure anything, she found, just as it has room for everything. Or *almost* everything . . . not, of course, for tolerance of Lottie's, she told herself hastily, hanging for dear life to her scorn.

The fact of having created with her own hands " the danger for Dids, to avoid which she now sentenced herself

275

to life-imprisonment, was, for a nature like hers, one more reason for not whimpering. She remembered Ralph's rough comment on his own trouble, and told herself in his words, 'I'm only getting what's coming to me.' To take standing up, the consequences of your own actions was the only decent thing. She *must* endure it. And hence could.

Some days later, when she thought she could speak quietly about it, she said to Ralph, 'I don't believe I'd better carry out that plan about going away to live by myself, after all. I've been thinking it over, and I think I'd better give it up.'

The momentary blankness in his face told her that he had not thought of it since she had spoken about it. But in an instant, he remembered. 'Oh, yes. Well, just as *you* say, Mother,' he told her kindly. 'I always want things fixed to suit you.'

Neither she nor Lottie ever spoke of it again.

Chapter 39

FROM almost the first days of Ralph's marriage, Mrs. Bascomb had been more or less aware of the existence of Lottie's father. She had known his quaint name, Alvah P. Hicks, his occupation (he was night-watchman in one of the large shoe-factories in Harristown), and had heard more than she cared to about the folly of his second marriage with a disagreeable woman, which took place shortly after Lottie's own. Her violent disapproval of this marriage had cut her off entirely from her father. Apparently there had been few regrets on her side. At least she had said nothing about feeling any regret at never seeing her father, and at bringing up her little girl with no knowledge of her grandfather. But one of the unregarded pieces of information about Lottie which was slowly dissolving in Mrs. Bascomb's mind was a notion that Lottie often felt things of which she did not speak : – perhaps because she was not clearly conscious that she felt them, perhaps because she did not know how to speak of them, perhaps because of the total absence in her early habit-forming years of anyone to whom it was possible to speak of feelings. Such unavowed currents of emotions beneath the surface might be the explanation (Mrs. Bascomb occasionally felt) of the inexplicable changes of mood in which Lottie had always been so baffling to her. Perhaps they had also been baffling to Lottie.

At least, nothing that Mrs. Bascomb had ever seen in Lottie could account for the startled pain she showed, when, about the time of Dids' graduation from high school, she received a letter from the district nurse of Harristown, appealing to her as the only discoverable relative of Mr. Hicks. He was dying, it seemed of an incurable wasting disease, and his wife having died a year or so ago, had no one to look out for him. The little pension given him since his illness by his employers was quite inadequate to provide proper care for a man so ill.

Dids had taken this letter up to her mother, whose hair was just being brushed and dressed by Mrs. Bascomb. Surprised at receiving a letter (for she had no correspondents), Lottie tore it open and read it quickly. It was to her mother-in-law she turned with a cry of distress. 'Oh, Momma, you must go to see him!' she exclaimed, clutching at Mrs. Bascomb's hand. 'Poor Poppa! All alone, and sick, and nobody to look out for him. Oh, Momma, do go right away and see about it. Poor Poppa!'

'If Granny's going, I'm going with her,' said Dids. 'He's no relation to her but he's my own grandfather.' For, long ago, Dids had figured out that there was more to relationships than she had thought, at first, and now knew quite accurately how the generation above her was tied together.

So it was a tall, upright girl of seventeen, and a tall bent woman of sixty, who went with the district nurse of Harristown, up the steps of the poor boarding-house, in the poor district. They were met at the door by the landlady who couldn't be bothered any longer with a moneyless, sick, old man.

An hour later, when they came down the steps, Dids' young face was white and her eyes reddened. She held

277

fast to her grandmother's hand as if she were still a little girl.

For a moment, Mrs. Bascomb and the nurse stood together, talking in business-like tones. 'I can't come for him till after four o'clock,' said the nurse. 'I can't leave the office till then. My assistant is taking her vacation and there's nobody to answer the 'phone. But if I get here with the ambulance at half-past four, I should think I'd have him at your house before dark, don't you think?'

'Yes,' said Mrs. Bascomb, making an inner calculation, 'and that'll be better for me. I can have everything ready for him by that time. I think we can catch the 11.20 train now, if we hurry.'

The nurse dropped her voice and said in a low tone, 'You can see for yourself, it won't be for long. You won't need to make any very permanent arrangements.' Then dismissing the subject with professional calm, she turned to the next thing and consulting her note-book said, 'I've got to step around the corner to a cancer case. So I'll have to leave you now.' She shook hands with them both, and walked briskly away from them.

Dids and her grandmother turned towards the station, Dids still clinging with all her might to Mrs. Bascomb's hand. 'Oh, Granny!' she said quaveringly. 'How awful! How awful! That miserable dark little room . . . so dirty . . . all alone. Only that terrible hating woman to fling him a mouthful of food once in a while. And he'd been there for months! How he looked at you when you said we'd take him home . . . oh, Granny, how *horribly* glad he was! It made me sick to see how glad. It made you realize how he'd been . . . but I was ashamed of myself to burst out crying so. Granny, you were just great. How can you keep so quiet and steady always?'

'It's part of what people learn, dear, as they get older . . . to stand things,' said her grandmother, turning to the girl's quivering distress a quiet, loving face. 'It makes up for some things you lose as you get older.'

She meant never to say such things to Dids, remembering very well the impatient incredulity of her own youth, when older people talked in that tiresome, sententious way. But sometimes, it seemed to her, that young as Dids

278

was and normal as she was, she was kinder, less hard to older people, more loving, than she herself had been in her youth. It did not occur to Mrs. Bascomb that she might have any part in this. She only thought humbly once in a while, 'Dids is so sweet, always, to her old Granny.' She thought of this as a merit of Dids, like her limpid unconsciousness of being looked up to by her comrades, and of being brilliant and strong.

On the train as they sat silent, their minds filled with what they had seen, Dids repeatedly stirred and turned towards her grandmother, opening her lips and shutting them again. Finally, 'Say, Granny . . . I don't know how to say it . . . but I just want you to know,' she began gruffly like an embarrassed boy. 'It's awfully white of you to take him right home. You're . . . you're just all *right*, Granny!'

'It's only what anybody would have done under the circumstances,' murmured Mrs. Bascomb in the accepted formula. But at Dids' praise a deep flush had come to her pale face which took for a moment, the girl thought, an expression so beautiful that she scarcely knew it for her grandmother's face.

But a moment later, she was saying practically, 'I am planning to move your father out of his room for the present. He's going to be away a good deal this summer anyhow. I'll make up a bed for him in the alcove off the living-room, on the couch there.'

'Let me give up *my* room,' cried Dids, eager to sacrifice herself, just as her grandmother knew that she would have given up anything her mother asked for. Thinking of this and squaring her shoulders once more under her staggering load, she answered, as if after reflection, that she thought Dids' room was up too many stairs to be convenient for a sick man.

As a matter of fact, the change, the good care, the sudden relief from anxiety, together with the energetic measures of Dr. Dewey gave the shrunken little old man a brief period of more strength than any of them had dreamed possible for him. (Mrs. Bascomb called in Dr. Dewey for him, as she always had for all the family except Lottie.

279

Her explanation of this to Lottie had been that for their simple ordinary complaints they did not need an expensive specialist like Dr. Pell).

Mr. Hicks, brought into the house on a litter, stricken, grey-faced, wasted away to a shred, his bony old hands lying as limp on the sheet as though he were already laid out for his grave, was in a week's time sitting up in bed and asking for his clothes. 'Only let me get my trousers on, doctor,' he said, 'and I'll feel like a man again.'

'Let him do whatever he likes,' said Dr. Dewey to Mrs. Bascomb one morning as she stood outside on the porch with him. 'It's a matter of a few weeks at the longest, and no harm done if he shortens it by doing what he takes a fancy to. All anybody can do for him is to make him as comfortable as possible.'

Mrs. Bascomb was astonished. 'Is it possible that he can ever get up on his feet again?' she asked.

'Didn't you ever see a dying candle flare up just before it went out?' he returned.

So Mr. Hicks was given his trousers, and leaning on his granddaughter's muscular arm, he shuffled his way in to see his bedridden daughter. Lottie cried a little when she first saw him, and he was embarrassed and did not know what to say to her. But before long, reminiscences unloosed their tongues, and Mrs. Bascomb, coming and going about the house, heard a steady murmur of talk from Lottie's room. . . 'Did you ever hear about what happened to that Wheeler boy that run away from home?' and 'The year when the flood came all the way up Mullin Avenue. . .' and, 'No, he married again and had two children, a boy and a girl.'

In this last flaring up of life, the old man even got himself downstairs, and once or twice out on the street, clinging for dear life to Dids, her straight tall body as strong as a young tree. The weight of his emaciated frame was no more for her than that of a dried leaf. 'I could pick you up with one hand and carry you upstairs, Grandfather,' she sometimes told him laughingly, to his great delight.

For she always called him 'Grandfather' and was on excellent joking terms with him. Closely as Mrs. Bascomb watched her, she never seemed to shrink from being seen on the street with the shabby old working-man, answering unabashed the greetings of her friends in his barbarous bad grammar. Mrs. Bascomb knew very well that when she had been seventeen, it would have been anguish for her to acknowledge as her grandfather a common, ignorant labouring man. But Dids, adolescent though she was, seemed never to think of this. There was apparently nothing in her heart at this time save a burning and indignant compassion. 'I only wish there was *something* I could think of that I could do to make it up to him!' she said once to her grandmother, rubbing the tears roughly away from her eyes. But to the old man, she showed only a droll, affectionate gaiety which enchanted him.

Mrs. Bascomb felt an almost reverent pride in Dids' bigness of heart. Watching the tenderness in the girl's bright face as she talked with her grandfather, Mrs. Bascomb often said to herself, 'Only a strong soul can pity like that . . . *purely*, without condescension or disdain.' Such stuff in the child! Such fine, straight, sound material there. Mrs. Bascomb knew whence it had come. In those days when they were waiting for death to enter the house it sometimes seemed to her that she saw Dids walking between two old men, her two grandfathers, who both bent upon her a shining look of confidence and hope.

The flash of renewed strength faded as quickly as it had flared up. By the end of July, Mr. Hicks rose no more from the bed, where he lay, spent and emptied, looking out of his open door into the passage. Ralph engaged a nurse to come in by the day, to give the old man the necessary medical care; but the old man's eyes turned constantly towards Mrs. Bascomb, and his grey face lighted up dimly when she went past his door.

'I suppose you always look to him the way you did when you went into that awful place and promised to take care of him,' said Dids to her grandmother. She put her arms suddenly around Mrs. Bascomb's neck. 'Well, you do to me, too,' she said in a trembling voice. Their hearts were all quivering and soft as the shadow slowly drew near.

The dying man never asked for a moment of Mrs. Bascomb's time, and indeed after the nurse went home every evening, never asked for anything at all. And there was nothing that need be done for him in the night. But Mrs. Bascomb, always a light sleeper, came down once in a while with a candle, in her wrapper and slippers, to make a round of the house to see that all was well and often found the old man awake, his eyes patiently turned toward the door as if he were hoping she might come in. If she put her candle on his table and sat down in the nurse's chair by his bedside, he showed an eager, remorseful pleasure. 'You'd ought to go back to your rest,' he told her. 'You do enough as 'tis, and more too.'

But when she settled herself in the chair as if to stay for a time, he gave a sigh of relief.

And yet he seemed to have little to say to her, and not to expect much talk from her. It was a comfort to him, he told her once, just to have her there, 'to keep him company.' Sometimes he seemed to doze off, but at the least stir from her, his eyes opened upon her, with a faint, apologetic smile, as if he wished to tell her that it would not be for long, his bothering of her. Once in a while he made some brief remark which showed that he spent many of his dark, wakeful hours in thinking about the household in which he found himself. He had evidently learned that praise of Dids would please her grandmother and it was usually to speak of her that he stirred himself from the silence in which he lay, slowly slipping over the brink of death. 'You've done an awful good job on Dids. She's as fine as they make 'em.' Or, 'That second time we went out on the street, we run into the head perfesser in her school and he said to me he said that he hadn't never *had* a better all 'round student than what Dids is.'

Of himself, he never spoke at all, beyond occasionally apologizing for being so much trouble. 'I hadn't ought to let you lose your sleep this way,' he said faintly one night; 'the nurse is all right. She's a good girl. But I know just how Lottie felt when she thought you were going away from her . . . like the bottom had fell out of every-thing.'

Mrs. Bascomb was surprised to know that Lottie had

spoken to him about that episode which was never mentioned between them. He saw the surprise in her face and misinterpreted it. 'Why, didn't you *know*,' he asked her, 'that Lottie felt perfectly terrible at the idea of not having you here? She told me she'd just give up and die if she lost you.' Mrs. Bascomb's look of surprise deepened to blankness, to amazement. In all her conjectures about that affair, the one idea which had never occurred to her was that it might have been *sorrow* which Lottie felt at the idea of her going away! The idea was as startling to her as if in a blank wall before her, a door had opened – and beyond the door a path leading to an unknown country. Lottie had given her one more surprise.

She was too much shaken to speak, and sat motionless, trying to take in the meaning of what she had heard, so strange an expression on her face that the dying man looked at her wonderingly. Presently in his husky voice, he said, 'I don't believe you've got the least idee, Mis' Bascomb, how much Lottie thinks of you!'

After a silence he murmured, 'Why wouldn't she? You're the best that ever come *her* way. Look at all you've done for her. And she appreciates it too. You're the only person she's ever really loved, I guess.'

At this, Mrs. Bascomb looked down and away to hide from the sick man the shamed, horrified pain which came into her face. He said no more that night.

Another time on one hot August night, as she sat there, her head tipped back against her chair, her eyes lifted to the ceiling, her mind full of wonder as to the meaning of her life, of anyone's life, her silent vitality filling the room with a stronger stimulant than any the nurse could give the dying man, he remarked gently, 'She never had no chance, my poor girl hadn't. If she'd a-ben looked out for, the way you've looked out for Dids . . .'

Later that night, in a faint, apologetic voice, 'But we didn't know no better, her mother and me.'

And finally, after a long time, so low that Mrs. Bascomb barely heard him, 'Nobody ever learned us any better.'

The next night when she stepped into his room, she saw him lying with the patient, waiting look on his face, his eyes turned towards the door. His eyes were open. But they were not alive.

Mrs. Bascomb set down her candle, closed the eyes gently, and straightening the skeleton-like old hands, folded them across his breast. After this, she sat by the bed, her own eyes closed, for a long time, before calling anyone.

Chapter 40

FLORENCE KING and her young brother were to come round for Dids in their Ford at nine o'clock that September morning, so that the two girls would have time to reach the University campus by daylight and have everything unpacked and in their rooms by supper-time. Florence, Dids, and Charlie were all to perch in the front seat, leaving the back free for the two steamer trunks, the sofa pillows, pennants, framed photographs, gramophone and records, curtains, rugs, table-cover, tennis-rackets . . . 'all the junk to make your room look right,' as Dids had said the night before, bringing it by armfuls down the stairs.

From the accumulations of the decade of years she had lived in that slant-ceilinged room, she picked out what suited her present taste, and turned her back as joyously on the rest as on her childhood. 'My! It'll be nice to have a room big enough to hang pictures up decently,' she exclaimed. 'Florence says we have drawn one of the dandiest rooms in the girls' dorm. I'm crazy to get there and see it, and begin to fix it up.' Without a pause she ran on rattlingly, 'Here, I believe I'll take those hanging bookshelves after all. Charlie could tie them on the running-board.' She laughed out delightedly. 'That old Ford'll look like a gipsy van all right. But they say everybody that knows his way round, rolls up on the campus with a lot of junk piled into an old car. The worse you look the more it shows you know what's what. I'd hate to go primping in with just a new, shiny suitcase. This way's lots more fun.'

It was so much fun that the house was filled from top to

bottom with the cheerful animation of the departure. Florence King came early to compare notes about what to take, and the two tall children raced up and down stairs, shouting questions and answers to each other, deciding on this, rejecting that and clutching at something else, laughing incessantly from high spirits. The golden clarity of the September sun poured in through open doors and windows on their shining heads, with a gaiety like that of their chiming, chattering voices. The bright air quivered about them, as they flung themselves here and there shouting – 'Have you your towels ready? You know we take our own towels?' And, 'Where did you put that volume of Masefield?' And, 'Oh, you've had your racket re-strung. Isn't it dandy!'

For Mrs. Bascomb, sitting in her attic-room, her hands folded on her lap, her dry eyes fixed on the distant sky, the noise and youth and gaiety were like a shimmering high tide. She knew that to-day marked its ebbing away from her for ever.

'There's Charlie coming with the car, now, and I haven't the teacups packed.'

'Never mind! He can begin carrying out what we *have* got ready and packing them in. It's going to take some packing, believe. *me*.'

Charlie's voice now came up to Mrs. Bascomb, adolescent and reedy. 'Gee whillikens, girls! You must be crazy! Why don't you take along the feather bed and the hen coop while you're about it!'

Rushing in and out, trampling of eager young feet, laughing voices screaming out of the windows . . . Mrs. Bascomb closed her eyes to hear it better. She would never hear it again. Dids was leaving home. Her life at home was ended.

'Hi, there, Flo,' squeaked Charlie's voice, 'what do you take me for? Heavyweight champion? You girls can just carry one end of this yourselves!'

Flutterings . . . laughing . . . shuffling feet, things dropped, things thrown downstairs. . . 'Here, *catch!* Oh, you muffed it!'

They were out on the front walk now, by the Ford. Mrs. Bascomb opened her eyes to watch them, climbing over the piled up bundles, stooping to rope on the boxes, pausing to sit back on their heels and shout with laughter over the preposterousness of the bulging, knobby car.

'It's a scream, a perfect picture of a scream!' They held their sides to laugh, their ha! ha! floating up through the still dreamy autumn air, to the open window of Mrs. Bascomb's attic-room.

'Say, seriously, girls,' said Charlie, 'we gotto get down to business, if we're not going to roll in to old Mother Alma after dark. Get a move on you, Dids!'

The girls were back in the house now, looking for their hats and wraps. 'Never mind. I don't care if I can't find it. I won't wear any. I hate a hat!'

'Oh, Dids, you must! Your hair'll look like . . .'

And now Dids was saying good-bye to her mother. Through the open doors Mrs. Bascomb could hear her voice as though she were in the room. 'We're actually on the move at last, Mother. *Good*-bye! I'll write the minute we get there. Take care of yourself now! I'll subscribe to the college paper for you, so you'll know all the news. *Good*-bye!'

The two girls were running down the front walk together, long-legged and graceful as young heifers.

'I'm going to sit in back on top of the pile.'

'Oh, Dids, you'll fall off. It wouldn't be safe.'

'No, I won't fall off. I can hang on to this rope. It's solid. It's tied fast at both ends. When you've got something solid to hang on to, you can't fall. I'm going to. . . oh, for heaven's sake! I forgot to say good-bye to Granny!' A rush back up the walk and into the house.

Through the window, Mrs. Bascomb heard the girl in the car remark to her brother, 'Dids is awfully good to her grandmother. Lots of girls never would have thought of that.'

Dids was there, filling the room like a gust of wind from an orchard in bloom . . . with her health, her youth, her lightness of heart. God bless her!

'Well, Granny, what do you think! in all the hullabaloo, didn't I 'most forget to come and give you a smacker!'

She flung herself on her knees beside the woman in the chair and put her young arms about the thin, old body. 'Good-bye, Granny! You're just an old brick, that's what you are, and don't forget it!'

She pressed the firm, fresh innocence of her girl's lips upon the other's withered cheek 'Good-bye. I'll write home just as soon as I get there. And don't you worry. I'll be all right always.'

'Good-bye, my darling,' said Mrs. Bascomb, smiling lovingly into the girl's face.

And then Dids was gone.

As she had sprung to her feet and turned away, her grandmother felt the girl's past life slip from her. By the time she was once more laughingly balancing herself on the tops of the trunks, she had forgotten that her grandmother existed. That was right. That was as it should be. Dids needed all she had for her airy, confident, joyous rush forward into her own future.

'Do the procession prosesh?' inquired Charlie. 'It do.'

The old car groaned, whirred, and rattlingly moved forward.

'Look out, Dids, you'll fall. Honest you will.'

'Oh, shucks! You can't fall when you've got something solid to hang on to, can you?'

The sound of their laughter, of their chatter, of the humorous clanking of their car grew less and less as they rolled away. Presently it could not be heard at all. In the street, in the listening house, in Mrs. Bascomb's room, there was an empty silence.

Was she alive? She did not seem to herself to draw a breath. She felt as though she had died.

This was the end. Now there was nothing left for her, nothing at all. Emptiness . . . emptiness . . . this was the end.

She heard a voice calling lamentably, 'Oh, Momma! Oh, Momma!' It was Lottie.

Mrs. Bascomb rose mechanically and went downstairs. Lottie was crying, her head buried in her pillows, her hands over her face.

Standing there at the door of that room, Mrs. Bascomb felt something strange come into her empty heart. As if it had been slowly seeping in and piling itself higher and higher against the barrier which shut it out from her life, it was there . . . a shining tide. At the sound of Lottie's disconsolate weeping it overflowed the barrier. She felt its bright healing waters pour into the parched and dusty places of her heart.

She looked in through the door, as she had looked so many thousand times before; and now, she saw standing there a forlorn little phantom, a helpless, desolate child who ought never to have been born, doomed from the hour she drew breath, ignorant, unprotected, warped, stunted. Had she come there, without knowing it, to look for help? Had she been standing there all these years waiting for a mother?

Strange that utter humility and remorse could have so sweet a savour! Was it because they were now perfumed with pity and love?

Lottie looked up and saw her standing there. 'Oh Momma, I haven't got anybody left but you,' she said, whimpering, and held out her arms.

Mrs. Bascomb stepped forward quickly. She said with a strong, comforting accent of affection, 'Yes, we two will have to stick together now, Lottie, dear.'

VIRAGO MODERN CLASSICS

The first Virago Modern Classic, *Frost in May* by Antonia White, was published in 1978. It launched a list dedicated to the celebration of women writers and to the rediscovery and reprinting of their works. Its aim was, and is, to demonstrate the existence of a female tradition in fiction which is both enriching and enjoyable. The Leavisite notion of the 'Great Tradition', and the narrow, academic definition of a 'classic', has meant the neglect of a large number of interesting secondary works of fiction. In calling the series 'Modern Classics' we do not necessarily mean 'great' — although this is often the case. Published with new critical and biographical introductions, books are chosen for many reasons: sometimes for their importance in literary history; sometimes because they illuminate particular aspects of womens' lives, both personal and public. They may be classics of comedy or storytelling; their interest can be historical, feminist, political or literary.

Initially the Virago Modern Classics concentrated on English novels and short stories published in the early decades of this century. As the series has grown it has broadened to include works of fiction from different centuries, different countries, cultures and literary traditions. In 1984 the Victorian Classics were launched; there are separate lists of Irish, Scottish, European, American, Australian and other English speaking countries; there are books written by Black women, by Catholic and Jewish women, and a few relevant novels by men. There is, too, a companion series of Non-Fiction Classics constituting biography, autobiography, travel, journalism, essays, poetry, letters and diaries.

By the end of 1986 over 250 titles will have been published in these two series, many of which have been suggested by our readers.

THE MOTHER'S RECOMPENSE

By Edith Wharton

New Introduction by Marilyn French

"She had left Anne when Anne was a baby of three; left her with a dreadful pang, a rending of the inmost fibres, and yet a sense of unutterable relief, because to do so was to escape from the oppression of her married life."

Kate Clephane lives alone in a second-rate hotel on the French Riviera. Nearly twenty years before she eloped with a man, fleeing her husband and home, and the rigidity of New York society. Now middle-aged, her years of raffish expatriate living have taken their toll. Then a telegram arrives from her daughter Anne, inviting her back to their Fifth Avenue mansion and the charmed circle of her old world. But Kate finds postwar New York a changed city of towering skyscrapers: though more liberal it is no less oppressive. And the joy of being with her daughter is soon threatened by the reappearance of the only man she ever passionately loved. This penetrating and moving study of mother daughter relations, of sexual mores, jealousy and exile, was first published in 1925.